WEIGHED AND WANTING

By

George MacDonald

A New Edition
Updated and Introduced by
Michael Phillips

The Cullen Collection
of the Fiction of George MacDonald
Volume 26

The Cullen Collection

of the Fiction of George MacDonald

New editions of George MacDonald's classic fiction works
updated and introduced by Michael Phillips

Weighed and Wanting, 1882
Published by Kegan Paul, Trench (U.K.), Lothrop (U.S.)

Weighed and Wanting: A New Edition

By George MacDonald, Michael Phillips, editor
© 2018 by Michael Phillips
October 2018
> A new and expanded edition of *The Gentlewoman's Choice*
> published by Bethany House Publishers, 1987.

Grateful appreciation is acknowledged for those who have contributed directly and indirectly to this set of new editions of George MacDonald's fiction, going all the way back to the folks at Bethany House publishers in the early 1980s who launched the most ambitious MacDonald publishing project since MacDonald's own lifetime. More recently, there have been many who have contributed in various ways to the research, counsel, design, and proofreading for *The Cullen Collection,* especially including David Hiatt, Lora Hattendorf, Joseph Dindinger of Wise Path Books, and of course Judy Phillips, a full co-laborer in every facet of this project. A special note of thanks is due our friend and colleague, Wheaton's Dr. Rolland Hein, the preeminent MacDonald scholar of our time, for his gracious permission to quote from his excellent biography, *George MacDonald: Victorian Mythmaker,* in the introductions to these volumes. More complete acknowledgements are found in Volume 38 of the series, *George MacDonald A Writer's Life,* which comprises the complete collection of introductions to the 37 fiction titles.

Interior title design by Joseph Dindinger of Wise Path Books.

The Cullen Collection of the Fiction of George MacDonald, Volume 26

Published by SUNRISE BOOKS in cooperation with WISE PATH BOOKS—
Preserving the works of George MacDonald for future generations

ISBN 978-1724147080

WEIGHED
AND WANTING

This updated edition of a 19th century literary gem,
first cut, polished, and set by George MacDonald,
is now presented in a fresh setting for a new generation

SUNRISE BOOKS
PUBLISHERS
in cooperation with Wise Path Books

The Cullen Collection of the Fiction of George MacDonald

1. Phantastes (1858)
2. David Elginbrod (1863)
3. The Portent (1864)
4. Adela Cathcart (1864)
5. Alec Forbes of Howglen (1865)
6. Annals of a Quiet Neighbourhood (1867)
7. Robert Falconer (1868)
8. Guild Court (1868)
9. The Seaboard Parish (1868)
10. At the Back of the North Wind (1871)
11. Ranald Bannerman's Boyhood (1871)
12. The Princess and the Goblin (1872)
13. Wilfrid Cumbermede (1872)
14. The Vicar's Daughter (1872)
15. Gutta Percha Willie (1873)
16. Malcolm (1875)
17. The Wise Woman (1875)
18. St. George and St. Michael (1876)
19. Thomas Wingfold Curate (1876)
20. The Marquis of Lossie (1877)
21. Paul Faber Surgeon (1879)

The introductions to the 37 volumes form a continuous picture of George MacDonald's literary life, viewed through the prism of the development of his written legacy of works. While each book can of course be read on its own, every introduction picks up where that to the previous volume left off, with special attention to the title under consideration. The introductions together, as a biography of MacDonald's life as a writer, are compiled in Volume 38.

CONTENTS

NOTE: As the introductions to the 37 volumes of *The Cullen Collection* form a continuous portrait of George MacDonald's life, and as many of the introductions contain comprehensive and detailed discussion and analysis of the title in question—its plot, themes, and circumstances of writing—some first-time readers may choose to skip ahead to the story itself, saving the introduction for later, so as not to "spoil the story."

"Papa seems so quietly happy."
 —Louisa MacDonald, May 4, 1872, from Deskford (near Cullen)

"Papa does enjoy this place so much."
 —Louisa MacDonald, May 6, 1872 from the Seafield Arms Hotel, Cullen

"Papa oh! so jolly & bright & happy…Papa was taken for Lord Seafield yesterday."
 —Louisa MacDonald, Sept. 2, 1873, from Cullen

"Papa is very poorly. He ought to go to Cullen for a week I think."
 —Louisa MacDonald, October 5, 1873, from London

The Cullen Collection
of the Fiction of George MacDonald

The series name for these works of Scotsman George MacDonald (1824-1905) has its origins in the 1830s when the boy MacDonald formed what would be a lifelong affection for the northeast Scottish village of Cullen.

The ocean became young George's delight. At the age of eleven, writing from Portsoy or Cullen, he announced to his father his intention to go to sea as a sailor—in his words, "as soon as possible." The broad white beach of Cullen Bay, the Seatown, the grounds of Cullen House, the temple of Psyche ("Temple of the Winds"), Cullen Burn, the dwellings along Grant Street, Scarnose, and especially Findlater Castle, all seized the youth's imagination with a love that never left him. MacDonald continued to visit Huntly and Cullen throughout his life, using his childhood love for his homeland as the backdrop for his richest novels, including what is arguably his greatest work of fiction, *Malcolm*, published in 1875.

We therefore honor MacDonald's unique relationship to Cullen with these newly updated editions of his novels. In Cullen, in certain respects more than in any other place, one finds the transcendent spirit of George MacDonald's life and the ongoing legacy of his work still magically alive after a century and a half. This release of *The Cullen Collection of the Fiction of George MacDonald* coincides with a memorial bench and plaque established on Cullen's Castle Hill commemorating MacDonald's visits to the region.

To those readers familiar with my previous editions of MacDonald's novels, I should make clear that eighteen of the volumes in this new series (including this one) are updated and expanded titles from the Bethany House series of the 1980s. Limitations of length dictated much about how those previous volumes were produced. To interest a publisher in the project during those years when MacDonald was a virtual unknown in the publishing world, certain sacrifices had to be made. Cuts to length had to be more severe than I would have preferred. Practicality drove the effort. Imperfect as they were in some respects, I am enormously grateful for those editions. They helped inaugurate a worldwide renaissance of interest in MacDonald. They were wonderful door-openers for many thousands into MacDonald's world.

Hopefully this new and more comprehensive set of MacDonald's fiction will take up where they left off. Not constrained by the limitations that dictated production of the former volumes, these new editions, though identical at many points, have been expanded—sometimes significantly. In that sense they reflect MacDonald's originals somewhat more closely, while still preserving the flavor, pace, and readability of their predecessors. Nineteen additional titles have been added. The thirteen realistic novels among these have been updated according to the same priorities that guided the earlier Bethany House series. That process will be explained in more detail in the introductions to the books of the series. The final six, which would more accurately be termed "fantasy," have not been edited in any way. They are faithful reproductions of the originals exactly as they were first published. These six—*Phantastes, At the Back of the North Wind, The Princess and the Goblin, The Wise Woman, The Princess and Curdie,* and *Lilith*—are so well known and have been published literally in hundreds of editions through the years, that it has seemed best to reproduce them for *The Cullen Collection* with the same texts by which they are generally known.*

Dedicated followers of all great men and women continually seek hints that reveal their inner being—the *true* man, the *true* woman. What were they *really* like? What made him or her tick? Many biographies and studies attempt to answer such questions. In George MacDonald's case, however, a panorama of windows exists that reveals far more about his person than the sum-total of everything that has been written about him over the years. Those are the novels that encompass his life's work. The volumes of this series represent the *true* spiritual biography of the man, a far more important biography than life's details can ever tell.

---

* A word of clarification at this point will hopefully alleviate minor confusions that may arise about certain usages of punctuation and capitalization. In speaking of the original texts of MacDonald's books, a phrase such as the "texts by which they are generally known," is not really accurate. For most of MacDonald's books there are no *absolutely* authoritative texts. Editions vary widely, even so-called "first editions." This is a theme that will be developed in the introductions to other editions of *The Cullen Collection,* and is a fascinating study in itself. Suffice it at this point to say that punctuation and capitalization varies. Sometimes the differences are between U.S. and U.K. editions—American publishers capitalizing lower case words from the British editions (in addition to changing words such as labour, honour, odour, parlour, neighbourhood, etc. to their American spellings). This is especially the case with the God-pronouns *He* and *Him*. MacDonald usually wrote these in the lower case, as he did nouns of direct address in dialogue—mother, father, aunt, uncle, your majesty, etc.—which are occasionally capitalized in U.S. editions.

The ambiguity is heightened, however, when MacDonald himself is inconsistent in his usage. Sometimes he *does* capitalize *He* and *Him*. Sometimes God is referred to as *father*, at other times as *Father*. But he is inconsistent (whether by intent or blunder I have never been able to ascertain)—with *he* and *Him* (both referring to God or Jesus), and *father* and *Father*, perhaps even occurring in the same sentence.

Punctuation, likewise, varies from edition to edition—colons, dashes, quotation marks, paragraph breaks being the most common differences. Quotation marks ('single') sometimes follow U.K. convention, at other times U.S. convention ("double"). But it is not so simple as whether a particular edition was published in the U.K. or U.S. Some U.K first editions use American quotation marks, and likewise some U.S. editions use British spellings. It is very confusing.

Most readers won't notice and won't care about such tiny details. But the occasional purist may say, "Hey, wait a minute, my original edition has a colon here, and this new edition has a comma!" Granted, there won't be many who will be so persnickety. But for those few of you, I will only say that I have made use of as many original editions as possible—for nearly every title at least two, sometimes more—to compare these minor distinctions. Then I have followed what I consider the "best" usage or punctuation under the circumstances (which is obviously my own judgment call) and that which I consider the most likely usage MacDonald himself originally would have employed. But obviously in some cases I may be mistaken.

In 1911, six years after his father's death, George MacDonald's son Ronald wrote of the man with whom he had spent his life:

> "The ideals of his didactic novels were the motive of his own life...a life of literal, and, which is more, imaginative consistency with his doctrine...There has probably never been a writer whose work was a better expression of his personal character. This I am not engaged to prove; but I very positively assert...that in his novels...and allegories...one encounters...the same rich imagination, the same generous lover of God and man, the same consistent practiser of his own preaching, the same tender charity to the sinner with the same uncompromising hostility to the sin, which were known in daily use and by his own people counted upon more surely than sunshine." [*]

Thirty years after the publication of my one-volume biography *George MacDonald Scotland's Beloved Storyteller,* it now gives me great pleasure to present this thirty-seven-volume "biography" of the man, the Scotsman, the prophetic spiritual voice who is George MacDonald. [†]

How fitting is the original title in which Ronald MacDonald's sketch of his father quoted above first appeared, *From A Northern Window.* For any attempted portrait of the man George MacDonald becomes at once a window into his homeland as well.

Therefore, I invite you to gaze back in time through the "northern windows" of these volumes. Picture yourself perhaps near the cheerful hearth described in the opening pages of *What's Mine's Mine,* looking out the window to the cold seas and mountains in the distance, where perhaps you get a fleeting glimpse of highlanders Ian and Alister Macruadh.

Or imagine yourself walking up Duke Street in Huntly from MacDonald's birth home, following in the footsteps of fictional Robert Falconer to the town square.

Or envision yourself on some windswept highland moor with Gibbie or Cosmo Warlock.

Or walk up the circular staircase of Fyvie Castle to Donal Grant's tiny tower hideaway where he began to unravel the mysteries of that ancient and spooky place.

Or walk from Cullen's Seatown alongside Malcolm selling the fish in his creel, turning at the Market Cross into Grant Street and continuing past Miss Horn's house and up the hill to the entrance of the Cullen House grounds.

Or perhaps climb Castle Hill to the George MacDonald memorial bench and gaze across the sweep of Cullen Bay to Scarnose as Malcolm's story comes to life before your eyes.

---

[*] "George MacDonald: A Personal Note" by Ronald MacDonald, Chapter 3 in *From A Northern Window,* James Nisbet & Co., 1911, reprinted in book form as *From A Northern Window,* Volume One in The Masterline Series, Sunrise Books, Eureka, CA 1989.

[†] For the texts of the books of the series, and quotes referenced from them, I have preserved most British spellings. In my introductions, when I am speaking for *myself,* I use American spellings. In quoting from other books and authors, I obviously retain the usage of the original source.

From any of these settings, whether real or imaginary, drift back through the years and gaze through the panoramic windows of these stories, and take in with pleasure the drama, relationships, images, characters, settings, and spiritual truths George MacDonald offers us as we are drawn into his world.

Michael Phillips
Cullen, Morayshire
Scotland, 2017

WEIGHED AND WANTING

A Heart of Ministry

A significant reason for the timelessness of George MacDonald's writings is that he kept himself from using his pen to inveigh on the multitude of transitory issues that plagued society in his day. MacDonald was a thinking man, widely read, socially conscious, with strong views. Yet he resisted the temptation—if indeed it was such—to sway public opinion, or to use his influence to right the world's transitory wrongs. His focus was always man's response to the eternal not the temporal, on the character of God, on personal growth, on what being a follower of Christ means practically in daily relationships, responses, and choices.

His focus on *eternal* themes thus retain their relevance, and keep his message vibrant and alive generation after generation, ever to be discovered anew by individual men and women. Meanwhile, the passing issues of 1860s Scotland or 1880s England, or 1900 America…industry, world wars, depressions, politics…as time raced on into the twentieth-century…these all rose and fell on the tides of time. Poverty, slums,

Photograph 1884.

war, and disease are still with us. Yet *individuals* are still being called out of the world to live in the higher air of Fatherhood. MacDonald's *eternal* message lives on, as vital and transformational today as it was in 1870. His vision never lost its clarity in pointing the men and women of God's creation toward life's true first causes.

It is not that MacDonald didn't care about the issues of his day. He simply realized where the precision and insight of his writing could do the most eternal good in men's hearts—turning individuals toward their heavenly Father rather than attempting to right the world's wrongs.

Yet *occasionally* MacDonald spoke to the world's pains he saw around him. It fell to one of his lesser-known novels, *Weighed and Wanting,* to manifest more fully than most of his other works one of the strongest driving forces in MacDonald's spiritual vision—the theme of godly service to the poor, working compatibly with his recognition of the deeper need of the human soul to address its sin. MacDonald stresses the necessity for Christian charity and sacrifice in a number of books, notably *The Vicar's Daughter, Robert Falconer,* and *Sir Gibbie,* and infuses nearly everything he wrote with the imperative of actively *living* one's faith. However, in *Weighed and Wanting,* such ministry becomes a dominant theme as the story progresses, alongside the equally prominent theme of *sin.* MacDonald thus achieves an extraordinary marriage between the social and salvationary halves of the gospel.

In *Weighed and Wanting,* MacDonald explores societal conditions and the plight of the poor more directly than is his normal custom, bringing into wonderful harmony the temporal and the eternal. He gives us here a vision of ministry to the poor, suffering, diseased, and dying—a ministry imbued with the power of eternal Fatherhood. It is a balance few social reformers and few preachers through the centuries have been able to grasp, as the pendulum of "ministry" swings to the extremes but rarely finds the calm and quiet center.

It is in that *center* (spiritual and temporal fusing in unity) where Jesus lived and which MacDonald articulated in his writings. I know of nowhere else outside the gospel itself, other than in the writings of George MacDonald, where the balance between love for God and care for one's neighbor is so profoundly illuminated. And though many consider *Weighed and Wanting* one of his minor works, it stands almost at the apex with one or two others in revealing, in a sense, this *societal* or *social* component of MacDonald's overall vision of life.

Indeed, it was a vision he *lived.* The principles and methods and priorities we read about here emerged out of the MacDonald's own lifestyle. Wherever they happened to be, with eleven children, he and Louisa always opened their home, not to *every* waif and stray and beggar of the city or they would have been inundated, but to those in need whom God brought them. They took in unofficial "foster" children and adults, and even, the very year this book was written, "adopted" (probably also unofficially, though the family used that word) two girls whose mother was dying of tuberculosis (whom they also cared for until her death). After moving to Italy, with their own brood gradually shrinking, their huge home in Bordighera was nevertheless nearly always full. [1] Perhaps this fact in some measure helps explain why they always seemed financially strapped.

MacDonald's was the practical perspective, not of attempting to change the whole world, but only his little corner of it. We can all be deeply thankful that he kept his focus on the essential bull's eye of God's Fatherhood. In so doing, living as he did, through his writings he changed the world as well.

In his final book of sermons (released a decade after *Weighed and Wanting*, in 1892), MacDonald would articulate this differentiation between man's spiritual and temporal need in his powerful address, "Salvation from Sin." He speaks pointedly about those who would "wage war on the evils" around them, declaring it *impossible* that the world can "be righted from the outside." MacDonald was not deaf to the crying needs of humanity. He simply recognized the clear dividing line between eternal and temporal.

> *I presume there is scarce a human being who...would not confess to having something that plagued him, something from which he would gladly be free...Most men...imagine that, free of such and such things antagonistic, life would be an unmingled satisfaction...Perhaps the greater part of the energy of this world's life goes forth in the endeavour to rid itself of discomfort...*
>
> *However absurd the statement may appear to one who has not yet discovered the fact for himself, the cause of every man's discomfort is evil, moral evil—first of all, evil in himself, his own sin, his own wrongness, his own unrightness...Foolish is the man, and there are many such men, who would rid himself or his fellows of discomfort by setting the world right, by waging war on the evils around him, while he neglects that integral part of the world where lies his business, his first business—namely, his own character and conduct. Were it possible—an absurd supposition—that the world should thus be righted from the outside, it would yet be impossible for the man who had contributed to the work, remaining what he was, ever to enjoy the perfection of the result...The philanthropist who regards the wrong as in the race, forgetting that the race is made up of conscious and wrong individuals, forgets also that...no evil can be cured in the race, except by its being cured in its individuals...There is no way of making three men right but by making right each one of the three; but a cure in one man who repents and turns, is a beginning of the cure of the whole human race...*

The one cure for any organism, is to be set right—to have all its parts brought into harmony with each other...Rightness alone is cure. The return of the organism to its true self, is its only possible ease. To free a man from suffering, he must be set right, put in health; and the health at the root of man's being, his rightness, is to be free from wrongness, that is, from sin. [2]

During the socially-active years of MacDonald's writing career, many middle and upper-class women were tiring of drawing room boredom and wanted to make a difference in people's lives. The suffrage movement had not yet come into full flower. Yet women were exerting themselves upon society and British culture in ever-expanding and visible ways. Women like the MacDonalds' friend and social activist Octavia Hill, founder of the National Trust, were on the front lines fighting for better living conditions for the poor.

The character of Miss Vavasor in *Weighed and Wanting* notes disparagingly:

> *"That kind of thing is spreading very much in our circle, too. I know many ladies who visit the poor. The custom came in with these women's-rights people. I fear they will upset everything before long. No one can tell where such things will end."*

Such was not MacDonald's primary fight. Though in sympathy with the so-called "Christian Socialism" of F.D. Maurice and others, MacDonald was no activist. He would, however, bring his *spiritual* perspectives to bear upon Victorian social conditions by telling the stories of Mary St. John's, Gibbie's, and Falconer's "inner-city ministries" to use a contemporary term. MacDonald's compassion for the poor of London was the same compassion Jesus felt—knowing, once they were fed and clothed, that their deepest need of all was to know God as their Father.

Elizabeth Saintsbury writes:

"In *Weighed and Wanting*...which shows the influence of Ruskin's socialistic ideas and work, he condemns the landlords who exploit their tenants and refuse to maintain their properties. In *Robert Falconer*...MacDonald paints a picture of poverty, degradation and squalor in the slums of London equalled only by Dickens in its lurid detail...But George did not agree that environment was the deciding factor in people's moral development." [3]

In the tradition of these characters who frequented the streets of London and Aberdeen's slums and tenements, Octavia Hill (and it was MacDonald's friend Ruskin who gave the building for one of Hill's slum-renovation projects) provided the inspiration for a new messenger of compassion, Hester Raymount of *Weighed and Wanting*.

Rolland Hein writes:

"MacDonald's thinking concerning the poor was influenced by Maurice as well as Ruskin and Hill. One of the reasons MacDonald was attracted to F.D. Maurice was his advocacy of what was known as Christian Socialism. The program these Christian (not Marxist) Socialists advocated emphasized individual responsibility as well as social reform by the application of Christian principles to all social relationships. With typical Scottish sternness MacDonald insisted on the need of the poor to better themselves. They must be given adequate opportunities, something many sadly lacked. When anyone whose life was at a low ebb needed to be taken in and helped to make a new start, The Retreat was open to them, while the MacDonalds did what they could to help them turn their lives around. It was not unusual for a penniless person or a drunkard trying to reform to live with the MacDonalds temporarily. Not all such attempts issued in successful rehabilitation, but many did." [4]

Weighed and Wanting also contains very personal elements, as do all his novels, for more reasons than Octavia Hill's fictionalization as Hester. The book's emphasis on entertainment—fixing up the great room for a concert—is surely an outgrowth of Louisa's expanded theatrical efforts during this period of their lives. There were apparently some among family and friends who were aghast at the family going on stage publically with their production of *Pilgrim's Progress.* Perhaps this book gave MacDonald a forum to respond to their criticisms.

Though Hester Raymount's single musical performance was on a different scale from those of the MacDonald family, the theme of "musical ministry" to the poor, elderly, and suffering that infuses *Weighed and Wanting* surely grew out of the experiences of the MacDonald family.

(The shared musical bent of Hester and Mary Marston, the two leading women whose books came almost in succession, is noteworthy. Nor can we help observing the oddly parallel names of Hester Raymount and Hester Redmain, though the two women could not have been more different. Indeed, MacDonald's penchant for repeating names is more than a little puzzling. These two similarly-named women coming in back-to-back years is certainly perplexing.)

These two novels offer fit opportunity to reflect on the MacDonald family's musical and dramatic productions—especially their performances of *Pilgrim's Progress*—spearheaded of course by Louisa and her music talents.

Louisa and her daughters had always had a flair for drama and music. Though the worldly atmosphere of the theater was off limits, the MacDonald's oldest daughter Lilia was, by all accounts, a talented actress. With Louisa's organizational skills, the MacDonald girls began performing for family and friends after moving to The Retreat in the late 1860s.

Looking back to those first productions, William Raeper, quoting occasionally from Greville, explains:

"Visitors came in abundance...Whatever the food was like, there was no doubt that the main attraction of the day was the play...

"'The coachhouse was converted into a theatre with a gas-lit stage...There we acted our plays; and friends came from afar, if only to see Lilia Scott MacDonald play Lady Macbeth to her father in the title role...'[5]

"The first of all these entertainments, with its performance of *Beauty and the Beast,* was so chaotic, that poor Ruskin went home without having had anything proper to eat.

"As the children grew more proficient in music, they would travel out to perform for Octavia Hill's tenants in a decorated entertainment room...Here her children would act or sing, Grace would play Beethoven on her piano, and Greville would scratch on his violin. Their specialty was Carols at Christmas time, punctuated by MacDonald's dramatic renderings of specially composed nativity verses...Lilia was generally the star of the show." [6]

The family's musical and dramatic presentations expanded, gradually involving everyone and becoming more sophisticated, with sets and costumes, as the children grew into their teen years. Eventually the repertoire settled most regularly on the dramatic presentation of *Pilgrim's Progress.* By the late 1870s, all the girls then in their twenties, the productions under Louisa's directorship had become lavish indeed, complete with George doing his part outfitted as Mr. Greatheart.

With the transition to Italy between 1878 and 1880, the MacDonald family productions continued at an even higher and more elaborate level. By then Greville was on his own living in England, but most of the others were still involved. Louisa often made arrangements for the family to accompany their own Mr. Greatheart during the summer months to England and Scotland, playing *Pilgrim's Progress* in conjunction with MacDonald's speaking schedule. *

Of one of these trips, William Raeper writes:

"Meanwhile, the MacDonalds decided that it was about time they returned to England. They returned there for the summer months [1879], but had to stage *Pilgrim's Progress* in order to pay for their traveling expenses. Louisa hired halls all over London and took the players as far afield as Malvern, Cheltenham, Nottingham, and Leicester. MacDonald wrote merrily to his American friend James Fields: 'We are now, as you may have heard, turned into a sort of company of acting strollers—I mean strolling actors—and have a good

---

* This dramatic side of the MacDonald "family story" is chronicled in much greater detail in other sources, including *George MacDonald and His Wife* Part 10, Chapter 1, Chapter 34 of Hein, *Mythmaker,* and Chapters 30-31 of Raeper, *MacDonald.*

reception and tolerable results. We have really hardly tried the country yet though people seem a good deal interested in our attempt.' [7]

"MacDonald began lecturing again on 28 May, while the family had fun, playing to captive audiences, and enjoying the attention given them. They were soon experts at hanging the curtains and striking up on the piano in the oddest places. Often MacDonald would sit in the wings, in his spangled costume, maniacally correcting proofs while the children tripped out one by one to play their roles. Greville…thought the acting interfered too much with schoolwork and routine life, and did not enjoy seeing his brothers and sisters sporting themselves on stage…flaunting themselves in costume." [8]

William Raeper speculates that the increase in the family's dramatic performances was almost entirely a financial enterprise. I have the feeling he may be considerably embellishing MacDonald's despondency and "anguish" and the financial motivation for the productions. The "financial martyrdom" theme so emphasized in MacDonald's biography continues as a somewhat dubious undercurrent to events.

"MacDonald was battling with severer problems that gathered over his head like stormclouds. As usual, his health was fitful, interrupting his work, and consequently affecting the family's income. To make matters worse, MacDonald's friend and publisher Strahan had separated from his partners, and could not offer MacDonald the prices for his books that he had been accustomed to. Strahan went as far as rejecting MacDonald's recently finished *Paul Faber Surgeon* as not being suitable for his newly-established journal *The Day of Rest,* and gave him only £400 for the three-volume edition—less than half of his previous prices. MacDonald was helpless and crestfallen. He needed more money, not less, as there was the burden of Mary's health to think of.

"Louisa was troubled at her husband's anguish and decided to take matters into her own hands. She devised of her own a startling scheme for bringing about an increase in the family's finances—she would put her children on the stage. She reckoned that the family had charmed friends and charity audiences for long enough, and determined to cull some income from their acting." [9]

It is my sense that, whatever extra money they may have produced, Louisa's dramatic efforts were more motivated by her own creative instincts than finances. Indeed, she had published a book of her own, *Dramas for Children*, long before (released by Strahan in 1870). Music and drama were in her blood.

And Greville speaks a little less glowingly of the family obsession with drama.

"For my own part," he writes, "being now able to earn my own living, and so taking no share in the dramatic representations, I could never rejoice in the work if only because the old peace and rest of the home was thenceforward, till 1887, made impossible by the exigencies of the drama. Although it was hardly successful economically, it certainly made more possible the half-yearly journeys to Italy. Physically the work seemed too much for my sisters, and was in danger of interfering with my brothers' prospects...

"As I have said already, many friends were sad about the enterprise, in spite of my father's whole-hearted endorsement of it." [10]

Perhaps the most personal aspect of *Weighed and Wanting* is the lovely haunting caricature of peaceful Mark Raymount, an obvious fictional portrayal of MacDonald's son Maurice, whose death two years before its writing (1879) caused MacDonald far more anguish than finances. In the writing of this novel, is MacDonald, in a sense, still working through his own grief? I think it likely, coming to terms with it perhaps by elevating Mark to the mysterious stature of a *child-Christ* whom God specially took because of his goodness. Nor can the character of Moxy be coincidental—another M-named boy who follows in beloved Maurice's footsteps. I cannot but wonder, however, what MacDonald's other sons thought, knowing that both Mark and Moxy were drawn after their brother Maurice, when they read in this novel, "The parents loved Moxy more tenderly than...his brothers."

There are other clear hints of autobiography woven through the book's pages.

MacDonald's love of mystery houses reappears, with secret doors and passageways and entrances and garrets.

There are echoes of daughter Lilia's broken engagement to a young aristocrat when she would not agree to the condition imposed by his aunt (fictionalized as Miss Vavasor) that she give up what she considered her creative calling. Lilia's passion was acting. Hester's was working with the poor. Neither young woman was willing to relinquish her pursuit, even to marry—which neither ever did.

Hester's fearlessness around smallpox perfectly reflects the MacDonald family's ministrations to friends. Indeed, the MacDonalds' work with those suffering from TB no doubt incurred criticism from family and friends, just as did Hester's. Years later, after her failed engagement, this ministry cost Lilia MacDonald her life at thirty-nine, after she contracted TB from a suffering friend whom she would not abandon.

I also find of particular interest—as one who has watched with some heartbreak many MacDonald enthusiasts lose themselves in the details of intellectual analysis while missing the true gold of his writings—MacDonald's own prophetic recognition of this unfortunate principle at work. He writes in *Weighed and Wanting*:

The ruin of a man's teaching comes of his followers, such as having never touched the foundation he has laid, build upon it wood, hay, and stubble, fit only to be burnt. Therefore, if only to avoid his worst foes, his admirers, a man should avoid system. The more correct a system the worse will it be misunderstood—its professed admirers will take both its errors and their misconceptions of its truths, and hold them forth as its essence.

Hester Raymount, along with Mary Marston, is one of MacDonald's few leading ladies who carries a book on her own. Hester's eventual recognition of the life God has marked out for her comes only with much soul-searching along the way, and some unpleasant revelations about herself. The quest of Falconer's heart had primarily to do with the truth of the gospel. Hester's choices, however, focus more specifically on what obedience to the gospel means regarding her fellow man. Interestingly, in the end she and Falconer find themselves engaged in almost the same work. The eventual parallel between Falconer and Mary St. John and Hester and Mr. Christopher is inescapable.

Judy and I find Hester's story particularly personal. As a musician, Judy was always taught—indeed such is the *assumption* for musicians, and the clear goal inherent in nearly all music training and studies— that *performance* is the validating objective of musical pursuits. Performance becomes the be-all and end-all. Judy was shy, however, and uncomfortable in that role. She *loved* music, but hated "performing."

After years in various symphonies and teaching (where even she found herself emphasizing performance to her students), it was not until she began taking her harp into hospital rooms to play for the sick and suffering and dying that she realized she had discovered her musical niche. Watching blood pressure numbers drop before her eyes, observing those in pain drift to sleep for a few minutes of peace, seeing tears of healing come to the eyes of a patient…suddenly she saw what had been the heart's desire of her music all along. It wasn't *performance*, but bringing the healing therapeutic power of music into the lives of the suffering.

The progression of Hester's ministry-vision is identical. She, too, is lauded and praised and encouraged to perform, and even puts on a concert, thinking it's what musicians are *supposed* to do. Not only is the concert a disaster, Hester's personality is not one that thrives on being in the spotlight.

Then comes a change. As she sits beside a woman and child with smallpox not knowing what to do or say, she softly begins to sing. Within minutes both are sleeping peacefully.

It is an epiphany for Hester. Performance is the *last* thing on her mind. Suddenly she realizes that her music can bring calm, comfort, peace, and even healing. With that eye-opening truth, her vision for help and service and ministry begins to coalesce into a reality.

Hester's family is a so-called religious one, yet without deep convictions. Hester has grown up in an environment where the *words* of life were present but had not penetrated into *life*. The words built up a mere hollow spiritual shell, the vacancy of which is exemplified by her father and the character of one of her brothers. It is this empty pretended spirituality—the unconverted heart that gives hypocritical lip service to faith—which has been "weighed" and found "wanting."

Hester ultimately discovers fulfillment in laying down her life in service to God's humanity. She thus personifies one of the most profound lessons MacDonald emphasizes in his books—letting God use you where you are, with the talents you possess, on behalf of those around you.

The gift God wanted Hester to use in his kingdom was a simple one—her music. At the time of MacDonald's writing, singing was not considered a great "witnessing" tool alongside the preaching of the mighty evangelists of the day. Yet Hester's music was the tool God had given *her*. It was the talent *she* had been given. It was *her* gift, and she faithfully put it to use. That was all God required.

In addition to MacDonald's constant theme of *living* faith, a number of sub-themes capture our attention. MacDonald reveals that his views of marriage ran counter to the accepted Victorian norms, and were a century ahead of his time. "You have very different ideas from such as were taught in my girlhood concerning the duties of wives," Miss Vavasor says to Hester. "A woman, I used to be told, was to fashion herself for her husband, fit her life to his life, her thoughts to his thoughts, her tastes to his tastes."

In one sense, this book summarizes MacDonald's message to Christendom—worry less about doctrine, theology, and the forms of religion, and *do* the work God has put before you. *Weighed and Wanting* is thus one of the least theological of MacDonald's works. It illustrates that faith without works is no faith at all. MacDonald brings this theme to a concise fulfillment at the book's close with the words, "Let every man or woman work out the thing that is in him. Whoever uses the means that he has, great or small, and does the work that is given him to do, stands by the side of Jesus and is a fellow worker with him."

MacDonald began writing *Weighed and Wanting* probably in the latter months of 1881, on the heels of the publication of the American edition of *Castle Warlock*. The writing no doubt continued through 1882 as it was being serialized in the U.K. from January to December in the *Sunday Magazine*. It was also serialized in the U.S. by the *Cottage Hearth Magazine*, also running throughout 1882, possibly extending into 1883.

An intriguing fact about the *Cottage Hearth* serialization is the statement made in the magazine that the copy is from "advance sheets" of the book from the author. [11] The conundrum of delivery to two different publishers on opposite sides of the Atlantic, at almost identical times, again rears its head. Coming as it does precisely between *Castle Warlock* and *Donal Grant*, whose varying editions are the subject of so much intriguing uncertainty, *Weighed and Wanting* sheds yet more light on the validity of American editions. As we have seen with the Lippincott publications, and of course in MacDonald's arrangement with Lothrop for *Castle Warlock*, the following hand-written note, accompanying the delivery of of *Weighed and Wanting*, establishes further evidence that authorized American editions of MacDonald's books were on the increase.

Referencing his delivery of an "authorized" manuscript to the magazine, in whatever form the "advance sheets" took, MacDonald wrote:

> *London, Nov. 7, 1881*
> *The copy of "Weighed and Wanting" is furnished by me to the "Cottage Hearth Magazine" of Boston, United States. And this American periodical is authorized to publish the same.*
> *George MacDonald.*

The triple decker book edition was published by Sampson Low late in 1882, probably in December as soon as the U.K. serialization was completed. (The first review of the book appeared in late November.) As mentioned in the introduction to *Castle Warlock*, the same publishing players were involved. Exactly as we saw with *Castle Warlock,* the Table of Contents varies significantly, with many differently-titled and combined chapters—60 chapters in the U.S. edition, 58 in the U.K. The text of the two editions, however, is *almost* identical except for U.S. spellings and punctuational changes.

The second sentence of the U.K. Sampson Low edition of *Weighed and Wanting*, for example, reads, "The sky and the sea were almost of the same colour..." The U.S. Lothrop edition changes *colour* to *color.*

Six sentences later, the U.K. "...to the labour-weary..." is changed in the U.S. edition to *labor weary*—including the spelling change and omitting the hyphen.

Obviously these are tiny changes. But there are other oddities and irregularities as well. Skipping ahead to the very end of the book, the last sentence of the U.K. edition, which reads, "...the woman who spends her strength on the poor..." is changed in the

U.S. edition to, "…the woman who spends her strength *for* the poor…"

How many more such small word substitutions might there be is anyone's guess. And given the sequence of publications for *Warlock*, on the other hand, if the U.S. edition of *Weighed and Wanting* came first, it may be the U.K. edition that was "changed."

I have noted elsewhere the inconsistent use of capitalizations, both between U.K. and U.S. editions, sometimes because of the apparent need U.S. publishers felt to capitalize God and Jesus pronouns, but also resulting from MacDonald's own varying usages. (This is a particularly fascinating case, MacDonald himself once insisting to a publisher that not so much as a single capital letter was to be changed. Yet alongside his insistence that every Capital or lower-case letter use mattered, must be placed his own inconsistent use of capitals visible throughout his books. That is, unless these inconsistencies are *not his at all*, but are the result of publisher changes!)

The following sentence occurs in the U.K. triple decker of *Weighed and Wanting*: "…her thoughts kept rising to him whose thought was the meaning of all she saw, the centre and citadel of its loveliness."

It is changed in the U.S. edition to, "…her thoughts kept rising to <u>Him</u> whose thought was the meaning of all she saw, the <u>center</u> and citadel of its loveliness."

Even the changes, however, are not made with complete consistency. Notwithstanding the examples noted, color and labor and center and neighbor, etc. are *not* consistently changed from U.K. spellings—*colour, labour, centre,* and *neighbour* exist throughout the U.S. Lothrop edition too.

These spelling and punctuational distinctions and inconsistencies exist in all MacDonald's titles. Most of them are so infinitesimal as not to be worth mentioning. I mention them here as illustrating how imperfect is the science of trying to analyze MacDonald's texts for uniformity. Irregularities are intrinsic to publishing—which itself is an inexact science.

As an indication of MacDonald's waning esteem among the literati and academic intelligentsia—a development which annoyed him in light of the overwhelmingly positive response of readers to the spiritual themes in his books—all the reviews of *Weighed and Wanting* were critical. The *Athenaeum* called it "ill-balanced." [12] The *Saturday Review* gave a long negative review and called it "one of the worst" of MacDonald's novels. [13] The *Spectator* thought it "probably the poorest and least pleasant" of his stories. [14]

This is but one more example of a sad fact—that the academic intelligentsia rarely "gets" the true essence of George MacDonald.

Needless to say, the reviewers during MacDonald's day did not have eyes to see the gold. Indeed, some of the personal transformations that begin to unfold as the book reaches its climax are among the most powerful MacDonald gives us. In working on this new edition, I found myself unexpectedly moved over and over as I was emotionally caught up into the unique character-births taking place before my eyes.

This may well be a book about which you may find yourself saying, "I need to read this *again!*"

Michael Phillips
Cullen, Morayshire
Scotland, 2017

NOTE ON FOOTNOTES: For the reader's ease in referencing frequently quoted titles, I have dispensed with the scholarly ciphers, more mystifying than helpful for the average fiction reader. These books will therefore be noted in the footnotes below as follows, rather than with the formal notations of op. cit., loc. cit., ibid., etc.

> Bulloch, *Bibliography*—"A Bibliography of George MacDonald," by John Malcolm Bulloch, *The Aberdeen University Library Bulletin,* February, 1925, Vol. V, No. 30.
> Greville, *Biography*—*George MacDonald and His Wife* by Greville MacDonald, George Allen & Unwin, London, 1924.
> Hein, *Mythmaker*—*George MacDonald, Victorian Mythmaker* by Rolland Hein, Star Song Publishing, Nashville, TN, 1993.
> Raeper, *MacDonald*—*George MacDonald* by William Raeper, Lion Publishing, Tring, England, 1987.

---

1 Such ministry may have been one of the reasons they built such a huge home. In his Footnote # 1 of Chapter 34, Rolland Hein says of Casa Coraggio: "Today, remodeled with a fifth story and terraces added, it is a modern apartment complex containing nearly forty units." (Hein, *Mythmaker*, p. 431)
2 The Hope of the Gospel, "Salvation from Sin."
3 Elizabeth Saintsbury, *George MacDonald, A Short Life*, 82-83.
4 Hein, *Mythmaker*, p. 206.
5 This quote-within-a-quote (from Raeper) is from Greville, *Biography*, p. 384.
6 Raeper, *MacDonald*, pp. 264-65.
7 Another quote-within-a-quote is this letter from MacDonald to James Fields, August 21, 1879, quoted in Raeper, p. 346.
8 Raeper, *MacDonald*, p. 346.
9 Raeper, *MacDonald*, p. 338.
10 Greville, *Biography*, p. 503.
11 First entry in Table of Contents for March 1882 issue reads: "WEIGHED AND WANTING (*illus.*), from advance sheets furnished by George MacDonald, LL. D."
12 The *Athenaeum*, Nov. 4, 1882, quoted in Bulloch, *Bibliography*.
13 The *Saturday Review*, Nov. 25, 1882, quoted in Bulloch, *Bibliography*.
14 The *Spectator*, March 24, 1883, quoted in Bulloch, *Bibliography*.

Weighed and Wanting

1882

The Cullen Collection
Volume 26

George MacDonald

— One —

A Bad Weather Holiday

It was a gray, windy noon at the beginning of autumn. The sky and the sea were almost the same colour. Across from the blurry horizon where they met came troops of waves that broke into white crests as they rushed at the shore. On land the trees and the smoke were greatly troubled—the trees because they would rather stand still, the smoke because it would rather ascend, while the wind kept tossing the former and beating down the latter. None of the hundreds of fishing boats belonging to the coast were to be seen, nor was a single sail visible—not even the smoke of a solitary steamer ploughing through the rain and fog south to London or north to Aberdeen.

To the thousands who had come to Burcliff to enjoy a holiday, the weather was depressing. But whether the labour weary had days

Image from frontispiece of 1882 Lothrop edition.

or weeks, the holiday had looked short from the beginning, and was growing shorter and shorter, while the dreary days seemed longer and longer.

The Raymounts had come to the east coast of England to enjoy the blue sky, the blue sea, and the bright sun overhead. So far, however, they had scarcely seen any of the three. Their moods were disagreeable.

They found themselves wrapped in a blanket of fog, out of which the water was every now and then squeezed down upon them in the wettest of rains. To those who hated work, this holiday, which by every right and reason belonged to them, seemed snatched away by that vague enemy against whom the grumbling of the world is continually directed. For were they not born to be happy, and how could a human being possibly fulfil that destiny in such miserable circumstances?

There are men and women who can be happy in such circumstances by securing the corner of a couch near a good fire. With the help of a good novel, they are able to forget the world around them. The noise of the waves on the sands, the storm resounding through the chimney, or the rain on the windows serves to deepen the calm of their spirits. Take the novel away, give the fire a black heart, let the smells of a lodging-house kitchen invade the sitting-room, and the man or woman who can then, on such a day, be patient and pleasant to other people, is one worth knowing. Mrs. Raymount, half the head and more than half the heart of the family staying in a certain lodging house in the forefront of Burcliff, was one of these.

It was not a large family, yet it contained perhaps as many varieties of character and temperament as some larger ones. These varieties gave rise to several ways of confronting such misfortunes as rainy weather. For misfortune it must seem to poor creatures who are slaves of the elements, especially when the weather ought to be sunny. When it is not, something is out of order, giving ground for complaint.

The father met it with tolerably good humour, but he was busy writing a paper for one of the monthly reviews and would have stayed inside no matter how fine a day it was. Therefore, he could take no credit for his genial mood, and his disposition must for the moment pass as unproven. But, if you had taken from the mother her piece of work—she was busy embroidering a lady's pinafore in the colours of a peacock's feather—and given her nothing to do, she would yet have been as peaceful as she now looked, for she knew who made her.

A tall lad stood at one of the windows in a mood of smouldering rebellion against the order of things. He was such a creature of moods that individual judgments of his character might well have proved irreconcilable. He had not yet begun to use his will—for he constantly mistook impulse for will—to blend the conflicting elements of his nature into one. As a man he was, therefore, much like the mass of flour and raisins, etc., before it becomes a plum pudding. He would have to pass through something analogous to boiling before he would become worthy of the name *man*. In his own estimate of himself, he claimed the virtues he was conscious of in his good moods, and let the bad ones slide without looking too closely into them. He substituted forgetfulness for repudiation, a return of good humour for repentance, and at best a joke for apology.

Mark, a pale, handsome boy of ten, and Josephine, a rosy girl of seven, sat on the opposite side of the fire amusing themselves with a puzzle. The gusts of wind and the great splashes of rain on the glass only made them feel cosier and more satisfied.

"Beastly weather!" said Cornelius as he turned toward the room rather than the persons in it.

"I'm sorry you don't like it, Corney," said his elder sister where she sat beside her mother trimming what promised to be a pretty bonnet. A concentrated effort to draw her needle through an accumulation of silken folds seemed to take something off the bloom of the smile with which she spoke.

"Oh, it's all very well for girls!" returned Cornelius. "You don't do anything worthwhile. And besides, you've got so many things you like to do, and so much time to do them in, that it's all the same to you whether you go out or stay home. But when a fellow has but a miserable three weeks and then it's back to a job he hates, it is rather hard to have it turn out like this. Day after day, as sure as the sun rises—if it does rise—the weather is as abominable as rain and wind can make it!"

"My dear boy!" said his mother without looking up.

"Oh yes, mother! I know! You're so good you would have had Job himself take it coolly. But I'm not like you. Only you needn't think me so very—what do you call it? It's only a breach in the laws of nature I'm grumbling at. I don't mean anything to offend you."

"Perhaps you mean more than you think," answered his mother with a deep sigh.

"Oh, I know," said the youth in a tone that roused his sister's anger, "you think I should be as thankful as the three children in the fiery furnace you are so fond of reminding me about."

"They would have been glad enough for some of the weather you call beastly," said Hester, again pulling through a stiff needle, this time without a smile, for sometimes her brother was more than she could bear.

"Oh, I daresay! But then, they knew when they got out they wouldn't have to go back to a beastly bank with nothing but notes and figures before their eyes from morning till night."

The mother's face grew sad.

"I am afraid, Cornelius, my dear son, that you may need the furnace yourself to teach you that the will of God, even in unpleasant weather, is a thing to be rejoiced in not abused. But I dread the fire for your sake, my boy!"

"I should have thought this weather, and the bank waiting after it, furnace enough, mother!" he answered, trying to laugh off her words.

"It does not seem to be," she said with some displeasure. "But then," she added with a sigh, "you do not have the same companion the three holy children had."

"Who is that?" rejoined Cornelius, for he had partly forgotten the story he knew well enough in childhood.

"We will not talk about him now," answered his mother. "He has been knocking at your chamber door for some time. When he comes to the furnace door, perhaps you will open that to him."

Cornelius returned no answer. He felt his mother's seriousness awkward, and said to himself she was unkind. Why couldn't she make some allowance for a fellow? He meant no harm.

Since going to work at the bank, he had become still less patient with his mother's infrequent admonitions, for, much as he disliked his work, he considered himself quite a man of the world because of it. But a thoroughgoing man of the world he was not—not yet at least—even though he was totally incapable of perceiving the kind of thing his mother cared about. This came not from moral lack alone, but from dullness and lack of imagination as well. He was like the child so sure he can run alone that he snatches his hand from his mother's and sets off through dirt and puddles, acting the part of the great person he considers himself.

With all her peace of soul, Mrs. Raymount was very anxious about her son, but she said no more to him now. She knew that a drenching shower is not the readiest way of making a child friendly with cold water.

"Well, for my part," said Cornelius at length, "I don't desire to be better than my neighbour. I think it downright selfish."

"Do you want to be as good as your neighbour, Corney?" said his mother. "There is a more important question still, and that is whether you are content with being as good as yourself, or do you want to be better?"

"To tell you the truth, mother, I don't trouble my head about such things. Philosophers are agreed that self-consciousness is the bane of the present age. Therefore, I mean to avoid it. If you had let me go into the army, I might have had some time to think about such matters, but that horrible bank takes everything out of me— except a burning desire to forget it at any cost till the time comes when I must endure it again. If I hadn't some amusement in between, I would kill myself, or take to opium or drinking. I wonder how the governor would like to be in *my* place!"

Hester rose and left the room, indignant with him for speaking so of his father.

"If your father were in your place, Cornelius," said his mother with dignity, "he would carry out his duties without grumbling, however irksome they might be."

"How do you know that, mother? He never had such a job."

"I know it because I know him," she answered.

Cornelius gave a grunt.

"If you think it hard," his mother resumed, "that you have to follow a way of life you did not choose, you must remember that we could get you to express no preference for anything. And your father had to strain everything to send you to college, with some

5

hardship to the rest of the family. I am sorry to say it, but you did not make it any easier by your mode of living while there."

"I didn't run up a single bill!" cried Cornelius with indignation.

"Your father knows that. But he also knows that your cousin Robert did not spend two-thirds of what you did, and made more of his time."

"He was in *rather* a different set," sneered the youth.

"And you know too," his mother went on, "that your father's main design for placing you in your uncle's bank was that you might gain a knowledge of the business that will help you to properly manage the money he will leave behind him. When you have gained that knowledge, there will be time to look for something else to do—you are young yet."

His father's money was a continual subject of annoyance to Cornelius, for it was no secret how he meant to dispose of it after he died. He intended, namely, to leave it under trustees, with his son as one of them until he married. At that time his estate was to be divided equally among his children, without any particular provision made for Cornelius.

The arrangement was an annoyance to Cornelius, who could see no advantage to him in being the eldest son of the family.

"Now, mother," he said, "do you think it fair that I should have to look after the whole family as if they were my own?"

This was by no means his real cause of complaint, but he chose to use it as his grievance for the present.

"You will not be the only trustee," said his mother. "It need not weigh on you."

"Well, of course, I could do better with it than anybody else of the family."

"If you have your father's love of fair play, Cornelius, you will. What you can do to prepare yourself is to make yourself thoroughly acquainted with business."

"A bank is hardly the place to get the business knowledge necessary for that sort of thing!"

"Your father has his reasons. How well prepared you are will depend on you. And when you marry, your responsibility will cease."

"What if I should marry before my father's death?"

"Indeed, I hope you will, Cornelius. The arrangement your father has made is merely a provision against the unlikely. When you are married, I don't doubt he will make an entirely new will to meet the new circumstances."

"I believe," Cornelius thought to himself, "that if I were to marry for money—and why shouldn't I—my father would divide my share among the rest and not leave me a farthing!"

Full of the injury of the idea, he rose and left the room. His mother wept as he vanished. She dared not allow herself to ask why she wept, dared not admit to herself that her firstborn was not lovely in her eyes, dared not ask where he could have gotten such a selfish nature, so selfish that he did not know he was selfish.

Although since coming to Burcliff, Cornelius attributed his sour spirits to the weather, and had expended them on the cooking, the couches, the beds, and twenty different things that displeased him, he had nevertheless brought his disposition with him. And his mother had sad doubts that the cause of it might lie in his own conduct—for the consciousness may be rendered uneasy without much rousing of the conscience proper.

He had always been fitful and wayward, but had only recently begun to behave so unpleasantly. Yet among his companions, he bore the character of the best-natured fellow in the world. To them he never showed any of the peevishness of his mental discomfort. He kept that for home, for those who loved him a thousand times better and would have cheerfully parted with their own happiness for his. Cornelius was but one of a large herd of youths who possessed no will of their own yet enjoyed the reputation of a strong one. He would become obstinate over any liking or foolish notion his pettiness decided to latch on to. And the common mind always takes obstinacy for strength of will, even when it springs from an utter inability to exercise the will as it was meant to be used, especially against liking.

Mr. Raymount knew little of the real nature of his son. The youth was afraid of his father—none the less that he spoke of him with so little respect. To his face he dared not show his true nature. He knew that his mother would not betray him—at least he would have considered it betrayal—to his father. And to be sure, no one who had ever heard Mr. Raymount give vent to his judgments would have wondered why either of them hesitated to mention the thing to him.

Whether in his own youth he would have done better in a position like his son's, as his worshipping wife believed, may be doubtful.

—Two —

An Eventful Walk

Gerald Raymount was a man of an unusual combination of qualities. His character contained such contradictions as to make one think there was almost a savage strain in him. On the other hand, he possessed a sharp mind, which seemed to indicate a heritage of culture. At the university he had read widely outside his specific requirements and thus had developed a broad faculty in literature.

From a long line of ancestors, he had inherited a few thousand pounds from his father, a country attorney. However, he had found that as his family had increased, his income was not sufficient for their accustomed style of living. There were no extravagant tastes among them, but neither did they possess the faculty for saving money and were rather too free with it in small things. The result was that Mr. Raymount was compelled to rouse himself out of his self-indulgence, and as the reader of many books now take himself to his study table, and try to discover whether he might be capable of writing articles that could add to his shrinking income.

Though Mr. Raymount was driven to this extreme by necessity, it did serve to some extent to make a man of him. The question is not whether a man works because he has to, but whether the work he does is good, honest work for which the world is better off. In this matter there are many first that shall be last. The work of a baker for instance, must stand higher in the judgment of the universe than that of a brewer, no matter how good his ale might be. Because the one trade brings in more money than the other, many in the world count it more honourable. But there is another judgment at hand.

In the exercise of his calling, Mr. Raymount was compelled to think more carefully than before, and so not only his mind but his moral and spiritual nature took a fresh start. More and more he wrote of the feelings and experiences of his own heart and history, and so, by degrees, gained power to rouse the will, not merely the emotions, or even the aspirations of men—the only true kind of power. The poetry of his college days now came to the service of his prose, and the deeper poetic nature, which is the prophetic in every man, awoke in him. His wife grew proud of him and of his work. Even though she looked upon her husband as a great man, she was still the practical wisdom of the house. He was not a great man—only a growing man. Yet she was nothing the worse for thinking so highly of him, because he *was* a growing man.

The daughter of a London barrister, of what is called a good family, she had known something of life before she married. From mere dissatisfaction she had early begun to withdraw from the show and self-assertion of social life, and sought within herself the door of that quiet chamber whose existence is unknown to most. For a time she had not heeded a certain soft knocking of one who would enter and share it with her. But now for a long time he who knocked had been her companion in the chamber whose walls are infinite. Why is it that men and women will welcome any romance or tale of love, devotion, and sacrifice from one to another of themselves, but turn from the least hint at the existence of a perfect love at the root of it all? Is it not because their natures are yet so far from the ideal, the natural, the true, that the words of the prophet rouse in them no vision, no poorest perception of spiritual fact?

Helen Raymount was now a little woman of fifty, clothed in a sweet dignity with plentiful gray hair and great, clear, dark eyes. She had the two daughters and two sons already introduced, of whom Hester was the eldest.

Wise as was the mother, and far-seeing as was the father, they had made the mistake common to many parents of putting off teaching their children obedience until it was more or less too late. If this is not begun at the first possible moment, it will be harder every hour it is postponed. The spiritual loss and injury caused to the child by their waiting till they fancy him fit to reason with is immense. Yet there is nothing in which parents are more stupid and cowardly, and even stubborn, than this. A home where children, even of parents of good conscience, are humoured and scolded and coaxed and punished instead of being taught obedience is like a moral slaughterhouse instead of the training ground it was meant to be.

The dawn of reason will no doubt help to develop obedience, but obedience is even more necessary to the development of reason. To require of a child only what that child can understand is simply to help him to make himself his own god—that is a devil. That some seem so little injured for their bad training is no justification for their parents' foolishness.

Cornelius was a youth of good abilities and a few good qualities. Naturally kind-hearted, he was full of self. He was not incapable of generosity, and was even tempted occasionally toward kindness. But he did not care whom he hurt as long as he did not see their suffering. He was incapable of controlling himself, yet was full of weak indignation whenever control was placed upon him. Supremely conceited, his view of the essentials of life were a good carriage, good manners, self-confidence, and plenty of money to spend freely. In his foolish brain he had fashioned a god into the likeness of what he considered a *gentleman*—and it was this image he was trying to become. To any wisdom in his father and mother he was so far blind that he even looked down upon it. Their opinion was hardly to be compared with that of one Reginald Vavasor, who, though so poor as to be one of his fellow clerks, was heir apparent to an earldom.

Leaving his mother, Cornelius took refuge in his room. Although he had occupied it but two weeks, the top of its chest was covered with cheap novels—the only literature he cared for. He read largely of these, if indeed his mode of swallowing could be called reading. But though he had read them all, he was too lazy to face the wind and rain between him and the nearest bookshop. None of his father's books interested him, whether science, philosophy, history, or poetry. A drearier soul in a drearier setting could hardly be imagined than the soul of this youth in that day's weather at Burcliff.

Though it may seem at first glance that one could hardly be blamed for such a reaction to his circumstances, in truth when a man cares for nothing that is worth caring for, the fault must indeed lie within himself—in the character the man has made, and is making, out of the nature God has given him. There is a moral reason why he does not and cannot care. If Cornelius had begun at any time to do something he knew he ought to do, he would not now have been the poor slave of circumstances he was—at the mercy of the weather. When men face a duty, not merely will that duty become less unpleasant to them, but life itself will *immediately* begin to gather interest. For in duty, and duty only, does an individual begin to come into real contact with life. Only then can he see what life is, and grow fit for it.

He threw himself on the bed—for he dared not smoke with his father so near—and dozed away the morning till lunch. He then returned to his room and fell asleep again till tea time. This was his only resource against the unpleasantness of the day. When tea was over, he rose and sauntered once more to the window.

"Hullo!" he cried. "I say, Hester, the sun's shining! The rain's over—at least for a quarter of an hour! Come, let's go out for a walk. We'll go hear the band at the castle gardens. I don't think there's anything going on at the theater."

The sight of the sun revives both men and midges.

"I would rather walk," said Hester.

Hester had a rather severe mode of speaking, especially to this brother. She was the only person in the house who could have done any thing with him, and she lost her opportunity by shouting to him from a distance, instead of coming close up to him and speaking in a whisper. But she did not love him enough for that, neither was she yet calm enough in herself to be able for it. I doubt much, however, if he would have been in any degree permanently the better for the best she could have done for him. He was too self-satisfied for any redemption. He was afraid of his father, resented the interference of his mother, was as cross as he pleased with his sister, and cared little whether she was vexed with him or not. He regarded the opinion of any girl, just because she was a girl, too little for her to establish any true relation with him.

She went to put on her hat and cloak, and soon they were in the street.

It was one of those misty clearings in which sometimes the day seems to gather up its careless skirts that have been sweeping the half-drowned world as it prepares for the waiting night. There was a great lump of orange colour half melted in the watery clouds of the west, but dreariness still hung everywhere else. As they walked along, Hester's eyes were drawn upward into the sky. Suddenly she cried out in pain when her foot turned awkwardly on a stone.

"That's what you get, Hester," said Cornelius, pulling her up like a horse that stumbled, "by your star gazing. You are always coming to grief by looking higher than your head!" He was always ready to criticize, and it was so much the easier for him that he had not the least inclination toward self-criticism.

"Oh, please stop a minute, Corney," returned Hester, for he continued to walk on as if nothing had happened. "My ankle hurts!"

"I didn't know it was that bad," he answered stopping. "There, take my arm."

After a few moments she said, "Now I can go on again. How stupid of me—on plain asphalt pavement!"

They walked on, but within minutes Hester stopped again.

"Corney," she said, "my ankle feels so weak I am afraid I will twist it again."

"Just my luck," rejoined her brother. "I thought we were going to have some fun!"

They stood silent—she looking nowhere in particular, and he staring about in all directions.

"What's this?" he cried, fixing his gaze on a large building opposite them. "*The Pilgrim's Progress,* it says on the board. It must be a lecture. Let's go in and see! We may at least sit there till your ankle is better. *Admission—sixpence.* Come along. We may get a good laugh, who knows?"

"I don't mind," Hester said as they crossed the road.

It was a large, dingy, dirty, water-stained and somewhat dilapidated hall to which the stone stair, ascending immediately from the door, led them. Some twenty-five or thirty people formed the company present in the gloomy place. An old man, like a broken-down clergyman, wearing a dirty white neckcloth, kept walking up and down the platform, flaunting a pretence of lecture on Bunyan's allegory. Whether he was a little drunk or greatly in his dotage, it was impossible to determine. A sample of his mode of lecturing will reveal that a few lingering rags of scholastic achievement yet fluttered about the poor fellow.

"And then came the terrible battle between Christian—or was it Faithful?—I used to know, but trouble has played old hookey with my memory. It's all here, you know"—and he tapped his bald head—"but there's Christian and Apollyon. When I was young, and that wasn't yesterday, I used to think, but that was before I could read, that Apollyon was one and the same with Bonaparty—Nappoleon, you know. And I wasn't just so far wrong neither, as I shall readily prove to those of my distinguished audience who have been to college like myself, and learned to read Greek like their mother tongue. For what is the very name Apollyon but a prophecy concerning the great conqueror of Europe! Nothing can be plainer. N stands for nothing—a mere veil to cover the prophecy till the time of revealing. In all languages it is the sign of negation—*no*, and *none*, and *never*, and *nothing*. Therefore cast it away as the nothing it is. Then what have you left but *apoleon*! Throw away another letter, and what have you but *poleon*! Throw away letter after letter, and what do you get but words—*Napoleon, apoleon, poleon, oleon, leon, eon*, or, if you like, *on*! Now these are all Greek words—and what, pray, do they mean? I will give you a literal translation, and I challenge any Greek scholar who may be here present to set me right, that is, to show me wrong: Napoleon the destroyer of cities, being a destroying lion! Now I should like to know a more sure word of prophecy than that! Would any one in the company oblige me? I take that now for an incontrovertible"—he stammered over the word—"proof of the truth of the Bible. But I am wandering from my subject, which error, I pray you, ladies and gentlemen, to excuse me."

He maundered on in this way, uttering even worse nonsense, and mingling with it soiled and dusty commonplaces of religion, every now and then dwelling for a moment or two upon his own mental and physical decline from the admirable being he once was.

Cornelius was in fits of near laughter. The only thing that kept his merriment within bounds was the dread that the dreary old soul, who smelled abominably of strong drink, might address him personally and so draw upon him the attention of the audience.

How different were Hester's thoughts. To the astonishment of Cornelius, when at last they rose to go, there were tears in her eyes. The misery of the wretched man, no doubt once a clergyman, had overcome her heart. Worst of all, to the heart of Hester, was the fact that so few people were present, many of them children at half-price, most of whom were far from satisfied with the amusement offered them. When the hall and the advertising were paid for, what would this poor, old remnant of humanity, with his yellowing neck-cloth, have left for his supper? Did he have anyone to look after him? The poor man! Hester's eyes were full of tears to think she could do nothing for him. She remembered the fat woman with curls hanging down her cheeks who had taken their money at the door. Apparently she was his wife. Alas for the misery of the whole thing!

When they emerged and breathed again the clean, rain-washed air instead of the musty smells of the hall, Hester's eyes involuntarily rose to the vault above her, the top of whose arch is the will of the Father, whose endless space alone is large enough to picture the heart of God. How was that old man to get up into the high regions and grow clean and wise? He must belong there as well as she! And were there not thousands equally and more miserable in the world—people who knew no tenderness, to whom none ministered, people who were pitifully alone? Was there nothing she could do to help, to comfort, to lift up one such person of her own human family, to rescue a heart from the misery of hopelessness, to make one feel there was a heart of love and refuge at the center of things?

Hester had a large, though not hitherto entirely active aspiration in her. And now, the moment she began to flutter her weak wings, she found the whole human family hanging upon her, and that she could not rise except in raising them along with her. For the necessities of our deepest nature are such as not to allow a mere private and individual satisfaction.

I well remember feeling as a child that I did not care for God to love me if he did not love everybody. The kind of love I needed was love essential to my nature—the love of me, a man, not of me a person—the love therefore that all men needed, the love that belonged to their nature as the children of the Father, a love he could not give me except he gave it to all men.

This was not the beginning of Hester's enthusiasm for her kind—only a crystallizing shock it received. And though at the age of twenty-three she had little fruit to show yet, the tree would be nonetheless abundant in the end. She was one of the strong ones that grow slowly.

"There you are again, staring up into the sky again!" said Cornelius. "You'll be spraining your other ankle any moment!"

"I had forgotten all about my ankle, Corney," returned Hester quietly. "But I will be careful."

"Well, I think between us we got the worth of our shilling! Did you ever see such a ridiculous old bloke?"

Hester did not reply, but heaved an inward sigh. What would be the use in trying to let her brother know how she felt inside so long as he recognized no dignity in life, never set himself *to be!* Why should anyone be taught to behave like a gentleman, so long as he is not a gentleman?

Cornelius burst out laughing.

"To think of that old codger trying to interpret the muffs going through the river, and the angels waiting for them on the bank like laundresses with their clean shirts! Ha, ha, ha!"

"The whole thing was pitiful," said Hester. "That old man made me very sad."

"How you could see anything pathetic, or 'pitiful,' as you call it, in that disreputable old humbug, I can't even imagine," replied her brother. "A more ludicrous specimen of broken-down humanity would be hard to find! A drunken old thief, I'll lay you anything!"

"And you don't count that pitiful, Cornelius? A man so low, so hopeless, yet you feel no pity for him?"

"Oh, don't trouble your head about him. He'll have his hot supper when he gets home, and his hot tumbler of whisky— swearing, too, if it's late."

"That seems to me the most pitiful of all," returned Hester, and was on the point of adding, "That is just the kind of pity I feel for you, Corney," but checked herself. "Is it not pitiful to see a human being, made in the image of God, sunk so low?"

"It's his own doing," returned Cornelius.

"And is not that the worst of it all? If he were not to blame, it would be sad enough. But to be as he is and to be to blame for it seems to me a misery unbearable."

Cornelius again burst into laughter, and Hester held her peace. That her own brother's one mode of relieving the suffering in the world should be to avoid as much as possible adding to his own was to her sisterly heart humiliating.

– Three –

Hester Alone

After the family separated for the night, Hester went to her room and fell to thinking again.

She was one of those women who, from the first dawn of consciousness, have all their lives tried, with varying degrees of success, to do the right thing. In this she followed in the footsteps of her mother, who also walked steadily along the true path of humanity. But Hester was young and did not consider herself as caring as she wanted to be, and was frequently irritated by her failure. For it is impossible to satisfy the hard master *Self.* While he flatters some, he requires of others more than they can give.

God seems to take pleasure in working by degrees. The progress of the truth is as the permeation of leaven, or the growth of a seed. A multitude of successive small sacrifices may work more good in the world than many a large one. What would even our Lord's death on the cross have been except as the crown of a life in which he died daily, giving himself, soul, body, and spirit, to his men and women? It is the Being that is precious.

Being is the mother to all little Doings as well as the grown-up Deeds and the mighty heroic Sacrifice. Hester had not had time, neither had she prayed enough to *be* quite yet, though she was growing well toward it. She was a good way up the hill, and the Lord was coming down to meet her, but they had not quite met yet so as to go up the rest of the way together.

In religious politics, Hester was what was called a good churchwoman, which in truth means a sectarian. She looked down upon those of all dissenting churches as from a superior social standing—that is, with the judgment of this world, and not that of Christ the carpenter's son. So she was scarcely in the kingdom of heaven yet, any more than thousands who regard themselves as good Christians. I do not say these feelings were especially active in her, but she did not love her dissenting neighbour as herself.

I well know that many good dissenters are equally and in precisely the same way sectarians, that is bad Christians. For my part I would rather cut off my right hand than be so cased and in a narrow garment of pride and satisfaction if I were condemned to keep company with myself instead of the Master as he goes everywhere—into the poorest companies of them that love each other, and so invite his presence.

The Lord of truth and beauty has died for us. Shall we turn up a Pharisaical nose toward our brothers and sisters? Casting from us our own faults first, let us cast from us and from him our neighbour's also.

That Hester's exclusiveness in favour of the Church of England was simply a form of that pride, justify or explain it as you will, which found its fullest embodiment in the Jewish Pharisee—the evil thing that Christ came to burn up with his lovely fire, and which yet so many of us who call ourselves by his name keep hugging to our bosoms—I mean the pride that says, "I am better than thou." If there be any who is in any true sense below us, it is Christ's call upon us to stoop and lay hold of and lift the sister soul nearer to the heart of the divine tenderness.

This tenderness, which has its roots in every human heart, had larger roots in the heart of Hester than in most. Whatever her failings, whatever ugly weeds grew in the neglected corners of her nature, the moment she came in contact with any of her kind in whatever condition of sadness or need, the pent-up love of God—I mean the love that came of God and was divine in her—would burst its barriers—even the barriers of her sectarian prejudices—and rush forth, sometimes almost overwhelming herself in its torrent. She would then be ready to die, nothing less, to help the poor and miserable.

The tide of action, in these later years flowing more swiftly in the hearts of women—whence has resulted so much that is noble, so much that is paltry, according to the nature of the heart in which it swells—had been rising in that of Hester also. She must not waste her life! She must do something! What should it be? Her deep sense of the misery around her had of course suggested that it must be something in the way of help. But what form was the help to take? "I have no money!" she said to herself—for this the last and feeblest of means for the doing of good is always the first to suggest itself to one who has not perceived the mind of God in the matter.

To me it seems that the first thing in regard to money is to prevent it from doing harm. The man who sets out to do good with his fortune is like one who would drive a team of tigers through the streets of a city, or hunt the fox with cheetahs. I would think of money as Christ thought of it, for no other way is true, however it may recommend itself to good men. Neither Christ nor his apostles did anything by means of money. Nay, he who would join them in their labours had to abandon his fortune.

That evening the thought of the miserable, ruinous old man kept haunting Hester, making her very sad. Her thoughts wandered abroad over the universe of misery. For was not the whole world full of men and women who groaned, not merely under poverty and cruelty, weakness and sickness, but under dullness and stupidity? And now, on this night for the first time, the idea came to Hester whether she might in some way make use of the one gift she was aware she possessed for the service she desired. Her passion for music had resulted in her training in both organ and piano. She was also gifted with a fine contralto voice which, she hoped, could comfort and uplift humanity.

But sheer pity for her kind was not the only impulse moving Hester in this direction. Hers was an honest and active mind. She could not have gone to church regularly as she did without gaining some glimpses of the mightiest truth of our being, that we belong to God in actual fact of spiritual property and profoundest relationship. She had much to learn in this direction yet. This night came back to her the memory of a sermon she had heard on the text, "Glorify God in your body, and in your spirit, which are God's." It was a dull enough sermon, yet not so dull that it hindered her from gleaning its truth. When she had gone out of the dark church into the sunshine on that day and heard the birds singing, a sense awoke in her such as she had never had before.

She saw that the voice lying like an unborn angel in her own throat belonged not to herself but to God, and must be used in some way for the working of his will in the world he had made. She had no real notion yet of what was meant by the glory of God. She had a lingering idea—a hideously frightful one—that God thought so much of himself that he required homage from his creations. Hence, she first thought of devoting her voice to some church choir. With her incomplete notion of God and of her relation to him, how could she yet have escaped the poor pagan fancy—good for a pagan, but beggarly for a Christian—that church and its goings-on are synonymous with serving God? She had not begun to ask how these were to do God any good, or how they were to do anything for God.

She had not begun to see that God is the one great servant of all, and that the only way to serve him is to be a fellow servant with him—to be, say, a nurse in his nursery, tending this or that lonely person, this or that sickly child of his. It is as absurd to call song and prayer serving God as it would be to say the thief on the cross did something for Christ in consenting to go with him to paradise.

But now some dim perception of this truth began to wake in her. Vaguely she began to feel that perhaps God had given her this voice and this marriage of delight and power in music and song for some reason like that for which he had made the birds the poets of the animal world.

What if her part also should be to drive dull care away? What if she too were intended to be a door-keeper in the house of God, and open or keep open windows in heaven that the air of the high places might reach the low swampy ground? If while she sang, her soul mounted on the wings of her song till it fluttered against the latticed doors of heaven as a bird flutters against the wires of its cage, and if also God had made of one blood all nations of men—then surely her song was capable of more than carrying merely herself up into the regions of delight!

Might there not from her throat go forth a trumpet-cry of truth among such as could hear and respond to the cry? Then, when the humblest servant should receive the reward of his well-doing, she would not be left outside, but enter into the joy of her Lord. How such work might be done by her she did not yet see, but the truth had drawn nigh her that, to serve God in any true sense, we must serve him where he needs service—among his children lying in the heart of lack, in sin and pain and sorrow. And she saw that, if she was to serve at all, it must be with her best, with her special equipment.

I need not follow the gradations, unmarked of herself, by which she at length came to a sort of conclusion. The immediate practical result was, that she gave herself more than ever to the cultivation of her gift, seeing in the distance the possibility of her becoming, in one mode or another, or in all modes perhaps together, a songstress to her generation.

– Four –

The Aquarium

The cry of the human heart in all ages and in every moment is, "Where is God and how shall I find him?" I know multitudes are incapable of knowing that this is their heart's cry. But if you are one of these, I would ask if you have ever yet made one discovery in your heart. To him who has been making discoveries in it for fifty years, the depths of his heart are yet a mystery. The roots of your heart go down beyond your knowledge—whole eternities beyond it—into the heart of God. I repeat, whether you know it or not, your heart in its depths is ever crying out for God.

Where the man does not know it, it is because the unfaithful Self, a would-be monarch, has usurped the consciousness—the demon-man, is uppermost, not the Christ-man. If ever the true cry of the heart reaches that Self, it calls it childish folly, and tries to trample it out. It does not know that a child crying to God is mightier than a warrior armed with steel.

If there was nothing but fine weather in our soul, the demon-self would be too much for the divine-Self, and would always keep it down. But bad weather, misfortune, ill-luck, adversity, or whatever name men may call it, sides with the Christ-self down below, and helps to make its voice heard.

To the people at Burcliff came at length a lovely morning, with sky and air like the face of a repentant child—a child who has repented so thoroughly that the sin has passed from him, and he is no longer even ashamed. The water seemed dancing in the joy of a new birth, and the wind, coming and going in gentle conscious organ-like swells, was at it with them, while the sun kept looking merrily down on the glad commotion his presence caused.

"Ah," thought the mother, as she looked from her windows before she began to dress for this new live day, "how would it be if the Light at the heart of the sun were shining thus on the worlds made in his image!"

She was thinking of her boy, whom perhaps, in all the world, only she was able to love heartily—there was so little in the personal being of the lad, that is, in the thing he was to himself, and was making of himself, to help anyone to love him! But in the absolute mere existence is reason for love, and upon that God does love—so love, that he will suffer and cause suffering for the development of that existence into a thing in its own full nature lovable, namely, an existence in its own will one with the perfect love whence it came. And the mother's heart more than any other God has made is like him in power of loving.

Alas that she is so seldom like him in wisdom—so often thwarting the work of God, and rendering more severe his measures with her child by her attempts to shield him from His law, and save him from saving sorrow. From his very infancy, she actively teaches him to be selfish, gets between him and the right consequences of his conduct, as if with her one feeble, loving hand she would stop the fly-wheel of the universe. It is the law that the man who does wrong shall suffer. It is the only hope for him and the neighbour he wrongs. When he forsakes his evil, one by one the dogs of his suffering will drop away from his track. He will find at last that they have but hounded him into the land of his nativity, into the home of his Father in heaven.

As soon as breakfast was over the whole family set out for a walk. Mr. Raymount seldom left the house till after lunch, but even he, who cared comparatively little for the open air, had grown eager for it. Streets, hills and the sandy beaches were swarming with human beings—all drawn out by the sun.

Mrs. Raymount saw her son, now cheerful from the change of weather, and looked upon him as good. She was one of the best of women herself—her lamp was sure to have oil in it. Yet ever since he first lay in her arms, I doubt if she had ever done anything to help the youth conquer himself. Now it was too late, even if she had known what could be done. The others had so far turned out well. Why should not this one also? The moment his surly disposition was temporarily over, she looked upon him as reformed. And when he spoke worldliness, she persuaded herself he was jesting. But, alas, she had no adequate notion—not even the shadow of an idea—of the selfishness of the man-child she had given to the world.

This matter of the black sheep in the white flock is one of the most mysterious facts of spiritual generation.

Sometimes, however, the sheep is by no means so black as the whiter ones—who perhaps think themselves whiter than they are—think. But on the other hand, he may be a great deal worse than some of his own family think him.

His father had just as little notion that Cornelius was a black sheep. He was not what the world would have called a black sheep, but his father, could he have seen into him, would have counted him a very black sheep indeed—and none the whiter that he recognized in the blackness certain shades that were of paternal origin. It was only to the rest of the family that Cornelius showed his true self. He was afraid of his father, and that father, being proud of his children, would have found it hard to believe anything bad of them—like his faults, they were his own! His faith in his children was in no small measure conceit of that which was his, and blinded him to their faults as it blinded him to some of his own. The discovery of any serious fault in one of them would be a sore wound to his vanity.

It never entered Mr. Raymount's mind that any member of his family might think differently than he did about anything. But both his wife and Hester were able to think, and did think for themselves, and there were considerable differences in the paths in which they walked from those he had trod. He supposed that both they and Cornelius read what he wrote and agreed with all of it. And while his wife and daughter did read most of it, his son read next to nothing of it, and what he did read, he read in silent contempt. The bond between the father and son was by no means so strong as the father thought. Indeed, because of Mr. Raymount's intentions regarding the division of his property, his son looked upon him as his enemy. And selfishness rarely fails of good arguments. Nor can anything destroy it but such a turning of things upside down as only he that made them can work.

"Let's go see the aquarium," said Cornelius.

"What do you think of that, Saffy?" the father asked the bright child walking hand in hand with him. Her name was Josephine, with eyes so blue he would have called her Sapphira but for the association. Between the two he contented himself with the pet name *Saffy*.

"Oh, yes, let's go see the fish, papa!"

As they were close, it did not take long before they entered and began the descent into the fascinating place. About halfway down, Cornelius gave a cry of recognition and darted down to the next landing. With a degree of respect he seldom manifested they saw him there accost a gentleman leaning over the balustrade, and shake hands with him. He was several years older than Cornelius, not a few inches taller, and much better-looking—one indeed who could hardly fail to attract notice even in a crowd. It was with almost a jeaous admiration that Cornelius cast a few glances at him. When the rest reached the landing, and Mr. Raymount, willing to know his son's friend, desired Corney to introduce him.

Cornelius had been now eighteen months in the bank, and had never even mentioned the name of a fellow clerk. He was one of those youths who take the only possible way for emptiness to make itself of consequence—that of concealment and affected mystery. Not even now but for his father's request, would he have presented his bank friend to him or any of the family.

The manners and approach of Mr. Vavasor were such as at once to recommend him to the friendly reception of all, from Mr. Raymount to little Saffy, who had the rare charm of being shy without being rude. If not genial, his manners were yet friendly, and his carriage if not graceful was easy. It was a kind of company bearing he had, but dashed with indifference, except where he desired to commend himself. He shook hands with little Saffy as respectfully as with her mother, but with neither altogether respectfully. Immediately, however, the pale-faced, cold, loving boy, Mark, unconsciously, disliked him. He was beyond question handsome, bearing an aristocratic look.

"Why didn't you tell me you were coming, Mr. Vavasor? I could have met you," said Cornelius, with just a little stretch of the degree of familiarity in use between them.

"I didn't know myself till the last minute," answered Vavasor. "It was a sudden decision of my aunt's. I had not the remotest idea you were here."

"Have you been looking at the fish?" asked Hester, at whose side their new acquaintance was walking, now that they had reached the subterranean level.

"Yes, but they are not very well kept. The glass is dirty and the water too. It seemed to me they look unhappy. I can hardly bear it. It would be a good deed to poison them all."

"Wouldn't it be better to give them fresh water?" said little Saffy. "That would make them happy."

To this wisdom there was no response.

"We were just talking," Hester said, "before we had the pleasure of meeting you, about people and fish—comparing them in a way."

"Look at that dogfish!" said Vavasor, pointing to the largest in the tank. "What a brute! I wouldn't want to be compared to him. Don't you just hate him, Miss Raymount?"

"I am not willing to hate any living thing," answered Hester.

"Why shouldn't you hate him? You would be doing the wretch no wrong."

"How can you tell that unless you knew all about his nature and past existence?"

"You seem to imply motive and choice, even for an ugly fish, where I see no ground for either. The ugly things are ugly just because they are ugly. We must take things as we find them. We ourselves are just what we are and cannot help it. We are made so."

"Then you think we are all just like the dogfish—except that destiny has made none of us quite so ugly?" asked Hester. "You do not believe in free will, then?"

"I see no ground for believing in it. We are but random forces. Everyone does just what is in him."

"I say *no*. Everyone is capable of acting better than he does," she replied.

"And why does he not then? How can he be made for it if he does not do it?"

"How indeed? That is the puzzle."

"Then you believe we can make ourselves different from what we are made?"

"Yes. We are made with the power to change. We are meant to take a share in our own making. We are made so and so, it is true, but not made *only* that way. We are made with a power inside us that can lay hold of the original power that made us. We are not made to remain as we are. We are bound to grow."

She spoke rapidly, her eyes glowing.

"You are too much of a philosopher for me, Miss Raymount," said Vavasor with a smile. "But just answer me one question. What if a man is too weak to change?"

"He must change," said Hester. "No one is too weak to change."

Beginning to feel the conversation was becoming much too serious, Vavasor asked, "But don't you think this is rather—ah—a bit too metaphysical for an aquarium?"

Hester did not reply. Nothing was too serious for her in any place. She was indeed a peculiar girl.

"Let us go see the octopus," said Vavasor.

Mr. Raymount followed and gradually drew even with his son's friend. He had heard the last turn of their conversation and now proceeded to pick up the edge of it, relating the ugliness of the fish around them to his rather oblique observations concerning art.

"A confoundedly peculiar family!" Vavasor thought to himself as they were leaving the place some time later. "There's a bee in every one of their bonnets! An odd, irreverent way the old fellow has about him—pretending to believe everything he says."

Vavasor was not one of the age who came out with a firm denial of God's existence. Like his fellows at the bank, he never took the trouble to deny him. They all took their own way and asked no questions. When a man has not the slightest intention that the answer shall influence his conduct, why should he bother to ask whether there be a God or not? Vavasor cared more about the top of his cane than the God whose being he did not take the trouble to deny. He believed a little less than the maiden aunt with whom he lived, she believed less than her mother, and her mother had believed less than hers. For generations the so-called faith of the family had been dying down, simply because all that time it had sent out no fresh root of obedience. It had in truth been no faith at all, only assent. Miss Vavasor went to church because it was the right thing to do. God was one of the heads of society, and his drawing rooms had to be attended. That she should come out of it all as well as other people when this life of family and incomes and match-making was over, she saw no reason to doubt. Ranters and canters might talk as they pleased, but God knew better than make the existence of thoroughly respectable people quite unendurable! She was kind-hearted, and treated her maid like an equal up to the moment of offense—then like a dog up to that of atonement. She had the power of keeping her temper even in family differences, and hence was regarded as a very model of wisdom, prudence and *tact*. She was devoted to her nephew, as she counted devotion, but would make sure that he made a correspondent return.

—Five —

Amy Amber

Some gently gradual crisis had arrived in the history of Hester, for in these days her heart was more sensitive and more sympathetic than ever before. It was ready to wake at every moan of the human sea around her. Unlike most women, she had not needed marriage and motherhood to open the great gate of her heart to her kind. Why the tide of human affliction should have begun to rise so rapidly in her just at this time, there is no need for conjecturing— much of every history must for the long present remain inexplicable.

Ever since her experience at the lecture on "The Pilgrim's Progress," she had seen the misery of the low of her kind as in a mirror, including her brother Cornelius. He had never before so plainly revealed to her his heartlessness, and the painful consequence of the revelation was, that now, with all her swelling love for human beings, she felt her heart shrink from him as if he were of another nature. Being several years older than he and having had a good deal to do with him as a baby and child, the infant motherhood of her heart had gathered about him, and nothing could destroy the relation between them. But as he grew up, the boy had undermined and weakened her affection, though hardly her devotion. And now the youth had given it a rude shock. But she did not yield to this decay of feeling, and every day grew more anxious and careful to carry herself toward him as a sister should.

The Raymounts could not afford one of the most expensive lodgings in Burcliff, but were content with a floor in an old house in an unfashionable part of town, looking across the red roofs of the port and out over the flocks of Neptune's white sheep on the blue-gray German ocean. It was kept by two old maids whose hearts had been flattened under the pressure of poverty—no, I am wrong. Our Lord never mentions poverty as one of the obstructions to his kingdom. It was *anxiety* over their poverty that caused the sisters Witherspin to wear away their lives in scraping together provision for an old age they were destined never to see.

They were a small, meager pair with hardly a smile between them. One waited and the other cooked. The one that waited had generally her chin tied up with a silk handkerchief, as if she had come to life again, but not quite, and could not do without the handkerchief. The other was rarely seen, but her existence was all day testified by the odours that ascended from the kitchen of her ever-recurrent labours. It was a marvel how from a region of such fumes could ascend the good dinners she provided.

Hester's heart was full of compassion for them. It looked as if God had forgotten them—toiling for so little all day long, but the fact was they had forgotten God. They should have sought the kingdom of heaven, and trusted him for their future while they did their work with might. Instead, they exhausted their spiritual resources by sending out armies of ravens, with hardly a dove among them, to find and secure a future still submerged in the waves of a friendly deluge. Nor was Hester's own faith in God so vital yet as to propagate itself in the minds of those she knew. She could only be compassionate and kind.

The morning after the visit to the aquarium, woeful Miss Witherspin, as Mark had epitheted her, entered to remove the ruins of breakfast with a more sad and injured expression of countenance than usual. It was a glorious day, and she was like a live shadow in the sunshine. Most of the Raymounts were already in the open air, and Hester was the only one in the room. The small, round-shouldered, cadaverous creature went moving about the table with a motion that suggested bed as fitter than labour, though she was strong enough to get through her work without more than occasional suffering. If she could only have left pitying herself and let God love her she would have got on well enough.

Hester, who had her own share of the same kind of fault, was rather moodily trimming her mother's bonnet with a new ribbon, glancing up from which she at once perceived that something in particular must have exceeded in wrongness the general wrongness of things in the poor little gnome's world. Her appearance was usually that of one with a headache. Her expression this morning suggested a mild indeed but all-pervading toothache.

"Is anything the matter, Miss Witherspin?" Hester asked.

"Indeed, miss. There never come nothing to sister and me but what's the matter. But it's the Lord's will and we can't help it." She ended with a great sigh.

"Is there some new trouble," Hester questioned further, "if you will excuse my asking?"

"Well, I don't know, miss, if trouble can ever be called new. But now our sister-in-law's passed on after her husband an' left her girl, brought up in her own way an' every other luxury, on our hands to take charge of. The responsibility will be the death of me."

"Is there no provision for her?"

"Oh yes, there's provision! Her mother kept a shop for fancy goods at Keswick—after John's death, that is—an' scraped together a good bit o' money, they do say. But that's under trustees—not a penny to be touched till the girl comes of age!"

"But the trustees must make you a proper allowance for bringing her up. And anyhow, you can refuse the charge if you choose, can't you?"

"No, miss, that we can't. It was John's wish, when he lay dyin', that if anything was to happen to Sarah, the child should come to us. It's the trouble of the young thing, the responsibility—havin' to keep your eyes on her every blessed moment for fear she'll do the thing she ought not to—that's weighing on me. Oh yes, they'll pay so much a quarter for her! It's not that. But to be always at the heels of a young sly miss after mischief—it's more'n I'm up to."

"When did you see her last?" asked Hester.

"Not since she was three years old!" answered Miss Witherspin.

"Then perhaps she may be wiser by this time," Hester suggested. "How old is she now?"

"Sixteen. It's awful to think of!"

"But how do you know she will be troublesome? You haven't seen her for thirteen years!"

"I'm sure of it. I know the breed, miss! She's took after her mother, you may take your mortal oath! The sly way she got round our John—an' all to take him away from his own family. You wouldn't believe it, miss!"

"Girls are not always like their mothers," said Hester. "I'm not half as good as my mother. When is she coming?"

"She'll be here this blessed day, miss!"

"Your house is filled with lodgers. Perhaps you will find her a help instead of a trouble. It won't be as if she had nothing to do."

"She'll be no good to mortal creature," sighed Miss Witherspin as she put the tablecloth on top of the breakfast things.

The girl did arrive that day. She sprang into the house like a loud sunbeam—loud for a sunbeam, not for a young woman of sixteen. She was small and bright and cheerful, with large, sparkling black eyes. Her face was rather small, her hair a dead brown, almost black. Her figure was, if not essentially graceful yet, thoroughly symmetrical, and her head, hands, and feet were all small and well-shaped. She had as little shyness as forwardness, being at once fearless and modest, gentle and merry, noiseless and swift—a pleasure to eyes, nerves, and mind. Her sudden appearance in rosebud print, to wait upon the Raymounts the next morning at breakfast, startled them all with a sweet surprise. Every time she left the room talk about her broke out all over again, and Hester's information about her was a welcome addition to their astonishment. A more striking contrast than that between her and her two aunts could hardly have been found in the whole town. She was like a star between two gray clouds of twilight. But she had not so much caused her own cheerfulness as her poor aunts had caused their misery. She so lived because she was so made. She was a joy to others as well as to herself, but as yet she had no merit in her own peace or its rippling gladness. So strong was the life in her that, although she cried often over the loss of her mother at night, she was fresh as a daisy in the morning, opening like that to the sun of life, ready not merely to give smile for smile but to give smile for frown.

In a word, she had one of those lovely natures that need but to recognize the eternal to fly straight to it. But, on the other hand, such natures are in general very hard to awaken to a recognition of that unseen eternal. They assent to every good thing, but for a long time seem unaware of the need of a perfect Father. To have their minds opened to the truth, they must suffer like other mortals less amiable. Suffering alone can develop in such any spiritual insight, or cause them to care that there should be a live God caring about them.

She was soon a favourite with every one of the family. Mrs. Raymount often talked to her. And on her side, Amy Amber was so much drawn to Hester that she never lost an opportunity to wait on her, and never once missed going to her room to see if she wanted anything, last of all before she went to bed.

The only one of the family that professed not to think much of her was Cornelius. Even Vavasor, who soon became a frequent caller, if he chanced to say some admiring word about the pretty creature after she had just flitted from the room, would only draw from his friend a grunt and a half sneer. Yet now and then he might have been caught looking at her, and would sometimes, in spite of himself, smile on her sudden appearance.

— Six —

Cornelius and Vavasor

If you had chanced to meet Cornelius in any other company than that of his own family, on all of whom he looked down upon with contempt, you would probably have taken him for an agreeable young man. The slouch and hands-in-pocket mood—those signals that self was at home to nobody but himself—vanished whenever he left his family. By going to the same tailor as Vavasor, he always managed to be well dressed in the latest European fashion—paying twice as much as his father for his irreproachable coats and linen shirts. His shirt-studs were simplicity itself—single pearls—and he was very particular about both the quantity and the quality of the linen showing beyond his coat-cuffs. Altogether he was nicely got up and pleasant to look upon. Stupid as the conventional European dress is, its trimness and clear contrast of white and black tends to level up all to the appearance of gentlemen, and I suspect this may be the real cause of its popularity.

Of course there are the manners suitable to strangers and those suitable to intimates, but politeness is the one essential of both. Watch a child and when he begins to grow rough you will see an evil spirit looking out of his eyes. It is a mean and bad thing to be ungentle with our own. Politeness is either a true face or a mask. If worn at one place and not at another, which of them is it? Neither is politeness inconsistent with thorough familiarity. I will go farther and say, that no true, or certainly no profound familiarity is attainable without it. The soul will not come forth to be roughly used. And where truth reigns familiarity only makes the manners strike deeper root in the being, and take a larger share in its regeneration.

35

But the pubicly agreeable side of his existence Cornelius kept hidden from his family. He never spoke to them about anything he did away from home. And he gloried in the thought that he did this or that of which neither the governor, the mother, nor Hester knew anything. He felt large and powerful and wise, and if he was only the more of a fool, what did it matter so long as he did not know it?

From Cornelius's first day at the bank, Mr. Vavasor, himself not the profoundest of men, had been taken with the youth's easy manners and his obvious worship of himself. Therefore he had allowed the one who aspired to his favour to enter by degrees into his charmed circle. He began to make Cornelius an occasional companion for the evening, and would sometimes take him home with him. There Cornelius at once laid himself out to please Miss Vavasor. Flattery went a long way with her, because she had grown to suspect herself no longer young or beautiful. Cornelius soon learned what he must admire and what he must look down on if he would be in Miss Vavasor's favour. As much energy as he expended on ingratiating himself to the man and his aunt, none of his own family had even heard of Mr. Vavasor before the encounter at the aquarium.

From Miss Vavasor's Cornelius had been invited to several other houses, and the consequence was that he looked from an ever growing height upon his own family, judging not one of them fit for the grand company to which his merits, unappreciated at home, had introduced him. He began to take private lessons in dancing and singing. As he possessed a certain natural grace, invisible when he was out of humour, but always appearing when he wanted to please, and a certain facility of imitation as well, he was soon able to dance excellently, and sing with more or less dullness a few songs of the sort fashionable at the time. But he took so little delight in music or singing for its own sake that in any allusion to his sister's practicing he would call it *an infernal row.*

Cornelius was inwardly astonished, even a little annoyed, at the seemingly favourable impression made by his family, Hester in particular, upon one in whose judgment he had placed unquestioned confidence. And he did not conceal from Vavasor his dissent from his opinion of them, for he felt that his friend's admiration of them gave him the advantage to be seen as a free-thinker, as one who disdained what his friend admired.

"My mother's the best of the lot," he said. "She's the best woman in the world, I do believe. But she's nobody except at home—don't you know? Why, just look at her and your aunt together! Pooh!"

What a fool! said Vavasor to himself, but he left his thought unsaid. He went on to give him a lecture, well meant and shallow, on what was good in a woman. In his view, not only Cornelius's mother, but Hester herself, possessed qualities which approached this strange virtue.

"Oh, she's a good girl—of her sort—Hester is," Cornelius continued, modifying his opposition somewhat. "I don't need you to tell me that. But she's too serious. Half an hour in one of her moods is enough to destroy one's peace of mind forever. And there's no telling when the fit may take her."

Vavasor laughed. But he said to himself what a woman might be made of her! To him she seemed fit—with a little developing assistance—to grace the best society in the world. It was not polish she needed, but experience and insight, he thought. He would have her learn to look on the world and its affairs as they who viewed them under the artificial light of fashion. Thus Vavasor almost immediately conceived the ambition of having a personal hand in the worldly education of this young woman, grooming her to shine as she deserved in the fashionable circles of the city—the only circles worth anyone's while. Through his aunt he could gain Hester's entrance where he pleased. Alongside her and her family, he seemed to himself a man of power and influence.

I wonder how Jesus Christ would carry himself in Mayfair. Perhaps he would not enter it. Perhaps he would only call to his own to come out of it, and turn away to go down among the money-lenders and sinners of the east end. I am only wondering.

Hester took to Vavasor from the first, in an external, meet-and-part sort of fashion. His bearing was so dignified, yet his manner so pleasing, that he brought out the best side of her nature. He roused none of that inclination to oppose, which poor, foolish Corney always roused in her. He could talk well about music and pictures and novels and plays. She not only let him talk freely, but was inclined to put a favourable interpretation on things that she did not

37

agree with, trying to see humour where another might find cynicism. For Vavasor, being in his own eyes the model of an honourable and well-behaved gentleman, had of course only the world's way of regarding and judging things. Had he been a man of fortune he would have given to charities with some freedom. But, his salary being very moderate, and his aunt just a little stingy as he thought, he would not have denied himself the smallest luxury for the highest betterment of a human soul. Instead of giving a poor woman in the street money for a pair of shoes, he would give her a half-worn pair of gloves while he was on his way to buy a new pair for himself.

It would have enlightened Hester a little to watch him for half an hour where he stood behind the counter of the bank. There he was the least courteous of proverbially discourteous bank-clerks, whose manners are about of the same breed with those of hotel-clerks in America. But he never forgot to take up his manners with his umbrella as he left the bank and resumed his airy, cheerful way of talking, which was more natural to him than his rudeness, and sparkled pleasantly against the more somber texture of Hester's consciousness. She suspected he was not profound, but that was no reason for not being pleasant to him and allowing him to be pleasant to her. So by the time Vavasor had spent three evenings with the Raymounts at Burcliff, Hester and he were on an external intimacy, if there be such a relation.

On the last of these evenings, he heard Hester sing for the first time. He had not even known she cared for music. For Hester, who did not regard her faculty as an accomplishment but as a gift, treated it as a treasure to be hidden for the day of the Lord rather than a flag to be flown in a public procession. She was jealously shy over it, as a thing it would be profanity to show to any but loving eyes. To utter in song to any but the right persons would have for her been immodest.

Yet she did sing, and Vavasor was astonished, yet delighted, at what he heard. He was in the presence of a power! But all he knew of power was society related. It was not a spirit of might he recognized, for the opening of minds and the strengthening of hearts, but only an influence of pleasing for self-aggrandizement. The best thing in him was his love of music. He did not really believe in music—he did not really believe in anything except himself. He professed to adore it, and imagined he did, because his greatest pleasure lay in hearing his own verses well sung by a pretty girl who would nod and then try to steal a glance at the poet from under her eyelids as she sang.

He had cultivated not a little what gift he had, but it was only a small power, not of production, but of mere reproduction like that of Cornelius, though both finer and stronger in quality.

On his way home he brooded over the delight of having his best songs sung by such a singer as Hester. From that night he fancied he had received a new revelation of what music was and could do, confessing to himself that a similar experience within the next fortnight would send him over head and ears in love with Hester—which must not be! Cornelius went half way with him.

"But why did you never tell me your sister was such a singer?" asked Vavasor

"Do you think so? She ought to feel very flattered! Why I didn't tell you?—Oh, I don't know. I never heard her sing like that before. I suppose it was because you were there. A brother's nobody, you know."

This flattered Vavasor, as how should it not? So he continued to go as often as he dared—that is, almost every night—to the Raymounts' lodging. But, as he thought, having discovered and learned thoroughly to understand her special passion, he was careful not to bring any of his own slight windy things of leaf-blowing poems under Hester's notice. It was not that he thought them such, but that he judged it prudent to postpone the pleasure of her singing them. She would require no small amount of training before she could quite enter into the spirit and special merit of them! He knew a good song, sometimes, when he heard it, and had himself a very tolerable voice and knew not a little about music.

Therefore, it came about by degrees that he found himself, to his satisfaction, relating to her as a pupil to a teacher. Hester gave herself to improving the quality of his singing—his style, his expression, and his tone. The relation between them became one which, had it then lasted, might have soon led to something like genuine intimacy. At least it might have led to some truer notion on the part of each of the kind of being the other was.

But the day of separation arrived first. And it was only on his way back to London that Vavasor began to discover what a hold the sister of his fellow-clerk had taken of his thoughts—indeed, of his heart, the existence of which organ he had never before had any very convincing proof.

—Seven —

Hester and Amy

Hester did not miss Vavasor quite so much as he hoped she might, or as much, perhaps, as he believed she did. She had been interested in him mainly because she found him both receptive and capable of development in the area of music—ready to understand, that is, and willing to be taught. To have such a man listen with respect to every word she said could not fail to be pleasant, even flattering to her. It is unfortunate how often a brother such as Cornelius and his rude behaviour at home will lead a sister such as Hester to place a higher value upon the civility of other men than they deserve. But the nearer persons come to each other in a family setting, the greater is the room and more are the occasions for courtesy.

Sad to say, such was not the case in the Raymount household. The Father cannot bear rudeness any more than wrong in his children—the comparison is unfit for rudeness is a great and profound wrong, a wrong to the noblest part of the human being. And a mere show of indifference is sometimes almost as bad as the rudest of words. The more guilty a man is of such faults, the less he is conscious of it.

But, despite his pleasant contrast with her brother, Vavasor did not move the deepest in Hester. How should he? With that deepest he had developed no relation. There were worlds of thought and feeling already in motion in Hester's universe, while the vaporous mass in him had hardly yet begun to stir. He was living on the surface of his being, all the more exposed to earthquake and volcanic eruption because he had never yet suspected the existence of the profound depths from which they rose. Hester, on the other hand, was already beginning to discover some of the abysses of the nature gradually unfolding in her. When Vavasor was gone she turned with greater diligence to her musical studies.

Amy Amber continued to be devoted to her, and when Hester was practicing would come about for as long as she could. Hester's singing seemed to enchant and fascinate the girl. But a change had already begun to show itself in Amy. The shadow of an unseen cloud was occasionally visible in her expression. As the days went by, the signs of her discomfort grew deeper. She moved about her work with less energy, and her smile did not come as readily. Both Hester and her mother saw the change. In the morning, when Amy was always the first one up, she was generally cheerful, but as the day passed, the cloud came. Happily, however, her diligence did not let up. Sound in health, and active by nature, she took a positive delight in work. In another household she would have been invaluable. But as it was, she was growing daily less and less happy.

One night she appeared in Hester's room, as usual, before going to bed. Her small face had lost, for the time, a great part of its beauty, and was dark as a thundercloud. She tried to smile, but only a wounded smile would come.

"My poor Amy! What is the matter?" cried Hester.

The girl burst into tears.

"Oh, miss, I *would* like to know what you would do in my place!"

"I'm afraid if I were in your place, I should do nothing so well as you do, Amy," said Hester. "But tell me what is the matter. What has made you so miserable?"

"It's not one thing nor two, nor even twenty things!" answered Amy, ceasing her crying and now looking sullen with the feeling of heaped-up wrong. "What *would* my mother say to see me treated so! *She* used to trust me. I don't understand how those two prying, suspicious old maids *can* be *my* mother's family!"

She spoke slowly and sadly, without raising her eyes.

"Don't they treat you well?"

"It's not that they watch every bite I put in my mouth," returned Amy. "I don't complain about that, for they're poor—at least they're always saying so. But not to be trusted one moment out of their sight—to be always suspected, and followed and watched, and me working my hardest—that's what drives me wild, Miss Raymount.

I'm afraid they'll make me hate them before long—and them my own flesh and blood, too. It was easier to take at first. I said to myself, 'They'll get to know me better!' But when I found they only got worse, I got tired of it altogether, and grew more and more cross, till now I can't stand it. If there isn't a change somehow soon, I shall run away—I shall, indeed, Miss Raymount. Oh, how I wish I could have kept the good temper I used to have—you're going away so soon, miss! Let me do your hair tonight."

"But you are tired, my poor child!" said Hester.

"Not too tired for that—it will relax me and bring back my good temper. Maybe some of yours will flow into me through your hair."

"No, no, Amy. I have none to spare. But do what you like with my hair."

As Amy lovingly brushed the long wavy overflow of Hester's beauty, Hester tried to help her understand that she must not think of a happy disposition merely as something that could be put into her and taken out of her. She tried to make her see that everyone has a large supply of good temper at hand, but that it was not theirs until it was made their own by choosing and willing to be good-tempered when inclined not to be—by holding it fast with the hand of determination when the hand of wrong would snatch it away.

"Because I have a book on my shelves," she said, "it is not therefore mine. When I have read and understood it, then it is a little mine. When I love it and do what it tells me, then it is altogether mine. It is like that with good temper—if you have it sometimes and not at others, then it is not yours. It lies in you like that book on my table—a thing priceless if it were your own, but as it is, a thing you can't even keep against your poor, weak old aunts."

As she said all this, Hester felt like a hypocrite, remembering her own weakness and sins. But Amy listened quietly, brushing steadily all the time. Yet scarcely a shadow of Hester's meaning crossed her mind. If she was in a good temper, she was in a good temper. If she was in a bad temper, she was in a bad temper. She had not a notion of the possibility of having a hand in making her own temper—not a notion that she was in any way accountable for the temper she might find herself in.

Hester kissed her, and though she had not understood, Amy went to bed a little comforted. When the Raymounts departed two or three days later, they left her at the top of the cliff-stair, weeping quietly.

Hester had no sooner reached home, hardly taking time to unpack her box, before she went to see her music teacher to make arrangements for taking up her study with her once again.

Miss Dasomma was one of God's angels, one of those live fountains that carry his gifts to their thirsting fellows. Of Italian descent, English birth, and German training, she had known well some of the greatest composers of her day. But the enthusiasm for her art was mainly the result of her own genius. It was natural, then, that she should exercise a great influence on every pupil who was worthy of her. Without her Hester could never have become what she was. Miss Dasomma was ready to begin at once, and Hester gradually increased her hours of practice, indulging her musical inclinations to the full.

They had not been home more than a week when, one Sunday afternoon, Mr. Vavasor called. This was not quite agreeable to Mrs. Raymount, who liked their Sundays kept quiet. But he was shown to Mr. Raymount's study.

"I am sorry," he said, "to call on a Sunday, but I am not so enviably situated as you, Mr. Raymount. I have so little time at my command."

Mr. Raymount was pleased with him afresh, for he spoke modestly and seemed by his manner to acknowledge the superior position of the elder man. They talked about the prominent questions of the day, and Mr. Raymount was even more pleased when he found the young aristocrat ready to receive enlightenment from his own lips. But the fact was that Vavasor cared very little about the matter. He simply had a light, easy way of touching on things, as if all his concessions, conclusions, concurrences were the merest matter of course. By this he made himself appear a master of a situation over which he merely skimmed on insect wing. Mr. Raymount took him not merely for a man of thought, but even of some originality—capable at least of forming an opinion of his own.

In relation to the wider circle of the country, Mr. Vavasor was so entirely a nobody that the acquaintance of a writer even so partially known as Mr. Raymount was something to him. There is a tinselly halo about the writer of books, and this attracted the young man.

Since his return he had instituted inquiries concerning Mr. Raymount, and finding both him and his family in good repute, he had told his aunt as much about them as he judged prudent. Miss Vavasor, however, being naturally skeptical of the opinions of young men, made inquiries for herself. From these she learned that there was a rather distinguished-looking girl in the family. Having, however, her own ideas for the nephew whose interests she had, for the sake of the impending title, made her own, she put off any visit, hoping his interest in the family would wane. But, though she declined to call, he went all the more often to see them.

On this, his first visit, he stayed for the evening and was installed as a friend of the family all over again. Although it was Sunday, and Hester's ideas were a little strict as to religious proprieties, she received him cordially while her mother received him with a somewhat detached kindness. Falling into the old ways, he took his part in the hymns, anthems, and what other forms of sacred music followed the family tea. And so the evening passed without annoyance—partly because Cornelius was spending it with a friend.

The tone, expression, and power of Hester's voice astonished Vavasor once again. After she had extemporized a sacred song on the piano, he was so moved as to feel more kindly disposed toward religion—by which he meant "going to church, and all that sort of thing"—than ever in his life before. He did not call the next Sunday, but came on Saturday. The only one present who was not pleased with him was Miss Dasomma, who happened also to spend the evening there.

Devout as well as enthusiastic, human as well as artistic, Hester's teacher was not an angel of music only, but had, for many years, been a power in the family for good. She did not find her atmosphere gladdened by Mr. Vavasor's presence. With tact enough to take his cue from the family, he treated her with studious politeness, but Miss Dasomma did not like Mr. Vavasor. She had to think before she could tell why, for there is a spiritual instinct which often takes the lead ahead of the understanding, and has to search and analyze itself for its own explanation. But once roused, she followed the question, and sitting off to the side while Hester played and watching his countenance, she tried to read it—trying to read, that is, what the owner of the face never meant to write. For what a man is lies as certainly upon his countenance as in his heart, though none of his friends may be able to read it.

Miss Dasomma's conclusion was, that Vavasor was a man of good instincts—as perhaps who is not?—but without moral development, pleased with himself, and desirous of pleasing others—at present more than moderately desirous of pleasing Hester Raymount.

"But," thought Miss Dasomma, "if this be his best, what might be his worst?" That he had some capacity for music was plain. But if, as she judged, the faculty was unassociated in him with truth of nature, it rendered him the more dangerous. For, at Hester's feet in the rare atmosphere and faint twilight of music, how could he fail to impress her with an opinion of himself more favourable than just? She knew well the character of his aunt, and the relation in which he stood to her. But for the present she could only keep a gentle watch over the mind of her pupil.

But that pupil had a better protection in the sacred ambition stirring in her. Hester had not yet told Miss Dasomma about it, even though she was the one best able to understand it. For Hester had already had sufficient experience to know that it is a killing thing to talk about what you mean to do. It is to let the wind in upon a delicate plant, requiring a long childhood under glass, open to sun and air, closed to wind and frost.

– Eight –

A Beginning in Hester

The Raymounts did not live in a highly fashionable part of London, but in a very serviceable house in Addison Square in the dingy, smoky, convenient, healthy district of Bloomsbury. One of the advantages of this location to a family with soul in it, that strange essence which will go out after its kind, was that on two sides it was closely pressed by poor neighbours. Artisans, small tradespeople, outdoor servants, poor actors and actresses lived in the narrow streets thickly branching away in certain directions. Hence, most happily for her, Hester had grown up with none of that uncomfortable feeling so many have when brought into contact with the poor. It was in a measure because since childhood she had been used to the sight of such that her sympathies were so soon and so thoroughly waked on the side of suffering humanity.

Those who would do good to the poor must attempt it in the way in which they could best do good to people of their own standing. They must make their acquaintance first. They must know something of the kind of the person they would help, to learn if help be possible from their hands. Only man can help man. Money without man can do little or nothing. As our Lord redeemed the world by being a man, the true Son of the true Father, so the only way for a man to help men is to be a true man to his neighbour. But to seek acquaintance with the poor with ulterior design is a perilous thing, likely to result in disappointment. We must follow the leadings of providence, and make acquaintance with the so-called lower classes by the natural working of the social laws that bring men together. What is the divine intent in the many needs of humanity, and the consequent dependence of the rich on the poor,

47

even greater than that of the poor on the rich, but to bring men together that in far-off ways at first they may be compelled to know each other? The man who treats his fellow as a mere means for the supply of his own desires, and not as a human being with whom his heart is to have interaction, is an obstructing clot in the human circulation.

Does anyone ask for rules of procedure in getting close to those about him? There are none to be had. Such must be discovered by each for himself. The only way to learn the rules of anything practical is to begin to do the thing. We have enough knowledge in us—call it insight, instinct, inspiration, or natural law—to begin anything required of us. The only way to deal with the profoundest mystery that is yet not too profound to draw us is to begin to do some duty revealed by the light from its golden fringe. If it reveals nothing to be *done,* there is nothing there for us.

Let the act of buying from the market, passing on the street, or meeting in the midst of some transaction, be recognized as a relation with, a meeting of that human soul. Let its outcome be in truth and friendliness. Allow nature her course, and next time let the relation go further.

To follow such a path is the way to find both the persons to help and the real modes of helping them. In fact, to be true to a man or woman in any way is to help him. He who goes out of common paths to look for opportunity leaves his own door and misses that of his neighbour. It is by following the paths we are in that we shall first reach somewhere. He who does this will find that his acquaintance widens and grows quickly. His heart will be full with the care of humanity, and his hands with its help. Such care will be death to one's own cares, such help balm to one's own wounds.

In a word, he must cultivate, in a simple human manner, the acquaintance of his neighbours. He must be a neighbour where a neighbour is needed. So shall he fulfill the part left behind of the work of the Master, which He desires to finish through him.

Of course I do not imagine that Hester understood all this. She had no theory toward the poor, and did not confine her hope of helping to the poor. There are as many in every other class needing help as among the poverty-stricken, and the need, although it wears different clothes, is essentially the same in all. To make the light go on in the heart of a rich man, if a more difficult task, is just as good a deed as to make it go on in the heart of a poor man. But with her strong desire to carry help where it was needed, and with her genuine feeling of the fundamental relationship between all human beings, Hester was in the right position to begin.

She went one morning into a small shop in Steven's Road to buy a few sheets of music paper. The woman who kept the shop had been an acquaintance almost from the day they had moved to the neighbourhood. In the course of their talk, Mrs. Baldwin mentioned that she was anxious about a woman in the house who was not well and whom she thought Mrs. Raymount would be interested in.

"Mama is always ready to help when she can," said Hester. "Tell me about her."

"Well, you see, miss," replied Mrs. Baldwin, "we're not in the way of having to do with such people, for my husband's rather particular about whom he rents the top rooms to. But, rent them we must, for times is hard an' children is many, an' it's all as we can do to pay our own way, only thank God we've done it up to this present. An' this man looked so decent, as well as the woman, but pitiful-like, that I didn't have the heart to send them away on such a drizzly, cold night as it was. They had four children with them, the smallest o' them ridin' pickaback on the biggest—an' it always goes straight to yer heart, to see one human being lookin' after another like that. But my husband, as was natural, he bein' a householder, was reluctant about the children. For children, you know, miss, 'cept they be yer own, ain't nice things about a house. An' them poor things wouldn't be a credit nowheres, for they were ragged enough—only they were pretty clean, as children go, an' there was nothing, as I said to him, in the top-rooms, as they could do much harm to. The man said theirs weren't like other children, for they had been brought up to do things as they were told, an' to remember that things belongin' to other people was to be handled as such. An', he said, they were always too busy earnin' their bread to be up to tricks, an' in fact were always too tired to have much spare powder to let off. So the long an' the short of it was we took 'em in, an' they've turned out as quiet an' well-behaved a family as you could desire. An' if they ain't got just the most respectable way o' earnin' their livin', that may be as much their misfortune as their fault, as my husband said."

"What is their employment, then?" asked Hester.

"Somethin' or other in the circus way, as far as I can make out from what they tell me. Anyway, they didn't seem to have no engagement when they come to the door, but they paid the first week down afore they entered. You see, miss, the poor woman she give me a kind of look up into the face that reminded me of my Susie, as I lost, you know, miss, a year ago—it was that as made me feel to hate the thought of sendin' her away, an' she was plainly in no condition to go wanderin' about, but I hardly knew how far her condition was. An' the very next day the doctor had to be sent for, an' there was a baby! The doctor come from the hospital, as nice a gentleman as you'd wish to see, miss, an' waited on her as if she'd been the first duchess in the land. 'I'm sure,' said my good husband to me, 'it's a lesson to all of us to see how he do look after her as'll never pay him a penny for the care he's taking of her!' But my husband he's that soft-hearted, miss, where anything in the baby-line's a goin' on! Now the poor mother's not at all strong, an' ain't gettin' back her strength, though we do what we can with her an' send her up what we can spare. You see, they pay for their house-room, an' then ain't got much over," added the woman in excuse of her goodness. "They're not out o' money yet quite, I'm glad to say, though he don't seem to have got nothing to do yet, so far as I can make out. That sort o' trade, ye see, miss, the demand's not steady in it. It's not like skilled labour, as my husband says—though to see what them young ones has to go through, it's labour enough. Would you mind goin' up an' havin' a look at her, miss?"

Hester told Mrs. Baldwin to lead the way, and followed her up the stairs.

The top rooms were two poor enough garret ones. In the largest, the ceiling sloped to the floor till there was only height enough for the small chest of drawers of painted pine to stand against the wall. A similar washstand and a low bed completed the furniture. The bed was immediately behind the door, and there lay the woman, with a bolster heightened by a thin petticoat and threadbare cloak under her head. Hester saw a pale, patient, worn face, with large eyes, thoughtful and troubled.

"Here's a kind lady come to see you," said her landlady.

It annoyed Hester to be called kind, but she spoke perhaps the more kindly to the poor woman because of Mrs. Baldwin's words.

"It must be dreary for you to lie here all alone," she said, taking the thin hand into hers. "May I sit a few minutes beside you? I was once in bed for a whole month and found it very wearisome. I was at school then. I don't mind being ill when I have my mother nearby."

The woman gazed up at her with eyes that looked like the dry wells of tears.

"It's very good of you, miss," she said. "It's a long stair to climb up."

She lay and gazed and said nothing more. Her child lay asleep on her arm, a poor little washed-out rag of humanity, but dear to the woman from the way she now and then tried to look at it, which was not easy for her.

Hester sat down and tried to talk, but found it hard to get on. After a few moments a dead silence came.

"What can be the good of a common creature like me going to visit people?" she said to herself. "I have nothing to say. I would help them if I could, but what can I do?"

For a few moments she sat silently, growing more and more uncomfortable, and thinking how to begin. The baby woke and began to whimper. The mother, who rarely let him off her arm, because then she was not able to get him till help came, drew him up to her, and began to nurse him. Suddenly the heart of the young, strong woman was pierced to the quick at the sight of how ill-fitted was the mother for what she had to do. "If only I could help her!"

She had yet to learn that the love of God is so deep he can be satisfied with nothing less than getting as near as it is possible for the Father to draw nigh to his children—and that is into absolute contact of heart with heart, love with love, being with being. And as that must be wrought out from the deepest inside, divine law working itself up through our nature into our consciousness and will, and claiming us as divine, who can tell by what slow certainties of approach God is drawing nigh to the most suffering of his creatures? Only, if we so comfort ourselves with such thoughts as to do nothing, we, when God and they meet, shall find ourselves out in the cold—a cold infinitely worse than any trouble this world has to show.

The baby made no complaint against the slow fountain of his life, but made the best he could of it, while his mother every now and then peered down on him as lovingly as ever a happy mother on her firstborn. The same God is at the heart of all mothers, and all sins against children are against the one Father of children, against the Life itself.

A few moments more passed, and then Hester began to sing—low and soft. Having no song planned for the occasion, she took a common hymn, sung in all churches and chapels. She put into it as much of sweetness and soothing strength as she could make the sounds hold. She sang with trembling voice, and with more shyness than she had ever experienced before. It was neither a well-instructed nor critically disposed audience she had, but the reason was that never before had she been so anxious for some measure of success. Not daring to look up, she sat with the music flowing over her lips like the slow water from the mouth of some statue of stone in a fountain.

And she had her reward. For when the hymn was done and at length she ventured to raise her eyes, she saw both mother and babe fast asleep. Her heart ascended on a wave of thanks to the giver of song. She rose softly, crept from the house, and hastened home to tell her mother what she had heard and seen. The same afternoon a basket of nice things arrived at the shop for the poor lodger in the top room.

The Raymounts did not relax their care until the woman was fairly on her feet again. And not till then did a day pass when Hester did not see her and sing to her and her baby. Several times she dressed the child, singing to him all the time. It was generally in the morning she went, because then she was almost sure to find them alone. Of the father she had seen next to nothing. All she had ever had time to see was that he was a man of middle height, with a strong face and frame, dressed like a workman. His three elder boys always left with him in the morning. The eldest was about twelve, the youngest about seven. They were rather sickly looking, but had intelligent faces and inoffensive expressions.

Mrs. Baldwin continued to bear the family good witness. She said they never seemed to have much to eat, but said they paid their lodgings regularly, and she had nothing to complain of. The place had indeed been untidy at first, but as soon as the mother was about again, it began to improve, and now, really, for people in their position, it was wonderfully well kept.

—Nine —

A Private Exhibition

Hester had not been near the woman and her child for two or three days. Dusk was approaching, but she would just run across the square and down the street, and look in upon them for a moment. It was but a few steps, and she knew almost every house she had to pass.

Tomorrow was Sunday and she felt as if she could not go to church without again seeing the little family committed, in a measure, to her humble charge. Finding Mrs. Baldwin busy in the shop, she nodded as she passed her and went up the stair. But she hesitated when she opened the door, and saw the father and the three boys standing together near the fire, like gentlemen on a hearth rug expecting visitors.

She glanced round in search of the mother. Some one was bending over the bed in the farther corner. The place was lighted with but a single candle, and a moment's gaze made it plain that the back was that of a man—was it the doctor?

She entered and approached the father, who then first seeing who it was that had knocked and looked in, pulled off the cap he invariably wore, and came forward with a bashful yet eager courtesy.

"I hope your wife is not worse," said Hester.

"No, miss, I hope not. She's took a bit bad. We can't always avoid it in our profession, miss."

"I don't understand you," she answered, feeling a little uneasy.

"If you will do us the honour to take a seat, miss, we shall be only too happy to show you as much as you may please to look upon with favor."

The man saw her hesitate, and resumed.

54

"You see, miss, this is how it was. Dr. Christopher—that's the gentleman there, a lookin' after mother—he's been that kind to her an' me an' all on us in our trouble, an' never a crown-piece to offer him—which I'm sure no lady in the land could ha' been better attended to than she've been—twixt him an' you, miss—so we thought as how we'd do our best for him, an' try an' see whether amongst us we couldn't give him a pleasant evenin' as it were, just to show as we was grateful. So we axed him to tea, an' he come, like the gen'leman he be, an' so we shoved the bed aside an' was showin' him a bit on our craft, just a trick or two, miss—me an' the boys here—stan' forward, Robert an' the rest of you an' make your bows to the distinguished company as honours you with their presence to cast an eye on you an' see what you can show yourselves capable of."

Mr. Franks had always hastened to disappear when Hester came, so she was astonished by his outpouring of information.

Here Mr. Christopher—Hester had heard his name before though she had never seen him—turned, and approached them.

"She'll be all right in a minute or two, Franks," he said.

"Evenin' to you, miss," came a soft voice from the bed. Hester walked over and greeted her.

Then flourishing a stage-bow, Franks immediately offered Hester a chair. She hesitated a moment, for she felt shy around Mr. Christopher. But as she had more fear of not behaving as she ought to the people she was visiting, she sat down, and became for the first time in her life a spectator of the feats of an acrobatic family.

"Now you be careful, John Franks!" said his wife. "Any more falls like that last one, cushion on the floor or no, an' I'll faint dead away.

The display may have seemed unremarkable to one in the habit of seeing such things. But to Hester it was positively astonishing at what each was capable of. As to the mother's anxiety over hard falls and broken bones, there hardly seemed any bones in the boys to break. Gelatine, at best, seemed to be what was inside their muscles, so wonderful were their feats and their pranks so strange. Amidst the marvels of their performance—broken by an occasional exclamation, followed by injunction to care from the doctor—in which their agile bodies responded to their wills, the occasional appearance of a strangely mingled touch of pathos chiefly interested Hester.

After some twenty or thirty minutes, the master of ceremonies suddenly drew himself up, wiped his forehead, then gave a deep sigh, as much as to say, "I have done my best, and if I have not pleased you, the more is my loss, for I have tried hard." The performance was over.

The doctor rose, and in a manly voice proceeded to point out to Franks one or two precautions which his knowledge of anatomy enabled him to suggest, especially regarding the training of the youngest. At the same time, he expressed himself greatly pleased with what his host had been so kind to show him.

"It mayn't be the best o' livin's for a family man," Franks replied, almost apologetically. "But at least I managed to keep life in the kids. It wasn't much more, you see, but life's life, though it be not tip-top style. An' if they're none o' them doin' just so well as they might, there's none o' them in trouble with the magistrate yet. An' that's a comfort as long as it lasts. An' when folk tell me I'm doin' no good, an' my trade's o' no use to nobody, I says to them, 'Beggin' your pardon, sir, or ma'am, but do you call it nothin' to fill four hungry bellies at home afore I was fifteen, after my mother and father died?' After that, they ain't in general said nothin'. An' one gentleman, watching me once perform on the street, he gave me half a crown."

"That was the best possible answer you could have given, Franks," rejoined Mr. Christopher. "But I think perhaps you hardly understood what such objectors meant to say. They might have gone on to explain, only they hadn't the heart after what you told them, that most trades did something on both sides. The trade not only fed the little ones at home, but did good to the persons for whom the work was done. The man, for instance, who cobbles shoes gives a pair of dry feet to some old man at the same time that he filled his own child's hungry little stomach."

Franks was silent for a moment, thinking.

"I understand you, sir," he said. "But I think I knows trades as makes a lot of money, and them they makes it from is the worse for it, not the better. It's better to stand on a fellow's own head like a clown as I do than to sell whiskey."

"You are quite right, there's not a doubt of it," answered Mr. Christopher. "But mind you," he went on, "I don't for a moment agree with those who tell you your trade is of no use. I was only explaining to you what they meant, for it's always best to know what people mean, even when they are wrong."

"Surely, sir, and I thank you kindly. Everybody's not so fair."

Here he broke into a quiet laugh, so pleased was he to have the doctor take his part.

"I think," Mr. Christopher went on, "that to amuse people innocently is often the only good you can do them. When done lovingly and honestly, it is a Christian service."

This rather shocked Hester—acrobatics a Christian service! With the grand ideas of service beginning to dawn within her, there still mingled some foolish notions. She still felt as if going to church and, while there, trying to fix her thoughts on the prayers and the sermons and the hymns was *serving* God. She felt that she ought to say something, but had no idea what. She was one of the few who know when they have nothing to say.

"Suppose," he went on, "somebody walking along Oxford Street was brooding over an injury that had been done to him by another, and thinking of how he might get his revenge. He passes many persons and things and takes no notice of anything. But then he comes upon a small crowd watching a man perform some tricks— we won't say as good as yours, Mr. Franks—he stops and stares and forgets for a moment or two that there is one brother-man he hates and would kill if he could."

Here Hester found words to respond. "But he would only go away as soon as he had had enough of it, and hate him all the same."

"I know very well," answered Christopher, turning now to her, "that it would not make a good man of him. Yet it must count for something to have the evil mood in a man stopped even for a moment, just as it is something to a life to stop a fever. It gives the godlike spark in the man, feeble, perhaps nearly exhausted, a fresh opportunity of revival. For the moment at least, the man is open to influences from a source other than his hate. If the devil may catch a man unawares when he is in a bad or unthinking mood, why should not the good Power take his opportunity when the evil spirit is asleep through the harping David or the feats of a Franks?"

Hester said nothing further, but still caught but a glimpse of the doctor's meaning. We are surrounded with things difficult to understand, and the way most people take it is to look away lest they should find out they have to understand them. Hester suspected scepticism in his remarks—most doctors, she believed, leaned in that direction. But she herself had begun to have a true notion of serving man. Therefore, there was no fear of her not coming to see, by and by, what serving God meant. She did serve him, therefore she could not fail to discover the word that belonged to the act. Only by serving can one find out what serving him means. Some people are constantly rubbing at their skylights, but if they do not keep their other windows clean also, there will not be much light in the house. God, like his body, the light, is all about us, and prefers to shine in upon us sideways, for we could not endure the power of his vertical glory. No mortal man can see God and live, and he who does not love his brother whom he has seen will not love his God whom he has not seen. He will come to us in the morning through the eyes of a child when we have been gazing all night at the stars in vain.

Hester rose. She was a little frightened at the very peculiar man and his talk. She had made several attempts in the dull light to see him as they watched the contortions of the acrobats.

Dr. Christopher was a thick-set man about thirty, in a rough coat of brownish gray with many pockets, a striped shirt, and a black necktie. His head was big, with rather thick, long and straggly hair. He had a large forehead and large gray eyes. The remaining features were well formed but rather fat, like the rest of his not elegant person, with a pale complexion. His voice was somewhat gruff but not unmusical, a thread of sadness in it. Hester declined his offer to see her home.

The next time she went to see the Frankses, which was not for four or five days, she found they were gone. They had told Mrs. Baldwin that they were sorry to leave, but they had to look for a cheaper place.

Hester was very disappointed. In later years the memory of them was always precious to her because it had been with Mrs. Franks that she had first experienced the hope of her calling by many times giving sleep and rest to her and her babe. And if it is a fine thing to delight the audience of a concert room of well-dined, well-dressed people, surely it is not a little thing to hand God's gift of sleep to a poor woman weary with the lot of women, and having so little pleasure in life.

Mrs. Franks would undoubtedly have differed from Hester in this judgment of her worldly condition, on the ground that she had a good husband and good children. Some people are always thinking others better off than themselves. Others feel as if the lot of many about them must be absolutely unbearable because they themselves could never bear it, they think. But things are unbearable only until we have them to bear. The possibility of carrying them comes with them. For we are not the roots of our own being.

—Ten —

Vavasor and Hester

The visits of Vavasor, in reality to Hester, continued. They became more frequent and he stayed longer. Her mother and Miss Dasomma noted with some anxiety, that he began to appear at the church they attended, a dull enough place, without any possible attraction of its own for a man like Vavasor. After two or three Sundays, he began to join them as they came out and walk part way home with them. Next, he went all the way and was asked to stay to lunch.

It may seem strange that Mrs. Raymount would allow things to go on like this if she was truly anxious about the result. But in the first place, she had thorough confidence in Hester and did not imagine it possible she should fall in love with a man like Vavasor.. In the second place, it is amazing what weakness may coexist with what strength, what worldliness stand side by side with what spirituality—for a time, that is, till one overcomes the other. Mrs. Raymount was pleased with the idea of a possible marriage of such distinction for her daughter, which would give her just the position she counted her fit for. These mutually destructive considerations were, with whatever logical inconsistency, both certainly operative in her.

Then again, they knew nothing against the young man! He made himself agreeable to every one in the house. In Addison Square he showed scarce the faintest shadow of the manner which made him at the bank almost hated. He was on his good behaviour in a private house, but his heart, and his self-respect, as he would have called his self-admiration, were equally concerned in his

60

looking his best—which always means looking better than one's best.

In Hester's company his best was always uppermost, and humility being no part of this best, he not merely felt comfortable and kindly disposed—which he was—but good in himself and considerate of others—which he was not. There was that in Hester and his feeling towards her which had upon him what elevating influence he was yet capable of receiving, and this fact said more for him than anything else.

She seemed gaining a power over him that could not be for other than good with any man who submitted to it. It had begun to bring out what was best in a disposition nearly ruined by evil influences on all sides. Both glad and proud to see her daughter exerting such influence, how could Mrs. Raymount interfere? It was plain he was improving. Not once now did they ever hear him jest on anything belonging to church!—As to anything belonging to religion, he scarcely knew enough to have any material for jesting.

Miss Dasomma was more awake. She knew better than Mrs. Raymount the kind of soil in which his human plant had been reared, and saw more danger ahead. She feared the young man was but amusing himself, or at best enjoying Hester's company as some wary winged thing enjoys the flame, courting a few singes, not quite avoiding even a slight plumous conflagration, but careful not to turn a delightful imagination into a consuming reality. She could not believe him as careless of himself as of her, but judged he was what he would to himself call flirting with her—which had the more danger for Hester that there was not in her mind the idea corresponding to the phrase.

I believe he avoided asking himself where the enjoyment of the hour was leading, and I fancy he found it more easy to set aside the question because of the difference between their social positions. Possibly he regarded himself as honouring the low neighborhood of Addison Square by the frequency of his shining presence. At the same time, he was feeling the good influences more than he realized or would have liked to acknowledge. For he had never turned his mind in the direction of good. It was far more from circumstance than refusal that he was not yet the more hurtful member of society which his no-principles were surely working to make him.

Hester was, of course, greatly interested in him. She had been but little in society, had not studied men in the least, and could not help being pleased with the power she plainly had over him. Even Corney, not very observant or penetrating, remarked on the gentleness of Vavasor's behaviour in their house. He followed every word of Hester's concerning his singing, and showed himself even anxious to win her praise by the pains he took to improve. He ceased to bring forward his heathenish notions about human helplessness and fate, and listened to her statements about the individual mission of every human being with an almost humble and attentive manner. Whether any desire of betterment was now awake in him through the power of her spiritual presence, I cannot tell. At first Hester thought only of doing him good. And it was not until she imagined some success in that vein that the true danger to her began.

After that, with every fresh encouragement the danger grew—for in equal proportion grew the danger of *self* coming in and getting the upper hand.

I do not suppose that Vavasor once consciously planned to actually deceive her, or make her think him better than he thought himself. With a woman of Hester's instincts, there might have been less danger if he had. But if he had any, he had but the most rudimentary notion of truth in the inward parts, and could deceive another all the better that he did not know he was deceiving. He had just as little notion of the nature of the person he was dealing with, or the reality to her of the things she spoke about—belief was, to him, the mere difference between opinions. She spoke the language of a world whose existence he was incapable of recognizing, for he had never obeyed one of its demands. His natural inborn proclivities to the light had, through his so seldom doing the deeds of the light, become so weak, that he hardly knew such a thing as reform was required of, possible to, or desirable in him. Nothing seemed to him to matter except "good form." To see and hear him for a few minutes after leaving her and entering his club, would have been safety to Hester. I do not mean that he was of the baser sort there, but whatever came up there, he would meet on its own grounds, and respond to in its own kind.

He was certainly falling more and more into what more people call *love*. As to what he meant he did not himself know. How little regard there may be in that for the *other* apart from the *self* I will not now inquire. When intoxicated with the idea of her, that is when thinking what a sensation she would make in his grand little circle, he felt it impossible to live without her. Some way must be found! Had he anything worthy the name of property coming with the title that would be his, he would have proposed to her at once, he told himself. But it would be raging madness, even with the most beautiful wife in the world, to encounter an earldom without a penny. And her family could not have great money. No one with anything would slave as the governor did from morning till night. To marry her would be to live on his salary, in a small house in St. John's wood, or Park Village, ride home in the omnibus every night like one in a tin of sardines, wear half-crown gloves, cotton socks, and cheap hats. The prospect was too hideous even to be ludicrous! No, there must be some way other than that. Thus would Vavasor's emotions work themselves back and forth.

It was some time before he risked an attempt to please her with a song of his own. There was just enough unconscious truth in him to make him a little afraid of Hester. Commonplace as were the channels in which his thoughts ran, he would still not risk encountering her scorn. He knew she was capable of it, for Hester had not yet gathered the sweet gentleness that comes of long breathing the air of the high countries. It is generally many years before a strong character learns to think of itself as it ought to think. While there is left in us the possibility of scorn, we know not quite the spirit we are of—still less if we imagine we may keep this or that little shadow of a fault.

But Vavasor had come to understand Hester so far as to know her likes and dislikes in a song. And so, by degrees, he had resolved to venture something that would please her. He flattered himself that he knew her *style*. He was very fond of the word, and imagined that all writers and speakers and musicians, to be of any worth, must fashion their style after this or that great master. How the master got it, and whether it might not be best to go back to the seed rather than propagate any more by cutting, it never occurred to him to ask. He never thought about having something worth saying or writing or singing. If you had told him this, and he had, as he thought, perceived the truth of it, he would immediately have desired some fine thing to say, in order that he might say it well! He could not have been persuaded that, if one has nothing worth saying, the best possible style for him is nothing but a foolish utterance from an empty skull. To make a good speech was the grand thing! What side it was on, the right or the wrong, mattered nothing. Even whether the speaker believed what he said was of no consequence—except that, if he did not, his speech would be the more admirable, as the greater *tour de force*, and himself the more admirable as the cleverer fellow.

Knowing that Hester was fond of a good ballad, he thought to try his hand at one, thinking it could not be so difficult. But he found that, like everything else, a ballad was easy enough if you could do it, and more than difficult if you could not. After several attempts he wisely yielded the ambition—his gift did not lie in that direction! He had, however, been so long in the habit of writing drawing-room verses that he had better ground for hoping he might produce something of the kind which might please her. It would be a great stroke toward placing him in a right position with her. It should be a love song, and he would present it as one he had written long ago. As such it would say the more for him while it would not seem that he had written it for her.

So one evening as he stood by her piano, he said all at once:

"By the bye, Miss Raymount, last night, as I was turning over some songs I wrote many years ago, I came upon one I thought I should like you just to look at—not the music—that is worth nothing, though I was proud enough of it then and thought it an achievement. But the words I still think are not so bad—considering. They are so far from me now that I am able to speak of them as if they were not mine at all!"

"Do let me see them!" said Hester, hiding none of the interest she felt, though fearing a little she might not be able to praise them so much as she would like.

He took the song from his pocket, and smoothed it out before her on the piano.

"Read it to me," said Hester.

"No, please," he answered with a little shyness, the rarest of phenomena in his spiritual atmosphere. "I could not read it aloud. But do not let it bore you if—"

64

He did not finish his sentence, and Hester was already busy with his manuscript.

When he was gone, leaving his manuscript behind him, Hester set to it again, and trying the music over, was by it so far enlightened that she despaired of finding anything in it, and felt a good deal disappointed.

Yet by degrees he continued to show her things. And if, as with the first, she saw little in their meaning, she hoped more meaning might be there than she was able to appreciate. For she was continuing to gather interest in Vavasor, though slowly, as was natural with a girl of her character. She had no suspicion of just how empty he was, even after she began reading some of his verses. It was impossible to imagine a person so indifferent to truth, or without interest in his own character and growth. Being of one piece herself, she had no conception of a nature all in pieces—with no unity except that of pleasing self. Though her nature did now and then receive a jar and a shock from him, she generally attributed it to his lack of development—a condition which she hoped her influence might change.

Women are being constantly misled by the fancy and hope of being the saviours of men! It is natural to goodness and innocence, but not the less is the error a disastrous one. There ought surely at least to be some probability of success as well founded as rare, to justify the sacrifices involved. Is it a good thing that a life of supreme suffering should be gone through for nothing but an increase of guilt?

It will be said that patience reaps its reward, but I fear too many patiences fail, and the number of resultant saints is small. The thing once done, the step no longer retrievable, fresh duty is born, and divine good will result from what suffering may arise in its fulfillment. The conceit or ambition itself which led to the fault, may have to be cured by its consequences.

Yet it may well be that a woman does more to redeem a man by *declining* than by encouraging his attentions. I dare not say how much a woman is capable of for the redemption of a man. But I think one who obeys God will scarcely imagine herself free to lay her person in the arms, and her happiness in the bosom of a man whose being is a denial of him.

Good Christians not Christians enough to understand this, may have to be taught by the change of what they took for love into what they know to be disgust. It is very hard for a woman to know whether her influence has any real power over a man. It is very hard for the man himself to know, for the passion having in itself a betterment, may deceive him as well as her. It might be well that a woman asked herself whether moral laxity or genuine self-devotion was the more persuasive in her to the sacrifice. If her best hope is to restrain the man within certain bounds, she is not one to imagine capable of any noble anxiety.

God cares nothing about keeping a man respectable. He will give his very self to make of him a true man. But that needs God—a woman is not enough for it. This cannot be God's way of saving bad men.

—Eleven —

The Concert Room

Vavasor at length realized that he must not continue to visit Hester so often, while not ready to go further, and that, much as he was in love—proportionately, that is, to his faculty for loving—he dared not do. But for the unconventionality of the Raymounts he would have reached the point long before. Therefore, he began to lessen the number, and shorten the length of his appearances in Addison Square.

But in so doing he became all the more aware of Hester's influence on him, and found that he had come to feel differently about certain things. He had not begun to change in a fundamental way, but was only a little infected with her goodness. He took the change, however, as one of great moral significance and was wonderfully pleased with himself. His natural kindness, for instance, toward the poor was quickened, causing him to give out a penny more often to those who begged. It was a good thing, and rooted in a better, but it did not indicate any advanced stage of goodness or any lessening of selfishness. On one occasion he prided himself that he had walked home in order to give his last shilling to a poor woman, whereas in truth he walked home because he found he had given her his last. Yet there was a little more movement of the sap of his nature, as even his behaviour in the bank would have testified.

Hester was annoyed to find herself disappointed when he did not appear, and took herself all the more diligently to her growing vocation. The question suggested itself whether it might not further her plans to be associated with a sisterhood, and indeed she began to widen her sphere a little by going about with a friend belonging to one. But in her own neighbourhood—not wishing her special work to be crossed by any prejudices—she always went alone, and seldom entered a house of the poor without singing in several of its rooms. To the children she would frequently tell a fairy tale, singing the little rhymes she made come into it. Of course, she had to encounter rudeness from time to time, but she set herself to get used to it and learn to let it pass.

The house in which the Raymounts lived, which was their own, was somewhat remarkable. Besides the ordinary accommodation of a good-sized London house with three drawing rooms on the first floor, it had unusual provisions for receiving guests. At the top of the first landing, rather more than halfway up the stair, there was a door through the original wall of the house to a long gallery, which led to a large and lofty room, apparently intended for concerts and dancing. Since they had owned the house, this room had been used only as a playroom for the children. Mr. Raymount always intended to furnish it, but had not yet done so.

The house itself was larger than they required, but Mr. Raymount had a great love for room and had obtained it at a low price. Beneath this concert room was another equally as large but so low it was difficult to find any use that could be made of it, and it continued even more neglected than the other. Below this again were cellars of alarming extent and obscurity, reached by a long vaulted passage. They would have held coal and wood and wine, everything natural to a cellar, enough for one generation at least. The history of the house was unknown. There was a nailed-up door in the second of the rooms I have mentioned, which was said to lead into the next house. But as the widow who lived there took every opportunity of making herself disagreeable, they had not ventured to investigate. There was no garden because of an addition that had been made to the original house. The great room was now haunting Hester's heart. If only her father would allow her to use it to give a concert to her lowly friends and acquaintances!

Questions concerning the condition of the poor in our large towns had, from the distance of speculation and the press, been of late occupying a good deal of Mr. Raymount's attention. He believed that he was enlightening the world on those most important perhaps of all the social questions of our day, their wrongs and their rights. He little suspected that his daughter was doing more for the poor, almost without knowing it, than he with all his conscious wisdom.

She could not, however, have made her request at a more auspicious moment, for he was just then feeling especially benevolent toward them for an article had just appeared in which he had expressed himself powerfully on behalf of the poor. Though he was far from being unprejudiced, he had a horror of prejudice, and hunted it as uncompromisingly in himself as in another. He was not like most people who, surmising a fault in themselves, rouse every individual bristle of their nature to defend and retain the very thing that degrades them.

He, therefore, speedily overcame his initial reluctance and agreed to his daughter's strange proposal. He was willing to make that much of an attempt toward the establishment of relations with the class he befriended in print. It was an approach which, if not altogether free of condescension, was still kindly meant.

Hester was greatly delighted with his ready compliance with her request, and for two weeks was busy preparing the house for the concert. A couple of charwomen were turned loose to thoroughly clean the great room. But before long, Mr. Raymount realized that no amount of cleaning could remove the dirty look of the place, so he committed the dingy room to painters and paperhangers. Under their hands it was wonderful to see how it gradually took on a gracious, lighter, and more colourful appearance.

The day for the concert was finally set for a week off, and Hester began to invite her poorer friends and neighbours to spend that evening at her father's house, when her mother would give them tea and she would sing to them. The married women were to bring their husbands if they would come, and each young woman might bring a friend. Most of the men turned up their noses at the invitation, but were nevertheless inclined to go out of curiosity. Some spoke doubtfully—they *might* be able to go, they were not sure. Some seemed to regard consent as a favour, if not a condescension. Of these, however, two or three were hampered by the uncertainty as to the redemption of their best clothes from the pawnbroker.

In requesting the presence of some of the small tradespeople, Hester asked it as a favour, begging their assistance in entertaining their poorer neighbours. And so put, the invitation was heartily accepted.

In one case at least, however, she forgot this precaution. The consequence was that the wife of a certain small furniture-broker began to fume once she saw that she was in the presence of the riff-raff of the neighbourhood. While she was drinking her second cup of tea her eyes kept roving. As she set it down, she caught sight of Long Tim, but a fortnight out of prison. She rose at once, made her way out fanning herself vigorously, and hurried home boiling over with wrath. The woman was not of a bad sort, only her dignity was hurt.

The hall and gallery were brilliantly lighted, and the room itself looked charming—at least in the eyes of those who had been so long watching the process of its resurrection. Tea was ready before the company began to arrive, and was served by men and women of the tradespeople. The meal went off well, with a good buzz of conversation. The only unpleasant thing was that several of the guests, mindful of their cubs at home, slipped large pieces of cake into their pockets to take to them. But this must not be judged without a just regard to their ways of thinking. It was, in reality, not a tenth part so bad as many of the ways in which well-bred persons appropriate slices of other people's cakes without once suspecting they are in the same category.

After the dinner, the huge urns and the remnants of food were removed, and the windows opened for a minute to freshen the air. A curtain rose at the end of the room, revealing a small stage decorated with green branches and artificial flowers. A piano had been placed in the center where Hester sat, now seen for the first time, having reserved her strength for her special duty.

When the assembly caught sight of her turning over the leaves of her music, a great silence fell. The moment she began to play, however, all began to talk again. But with the first tone of her voice, they quieted again, for she had chosen a ballad with a sudden and powerful opening, and, further, nervous and a little irritated at the same time with their talking while she played, had begun in a voice that would have compelled attention from a herd of cattle.

But the ballad was a little too long for them, so by the time it was half sung they had resumed talking again and exchanging opinions concerning the song. All agreed that Miss Raymount had a splendid voice. But several, who were there by second-hand invitation, said they could find a woman to beat her easily! I believe most of this group regarded their presence as a favour to her, providing her an audience that she might show off her talents. Among the poor, you see, as in more so-called respectable circles, the most refined and the coarsest-grained natures are to be met side by side.

Vavasor had not heard about the gathering. In part from doubt of his sympathy, in part from dislike of talking instead of doing, Hester had said nothing to him about it. When she lifted her eyes at the close of her ballad, a little disappointed in having failed to interest her audience, a gush of pleasure swept through her to see him standing near the door. She assumed that he had heard of her purpose and had come to help her. Even at that distance she could see that he was looking very uncomfortable—annoyed, she did not doubt, by the behaviour of her guests. A rush of new strength and courage went from heart to brain. She rose, advanced to the front of the little stage, and called out in a clear voice,

"Mr. Vavasor, will you come and help me?"

Now Vavasor was in reality a little disgusted at what he beheld. He had called without a notion of what was going on, and, seeing the lights along the gallery as he was heading for the drawing room, he had changed his direction, knowing nothing about the room to which it led. Partially blinded by the glare and bewildered by the unexpectedness of the sight, he did not at first discern the kind of company he had entered. For a moment it seemed as if, thinking to enter Paradise, he had mistaken and opened the left-hand door.

Presently his eyes came to themselves and confirmed the fact that he was in the midst of a great number of the unwashed. He had often talked with Hester about the poor, for they were now even a rather fashionable subject in some of the minor circles of the world's elect. But in the poor themselves he could hardly be said to have the most rudimentary interest, and that a lady should so degrade herself by singing to them and exposing both her voice and her person to their abominable remarks was to him simply incomprehensible. The admission of such people to a respectable house, and the entertainment of them as at a music hall, could have its origin only in some wild semi-political scheme of the old fellow, who had more eccentricities in his head than brain could well hold! It was a proceeding as disgraceful as extraordinary!

And then, of all things, with the ballad at an end, the voice he had grown so to delight in came to him across the hall, clear and brave and quiet, asking him, the future earl of Gartley, to come and help the singer! Was she in trouble? Had her father forced her into the awkward situation in which she found herself? These reflections flashing through his brain caused a moment's delay in Vavasor's response. Then with perfect command, and with no shadow of expression on his face beyond that of a perfect equanimity, he proceeded toward the stage through the malodourous air.

With smiling face but shrinking soul he walked forward, hiding his inner disgust, and sprang on the stage, making her a rather low bow.

"Come and sing a duet with me," she said, indicating one on the piano before her that they had sung together several times.

He smiled but said nothing, and almost immediately the duet began. They sang well, and the assembly, for whatever reason, acted a little more like an audience than before.

Hester next requested Vavasor to sing a certain ballad she knew was a great favourite with him. Inwardly protesting, he obeyed, and rendered it as expressively as could be expected under the circumstances. Even so, they were all talking again before he had finished.

After a brief pause, Hester invited a gentleman prepared for the occasion to sing them something patriotic. He responded with Campbell's magnificent song, "Ye Mariners of England!", which was received with hearty cheers. He was followed by another who, well acquainted with the predilections of his audience, gave them another to their liking, which was not only heard in silence but followed by tremendous cheering. Thus the occasion was gradually sinking to the intellectual level of the company—with an unforeseen consequence.

Now that the tail of the music-kite had descended near enough to the earth to be a temptation to some of the walkers afoot, they must try to catch it! The moment the last song was ended, one of the uninvited friends was on his feet. Without a word of permission he called out in a loud voice, "Ladies an' gen'lemen, Mr. William Blaney will now favour the company with a song."

Immediately a pale pock-marked man, with high retreating forehead and long, thin hair, rose and at once proceeded to make his way through the crowd. He would sing from the stage, of course! Hester and Vavasor looked at each other, one whisper passing between them, after which they waited the result in silence. After the singing one sometimes hears in drawing-rooms, there is little occasion for surprise that some of less education should think themselves more capable of fine things than they are.

Scrambling with knee and hand upon the stage, the poor, feeble fellow stood erect and faced the audience with glowing anticipated triumph. Plunging into his song, if song it could be called, he executed it in a cracked and strained falsetto. The result, enhanced by the nature of the song, which was pathetic and dubiously moral, must have been excruciation to every good ear in the place. Long before it was over Hester had made up her mind, the moment the end came, to let loose the most thunderous music of which she was capable.

But vanity is suspicious as well as vain, and Mr. Blaney, stopping abruptly in the middle of his song's final note, changed from the sung to the spoken word without a pause before she could strike the first chord, and screeched aloud,

"I will now favour the company with a song of my own composure!"

But before he had gotten his mouth into its singing place in his left cheek, Hester had risen—when she knew what had to be done, she never hesitated.

"I am sorry to have to interfere," she said, "but my friends are in my house and I am accountable for their entertainment. Mr. Blaney must excuse me if I insist on keeping the management of the evening in my own hands."

The vanity of the would-be singer was sorely hurt.

"The friends as knows me and knows what I can do will back me up. I have no right to be treated as if I didn't know what I was about. I can warrant the song homemade and of the best quality. So here goes."

73

Vavasor made a stride toward him, but a second later Mr. Raymount spoke from somewhere near the door.

"Come off the stage!" he shouted, making his way through the company as fast as he could.

Vavasor drew back and stood like a sentinel on guard. Hester resumed her seat at the piano. Blaney, fancying that he would be allowed to finish if he began before Mr. Raymount reached him, got his mouth into position and began to howl. But his host jumped on the stage from behind, reached him at his third note, took him by the back of the neck, and proceeded to walk him through the company and out of the room like a naughty boy. Propelling him thus out of the house, Mr. Raymount reentered the concert room and was greeted by a great clapping of hands as if he had performed a deed of valour. But in spite of the man's impudence, seeing his puny form in the mighty clutch of her father had gone right to Hester's heart.

The moment silence was restored, up rose a burly honest-looking bricklayer.

"I beg your pardon, miss, but will you allow me to make one remark?"

"Certainly, Mr. Jones," answered Hester.

"It seems to me, miss," said Jones, "as it's only fair on my part as brought Blaney here, to make my apologies and to say for him that I know he never would have done what he done if he hadn't had a drop as we come along to this 'ere tea party. That was the cause, miss, an' I hope as it'll be taken into account as poor enough reason of his conduct. It takes very little, I'm sorry to say, miss, to upset his behaviour—not more'n a pint. But there's not a morsel of harm in him, poor fellow. I know him well, bein' my wife's brother—leastways half brother. When he's got a drop in his nob, it's always for singing, he is—an' that's the worst of him. Thank you kindly, miss."

"Thank you, Mr. Jones," returned Hester. "We'll think no more of it."

Loud applause followed, and Jones sat down, well satisfied.

The order of the evening was resumed, but once the harmony of the assembly was disturbed, all hope of quiet was gone. They now had something to talk about!

74

Hester sang again, but no song seemed quite right. Vavasor also sang several times—as often as Hester asked him. But inwardly he was disgusted by the whole affair—as was natural, for could any fish have found itself more out of the water than he? Everything annoyed him—most of all that the lady of his thoughts should have addressed herself to such an assembly. If it was not degrading enough to appear before such a throng, surely to sing to them was! How could a woman of refinement seek appreciation for her songs from such a repulsive assemblage!

One main test of our dealings in the world is whether the men and women we associate with are better or worse for it. Vavasor had often been where at least he was the worse and no one the better for his presence. For days a cloud hung over the fair image of Hester in his mind.

He called on the first possible opportunity to inquire how she was after her exertions, but avoided any further allusion to the events of the evening. She thanked him for the help he had given her, but was so far from satisfied with her experiment that she too let the subject rest.

Mr. Raymount was so disgusted that he said nothing of the kind should ever again take place in his house. He had not bought it to make a music hall out of it!

If any change was about to appear in Vavasor, a change in the fortunes of the Raymounts prevented it.

What people call *luck* seems to have odd predilections and prejudices regarding families as well as individuals. Some seem invariably successful, whatever they take in hand. Others go on, generation after generation, struggling without a ray of success. On the surface there appears no reason for inequality. But there is one thing in which preeminently I do not believe—that same luck, namely, or chance, or fortune.

The Father of families looks after his families—and his children too.

—Twelve —

Sudden Change

Light and shade, sunshine and shadow pursue each other over the moral as well as the material world. Every soul has a landscape that changes with the wind that sweeps its sky, with the clouds that return after its rain.

The middle day of March had been dreary all over England—dreariest of all, perhaps, in London. Great blasts had blown under a sky whose miles-thick vault of clouds they never touched, but instead hunted and drove and dashed earth clouds of dust into all unwelcoming places, throats and eyes included. Now and then a few drops would fall on the stones as if the day's fierce misery were about to yield to sadness. But it did not so yield. Up rose again a great blundering gust, and repentance was lost in rage. The sun went down on its wrath, and its night was tempestuous.

But the next morning rose bright and glad, looking as if it would make up for its father's wildness by a gentler treatment of the world. The wind was still high, but the hate seemed to have gone out of it. It swept huge clouds across the sky, never granting a pause of motion. But the sky was blue and the clouds were white, and the dungeon-vault of the world was broken up and being carried away.

Everything in the room stood ready when the Raymounts assembled for breakfast—the fire in the hearth, crocuses in a vase on the table. Mr. Raymount was very silent, almost gloomy. Mrs. Raymount's face, in consequence, was a shade less peaceful. There was nothing the matter, only he had not yet learned to radiate. It is hard for some natures to let their light shine. Mr. Raymount had some light, but he let it shine mostly in reviews, not much at home.

The children were rosy, fresh from their baths, and ready to eat like breakfast-loving English. Cornelius was half of his breakfast ahead of the rest, for he had daily to endure the hardship of being at the bank by nine o'clock, and made the best of it by claiming immunity from the niceties of the breakfast table. Never did he lose a moment in helping anybody. Even little Saffy had to stretch out a very long arm after the butter without his even looking up—except indeed it happened to cross his plate, when he would sharply rebuke her breach of manners. Mark would sooner have gone without salt for his egg than ask Corney to pass it.

This morning the pale boy sat staring at the crocuses.

"Why don't you eat your breakfast, Mark, dear?" said his mother.

"I'm not hungry, mama," he answered.

The mother looked at him a little anxiously. He was not a very vigorous boy physically. But unlike his father's, his light was almost always shining, making the faces about him shine.

After a few minutes unconsciously staring at the crocuses, he said,

"I can't imagine how they come."

"They grow!" said Saffy.

"Didn't you see Hester make the paper flowers for her party?" added their father, willing to set them thinking.

"Yes," replied Saffy, "but it would take such a long time to make all the flowers in the world that way!"

"So it would. But if a great many angels took it in hand, I suppose they could do it."

"That can't be how," Saffy laughed. "You know the flowers come up out of the earth, and there isn't room to cut them out there."

"I think they must be cut and put together before they are made!" said Mark, very slowly and thoughtfully.

The supposition was greeted with a great burst of laughter from Cornelius. In the midst of a refined family he behaved as the blind and stupid generally behave to those who see what they cannot see. Mockery is the share they choose in the motions of life eternal.

"Stop, Cornelius!" said his father. "I suspect we have a young philosopher where you see only the silly little brother. He has, I fancy, got a glimpse of something he does not yet know how to say."

"In that case," said Cornelius, "he had better hold his tongue till he does know how to say it."

It was not often he dared to speak so to his father, but he was growing less afraid of him, though not through increase of love.

"They take everything for clever the little idiot says,? he thought to himself. "Nobody made anything of me when I was his age!"

The mail was soon brought in. Among them was one for Mr. Raymount with a broad black border. He looked at the postmark.

"This must be the announcement of cousin Strafford's death!" he said. "Someone told me she was not expected to live."

"You did not tell me she was ill," said his wife.

"I forgot to. It has been so many years since I had the least communication with her, or even heard anything of her. She was a strange old soul!"

"You used to be close to her, didn't you, papa?" asked Hester.

"Yes, at one time. But we differed so entirely it was impossible it should last. She would think the most peculiar things about what I thought and meant, and then fall out upon me as being in favour of things I disliked quite as much as she did. She took no trouble to try to understand what I was really saying. But that is often the way with people. They hardly know what they think themselves and can hardly be expected to know what other people mean."

"I can't understand why people should quarrel so about their opinions," said Mrs. Raymount.

Her husband took up the letter, slowly broke the large black seal and began to read. His wife sat looking at him, waiting in expectation.

He had scarcely read half the first page when she saw his countenance change a little, then flush. He folded the letter, laid it down by the side of his plate, and began to eat again, with a fixed expression on his face.

"Well, dear?" said his wife.

"It is not quite what I thought," he answered with a curious smile, then ate his toast in a brooding silence. Never in the habit of making secrets like his son, he nevertheless had a strong dislike of showing his feelings. Besides, he was too proud to reveal his interest in the special contents of this letter.

The poor, yet hopeless and hardly indulged, ambition of Mr. Raymount's life was to possess a portion of earth—even if only an acre or two. He came of families possessing property, but none of it had come anywhere near him except what belonged to cousin Strafford. He was her nearest relation, but he had never hoped to inherit anything from her. After a final quarrel had put an end to their quarrelling, he had stopped seeing her altogether. For many years there had not been the slightest communication between the cousins. But in the course of those years, all the other relatives of the old lady had died, and, as the letter he now held informed him, he was after all heir to her property—a small estate in a lovely spot among the roots of the Cumberland hills. Quite a few thousand pounds in government securities accompanied the property.

But while Mr. Raymount was not a money lover in any notable sense, his delight in having land of his own was almost beyond utterance. This delight had nothing to do with the money value of the property—he scarcely thought of that. It came in large part because of a new sense of room and freedom. It made him so filled with gladness he could hardly get his toast down.

Mrs. Raymount was by this time tolerably familiar with her husband's moods, but she had never before seen him look just the way he looked now, and was puzzled. The fact was, he had never before had such a pleasant surprise, and sat absorbed in a foretaste of bliss in which the ray of March sun that lighted up the delicate transparencies of the veined crocuses purple and golden, might seem the announcing angel.

Presently he rose and left the room, his wife following him. The moment she entered his study behind him, he turned and took her in his arms.

"Here's news, my dear!" he said. "You'll be just as glad of it as I. Yrndale is ours—at least so my old friend Heron says, and he ought to know. Cousin Strafford left no will. He is certain there is none. She persistently put off making one, with the full intention, he believes, that the property should come to me, her lawful heir and next of kin. He thinks she did not have the heart to leave it to anyone else. Thank God! It is a lovely place. Nothing could have given me more pleasure."

"I am indeed glad, Raymount," said his wife—who called him by his family name on important occasions. "You always had a fancy for playing the squire."

"A great fancy for a little room, rather," replied her husband—"not much, I fear, for the duties of a squire. There is money as well, I am glad to say—enough to keep the place up, anyhow."

"I have no doubt you will develop into a model farmer and landlord," replied his wife.

"You must take the business part," he returned, "at least till Corney is fit to look after it."

But his wife's main thought was what influence the change would have on Hester's marriage prospects. In her heart she hated the thought that property should have anything to do with marriage—yet this was almost her first thought. Inside us are played more fantastic tricks than any we play in the face of the world.

"Are the children to be told?" she asked.

"I suppose so. It would be a shame not to let them share in our gladness. And yet I hate to think of them talking about it, as children will."

"I am not afraid of the children," returned his wife. "I must simply tell them not to talk about it. I am as confident in Mark as if he were fifty. Saffy might forget, but Mark will keep her in line."

When she returned to the dining room, Cornelius was gone, but the rest were still at the table. She told them that God had given them a beautiful house in the country with hills and woods and a swift flowing river. Saffy clapped her hands, crying, "Oh, mama!" and could hardly sit on her chair. Mark was perfectly still, but his eyes looked like ears. The moment her mother ceased, Saffy jumped down and made a rush for the door.

"Saffy, Saffy, where are you going?" cried her mother.

"To tell Sarah," answered Saffy.

"Come back, my child. Your papa and I wish you to say nothing whatever about it to anyone."

"O-oh!" returned Saffy. Both her look and tone said, "What's the good of it then?"

Not a word did Mark utter, but his face shone as if it had been heaven he was going to. No colour, only light came to the surface of it, and broke into the loveliest smile. When Mark smiled, his whole body and being smiled.

Hester's face flushed a rose red. Her first thought was of the lovely things of the country and the joy of them. Her next thought was of the poor: "Now I shall be able to do something for them!" But quickly followed the thought that now she would be able to do less than ever for them.

Yrndale was far from London. Maybe her father and mother would let her stay behind, but she hardly dared even hope for that. Perhaps it was God's will to remove her from London because she was doing more harm than good. Now her endeavours would be at an end!

"You don't like the thought of leaving London, Hester?" said her mother with concern, thinking it was because of Vavasor.

"I am very glad for you and papa, mother," answered Hester. "I was thinking of my poor people and what they would do without me."

"I have sometimes found," returned her mother, "that the things I dreaded most serve me best in the end. I don't mean because I got used to them, or because they did me good. I mean they furthered what I thought they would ruin."

"Thank you, mother! You always comfort me. For myself I could not imagine anything more pleasant. If only it were near London!"

She was still thinking of her poor, but her mother suspected another reason.

"I suppose, father," said Cornelius when his father told him the news that same evening, "that there will be no more occasion for me to work at the bank."

"There will be more occasion than ever," answered his father. "There will be far more to look after when I am gone. What do you imagine you could employ yourself with down there? You have never taken to study, otherwise, as you know, I would have sent you to Oxford. When you leave the bank, it will be to learn farming and the management of an estate."

Cornelius made no reply. His father's words annoyed him. He was hardly good at anything except taking offense, and already he looked on the estate as nearly as much his as his father's. What right had his father to keep from him what he deserved—a share in the good fortunes of the family? He left the study almost hating his father because of what he counted his injustice. Despite his father's request that he would say nothing of the matter until things were more settled, he made not the slightest effort to obey him, and took the first opportunity to pour out his righteous indignation to Vavasor.

His friend responded to the communication very sensibly, trying, without exactly saying it, and without a shadow of success, to make him see what a fool he was. He congratulated him all the more warmly on his good fortune that a vague hope went up in him of a share in the same. For Cornelius had not failed to use large words in making mention of the estate and the fortune accompanying it. In the higher position, as Vavasor considered it, which Mr. Raymount would henceforth occupy as one of the proprietors of England, therefore as a man of influence in his country and its politics, he saw something like an approximative movement in the edges of the gulf that divided him from Hester. She would likely come in for a personal share in this large fortune. And if he could but see a possibility of existence without his aunt's money, he would, he *almost* said to himself, marry Hester, and take the risk of his aunt's displeasure. At the same time she would doubtless now look with more favour on Hester. There could be nothing offensive to her aunt's pride at least in his proposing to marry the daughter of a country squire. If she were the heiress of a rich brewer, that is, of a brewer rich enough, his aunt would, like the rest of them, get over it fast enough!

Mr. Raymount went to look at his property, returning more delighted with house, land, and landscape than he had expected. He seldom spoke of his good fortune, however, except to his wife, or betrayed his pleasure except by the glistening of his eyes. As soon as the warm weather came, they would migrate. Immediately they began their preparations—the young ones by packing and unpacking several times a day a most unlikely assemblage of things. The house was to be left in charge of old Sarah, who would also wait on Cornelius.

—Thirteen —

Yrndale

It was a lovely morning when they left London. The trains did not then travel so fast as now, and it was late in the afternoon when they reached the station at which they must leave the railway for the road. Before that the weather had changed, or they had changed their weather, for the sky was one mass of cloud, and rain was falling persistently. They had been for some time in the region of hills, but those they were passing through, though not without wonder and strange interest, were but an inferior clan, neither lofty nor lovely. Through the rain and the mist they looked lost and dreary. They were mostly bare, except for a little grass, and broken with huge brown and yellow gulleys, worn by such little torrents as were now rushing along them straight from the clouded heavens. It was a vague sorrowful region of tears, whence the streams in the valleys below were forever fed.

Saffy had been sound asleep through this part of the journey, but Mark had been standing at the window of the railway carriage, gazing out on an awful world. What would he do, he thought, if he were lost there? Would he be able to sit still all night without being frightened, waiting for God to come and take him? As they rushed along, it was not through the brain alone of the child the panorama flitted, but through his mind and heart as well. There, like a glacier, it scored its passage, or rather, it left its ghosts behind it, ever shifting forms and shadows, each atmosphered in its own ethereal mood. They were hardly thoughts, but a strange other consciousness of life and being.

Hills and woods and valleys and plains and rivers and seas, entering by the gates of sight into the live mirror of the human, are transformed into another nature—to a living wonder, a joy, a pain, a breathless marvel as they pass. Nothing can receive another thing—not even a glass can take into its depth a face without altering it. In the mirror of man, things become thoughts, feelings, life, and send their streams down the cheeks, or their sunshine over the countenance.

Before Mark reached the end of that journey, he had gathered a great amount of fuel in the bottom of his heart, stored there for the future consumption of thinking and for reproduction in forms of power. He took nothing consciously. Things just kept sinking into him. The sole sign of his reception was an occasional sigh—of which he could not have told either the cause or the meaning.

Arriving at the station, they got into their own carriage. The drive was a long and tedious one, for the roads were rough, muddy and often steep. For some time they drove along the side of a hill and could see next to nothing except in one direction. When at length the road ran into a valley and along the course of the swollen river, it was getting so dark and the rain was coming down so fast that they could see nothing at all. Long before they reached their new home, Saffy and Mark were sound asleep, Hester was sunk in her own thoughts, and the father and mother sat in unbroken silence hand in hand.

Hester's mind was on the places they had left. Ah, that city—so full of fellow creatures struggling in the toils of numerous foes! Many sorrows had entered in at Hester's ears—tales of oppression and want, giving rise to sympathy in her bosom. From the spray that reached her on its borders, she knew how that human sea tossed and raged afar. Yet now she was gone away from it, unable to plunge into its midst with what little help she was able to give.

It was pitch dark when they arrived at their destination. They turned and went through a gate, then passed through the trees, which made the night yet darker. By and by the faint lights of the house appeared, with blotchy pallours thinning the mist and darkness. Presently the carriage stopped.

Both the children continued sound asleep and were carried off to bed. The father and mother knew the house from times past and revived for each other old memories. But to Hester all was strange. With the long journey, the weariness, the sadness, and the strangeness, she entered the old hall as if walking in a dream. It had a quiet, dull, dignified look, as if it expected nobody, as if it was here itself because it could not help it and would rather not be here, as if it had seen so many generations come and go that it had ceased to care much about new faces. Everything in the house looked somber and solemn, as if it had not forgotten its old mistress.

They had supper in a long, low room, with furniture almost black, against whose window heavy roses every now and then softly patted, caught in the fringes of the rain gusts. The dusky room, the perfect stillness inside, the low mingled sounds of swaying trees and pattering rain outside, the sense of the great darkness—all grew together into one possessing mood, which rose and sank, like the water in a sea-cave, in the mind of Hester. But who by words can fix the mood that comes and goes unbidden? A single happy phrase, the sound of a wind, the odour of the mere earth may send us into some lonely, dusky realm of being. I doubt if even the poet ever conveys just what he means to the mind of his fellow. Sisters, brothers, we can meet only in God.

But the nearest mediator of feeling, the most potent, the most delicate, and perhaps the likest to the breath moving upon the soft face of the waters of chaos, is music. It rose like a soft, irrepressible tide in the heart of Hester. It mingled and became one with her mood. Together they beat at the gates of silence. She rose and looked around her for such an instrument as had always been within her reach—walked about the shadowy room searching. But there was no creature among the aged furniture. She returned and sat again at the table, the mood vanishing in weariness.

But they did not linger there long. Fatigue made the ladies glad to be shown to the rooms prepared for them. The housekeeper, the ancient authority of the place, in every motion and tone expressing herself wronged by their intrusion, conducted them. Every spot they passed was plainly far more hers than theirs, only the law was a tyrant, and she dared not assert her rights!

Tired as she was, Hester was charmed with her room, and the more charmed the more she looked about. It was old fashioned to her heart's content, and seemed full of shadowy histories, as if each succeeding occupant had left behind an ethereal record, a memorial imprint of presence of walls and furniture—to which she would now add hers. In weary haste she undressed, ascending with some difficulty the high four-post bed which stood waiting for her like an altar of sleep.

She awoke to a blaze of sunlight. The night had passed and carried the tears of the day with it. Ah, how much is done in the night when we sleep and know nothing! Things never stop. The sun was shining as if he too had wept and repented. All the earth beneath him was like the face of a child who has ceased to weep and begun to smile, but has not yet wiped away his tears.

Raindrops everywhere! millions upon millions of them! every one of them with a sun in it! Hester had sprung from her bed and opened the curtains. How different was the sight from what she saw when she looked out in Addison Square. If heaven be as different from this earth, and as much better than it, we shall indeed be happy children. On each side she saw green, undulating lawn, with trees and meadows beyond. Just in front, the grassy lawn sloped rapidly, grew steep, and fell into the swift river—which, now swollen from the rains, went rolling and sliding, brown and heavy toward the far-off sea. Beyond the river, the bank rose into a wooded hill. She could see walks winding through the wood, here appearing, there vanishing, and a little way up the valley, the rails of a rustic bridge that led them to it.

It was a paradise! In place of the roar of London along Oxford Street, there was the sound of the river. In place of the cries of rough human voices, the soprano of birds and the soft mellow bass of the cattle in the meadows. The sky was a shining blue. Not a cloud was to be seen upon it. Quietly it looked down as if saying to the world over which it stood, "Yes, you are welcome to it all!"

She thanked God for the country, but soon was praying for the town. The neighbourly country offered to console her for the loss of the town she received, but then she remembered that God cared more for one miserable, selfish, wife-and-donkey-beating ironmonger in London than for all the hills and dales of Cumberland, and all the starry things of his heavens.

Dressing quickly, she went to her mother's room. Her father was already outdoors, but her mother was having breakfast in bed.

"What a *lovely* place it is, mama! You did not say half enough about it," exclaimed Hester.

"Wasn't it better to let you discover for yourself, my child," answered her mother. "You were so sorry to leave London that I did not want to praise Yrndale for fear of prejudicing you against it."

"Yes, it was hard for me to leave," said Hester. "I was never one to turn easily to new things. And perhaps I need hardly tell you that the conviction has been growing upon me that my calling is among my fellow creatures in London."

She had never yet, even to her mother, spoken so plainly about the things on her heart and mind. She was a little timid to do so even now. What if her mother thought the mere idea of having a calling was presumptuous?

"Two things, I think, go to make up a *call*," said her mother, to Hester's relief. "You must not imagine that because you have said nothing, I have not known what you were thinking. Mother and daughter are too near not to be able to hear each other without words. There is between you and me a constant undercurrent of communication."

"Oh, mother!" cried Hester, overjoyed to find her mother felt close to her, "I am so glad. Please tell me the two things you mean."

"I think, to make up a true call," replied Mrs. Raymount, "both desire and possibility are required. The first you know well, but have you considered the second? Even if you have a desire to help people, the other half of being so used needs an open door. And in addition, a desire to do a thing in itself does not always determine fitness to do it."

"I can't believe, mama, that God would give any gift, especially when accompanied by a desire to use it for some special purpose, without intending it should be used."

"You must admit there are some who never find a use for their special gifts."

"Yes, but may that not be because they have not sufficiently cultivated their gifts or have not done their best to bring them into use? Or could they have wanted to use them for their own ends instead of God's? I feel as if I must stand up against every difficulty lest God should be disappointed in me. Surely any frustration of the ends to which their very being points must be their own fault. May it be that they have nothing but unsatisfied longings because they have not yielded to the calling voice? They have gone picking and choosing what *they* would like to do instead of obeying?"

"There must be truth in what you say, Hester, but it cannot explain every case. Sometimes there might be delay in carrying out a calling without that calling being frustrated. You think yours is to help the poor. But is it for you to say when you are *ready*? Willingness is not everything. Might one not fancy her hour come when it was not come? May not part of the preparation for work be the mental discipline involved in the imagined postponements? And what about our life beyond the grave? This life is but a beginning. While cultivating your gift and waiting the call, you may be in active preparation for the work in the coming life for which God intended you when he made you."

Hester gave a great sigh. Indefinite postponement is terrible to the young and eager.

"That is a dreary thought, mother," she said.

"Is it, my child?" returned the mother. "Painful the will of God may be—that I well know. But *dreary,* no. Have patience, my love. Your heart's deepest desire must be the will of God, for he cannot have made you so that your heart should run counter to his will. Let him have his own way with you and he will give you your desire. He delights in his children. As soon as they can be indulged without ruin, he will heap upon them their desires. They are his too."

Hester was astonished at her mother's grasp and wisdom. The child may for years have but little idea of the thought and life within the form and face he knows and loves better than any. But at last the predestined moment arrives, the two minds meet, and the child understands the parent.

Hester threw her arms around her mother, kissed her, and went to her own room, understanding that if God has called, he will also open the door.

Scarcely had she reached it, however, when she heard the voices of the children shouting along the same corridor on their way to breakfast. In their eagerness to rush into the new creation, the garden of Eden around them, they could hardly be prevented from bolting their breakfast like puppies.

I will attempt no description of the beauties that met them at every turn. I doubt if some of the children in heaven are always happier than Saffy and Mark were that day. Hester had thoughts which kept her from being so happy as they, but she was more blessed. Glorious as is the child's delight, the child-heart in the grown woman is capable of tenfold the bliss. Saffy pounced on a flower like a wild beast on its prey—she never stood and gazed at one like Mark. Hester would gaze until tears came to her eyes.

Mark was in many things an exception—a curious mixture of child and youth. He had never been strong and had always been thoughtful. God is the God of little children, and is at home with them.

Saffy was a thing of smiles and tears just as they chose to come. She had not a suspicion yet that the exercise of any operative power on herself was possible to her—not to say required of her. Many men and women are in the same condition who have grown cold and hard in it. She was soft and warm, on the way to wakefulness and action. Even now, when a good thought came she would give it a stranger's welcome, but the first appeal to her sense would drive it out-of-doors again.

Before the three had done with their ramble, what with the sweet twilight gladness of Mark, the merry noonday brightness of Saffy, and the loveliness all around, the heart of Hester was quiet and hopeful as if waiting in the blue night for the rising of the moon. She had some things to trouble her, but none of them had touched the quick of her being. She was at last beginning to see that it is God who means everything as we read it, however poor or mingled with mistake our reading may be. And the soothing of his presence in what we call nature was now coming to work on Hester, helping her toward that quietness of spirit without which the will of God can scarce be perceived.

—Fourteen —

Down the Hill

When Franks, the acrobat, and his family left Mrs. Baldwin's garret to go to another yet poorer lodging, it was with heavy hearts. They crept silently away to go down another step of the world's stair. And yet how often on the steps of this world, when you think you are going down, you are really ascending. I think it was so with the Frankses and the stair they were on.

I think God has more to do with the fortunes of the poor a thousand fold than with those of the rich. In the fortunes of the poor there are many more changes, and they are of greater import as coming closer to the heart of their condition. They have more variations of weather, more sunshine and shade, more storms and calms, than lives passed on airier slopes. Who could think of God as a God like Christ and imagine he would not care as much for the family of John Franks as for the family of Gerald Raymount?

It is perhaps true that the God of truth cannot love the unlovely in the same way as he loves the lovely. The one he loves for what he is and what he has begun to be. The other he loves because he sorely needs love—as sorely as the other, and must begin to grow lovely one day. Nor dare we forget that the celestial human thing is in itself lovely as made by God, and pitiably lovely as spoiled by man. That is the Christ-thing which is the root of every man, created in his image—that which, when he enters the men, he possesses. The true earthly father must always love those children more who are obedient and loving—but he will not neglect one bad one for twenty good ones. "There is more joy in heaven over one sinner that repenteth than over ninety and nine that need no repentance."

The Frankses were on the down-going side of the hill Difficulty, and down they must go, unable to help themselves. They had found a cheaper lodging, but entered it with misgiving. Their income had been very moderate since their arrival in London, and their expenses greater than in the country. Also Franks was beginning to feel or to fancy his strength and elasticity not quite what they had been.

The first suspicion of the approach of old age and the beginning of that weakness whose end is sure, may well be a startling one. The man has begun to be a nobody in the world's race—is henceforth himself but the course of the race between age and death—a race in which the victor is known before the start. Life with its self-discipline withdraws itself more to the inside. The man has now to trust and yield constantly. He is coming to know the fact that he was never his own strength, had never the smallest power in himself at his strongest. He is learning to lay hold of the true strength, to make it his by laying hold of it. He is coming to trust in the unchangeable thing at the root of all his strength. Strength has ever to be made perfect in weakness, and old age is one of the weaknesses in which it is perfected.

But poor Franks had not got so far yet as to see this, and the feeling of the approach of old age helped to relax the springs of his hopefulness. Also, his wife had not recovered from her last confinement. The baby, too, was sickly. And there was little receptivity for acrobatics in the streets—coppers came in slowly. But his wife's words were always cheerful, though their tone was a little mournful. Their tone came of temperament, the words of love and its courage. The daughter of a gamekeeper, she was regarded by the neighbours as throwing herself away when she married Franks. But her husband was an honest and brave man, and she never repented of giving herself to him, even when life was the hardest.

For a few weeks they did pretty well in their new lodging. They managed to pay their way, and had food enough—though not quite so good as husband and wife wished each for the other and both for their children. The boys had a good enough time of it. They had not yet exhausted their own wonder in London. The constant changes around made of their lives a continuous novel, a romance, and being happy they could eat anything and thrive on it.

The lives of father and mother are like an umbrella over those of their children, shutting out all care if not all sorrow, and every change is welcomed as a new delight. This is true in all classes, yet I suspect perhaps that imagination, fancy, perception, insight into character, the sense of adventure, and many other powers and feelings are more likely to be active in the children of the poor, to the greater joy of their existence, than in others.

John Franks, according to his light, was a careful and conscientious parent. His boys were strongly attached to him, never thought of shirking their work, and endured a good deal of hardness and fatigue without grumbling. Their mother opened their eyes to see that their father took more than his full share and did his best for them. They were greatly proud of their father and believed him not only the top man in his profession, but the best man that ever lived in the world besides. To believe so of one's parent is a stronger aid to righteousness than all other things whatever, until the day-star of the knowledge of the great Father rises in the heart to know whom, in like but better fashion, as the best more than man and the perfect Father of men, is the only thing to redeem us from misery and wrong, and lift us into the glorious liberty of the sons and daughters of God.

They were now reduced to one room, with the boys sleeping on the floor. This was no hardship now that summer was near, only the parents found it interfered a little with their freedom of speech. Nor did it change anything to send them to bed early, for the earlier they went to bed, the longer they were in going to sleep.

One evening after the boys were in bed, the father and mother sat talking. The mother was busy patching young Moxy's garment. The man's work for the day was over, but not the woman's!

"Well, I dunno— he said at last, and stopped.

"What don ye know, John?" asked his wife.

"I was jist thinkin' that Mr. Christopher was such a friend. You remember as how he used to say a man could no more get out o' the sight o' the eyes o' the Almighty than a child could get out o' sight o' the eyes o' his mother as was watchin' him?"

"Yes, John, I do remember, and a great comfort it was to me at the time."

"Well, I dunno!" said Franks again, and paused. But this time he resumed. "What troubles me is that if there was a mother lookin' after yer child an' was to see him doin' no better'n you an' me, an' day by day gettin' further an' further behind, I should say she wasn't much of a mother to let us go on in that way."

"She might have got her reasons for it, John," returned his wife. "Perhaps she might see a little farther down the road, and might know that the child was in no danger o' harm. When the children want their dinner very bad, I have heard you say to them sometimes, 'Now, kids, have patience. Patience is a fine thing. What if ye do be hungry? You ain't dyin' o' hunger. You'll wear a bit longer yet!' Ain't I heard you say that, John?"

"I ain't goin' to deny it. But you must allow this is drivin' it jist a little too far. Here we come to Lon'on thinkin' to better ourselves— not wantin' no great things, but jist thinkin' as how it were time to lay a shillin' or two to keep us out o' the workhouse—that's all we was after. An' here sin' we come, first one shillin' goes, an' then another, till we ain't got one, as I may almost say, left! Instead o' gettin' more we get less, an' that with harder work, as is wearin' me an' the boys out, an'—"

"I ain't wore out, father. I'm good for another go," said little Moxy from the bed.

"I ain't neither, gov'nor. I got a lot more work in me!"

"No, nor me!" cried the third. "I likes London. I can stand on my head twice as long as Tommy Blake, an' he's a year older'n me."

"Hold yer tongues, you rascals, an' go to sleep," growled the father, pretending to be angry with them. "What right have you to be awake at this time o' the night—an' in Lon'on too? It's not like the country, you know. In the country you can do much as you like, but not in the town! You've no call to be awake listenin' to what yer father an' mother was sayin' to theirselves."

"We wasn't listenin', father. We was only hearin' 'cause we wasn't asleep. An' you didn't speak down as if it was secrets."

"Well, you know there's things as fathers and mothers can understand an' talk about as no boys can see to the end. So they better go to sleep and wait till their turn comes to be fathers and mothers theirselves. Go to sleep direc'ly, or I'll break every bone in your bodies!"

"Yes, father," they answered together, in no way terrified by the awful threat—which was not a little weakened by the fact that they had heard it every day of their lives and not yet known it to be carried out.

But having become aware that his children were awake, the father, without the least hypocrisy, conscious or unconscious, changed his tone: in the presence of his children he preferred looking at the other side of the argument. After a few moments' silence he began again.

"Yes, as you was sayin', wife, an' I knows as yer always in the right, if the right be anyhows to be got at—there's no sayin' when that same as we was speakin' of—the Almighty is the man I mean—no sayin', I say, when he may come to see as we have, as I may say, had enough o' it, an' turn an' let us have a taste o' luck again."

"So it do seem to me, John," answered the mother.

"Well," said Franks, apparently, now that he had taken up the defense of the ways of the Supreme with men, warming to his subject, "I daresay he do the best he can, an' give us as much luck as is good for us. Leastways that's how the rest of us would do. We can't always do as well as we would like for to do for our little ones, but we always do the best we can. We'll suppose yet a little while, anyhow, as how he's a lookin' after us. It can't be for nothin', as he counts the hairs on our head, as the sayin' is!"

There are many who think to reverence the Most High by assuming that he can and should do anything or everything that pleases him in a mere moment. In their eyes power is a grander thing than love. But his Love is higher than his omnipotence. Nowhere is it said in the Book that God is omnipotence. But because they are told that he is omnipotent, such call him Omnipotence. But when told that he is Love, they do not care to argue that he must then be loving? But as to doing what he wills in an instant—see what it cost him to redeem the world! He did not find that easy, or to be done in a moment without pain or toil. Yea, awfully omnipotent is God. For he wills, effects and perfects the thing which, because of the bad in us, he has to carry out in suffering and sorrow, his own and his Son's. Evil is a hard thing for God himself to overcome. Yet thoroughly and altogether and triumphantly will he overcome it. And not by crushing it underfoot—any god of man's idea could do that!—but by conquest of heart over heart, of life in life, of life over death. Nothing shall be too hard for the God that fears not pain, but will deliver and make true and blessed at his own severest cost.

For a time, then, the Frankses went on, with food to eat and money to pay their way, but going slowly down the hill, and finding it harder and harder to keep their footing. By and by the baby grew worse. They sought help at the hospital, but saw no Mr. Christopher. The baby did not improve. Still they kept on, and every day the husband brought home a little money. Several times they seemed on the point of an engagement, but every time something happened to prevent it, until at length Franks almost ceased to hope, and grew more and more silent.

Poor Franks, struggling in his own way with the conflicts of life but having little philosophy to assist him, yet had much affection, which is indeed the present God in a man—and so he did not go far in the evil direction. The worst sign of his degenerating temper was the more frequently muttered oath of impatience with his boys— never with his wife. But not one of them was a moment uneasy in consequence—except when the *guv'nor* wasn't jolly, neither were they.

—Fifteen —

Out of the Frying Pan

There is another person in my narrative whom the tide of destiny seemed now to have caught and was bearing more swiftly somewhither. Unable, as she concluded, any longer to endure a life of espionage, distrust, and ill-tempered rebuke from her two aunts, Amy Amber did at last as she had threatened.

One morning when, in amazement that she was so late, they called her, they received no answer, neither could find her in or out of the house. She had applied to a friend in London, and following her advice, had taken the cheap train overnight, and gone to her. She met her, took her home, and helped her in seeking a situation. The result was that before many days were over, her appearance and manners being altogether in her favour, she obtained a place behind a counter in one of the largest shops. There she was kept hard at work, and the hours of business were long. But the labour was by no means too much for the fine health and spirits which now blossomed in her.

Her aunts raised an outcry of horror and dismay first, then of reprobation, accusing her of many things, and among the rest of those faults of which they were in reality themselves guilty toward her. For as to the gratitude and affection we are so ready to claim and so slow to pay, the debt was great on their part, and very small indeed on hers. They wrote to her guardians of course to acquaint them with the shocking fact of her flight, but dwelt far more upon the badness of her behaviour, the rapidity with which she had deteriorated, and their convictions as to the depth of the degradation she had preferred to the shelter of their—very moth-eaten—wings.

The younger of the two guardians was a man of business, and at once took proper measures to find her. It was not, however, before the lapse of several months that he succeeded. By that time her employers were so satisfied with her that, after an interview with them, followed by one with the girl herself, he was convinced that she was much better off where she was than with her aunts, whose dispositions were not unknown to him. So he left her in peace.

Knowing nothing of London and busy with her new way of life, Amy did not go at once to find Miss Raymount. She often recalled her kindness and always intended to seek her out as soon as she had the time. But the days and weeks wore away, and still she had not gone.

She continued a well-behaved girl, went regularly to church on Sundays, had many friends but few close ones, and lived with the girl who had been her friend before her mother's death. Her new life was, no doubt, from its lack of ties to a home and the restraining influences of older people, dangerous—no kite can soar without the pull of the string. But danger leads less often to ruin than some people think. He who can walk without falling will learn to walk the better that his road is not always smooth.

Such were the respective conditions of Amy Amber and the Frankses when the Raymounts left London. Hester knew nothing of the state of either, nor had they ever belonged to her flock. It was not for them that she was troubled in the midst of the peace and rest of her new life, when she felt like a shepherd compelled to leave his sheep in the wilderness. One good thing, however, that came of the change was that she and her father were drawn closer together through the quiet of this country life. When Mr. Raymount's hours of writing were over, he missed the more busy life into which he had been able to turn at will, and needed a companion. His wife not wishing to go with him, he naturally turned to his daughter, and they took many walks together.

During these walks Hester learned much. Though her father was not chiefly occupied with the best things, he did have both a learning and a teaching nature. There are few who can be said to be truly alive. Of Mr. Raymount it might be said that he was coming alive, and it was no small consolation to Hester to get nearer to him.

Like the rest of his children, she had been a little afraid of him. Fear, though it may dig deeper foundations of love, chokes its passages. Before a month was over, she was astonished to find how much of companions as well as friends they had become to each other.

Most fathers know little of their sons and less of their daughters. Because they are familiar with every feature of their children's faces and every movement of their bodies, they take it for granted they know them. But now Mr. Raymount began to make some discoveries of a deeper nature in Hester.

She kept up a steady correspondence with Miss Dasomma, and that also was a great help to her. She had a note now and then from Mr. Vavasor, but that was not a help. A little present of music was generally its pretext. He dared not trust himself to write to her about anything else. Hester was always glad when she saw his writing, and always disappointed with the letter—she could hardly have said why, for she never expected it to go beyond the surface of things.

In her absence Vavasor found himself haunted with her face, her form, her voice, her music, and the uplifting influence she exercised upon him. It is possible for a man to fall in love with a woman he is centuries from being able to understand. But how the form of such a woman must be dwarfed in the camera of such a man's mind. He is but a telescope turned wrong end upon her. If such a man could see such a woman after her true proportions, and not as the puppet he imagines her, thinking his own small great-things of her, he would not be able to love her at all. To see how he sees her—to get a glimpse of the shrunken creature he has to make her before he can get her through the proud door into the straightened cellar of his poor, pinched heart—would be enough in itself to keep any such woman from the possibility of falling in love with such a man. Hester knew that in some directions he was much undeveloped, but she thought she could help him. And had he thoroughly believed in and loved her, which he was not capable of doing, she could have helped him.

At length, in one of his brief communications, he mentioned that his yearly resurrection was at hand—a month of holiday. He must go northward, he said, to brace him for the heat of the autumn city. The memories of Burcliff drew him. He had an invitation to the opposite coast, which he thought he might accept instead. He did not know exactly where Yrndale lay, but if he found it within accessible distance, he hoped her parents would allow him to call some morning for an hour or two.

Hester answered that her father and mother would be glad to see him, and that if he were inclined to spend a day or two, there was a beautiful country to show him. If his holiday happened to coincide with Corney's, perhaps they would come together.

By return mail came a grateful acceptance. About a week after, they heard from Cornelius that he could not take a holiday before November. He did not inform them that he had exchanged vacations with another clerk whose time fell in the undesirable month late in the year.

One lovely evening in the beginning of June, when her turn came to get away a little earlier, Amy Amber thought that she woud at last make an effort to find Miss Raymount. She learned the address from a directory and was now well-enough acquainted with London to know how to reach Addison Square.

In every motion and feeling Amy Amber was a little lady—from her stylish dress to the daintiest little bonnet, to her gloves that clung closer to her small short hands than they had clung to the bodies of the rodents from which they came. She did not have much experience, and therefore was ignorant of some of the small ways and customs of the higher social strata. But such knowledge is not essential to ladyhood, though half ladies think themselves whole ladies because they have it. To become ladies indeed, they have to learn what those things and the knowledge of them are really worth. Another way in which Amy was unlike many who would have counted themselves her superiors—she was incapable of being disagreeable. Without knowing it, she held the main secret of all good manners—she was simple. She never put anything on, never wished to *appear* anything other than what she was. She tried to *be* pleasant.

She got into an omnibus and found Addison Square and the Raymount house. It looked dingy and dull—for many of its shutters were closed—and held an indescribable air of departure about it. Nevertheless, she knocked and the door was opened. She asked if Miss Raymount was at home.

Now Sarah, with most of the good qualities of an old trustworthy family-servant, had all the faults as well, and one or two besides. She had not been to Burcliff, consequently did not know Amy. Many householders have not an idea how abominably the servants they count patterns of excellence comport themselves to those even to whom special attention is owing.

"They are all out of town, miss," replied Sarah, "—except Mr. Cornelius, of course."

At that moment Mr. Cornelius, on his way to go out, stepped on the landing of the stair and stood for an instant looking down into the hall, wondering who might be at the door. He could not see Amy's face, and had he seen it, I doubt if he would have recognized her, but the moment he heard her voice he knew it, and hurried down, his face in a glow of pleasure. But as he drew near, the change in her seemed to him so great that he could hardly believe with his eyes what his ears had told him.

From the first, Corney, like everyone else of the family, was taken with Amy, and Amy was not less than a little taken with him. He was good-looking and, except with his own people, ready enough to make himself agreeable. Amy's face beamed with pleasure at the sight of him, and she almost involuntarily stepped within the door to meet him.

"Amy! Who would have thought of seeing you here? When did you come to town?" he asked, shaking her hand.

"I have been in London a long time," she answered.

Corney thought she indeed looked as if she had.

"How deuced pretty she is!" he said to himself. "Quite ladylike, by Jove."

"Come upstairs," he said, "and tell me all about it."

He turned and led the way. Without a second thought, Amy followed him. Sarah stood for a moment staring, wondering who the lady could be. "A cousin from Australia," she concluded. They had cousins there.

Cornelius went into the drawing room, Amy following him, and opened the shutters of a window, congratulating himself on his good luck. Not often did anything so pleasant enter the stupid old place! He made her sit on the sofa in the half dark, sat down beside her, and in a few minutes had all her story. Moved by her sweet bright face and pretty manners, pleased with the deference, amounting to respect, which she showed him, he began to think her the nicest girl he had ever known. After a conversation of about half an hour, she rose.

"What!" said Corney, "you're not going already, Amy?"

"Yes, sir," replied Amy. "I think I had better go. I am sorry not to see Miss Raymount. She was very kind to me."

"You mustn't go yet," said Corney. "Sit down and rest a little. Come—you used to like music. I will sing to you and you shall tell me whether I have improved since you heard me last."

Amy sat down again as he went to the piano and sang her half a dozen songs, then showed her a book of photographs, chiefly portraits of the more famous actresses of the day, and told her about them. He kept her occupied with one thing and another until Sarah grew fidgety and was on the point of stalking up from the kitchen when she heard them coming down.

Cornelius took his hat and stick, and said he would walk with her. Amy made no objection. She was pleased to have his company. He went with her all the way to the lodging she shared with her friend in a quiet little street in Kensington. Before they parted, her manner and behaviour had begun to fill what little there was of Corney's imagination, and he left her with a feeling that he knew where a treasure lay. He walked with an enlargement of strut as he went home through the park, and swung his cane with the air of a man who had made a conquest of which he had reason to be proud.

—Sixteen —

Waiting a Purpose

The hot, dreamy days rose and sank in Yrndale. Hester would wake in the morning oppressed with the feeling that there was something she ought to have begun long ago, and must positively set about this new day. Then as her inner day cleared, she would afresh recognize her duty as that of those who stand and wait. She had no great work to do—only the common family duties of the day, and her own education for what might be the will of Him who, having made her for something, would see that the possibility of that something should not be wanting.

In the heat of the day she would seek a shady spot with a book for her companion. Under the shadow of some rock, the tent-roof of some great beech tree, or the solemn gloom of some pine grove, the brooding spirit of the summer would day after day find her when the sun was at the height of his great bridge and fill her with a sense of repose. Then would such a quiescence pervade Hester's spirit, such a sweet spiritual sleep creep over her, that nothing seemed required of her but to live—mere existence was conscious well-being. On and off, however, she would he haunted with a vague sense of guilt at enjoying the leisure, but then faith would rouse itself and say: "But God will take care of you in this thing, too. You do not have to watch lest he should forget, only be ready when he gives the lightest call. You have to keep listening."

Every evening Hester would regularly sit at her piano, which had by then arrived. There, through all the sweet atmospheric changes of the brain—for the brain has its morning and evening, its summer and winter as well as the day and the year—she would meditate aloud. And, oftener than she knew, especially in the twilight when the days had grown shorter, Mark would be somewhere in the dusk listening to her, a lurking cherub, feeding on her music—sometimes ascending on its upward torrent to a solitude where only God would find him.

Occasionally a thought of Vavasor would come, but chiefly as one who would be a welcome helper in her work. And when for a time she had had enough of music, she would softly close her piano as she would have covered a child, and glide into the night to wander about through the gloom without conscious choice. At such times she would think what it would be to have a man for a friend, one who would strengthen her heart and make her bold to do what was needful and right.

To cherish the ideal of a man with whom to walk on her way through life is as right for a woman as it was for God to make them male and female. It is not the building of castles in the steepest heights of air that is to be blamed, but the building of such as inspector conscience is not invited to enter. And if occasionally Hester did indulge in such along the lines of the natural architecture of most young maidens, and if through these airy castles went flitting the form of Vavasor, who will wonder?

One evening, toward the end of July, when the summer is at its heat and makes the world feel as if there had never been and never ought to be anything but summer, Hester was sitting under a fir tree on the gathered leaves of numberless years, pine odours filling the air around her, as if they, too, stole out with the things of the night when the sun was gone. The sweet melancholy of the hour moved her spirit. So close was her heart to nature that when alone with it, she seldom longed for her piano. She *had* the music and did not need to hear it. When we are very near to God, we do not desire the Bible. When we feel far from him, we may well make haste to it. Most people, I fear, wait till they are inclined to seek him. They do not stir themselves up to lay hold on God. They breathe the dark airs of the tomb till the morning break, instead of rising at once and setting out on their journey to meet it.

As she sat she heard a slight rustle on the dry carpet around her feet. The next moment in the gloom she saw the dark form of a man. She was startled, but he spoke instantly. It was Vavasor. She could not answer for a moment.

"I am sorry I frightened you," he said.

"It is nothing," she returned. "But how did you find me?"

"They told me at the house you were somewhere in this direction. Mark had apparently followed you some distance. So I ventured to come and look for you, and something led me right."

"I hardly know myself where I am going sometimes. And it is so dark we ought to be moving back to the house before we can't see at all."

"Do let us risk it a few minutes longer," said Vavasor. "This is my first escape out of the dungeon-land of London for a whole year! This is paradise. I could imagine I am dreaming of fairyland."

Vavasor seated himself on the fir leaves beside her. She asked him about his journey and about Cornelius. Presently they rose, found their way without difficulty back to the house, and were soon at the piano.

Vavasor remained the next two weeks at Yrndale. In those days Nature had the best chance with him she had ever had. For a man is a man however he may have been injured by society trying to substitute itself for both God and Nature. A man is potentially a man however far he may be from actual manhood. Who knows what may be awakened in him?

During that fortnight, sensations came upon Vavasor of which he had had no previous consciousness The most remarkable event of the time, which would have seemed incredible to those who knew him best in London, was that one morning he got up in time to see—and *for the purpose of seeing*—the sun rise. It was a great stride forward. And that was not all—he really enjoyed it! He had poetry enough to feel something of the indwelling greatness that belonged to the vision itself. He felt a power of some kind present to his soul in the sight—though he set it down to poetic feeling. It was, in fact, the drawing of the naturing Eternal, whom he was made to understand, but of whom he knew so little.

Hester's thoughts dwelling so much on the people of her London neighbourhood, it could not be helped that their conversation often drifted in that direction. Yet notwithstanding the influences of nature around him, Vavasor was almost as far from understanding Hester's heart in the matter as he had been the night of the ill-fated concert. To him, Hester's calling was a mere fancy that would pass in time.

"I confess," said Vavasor as they chatted easily one day, "the condition of our poor in our large towns is the great question of the day."

"—which every one is waking up to talk about," said Hester, and said no more.

For, as one who tried to do something, she did not want to go on and say that if all who found the question interesting, would instead of talking about it do what they could, not to its solution but to its removal, they would at least make their mark on the poverty they claimed to be concerned about, of which not all the wind of words would in ten thousand years blow away the tiniest fragment. Love, and love alone, as from the first it is the source of all life, love alone, wise at once and foolish as a child, can work redemption. It is life drawing nigh to life, person to person, the human to human, that conquers death. This—therefore urges people to combine, seeking the strength of men, not the strength of God. Love alone, and the obligation thereto between the members of Christ's body, is the one eternal unbreakable bond. It is only where love is not that law must go. Law is indeed necessary, but woe to the community where love does not cast out—where at least love is not casting out law. Not all the laws in the universe can save a man from poverty, not to say from sin, not to say from conscious misery.

Work on, ye who cannot see this. Do your best. You will be rewarded according to your honesty. You will be saved by the fire that will destroy your work, and will one day come to see that Christ's way, and no other whatever, can either redeem your own life, or render the condition of the poorest or the richest wretch such as would justify his creation. If by the passing of this or that more or less wise law, you could, in the person of his descendant of the third or fourth generation, make a well-to-do man of him, he would probably be a good deal farther from the kingdom of heaven than the beggar or the thief over whom you now lament.

Vavasor began to think that if ever the day came when he might approach Hester "as a suitor for her hand," he must be very careful over what he called her philanthropic craze. But if ever he should in earnest set about winning her, he had full confidence in the artillery he could bring to the siege. He had not yet made any real effort to gain her affections.

Neither had he a doubt that, having succeeded, all would be easy, and he could do with her much as he pleased. He had no anxiety concerning the philanthropic craze thereafter. His wife, once introduced to such society as would then be her right, would speedily be cured of her extravagances and enthusiasms about the poor that were to him no less than folly.

Under the influence of the lovely place, of the lovely weather, and of his admiration for Hester, notwithstanding this folly, as he considered it, the latent poetry of Vavasor's nature awoke more rapidly, with the result that he was growing more and more in love with Hester. It was a pleasant experience to him. It began to grow plain to him that now his aunt could no longer look upon the idea of such an alliance in the same unfavourable light that she would naturally have before. It was very different to see Hester, now, in the midst of such grounds and in such a house, with all the old-fashioned comforts and luxuries of an ancient and prosperous family around her. If he could get his aunt to see her in the midst of these surroundings, then her beauty would have a chance to work its natural effect upon her.

By degrees, therefore, and without any transition noticed by Hester, emboldened mainly by the influences of the soft dusky twilight, he came to speak with more warmth and nearer approach.

"How strangely this loveliness seems to sink into the soul," he said one evening. "For when one loves, how it exalts his whole being, yet in the presence of the woman he worships, how small and unworthy he feels."

Hester sat silent. There are women like Hester who have had their minds constantly filled with true and earnest things and so have, over the years, come to woman's full dignity without having even speculated on what it may be to be in love. Such women, therefore, are somewhat in the dark when it first begins to show itself within them. Having never invited its presence, finding it within them adds to their perplexity. Yet, though Vavasor's experience was scarcely so valuable as her ignorance, he judged he might venture a little further. But with all his experience in the manufacture of compliments, he was now at a loss—he had no fine theories of love to talk from!

"If one might sit forever like this," he said in almost a whisper, "—forever and ever, needing nothing, desiring nothing! lost in perfect bliss! If only God would make this moment eternal."

He ceased and was silent.

Hester could not help being moved by the hint of the poetic thought that pervaded the utterance. But she was not altogether pleased. Never had she ever felt, even in a transient mood, like praying, "Let it last forever!"

"I do not *quite* understand you," she said. "I can scarcely imagine the time should ever come when I would wish it to last forever."

"Have you had so little happiness?" he asked sympathetically.

"I do not mean that," she replied. "Indeed, I think I have had a great deal. But I do not think much of happiness. And no amount of happiness that I have known yet should make me wish to stand still. I want to be always growing—and while one is growing Time cannot stand if he would: you drag him on with you! I want to be always becoming more and more capable of happiness."

"Ah!" returned Vavasor, "as usual you are out of sight beyond me. You must take pity on me and pull me along with you or else you will leave me miles behind and I shall never be able to look at you again, and what eternity would be to me without your face to look at, God only knows."

"But why should it be so?" answered Hester, almost tenderly. "Our fate is in our own hands. It is ours to determine the direction in which we shall go. I don't want to preach to you, dear Mr. Vavasor, but why should not every one be reasonable enough to seek the one best thing, and then there would be no parting? All the love and friendship in the world would not suffice to keep people together if they were inwardly parted by such difference as you imply."

Vavasor's heart was touched in two ways by this simple speech. First, in the best way in which it was at the moment capable of being touched—he could not help thinking for a moment what a blessed thing it must be to live in perfect peace, as Hester plainly did, about whatever might happen to you. Religion would be better than endurable in the company of such people as Hester! Secondly, he was pleased in the way of self-satisfaction, for clearly she was not opposed to terms of closer intimacy with him. And as she made the advance, why should he not accept, if not the help yet the offer of the help she had *almost* made? It would bind him to nothing. He understood her well enough to have no slightest suspicion of any coquetry such as a fool like Cornelius would have imagined. He was nevertheless a fool, also, only of another and deeper sort. It needs brains to be a real fool!

From that night he placed himself more than ever in the position of a pupil toward her, hoping in the natural effect of the intimacy. To keep up and deepen the relation, he would go on imagining himself in this and that difficulty. He was no conscious hypocrite in the matter—only his intellect alone was concerned, while he talked as if his whole being was. No answer given to him would have had the smallest effect on the man—Vavasor only thought about what he would say next. Hester kept trying to meet him as simply and directly as she could, never supposing that what she said made no difference to him. So long as she would talk, he cared not a straw whether she understood what he had said. Thus her desire to wake something better in him brought her into relations with him which had an earthly side, as everything heavenly of necessity has. For this life also is God's, and the very hairs of our head are numbered.

—Seventeen —

Major H.G. Marvel

One afternoon Vavasor was in his room, writing a letter to his aunt, in which he described in not too glowing terms, for he knew exaggeration would only give her a handle, the loveliness of the retreat among the hills where he was spending his holiday. Mr. Raymount was in his study, his wife in her own room, and the children out-of-doors—a gentleman was shown into the drawing room as Hester sat alone at her piano.

The servant apologized, saying he thought she was out. Since the visitor was already in the room, the glance she threw at the card the servant had given her informed her little as to the man's identity. The card simply read *Major H. G. Marvel*. She vaguely thought she had heard it, but in the suddenness of the meeting was unable to recall a single clue concerning the owner.

Advancing to meet him, she saw before her a man whose decidedly podgy figure yet bore a military air and was not without a certain grace of confidence. His bearing was marked by the total absence of any embarrassment, anxiety, or air of apology. His carriage spoke of self-assertion, and his person beamed with friendship. Notably above average height, his head looked a little too small for the base from which it rose, all the smaller that it was round and smooth and shining bald like ivory, and the face upon it was brought by the help of the razor into as close a resemblance with the rest of the ball as possible. His was a pleasant face to look at, in spite of—or maybe because of—his irregular features. A retreating and narrow forehead sat above keen gray eyes that sparkled with intelligence and fun.

"Cousin Hester!" he said as he approached her, holding out his hand.

Mechanically she gave him hers. The voice that addressed her was a little husky, and very cheery. The hand that took hers was small and soft, yet kind and firm. A merry, friendly smile lit up his eyes and face as he spoke. Hester could not help liking him at first sight—yet felt a little shy of him. She thought she had heard her mother speak of a cousin somewhere abroad. This must be he.

"You don't remember me," he said, "seeing you were not yet in this world for a year or two after I left the country. And, to tell the truth, had I been asked, I should have objected to your appearance on any terms."

As his words did not seem to carry much enlightenment, he went on to explain. "The fact is, my dear young lady, that I left the country because your mother and I were too much of one mind."

"Of one mind?" said Hester bewildered.

"The thing, you see," said the major, standing before her with polite yet confident bearing, "was that I loved your mother better than myself, but it was not to be. It was not an arrangement for my happiness. I had the choice between two things—staying at home and breaking my heart by seeing her marry another man, or going away and getting over it the best I could. So I must, by nature, be your sworn enemy—only it's of no use, for I've fallen in love with you at first sight. So now if you will ask me to sit down, I will swear to let bygones be bygones, and be your true knight and devoted servant as long as I live. How you do remind me of your mother, only by Jove, you're twice as lovely!"

"Do please sit down, Mr. Marley—"

"Marvel," interrupted the major, "and if you could let me have a glass of water with a little sherry just to take the taste off it, I should be greatly obliged to you."

As he spoke he wiped his round head with a red silk handkerchief.

"I will get it at once, and let my mother know you are here," said Hester, turning to the door.

"No, no, never mind your mother. I daresay she is busy or lying down. She always went to lie down at this time of the day. I shouldn't wonder if she thought me troublesome in those days. But I bear no malice now, and I hope she doesn't, either. Tell her I say so. It's more than twenty-five years ago, though to me it hardly seems more than so many weeks. Don't disturb your mother, my dear. But if you insist on doing so, tell her old Harry has come to see her—very much improved since she sent him about his business."

Hester told a servant to take the sherry and the water to the drawing room, and, much amused, ran to find her mother.

"There's the most interesting gentleman downstairs, Mama, calling himself old Harry. He's having some sherry and water in the drawing room. I never saw such an odd man!"

Her mother laughed—a pleased little laugh.

"Go and tell him I shall be down directly."

"Is he really a cousin, mama?"

"To be sure—my second cousin. He was very fond of me once."

"Oh, he has told me all about that already. He says you sent him about his business."

"If that means that I wouldn't marry him, it is true enough. But he doesn't know what I went through for taking his part. I always stood up for him, though I could never bear him near me. He was such an odd, good-natured bear! Such a rough sort of creature, always saying the thing he ought not to and making everybody, ladies especially, uncomfortable. He never meant any harm, but never saw where fun should stop. I daresay he's much improved by this time."

"He told me to tell you he was. But I like him, mama, so don't be too hard on him."

"I won't, dear. Did he tell you that since he left he has been married to a black, or at least a very brown, Hindu woman?"

"No. Has he brought her home with him, I wonder?"

"She has been dead now for some ten years. I believe he had a large fortune which by judicious management he has increased considerably. He is really a good-hearted fellow."

The major's wife was the daughter of an English merchant by a Hindoo wife, a very young girl when he first made her acquaintance. She had been kept almost in slavery by the relatives of her deceased father, who had left her all his property. Major Marvel had become interested in her when her relatives attempted to lay the death of her father at her door. The major had taken her part and helped win her complete acquittal. But, though nobody believed her in the smallest degree guilty, society looked askance upon her. True, she was rich, but was she not black? And had she not been accused of a crime? So the major said to himself, "Here I am a useless old fellow, living for nobody but myself. It would make one life at least happier if I took the poor thing home with me. She's too old for adoption, but perhaps she would marry me."

He did not know, even then, what a large fortune she had. That the major rejoiced over what he found when he came to inquire into things, I do not doubt. But I am entirely sure he would have been an honourable husband had he found she had nothing. When she left him the widowed father of a little girl, he mourned sincerely for her. When the child followed her mother, he was for some time a sad man indeed. He had now returned to his country to find almost every one of his old friends dead, or so changed as to make them all but dead to him.

Little as anyone would have imagined it from his conversation or manner, it was with a kind of heart-despair that he sought the cousin he had loved. And scarcely had he seen the daughter of his old love than he was immediately taken with her. He saw at once that she was a grand sort of person and gracious—different from anyone he had ever seen before. At the same time he unconsciously began to feel a claim toward her—to have loved the mother seemed to give him a right in the daughter. But all this was as yet only in the region of the feelings, not at all in that of the thinking.

"Well," said Hester, "I shall go back to him, mama, and tell him you are coming as soon as you have got your wig and your newest lace-cap on, and your cheeks rouged and pearl-powdered, to look as much like the young lady he left as you can."

Her mother laughed merrily and pretended to give her daughter a box on the ears. It was not often any mood like this rose between them, for not only were they serious in heart, but from temperament and history and modes and directions of thought, their ways were serious as well.

"Look what I have brought you, cousin," said major Marvel the moment Hester reentered the room, holding out to her a small necklace. "You don't mind such a gift from an old fellow like me. Of course I don't mean that I want to marry you straightaway before I know what sort of temper you've got. Here, take them."

Hester drew near and looked at the necklace.

"Take it," said the major again.

"How strangely beautiful it is!—all red, pear-shaped, dull, scratched stones, hanging from a savage-looking gold chain. What are they, Mr. Marvel?"

"You have described it like a book!" he said. "It is a barbarous native necklace, but they are fine rubies—only rough, neither cut nor polished."

"It is beautiful," repeated Hester. "Did you really mean it for me?"

"Of course I did!"

"I will ask mama if I can keep it."

"Why do that? I hope you don't think I stole it?—But here comes your mother!—Helen, I'm so glad to see you again!"

Hester slipped away with the necklace in her hand, and left her mother to welcome her old admirer before she would trouble her about the offered gift. They met like trusting friends whom the years had done nothing to separate. While they were still talking of times gone by, Mr. Raymount entered, received him cordially, and insisted on his remaining with them as long as he could. They were old friends, although rivals, and there had never been any bitterness between them. The major readily agreed, as Mr. Raymount sent to the station for his luggage, and showed him to a room.

—Eighteen —

The Major and Vavasor

Major Marvel was, in one sense, and that not a slight one, a true man. There was no discrepancy between his mental condition and the clothing in which he presented that condition to others. His words, looks, manners, tones, and everything that goes to express man to man expressed what was inside him. What he felt, he showed. I think he was unaware of the possibility of doing otherwise.

At the same time, he had little insight into the feelings of others, and almost no sense of the possibility that the things he was saying might affect his listeners otherwise than they affected him. If he boasted, he meant to boast. He had no very ready sympathy with other people, especially in any suffering he had never himself experienced. But he was scrupulously fair in what he said or did in regard of them, and nothing was so ready to make him angry as any appearance of injustice or show of deception. He would have said that a man's first business was to take care of himself, as so many think but do not have the courage to say—and so many more who do not think it. But one thing caused him to dislike another quicker than anything—that was when they found the heel of his all but invulnerable vanity and wounded it. Not accustomed to being hurt, he resented hurt all the more sorely when it came.

During dinner he dominated the conversation and evidently expected to be heard. But that was nearly all he wanted. Let him talk, and hear you laugh when he was funny, and he was satisfied. He was fond of telling tales of adventure, some wonderful, some absurd, and just as willing to tell a joke against himself as at the expense of another. Like many of his day who had spent their early years in India, he was full of the amusements and sports with which so much otherwise idle time is passed by Englishmen in the East, and seemed to think nothing connected with the habits of their countrymen there could fail to interest those at home.

Every now and then throughout the dinner he would say, "Oh, that reminds me!" and then tell something that happened when he was at such-and-such a place, when so-and-so "of our regiment" was out tiger-shooting, or pig-sticking, or whatever the sport might be. "And if Mr. Raymount will take a glass of wine with me, I will tell him the story," he would say, for he was constantly drinking wine, after the old fashion, with this or that one of the company.

When he and Vavasor were introduced to each other, he glanced at him, drew his eyebrows together, made his military bow, and included him among the listeners to his tales of exploit and adventure by sea and land.

Vavasor was much annoyed by his presence. So while he retained the blandest expression and was ready to drink as many glasses of wine with the newcomer as he wished, he set him down in his own mind not only as an ill-bred man and a boaster, in which there was some truth, but as a liar and a vulgar-minded man as well, in which there was little or no truth.

Now, although major Marvel had not much ordinary insight into character because of his inability to feel a deep enough interest in his neighbour, if his suspicion or dislike was roused, he was just as likely as anyone to arrive at a correct judgment concerning a man he did not love.

He had been relating a thrilling adventure with a man-eating tiger. He saw, as they listened, the eyes of little Mark and Saffy almost surpassing the use of eyes and becoming ears as well. He saw Hester also, who was still child enough to prefer a story of adventure to a love tale, sitting entranced as if her hair would stand on end. But at one moment he caught also a certain expression on the face of Vavasor, which that experienced man of the world certainly never intended to be seen, only at the moment he was annoyed to see Hester's attentiveness—she seemed to have eyes for no one but the man who shot tigers as Vavasor would have shot grouse.

The major, who, upon fitting occasion, could be as quarrelsome as any turkey cock, said, but not quite so carelessly as he had intended:

"Ha, ha, I see by your eyes, Mr. Passover, you think I'm drawing the long bow—drawing the arrow to the head, eh?"

"No, upon my word!" said Vavasor earnestly. "Nothing was further from my thoughts. I was only admiring the coolness of the man who would actually creep into the mouth of the—the jungle after a—what-do-you-call-him?—a man-eating tiger."

"Well, you see, what was a fellow to do," returned the major suspiciously. "The fellow wouldn't come out! and, by Jove, I wasn't the only one that wanted him out! Besides, I didn't creep in. I only looked in to see whether he was really there. That I could tell by his shining eyes."

"But is not a man-eating tiger a horrifying beast? Once he takes to that kind of diet, don't you know—they say he likes nothing else half so well. Good beef and mutton will no longer serve him, so I've been told at the club."

"It is true he does not care for other food after once getting a passion for the more delicate, but it does not increase either his courage or his fierceness. The fact is, it ruins his moral nature. He does not get many Englishmen to eat, and it seems as if the flesh of women and children and poor cowardly natives undermines his natural courage. He is well known as a sneak. I sometimes can't help thinking the ruffian knows he is a rebel against the law of his Maker, and a traitor to his natural master. The man-eating tiger and rogue-elephant are the devils of their kind. The others leave you alone except you attack them—then they show fight. These attack you—but run when you go out after them. You can never get any sport out of him. If there's a creature on earth I hate, it's a coward!" concluded the major.

"But why should you hate a coward so?" asked Hester, feeling at the moment, with the vision of the man-eating tiger in her mind, that she must herself come under the category. "How can a poor creature made without courage help being one?"

"Such as you mean, I wouldn't call cowards," returned the major. "Nobody thinks worse of the hare or the fox for running away from the hounds. Even men whose business it is to fight will run from the enemy when they have no chance, and when it would do no good to stand and be cut down. There is a time to run and a time to fight. But the man will run like a man, and the coward like a coward."

Vavasor's only reply was to himself, but he took care not to allow the slightest expression cross his face which the major might detect.

"What can harmless creatures do but run?" resumed the major, filling his glass with old port. "But when the wretch that has done all the hurt he could will not show fight for it, but turns tail the moment danger appears, I call him a contemptible coward. That's what made me go into the place to find the brute."

"But he might have killed you, though he was a coward," said Hester, "when you did not leave him room to run."

"Of course he might have, my dear! What else would be the fun of it? Without that the thing would be no better than this shooting of pigeons and pheasants that men do in this country under the so-called name of sport. You *had* to kill him, you know. He's first cousin—the man-eating, or rather woman-eating tiger—to a sort that I understand abounds in the Zoological Gardens called English society. If the woman be poor, he devours her at once. If she be rich he marries her, and eats her slowly up at his ease in his den."

As much as he was taken with the daughter of the house, the major disliked the fine gentleman visitor that seemed to be dangling after her. Who he was, or in what capacity he was there, he did not know, but almost from first sight, he profoundly disliked him. His dislike grew as he saw more of Vavasor's admiration for Hester. He might be a woman-eater himself, like the tiger, and after her money—if she had any. Such suspects must be watched and followed and their haunts marked.

"But," said Hester, "I should like to understand the thing a little better. I am not willing to set myself down as a coward. Tell me, major Marvel—when you know that a beast may have you down, and begin eating you at any moment, what is it that keeps you up? What have you to fall back upon? Is it principle, or faith, or what is it?"

"Ho, ho!" laughed the major, "a metaphysician in the very bosom of my family! I had not reckoned upon that! I cannot exactly say that it is principle, and I am sure it is not faith. You don't think about it at all. Well, I daresay there comes in something of principle!—that as an Englishman you are sent to that benighted quarter of the world to kill their big vermin for them, poor things!

But no, you don't think of it at the time. You've got to kill him—that's all. And then when he comes roaring on, your rifle jumps to your shoulder of itself."

"Do you make up your mind beforehand that if the animal should kill you, it is all right?" asked Hester.

"By no means," answered the major laughing.

"Unless I had made up my mind that if I was killed it was all right," said Hester, "I couldn't meet the tiger."

"But you see, my dear," said the major, "you do not know what it is like to have confidence in your eye and your rifle. It is a form of power that you soon come to feel as resting in yourself—a power to destroy the thing that opposes you."

Hester fell to thinking and the talk went on without her. She never heard the end of the story, but was roused by the laughter that followed it.

"It was no tiger at all—that was the joke of the thing," said the major. "Everyone roared with laughter when the brute—a great lumbering, floundering hyena, rushed into the daylight."

"And what became of the man-eater?" asked Mark, looking disappointed.

"Lost in the jungle till it was safe to come out and go on with his delicate meals."

"Just imagine that horrible growl behind you when you didn't suspect it."

"By George! for a young lady," said the major, "you have an imagination! Too much of that, you know, won't make you a good hunter of tigers."

"Then perhaps you own your coolness to lack of imagination?" suggested Hester.

"Perhaps so. Perhaps after all," returned the major with a merry twinkle in his eye, "we hunters are but a set of stupid fellows—too stupid to be frightened."

"I didn't mean that exactly. I think that perhaps you do not know so well as you might where your courage comes from. For my part I would rather be courageous to help the good than to destroy the bad."

"Ah, but we're not all good enough ourselves for that," said the major with a serious expression, looking at her out of his clear eyes, from which their habitual twinkle of fun had for the moment vanished. "Some of us are only fit to destroy what is yet worse than ourselves."

"To be sure we can't *make* anything," said Hester thoughtfully, "but we can help God to make. To destroy evil things is good, but the worst things can only be destroyed by being good, and that is so hard!"

"It *is* hard," said the major—"so hard that most people never try it!" he added with a sigh and a gulp of his wine.

Mrs. Raymount rose, and with Hester and the children, withdrew. After they were gone the major rattled on again, his host putting in a word now and then, while Vavasor sat silently with an expression that seemed to say, "I am amused, but I don't eat all that is put on my plate."

—Nineteen —

A Walk Along the River

The major had taken a strong fancy to Hester, and during the whole of his visit kept as near her as he could, much to the annoyance of Vavasor. Doubtless it was, in part, to keep the major from her that he himself sought her, for there was a natural repulsion between the two men. Vavasor thought the major a most objectionable, indeed low fellow, a vulgar braggart, and the major thought Vavasor a supercillious idiot. It is curious how differently a man's character will be read by two people in the same company. If you like a man, you will judge him with more or less fairness. If you dislike him, you cannot fail to judge him unjustly.

Without ceasing for a moment to be conventionally polite, Vavasor allowed major Marvel to see unmistakably that his society was not welcome to him. Entirely ignorant each of the other's pursuits, and nearly incapable of agreement on any point, each would gladly have shown the other to be the fool he counted him. Each watched the other—the major annoyed with the other's silent pretention, and Vavasor regarding the major as a narrow-minded and overgrown schoolboy—though, in fact, his horizon was very much wider than his own.

After breakfast the next day, all but Mr. Raymount went out for a little walk together.

It seemed destined to be a morning of small adventures. As they passed the gate of a nearby farm, out rushed a half-grown pig. Heading right for the major, the animal shot between the well-parted legs of the man, throwing him backwards into a humiliating heap. A look of keen gratification rose in Vavasor's face, but he was too well-bred to allow it to remain. He proceeded to offer assistance to the fallen hero. Marvel, however, heavy as he was, did not require it, but got on his feet again with a cheerfulness which showed either a sweetness or a control over his temper, which gave him a great lift in Hester's estimation.

"Confound the brute!" he laughed. "He can't know how many of his wild relatives I have stuck, else he should never have done it. What a mess he has made of me!"

Saffy laughed merrily over the fun he made of his fall, but Mark looked concerned. He ran and pulled some grass and proceeded to brush him off.

"Let us go into the farmhouse," said Mrs. Raymount. "Mrs. Stokes will give us some assistance."

"No, no," returned the major. "Better let the mud dry. It will come off much better then. Why shouldn't piggy have his fun as well as another, eh, Mark? Come along. You shan't have your walk spoiled by my carelessness."

There seemed to be more creatures than the pig wanting to escape the bounds. A spirit of liberty was abroad. Mark and Saffy went rushing away like wild rabbits every now and then, making a round and returning. It was one of those cooler of warm mornings that rouse all the life in heart, brain, and nerves, making every breath a pleasure and every movement a joy.

They had not gone much farther when, just as they approached the paling of a paddock, a horse which had been turned into the fenced field to graze came sailing over the fence, and would presently have been ranging free. Unaccustomed to horses, except when equipped and held ready by the hand of the groom, the ladies and children started and jumped back. Vavasor also stepped a little aside, making way for the animal. But as he alighted from his jump, carrying with him the top bar of the fence, the horse stumbled and almost fell. While he was yet a little bewildered, the major hurried up to him, and before the animal could recover his wits, had him by the nose and ear and was leading him to the gap in the fence. He made the horse jump in again and replaced the bar that had been knocked off.

"Thank you! How brave of you, major Marvel!" said Mrs. Raymount.

The major laughed with his usual merriment.

"If it had been the horse of the Rajah of Rumtool," he said, "I should have been brave indeed! Only by this time there would have been nothing left of me to thank. A man would have needed courage to take him by the head! But a quiet, good-tempered carriage-horse like this one none but a cockney would be frightened of him!"

With that, to the delight of the children, he began telling them the most amazing and, indeed, horrible tales about the Rajah's horse as they continued their walk. Whether it was all true or not I cannot tell. All I can say is that the major only told what he heard and believed, or had himself seen.

Vavasor was annoyed with himself for the very natural nervousness he had shown, for it was nothing more, and turned his annoyance on the major, who, by such an insignificant display of coolness had gained a great advantage over him in the eyes of the ladies.

Following the course of the river, the group gradually descended from the higher grounds to the immediate banks, which spread out into a small meadow on each side. There were not now many flowers, but Saffy was pulling stalks of feathery-headed grasses, while Mark was walking quietly along by the brink of the stream, stopping every now and then to look into it. The bank was covered with long grass hanging over, here and there a bush of rushes amongst it. On the opposite side lower down was a meal-mill, and nearly opposite, a little below, was the head of the mill-lade, whose weir, turning the water into it, dammed back the river, and made it deeper here than in any other part—some seven feet at least, and that close to the shore. It was still as a lake, and looked, as deep as it was.

The two ladies and two gentlemen were walking along the meadow, some distance behind the children, and a little way from the bank, when they were startled by a scream of agony from Saffy. She was running shrieking towards them. No Mark was to be seen. All broke into a run to meet her, but presently Mrs. Raymount sank on the grass. Hester would have stayed with her, but she motioned her on.

Vavasor outran the major, and reached Saffy first, but to his anxious questions—"Where is he? Where did you leave him? Where did you see him last?" she only continued shrieking.

When the major came up, he heard enough to know that he must use his wits and lose no time in trying to draw information from a creature whom terror had made for the moment insane. He kept close to the bank, looking for some sign of the spot where Mark had fallen in.

He had indeed overrun the place, and was still intent on the bank when he heard a cry behind him. It was the voice of Hester, screaming "Across, across!"

He looked across, and saw half-way over, slowly drifting towards the mill-lade, a something dark, now appearing for a little above the water, now sinking out of sight. The major's experienced eye saw at once it must be the body, dead or alive—only he could hardly be dead yet—of poor Mark. He threw off his coat, and plunged in, found the water deep enough for good swimming, and made in his direction.

In the meantime, Hester, followed by Vavasor, sped along the bank till she came to the weir, over which hardly any water was running. The footing was uncertain, with deep water on one side up to a level with the stones, and a steep descent to more deep water on the other. In one or two spots the water ran over, and those spots were slippery. But, rendered fearless by her terrible fear, Hester flew across without a slip, leaving Vavasor some little way behind, for he was neither very sure-footed nor very sure-headed.

By the time she had reached the other side and turned back up river, the major was already trying to get the unconscious form of Mark on to the bank. The poor man had not swum so far for many years, and was nearly spent.

He gave a great heave, got the body half on the shore, and was just able to scramble out himself. When Hester reached him, he was doing all he could to bring back the boy's life. She knelt down and caught the child up in her arms.

"Come, come!" she cried, and ran with him back to the mill. The major followed, running, panting, dripping. When they met Vavasor, he would have taken him from her, but she would not give him up.

"Go back across to my mother," she said. "Tell her we have got him, and he is at the mill. Then go and tell my father, and ask him to send for the doctor."

Vavasor obeyed, feeling again a little small. But Hester had never thought that he might have acted differently than he had.

In a few minutes they had him in the miller's blankets, with hot water about him, while the major, who knew well what ought to be done, for he had been tried in almost every emergency under the sun, went through the various movements of the arms prescribed, inflated the chest again and again with his own breath, and did all he could to bring back the action of the breathing muscles.

Vavasor took upon him to assure Mrs. Raymount that Mark was safe and would be all right in a little while. She rose and with Saffy's help managed to walk home. But after that day she was never so well again. Vavasor ran on to the house and before long Mr. Raymount was at the mill—just as the first signs of returning life appeared. After about half an hour the boy opened his eyes, looked at his father, smiled in his own angelic way, and closed them again with a deep sigh. They covered him up as warm as they could and left him to sleep until the doctor came.

That same night, as Hester was sitting beside him, she heard him talking in his sleep:

"When may I go and play with the rest by the river? Oh, how sweetly it talks! it runs all the way through me and through me! It was such a nice way, God, of fetching me home! I rode home on a water-horse!"

He thought he was dead, that God sent him home, and that he was now safe, only tired. It sent a pang to Hester's heart. What if, after all, he was going to leave them! For the child had always seemed fitter for heaven than earth, and any day it seemed, he might be sent for.

Mark recovered by degrees, but continued very sleepy and tired. He never fretted or complained, received every attention with a smile, and told his mother not to worry, for he was not going away yet. He had been told that under the water, he said. Before winter he was able to go about the house and was soon reading all his favourite books again, especially *Pilgrim's Progess,* which he had already read through five times.

The major left Yrndale the next morning, but Vavasor stayed a day or two longer. He could not go until he saw Mark well on the road to recovery.

In reality, the major went because he could no longer endure the sight of "that idiot," as he called Vavasor, assured that in London he had only to inquire to find out enough to discredit the fellow. He told them to tell Mark he was gone to fetch tiger skins and a little statue with diamond eyes and would tell him all about them as soon as he was well again.

He told Mr. Raymount that he had no end of business to look after, but now that he knew the way to Yrndale he might be back any day. He told Mrs. Raymount about some pearls he had for her— he knew she was fond of pearls—and was going away to fetch them. He made Hester promise to write to him at the Army and Navy Club every day till Mark was well. And so he departed, much blessed by all the family for saving the life of their precious boy.

When he reached London the major hunted up some of his old friends, and through them sent out inquiry after inquiry concerning Vavasor. He learned some things about him—nothing very bad, and nothing especially to his credit. That he was heir to an earldom he liked least of all, for he was only the more likely to marry his beautiful cousin, and he thought her a great deal too good for him.

Vavasor was relieved when he was gone, but as the days passed and he expected the enthusiasm for the major's heroics to have died down, he was annoyed to find that Hester was just as impressed with the objectionable character of the man. That Hester should not be shocked with him was almost more than he could bear. He could not understand that just as to the pure all things are pure, so the common mind sees far more vulgarity in others than the mind developed to genuine refinement. It understands, therefore forgives. Hester was able to look deeper than he, and she saw much that was good and honourable in the man, however he might have the bridle of his tongue too loose for safe riding in the crowded paths of society.

A day or two before the end of Vavasor's visit, as he was sitting together in the old-fashioned garden with Mrs. Raymount and Hester, the mail was brought to them—one letter for Vavasor with a great black seal. He read it through, then said quietly:

"I am sorry I must leave you tomorrow. Or is there a train tonight? But I daresay it does not matter, only I ought to be present at the funeral of my uncle, Lord Gartley. He died yesterday, from what I can make out. It is a tiresome thing to succeed to a title with hardly property enough to pay the servants."

"Very tiresome," assented Mrs. Raymount. "But a title is not like an illness. If you can live without, you can live with one."

"True. But there's society, you see. There's so much expected of a man in my position. What do you think, Miss Raymount?" he asked, turning toward Hester.

"I do not see why a mere name could have any power to alter one's mode of life. Of course if the change brings new duties, they must be attended to, but if the property be so small as you say, it cannot need much looking after. To be sure, there are the servants, but they cannot be many. Why shouldn't you go on as you are?"

"I must go a good deal by what my aunt thinks best. She has a sort of right, you see. Her one fixed idea, knowing that I was likely to succeed, has been the rehabilitation of the earldom. She has been like a mother to me, and will more than likely make me her heir too, though she might change her mind at any moment. She is a kindhearted woman, but a little peculiar. I wish you knew my aunt, Mrs. Raymount."

"I should be very pleased to know her."

"She would be delighted with this lovely place of yours. It is a perfect paradise. I feel its loveliness even more that I am so soon to hear its gates close behind me."

"You must bring your aunt some time, Mr. Vavasor. We should make her very welcome," said Mrs. Raymount.

"Unfortunately, with all her good qualities, my aunt, as I have said, is a little peculiar. For one thing, she shrinks from making new acquaintances."

By this time Vavasor had resolved to make an attempt to gain his aunt's approval of Hester and felt sure she could not fail to be taken with her if only she saw her in fit surroundings. With her the frame was more than half the picture. And now, in the setting of Yrndale, the family would be of so much more importance in her eyes. He also had the advantage of greater importance with the title in his possession—he was the Earl of Gartley. She must either be of one mind with him now, or lose the cherished purpose of so many years.

That same evening he left them in high spirits, and without any pretence of decent regret for the death of one whom he had never seen. It would be untrue to say that Hester was not interested in the news. She and Vavasor had been so much thrown together, and in circumstances so favourable to intimacy, that she could hardly have been a woman at all and not care what might happen to him. Neither was she altogether indifferent to the idea of wearing a distinguished historical name, or of occupying an exalted position in the eyes of the world. Her nature was not yet so thoroughly possessed with the things that *are* as distinguished from the things that only appear, as not to feel some pleasure in being a countess of this world, while waiting the inheritance of the saints in light. Of course this was just as far unworthy of her as it is unworthy of any one who has seen the hid treasure not to have sold all that he has to buy it—not to have counted, with Paul, everything but dross to the winning of Christ—not even worth being picked up on the way as he presses towards the mark of the high calling

But I must say this for her, she thought of it first of all as a buttressing help to the labour which, come what might, it remained her chief hope to follow among her poor friends in London. To be a countess would make many things easier for her, she thought. Little she knew how immeasurably more difficult it would make it to do anything whatever worth doing!

So, again, the days passed quietly. Mark grew a little better. Hester wrote brief but regular bulletins to the major, which were seldom acknowledged. The new earl wrote that he had been to the funeral, and described, with would-be humour, the house and lands to which he had fallen heir. The house might, he said, with unlimited money, be made fit to live in, but what was left of the estate was merely a savage mountain.

—Twenty —

An Unpleasant Interview

Mr. Raymount went to London now and then but never stayed long. In the autumn he had his books brought to Yrndale, saying in London he could always get what books he wanted, but must have his own about him in the country. When they were all accommodated and arranged to his mind, he began to feel for the first time in his life as if he had a permanent home, and talked of selling the house in Addison Square.

In the month of October, when the sun shone a little sadly and the hints of the coming winter might be felt hovering in the air, major Marvel again made his appearance at Yrndale. But this time he had a troubled expression on his face that Mrs. Raymount had never seen before. It was the look of one who had an unpleasant duty to discharge—a thing he would rather not do, but felt compelled to do just the same. He had brought the things he promised, and at the sight of them Mark brightened up amazingly. At the dinner table he tried to be merry as before, but failed rather conspicuously. He drank more wine than usual, and laid the blame on the climate. In the morning he appeared at the usual hour, but showed plain marks of a sleepless night. He said he must seek a warmer climate, for if it was like this already, what would it be in January?

It was in reality a perfect autumn morning, of which every one except the major felt the enlivening influence—the morning of all mornings for a walk!

After breakfast the major followed Hester out of the dining room. He humbly whispered the request for her to walk with him alone, as he wished a private conversation with her. With an undefined anxiety, Hester at once consented, but first ran to her mother.

"What can he want to talk to me about, mama?"

"How can I tell, my dear?" answered her mother with a smile. "Perhaps he will dare the daughter's refusal too."

"Oh, mama! How can you joke about such a thing! I shouldn't go with him."

"You had better go, dear. You need not be afraid. He really is a gentleman, and you must not forget how much we owe him for saving Mark's life."

"Do you mean, mama, that I ought to marry him if he asks me?" Hester was sometimes oddly dense for a moment as to the intent of those she knew best.

Her mother laughed heartily.

"What a goose you are, my darling! Don't you know your mother from a villain yet?"

But in truth her mother so rarely jested that there was some excuse for her. Relieved by her mother's laugh, she still was not comfortable about going, but put on her bonnet and went without more words. Until they were some distance from the house, she and the major walked in absolute silence. How changed the poor man was, she thought. He marched steadily along, his stick under his arm like a sword, his eyes straight before him.

"Cousin Hester," he said at length, "I am about to talk to you very strangely. Can you imagine a man making himself intensely, unpardonably disagreeable, from the very best of motives?"

They were words very different from what she expected.

"I think I could," answered Hester, thinking whatever he had to say, the sooner it was said the better.

"Tell me," he said suddenly then paused awkwardly. "Let me ask you first," he resumed, "whether you are able to trust me a little. I am old enough to be your father—let me say your grandfather. Imagine I am your grandfather. In my soul I believe neither could wish you well more truly than I do myself. Will you trust me and tell me what there is between you and Mr. Vavasor?"

Hester was silent.

Before she had time to consider an answer, he resumed.

"I know," he said, "ladies think such things are not to be talked about with gentlemen, but there are exceptions to every rule." He paused, then spoke directly. "Are you engaged to Mr. Vavasor?"

"No," answered Hester promptly.

"What is it, then? Are you going to be?"

"I don't know—how can I say?" replied Hester.

"Thank God you are still free!"

"But why should you be so anxious about it?"

"Has he never said he loved you?" asked the major eagerly.

"No," she said a little hurriedly. She felt instinctively it was best to answer directly. But her voice trembled a little, wondering whether though literally it was strictly true. "We are friends," she added. "We trust each other a good deal."

"Trust him with nothing, least of all your heart, my dear," said the major earnestly. "He is not worthy of you."

"Do you say that to flatter me or to disparage him?"

"Entirely to disparage him. I never flatter."

"Major Marvel, you surely did not bring me out to say evil things of one of my best friends?" said Hester, growing angry.

"I certainly did—if the truth be evil—but only for your sake. The man is a nobody."

"That only proves you do not know him. You would not speak so if you did."

"I am sure I would have worse to say if I knew him better. It is you who do not know him. It astonishes me that sensible people like your father and mother let a fellow like that come prowling after you."

"Major Marvel, if you are going to abuse my father and mother as well as Lord Gartley—" cried Hester, but he interrupted her.

"Ah, there it is!" he exclaimed. "Lord Gartley! I have no business to interfere—no more than your gardener or coachman—but to think of an angel like you in the arms of a—"

"Major Marvel!"

"I beg ten thousand pardons, cousin Hester! But I am so desperately in earnest I can't pick and choose my phrases. Believe me, the man is not worthy of you."

"As his friend I ask you, what do you have against him?"

"That's the pity of it. I can't tell you anything specifically very bad of him, other than that no one has anything good to say—of whom never a warm word is uttered. I do not say he has disgraced himself openly—he has not."

"I assure you, major Marvel, he is a man of uncommon gifts and—"

"Great attractions, no doubt—to me invisible," blurted the major.

Hester turned from him.

"I am going home," she said. "Luncheon is at the usual hour."

"Just one word more," he begged hurrying after her. "I swear I have no purpose in interfering but to save you from a miserable future. Promise me not to marry this man and I will settle on you a thousand pounds a year."

At those words she turned on him with a glance of contempt. But there were tears in her eyes and her heart smote her. Though he had abused her friend he was plainly being honest. Her countenance softened as she looked at him. She stopped and he came up to her. She laid her hand on his arm.

"Dear major Marvel," she said, "I will speak to you without anger. What would you think of one who took money to do the thing she ought or ought not to do? Such a promise I cannot give, whether it be an earl or a beggar. How am I to know the will of God for the remainder of my life?"

"Yes, yes, my dear! You are quite right—absolutely right," the major agreed humbly. "I only wanted to make you financially independent. But will you have liberty otherwise? Will your father settle any of his estate upon you?"

"I don't know. I have never thought about anything of the kind."

"How could they let you go about with him so much and never ask what he meant by it?"

"They could easier have asked me what I meant by it. Would you have them shut me up and make my life miserable to make it safe? If a woman has any sense, major Marvel, she can take care of herself. If she has not, she must learn the need of it."

"Ah!" said the major sadly, "but the thousand pangs and aches and heart-sickenings. I would sooner see my child dead with a husband she loved than living a merry life with one she did not."

Hester began to feel she had not been doing the major justice.

"So would I!" she said heartily. "You mean me well, and I shall not forget how kind you have been. Now, let us go back."

"Just one thing more: if you ever think I can help you, you *will* let me know?"

"That I promise with all my heart," she answered. "I mean if it be a thing I think it right to trouble you about."

The major's face fell.

"I see!" he said. "You won't promise anything. Well, stick to that, and *don't* promise."

"You wouldn't have me come to you for a new bonnet, would you?"

"By George! shouldn't I be proud to fetch you the best one in Regent Street!"

"Or saddle the pony for me?"

"Try me. But I trust you to remember there is an old man that loves you, and has more money than he knows what to do with."

"I think," said Hester, "that the day is sure to come when I shall ask your help. In the meantime, if it will be any pleasure to you to know it, I trust you heartily. You are all wrong about Lord Gartley, though. He is not what you think him."

"I sincerely hope you are right, for your sake."

She gave him her hand. He took it in his own and pressed it to his lips. She did not draw it away, and he felt she trusted him.

Now that the hard duty was done, and if not much good yet no harm had resulted, he went home a more peaceful man. His host congratulated him on looking so much better as a result of his walk, and Hester recounted to her mother their strange conversation.

"Just think, mama," she said, "he offered me a thousand a year not to marry Lord Gartley!"

"Hester!"

"He does not like the earl, and he does like me. So he wants me not to marry him. That is all!"

"I thought I could have believed anything of him, but this goes almost beyond belief!"

"Why should it, mama? The odd thing is that instead of hating him for it, I like him better than before."

"Are you sure he has no notion of making room for himself?"

"Quite sure. He said he was old enough to be my grandfather. But you know he is not that!"

"Maybe it is time we knew what Lord Gartley intends," said her mother in a more serious vein.

"Oh, mama, don't talk like that!"

"It does sound disagreeable, but I cannot help being anxious about you. If he does not love you, he has no right to court your company so much."

"I encourage it, mama. I like him."

"That is what makes me afraid."

"There will be time enough to think about it if he continues to come and visit now that he has the earldom."

"Would you like to be a countess, Hester?"

"I would rather not think about it, mother. It may never make any difference whether I like it or not."

"I can't help thinking it strange he should be so much with you and never say a word of his intentions."

"It is no more strange than that I am so often with him, or that you let him come so often to the house."

"It was neither your place nor mine to say anything. Your father has always said he would not ask a man his intentions—either he was fit to be in his daughter's company or he was not. Either he must get rid of him or leave his daughter to manage her own affairs. He is quite American in his way of looking at such matters."

"Don't you think he is right, mother? If I let Lord Gartley come, surely he is not to blame for coming!"

"Only if you became fond of him and it were to come to nothing."

"Well, I don't even know myself exactly what I think. I am afraid you must think me very cool. But all I can do is try to do right as things come up, and leave my understanding of things to follow in time. But of one thing you may be sure, mother. I will try to do what is right."

"I am sure of that, my dear—quite sure. And I won't trouble you more about it."

—Twenty-One —

Corney's Holiday

Major Marvel was in no haste to leave, but he spent most of his time with Mark, and was in nobody's way. Mark was very happy with the major. The nature of the man was so childlike that, although he knew little of the deep things in which Mark was at home, his presence was never an interruption to the child's thoughts. When the boy made a remark in the upward direction, he would look so grave and hold such a peace that the child never missed the lacking words of response. Who knows what the man may have gained even from silent communication with the child?

One day he was telling the boy how he had been out alone on a desolate hill all night, how he heard the beasts roaring round him, and not one of them came near him. "Did you see *him?*" asked Mark.

"See who, sonny?" returned the major.

"The one between you and them," answered Mark, in a subdued tone. From his tone the major understood.

"No," he answered, and taking into his the spirit of the child, went on. "I don't think anyone sees him nowadays."

"Isn't it a pity?" said Mark. "But I fancy sometimes I must have seen him with my eyes when I was young, and that's why I keep always expecting to see him again—some day, you know. I wish God would call me. I know he calls some children, for he said, 'Samuel, Samuel!'"

"What would you say?" asked the major.

"I would say, 'Here I am, God! What is it?' We mustn't keep God waiting, you know!"

The major wondered if God could ever have called him and he had not listened? Of course it was all a fancy! And yet as he looked at the child and met his simple, believing eyes, he could not help wondering if there were things in the world of which he was unaware. Could there be things this child understood but he did not? Happily there were no conventional religious phrases in the mouth of the child to repel him. His father and mother had a horror of formal Christianity. They had both seen in their youth too many religious prigs to endure temple white-wash on their children. Except what they heard at church, hardly a specially religious phrase ever entered their ears. Those of the New Testament were avoided from reverence, lest they should grow too common and fail their purpose when the children read them for themselves.

How such a plan could have succeeded with Hester and Mark and not with Cornelius is a hard question which cannot be answered without considering each person's own bent of choice, and how they respond to the influences before them. Hester and Mark had responded by making right choices, that is, unselfish ones. Cornelius had responded by making wrong, that is, selfish ones. But had the common forms of a so-called religious education been added to that youth's upbringing, he would have been a far more offensive fellow, and harder to influence for the good. The best true teaching for children is persons, history, and doctrine in the old sense of the New Testament—instruction in righteousness, that is—not human theory about divine facts.

The major was still at Yrndale when, in the gloomy month of November, Cornelius arrived for his holiday. He was more than usually polite to the major. He was, after all, in the army, the goal of Corney's aspiration! But he laughed in private at what he called the major's vulgarity. Because Cornelius prized nothing of the kind, he could see nothing of his essential worth, and took note merely of his blunders, personal ways, and oddities. The major was not truly vulgar, only ill-bred, for there are many ladylike mothers whose children do not turn out to be ladies and gentlemen because they do not teach them as they were taught themselves. But the feelings of the major went far deeper than those of Cornelius, though the latter's surface manners may have shown to better effect in the society of London. The one was capable of genuine sympathy, the other not yet of any. The major would have been sorry to find he had hurt the feelings of a dog, Cornelius would have whistled on learning that he had hurt the feelings of a woman.

If the major was a clown, Cornelius was a cad. The one was capable of genuine sympathy, the other not yet of any. The latter loved his own paltry self, counting it the most precious thing in creation. The former was conceited it is true, but had no lofty opinion of himself. Hence it was that he thought so much of his small successes. His boasting of them was mainly an uneasy effort at establishing himself comfortably in his own eyes and the eyes of friends. It was little more than a dog's turning of himself round and round before he lies down. He knew they were small things he boasted about, but he had no other. His great things, those in which he had shown himself a true and generous man, he looked on as matters of course, nor recognized anything in them worth thinking of. He was not a great man, but had elements of greatness. He had no vision of truth, but obeyed his moral instincts. When those should blossom into true intents, as one day they must, he would be a great man.

How blessed a thing that God will judge us and man shall not! Where we see no difference, he sees ages of difference. The very thing that looks to us for condemnation may to the eyes of God show in its heart ground for excuse, yea, of partial justification. Only God's excuse is, I suspect, seldom coincident with the excuse a man makes for himself. If anyone thinks that God will not search closely into things, I say there could not be such a God. He will see the uttermost farthing paid. His excuses are as just as his condemnations.

In respect of Cornelius the major was more careful than usual not to make himself disagreeable, for his feelings against the conceit of the lad put him on his guard. Many behave better to those they do not like than to those they do. By this he flattered, without intending it, the vanity of the youth, who did not, therefore, spare his criticism behind his back. Hester usually answered in the major's defence, but tried to do so calmly.

One day she lost her temper with her beam-eyed brother. "Cornelius, the major may have his faults," she said, "but you are not the man to find them out. He is ten times the gentleman you are."

As she spoke, the major had entered the room but she did not see him. Afterward he made himself known and asked Cornelius to go with him for a walk. Hoping he had only just come in, but a little anxious, Cornelius agreed. As they walked, he behaved better than usual—until he had persuaded himself that the major had heard nothing. He then relapsed into his former manner—one of condescension and thin offense. But all the time the major was studying him, and saw into him deeper than his mother or Hester—making out a certain furtive anxiety in the youth's eyes when he was silent, an unrest as of trouble he would not show. "The rascal has been doing something wrong," he thought to himself. "He is afraid of being found out."

The weeks went on. Cornelius's month ran out, but he seemed restless for it to be over, making no response to the lamentations of the children that Christmas was so near and their new home such a grand one for keeping it in, and Corney not to be with them! He did not show them much kindness, but a little went a long way with them, and they loved him.

"Mind you are well before I come again, Markie," he said as he left. "You're not a pleasant sight moping about the house!" Tears came to the child's eyes. He was not moping. He only looked a little sad, even when he was quite happy.

"Never mind, Markie dear," said Hester to him later. "He meant no harm. It's only that you are not very strong—not up to a game of romps as you used to be. You will be merry again one day."

"I am merry enough," replied Mark, "only somehow the merry goes all about inside me and doesn't want to come out—like the little bird, you know, that wouldn't go out of its cage though I left the door open for it."

He was indeed happy enough—more than happy when the major was there. They would be together most days all day long. And the amount of stories Mark, with all his contemplativeness, could swallow was amazing.

But the family party was soon to be broken up—not by subtraction but by addition. The presence of the major had done nothing to spoil the homeness of home, but that very homeness was now for a time to be disturbed.

There is something wrong with anyone who, visiting a house of any kind, makes it less of a home. The angel-stranger makes the children of a house all the more aware of their home. They delight in showing it to him, for he takes an interest in all that belongs to its family life, and sees the things as the children see them. But the stranger of this world makes the very home by his presence feel chilly and less comfortable and homey than before.

—Twenty-Two —

A Distinguished Guest

A letter came from Lord Gartley, begging Mrs. Raymount to excuse the liberty he took, and allow him to ask whether he might presume upon her wish, casually expressed, to welcome his aunt to the hospitality of Yrndale.

"I am well aware of the seeming rudeness of this suggestion," he wrote. "If you have not room for us, or if our presence would spoil your Christmas party, do not hesitate to put us off, I beg. I shall understand you, dear Mrs. Raymount, and say nothing to my rather peculiar but most worthy aunt, waiting a more convenient season."

An invitation was immediately dispatched—with some wry faces on the part of the head of the house who, however, would not oppose what his wife wished.

Despite his knowledge of human nature, Mr. Raymount was not good at reading a man who made himself agreeable and did not tread on the toes of any of his theories. I would not have you think of him as a man of theory only, but while he thought of the practice, he too sparingly practiced the thought. He laid too much upon words altogether, especially words in print, attributing more power to them for the regeneration of the world than was reasonable. Perhaps knowing how few of those who admired his words acted upon them would have made him think how little he struggled *himself* to do the things which, by persuasion and argument, he drove home upon the consciences of others. He had not yet believed that to do right does more for the regeneration of the world than any quality or amount of teaching can. The printed word no doubt has a great power for good, but every man possesses, in the very fact of his consciousness, a greater power than any verbal utterance of truth whatever. It is righteousness—not of words, not of theories, but in being, that is, in vital action, which alone is the prince of the power of the spirit. Where that is, everything has its perfect work. Where that is not, the man is not a power—is but a walker in a vain show.

He did not see deeply into Gartley, who was by no means an intentional hypocrite. But Vavasor was a gentlemanly fellow, and that went a long way with him. He did not oppose him, and that went another long way—of all things he could not bear to be opposed in what he so plainly saw to be true, nor could think why every other honest man should not at once also see it true. He forgot that the difficulty is not so much in recognizing the truth of a proposition, as in recognizing what the proposition is. In the higher regions of thought, the recognition of what a proposition is, and the recognition of its truth are the same thing.

The ruin of a man's teaching comes of his followers, such as having never touched the foundation he has laid, build upon it wood, hay, and stubble, fit only to be burnt. Therefore, if only to avoid his worst foes, his admirers, a man should avoid system. The more correct a system the worse will it be misunderstood—its professed admirers will take both its errors and their misconceptions of its truths, and hold them forth as its essence. Mr. Raymount, then, was not the man to take care of his daughter.

The day before Christmas Eve the expected visitors arrived—just in time to dress for dinner.

The family was assembled in the large, old drawing room of dingy white and tarnished gold when Miss Vavasor entered. She was tall and handsome and had been handsomer, for she was not of those who, growing within, grow more beautiful without as they grow older. She was dressed in the plainest, handsomest fashion—in black velvet, fitting well her fine figure, and half covered with lace. The only stones she wore were diamonds. Her features were regular, her eyes a clear gray, her expression very still, and her hair more than half gray but very plentiful. She had a look of distinction and to the merest glance showed herself wellborn, well nurtured, well trained, and well kept, hence well preserved. Her manner was as simple as her dress—without a trace of condescension or more stiffness than was becoming with persons she had just met. She spoke with readiness and simplicity, looked with interest but without curiosity at Hester, and had the sweetest smile at hand for use as often as wanted. The world had given her the appearance of much of which Christ gives the reality. For the world very oddly prizes the form whose informing reality it despises.

Lord Gartley was in fine humour. He had never before appeared to so great an advantage. Vavasor had not put off his company manner with Hester's family, however Gartley was almost merry, quite graciously familiar. But how shall I describe his face when major Marvel entered! He had never even suspected his presence. A blank dismay came over him, hardly visible, a strange mingling of annoyance, contempt and fear. But in a moment he had overcome the unworthy sensation and was again seemingly cool.

The major was presented to Miss Vavasor by their hostess as her cousin. Seated next to her at dinner, he did not once allude to pig-sticking or tiger-shooting, to elephants or Hindoos, or even to his regiment or India, but talked about the last opera and the last play, with some good criticisms on the acting he had seen. He conducted himself in such manner as would have made Lord Gartley quite grateful to him had he not put it down to the imperial presence of his high-born aunt and the major's cowering inferior nature.

All day the major had been tempted toward very different behaviour. Remembering what he had heard of the character of the lady and of the relation between her and her nephew, he knew at once that Lord Gartley was bringing her down with the hope of gaining her consent to his asking Hester to marry him. *The rascal!* he thought. And with this realization arose his temptation to so behave before the aunt as to disgust her with the family and save his lovely cousin from being sacrificed to a heartless noodle.

"I'll settle the young ape's hash for him!" he said to himself. "What jolly fun it will be to send her out of the house in a rage—and a good deed done too!"

But before the day was through he had begun to have his doubts. Would it not be dishonourable? He would turn Mark and Hester away from him in the very process. His heart continued to go against his plans, and by the time he dressed for dinner he had resolved to leave the fancy alone and behave like a gentleman. But now as they sat at the table, with every sip of wine the temptation came stronger and stronger. The spirit of fun kept stirring in him. Not merely for the sake of Hester, but for the joke of the thing, he was tempted, and had to keep fighting the impulse all evening. And thus came the subdued character of his demeanour. What threatened to destroy his manners for the evening turned out to correct his usual behaviour. Miss Vavasor, being good-natured, was soon interested and by and by pleased with him. This reacted upon him and he began to feel pleased with her and more at his ease. And with his ease came the danger some at the table had foreseen—he began to tell one of his stories. But he saw Hester look anxious and that was enough to put him back on his careful honour. Before dinner was over he said to himself that if only the nephew were half as good as the aunt, he would be happy to give the young people his blessing.

"By Jove!" thought Gartley, "the scoundrel is not such a low fellow after all."

Now and then he would listen across the table to their talk, and everything the major said that pleased his aunt pleased him as well. At one little witticism of hers in answer to one of the major's, he burst into such a hearty laugh that his aunt looked up.

"You are amused, Gartley," she said.

"You are so clever, Aunt," he returned.

"Major Marvel has all the merit of my wit," she answered.

After dinner they sat down to whist and cribbage and within another hour the fear of Lord Gartley as to the malign influence of the major vanished entirely.

Now that he was more at his ease, and saw that his aunt was pleased with both Hester and the major, Lord Gartley began to radiate his fascinations. All his finer nature appeared. He grew playful, even teasing, gave again and again a quick repartee, and sang as his aunt had never heard him sing before. But when Hester sang, the thing was done. The aunt perceived at once what a sensation such a singer would make in her circle! She would be a decided gain to the family, even contributing in herself an added luster to the title. Then who could tell but this cousin of hers—who seemed to have plenty of money the way he so cheerfully parted with it at the gaming table—might be moved to make a poor countess a rich one. The thing was settled, so far as Gartley was concerned.

—Twenty-Three —

Courtship in Earnest

Christmas was a merry day to all but the major, who did not like things any better than before. He found refuge and consolation with Mark, who was merry in a mild and reflective way.

Lord Gartley now began to pursue his courtship in earnest, with full intent and purpose. "How could she listen to him?" I can hear some reader say. But to explain the thing is more than I am bound to undertake. As I may have said twenty times before, how this woman will have this man is one of the deeper mysteries of the world—yea, of the maker of the world, perhaps.

One thing I may suggest—that where men see no reason why a woman should love this or that man, she may see something in him which they do not see, or do not value as she does. Alas for her if she only imagines it! One thing more I would touch upon which men are more likely never to have thought of than to have forgotten— that the love which a beautiful woman gives a man, is in itself not an atom more precious than that which a plain woman gives. In the two hearts they are the same, if the hearts be like. If not, the advantage may well be with the plain woman. The love of a beautiful woman is no more thrown away than the love of the plainest. The same holds with regard to women of differing intellectual developments or endowment.

But when a woman of high hopes and aims—a woman filled with eternal aspirations after life, and unity with her divine original gives herself to such a one as lord Gartley, I cannot help thinking she must have seriously mistaken some things both in him and in herself, the consequence, probably, of some self-sufficiency, ambition, or other fault in her, which requires the correction of suffering.

Hester found her lover now very pleasant. If sometimes he struck a jarring chord, she was always able to find some way of accounting for it or explaining it away so far that she was able to go on hoping. Like most self-deceiving women, she was sure she would have greater influence over him as his wife. But where there is not already a far deeper unity than marriage can give, marriage itself can do little to bring two souls together—and may do much to drive them apart. She began to put him in training, as she thought, for the help he was to give her with her loved poor. Lord Gartley had no real conception of her outlook on life, and regarded all her endeavour as born of the desire to perfect his voice and singing.

For Hester the days now passed in pleasure, though I fear the closer contact with Lord Gartley could not help but negatively influence the rate of her growth toward the upper regions. We cannot be heart and soul and self in the company of the untrue without loss. Her prayers were not so fervent, her aspiration not so strong. But the Lord is mindful of his own. He does not forget because we forget. Pain may come, but not because he forgets—nay, just because he does not forget. That is a thing God never does.

There are many women who would have bewitched Gartley more, yet great was his delight in the presence of Hester, and he yielded himself with pleasing grace. Inclined to rebel at times when wearied with her demands on his attention and endeavour, he yet condescended to them with something of the playfulness with which one would humour a child. His turn would come by and by. Then he would instruct her in many things she was now ignorant of. She had never moved in his great world—he must teach her its laws, instruct her how to shine, how to make the most of herself, how to do him honour! He had but the vaguest idea of the *folly* that possessed her about ministry. He thought of her relation to the poor as but a passing phase of a previously objectless life. That she should even imagine continuing her former pursuits after they were married would have seemed utterly incredible to him. And Hester would have been equally staggered to find that he had so totally failed to understand her after the way she had opened her heart to him. So things went on upon a mutual misunderstanding—each falling more and more in love with the other, while in reality they were separating further and further, each caught up in thoughts and motives that were alien to the other.

Miss Vavasor continued the most pleasant and unexacting of guests. She found the company of the major agreeable for her nephew's sake. Mr. Raymount would not leave what he counted his work for any goddess in creation. Hester had inherited her fixedness of purpose through him, and its direction through her mother. But it was good he did not give Miss Vavasor much of his company. If they had been alone together for a quarter of an hour discussing almost anything imaginable, they would have parted sworn foes. So the major, instead of putting a stop to the unworthy alliance, found himself actually furthering the affair, doing his part with the lady on whom the success of the enemy depended. He was still now and then tempted to break through his self-imposed shell of restraint, yet he remained a man of honour and behaved like one.

After almost two weeks, Miss Vavasor took her leave for a round of visits, and Lord Gartley went back to town, with intention thereafter to pay a visit to his property, such as it was. He would return to Yrndale in three or four weeks, when the final arrangements for the marriage would be made.

A correspondence naturally commenced and Hester received his first letter joyfully. But the letter was nothing like the man's presence. There was no *life* in it. With Hester in person, she suggesting and leading, his talk seemed to indicate the presence of what she would have in him. But alone with his own thoughts, without the stimulus of her presence or the sense of her moral atmosphere, the best things he could write were poor enough. They had no bones in them, and no other fire than that which the thought of Hester's loveliness could supply. So his letters were disappointing. Had they been those of a person indifferent to her, she would have thrown them down, called them stupid, and thought no more of them.

But all would be well, she said to herself, when they met again. It was her absence that oppressed him, poor fellow! He was out of spirits, and could not write! He did not possess the faculty for writing that some had! Her father had told her of men that were excellent talkers, but set them down pen in hand and not a thought would come! Was not the presence of a man's own kind the best inspirer of his speech? It was his loving human nature—she would have persuaded herself, but never quite succeeded—that made utterance in a letter impossible to him.

Yet she *would* have liked a little genuine, definite response to the things she wrote! He seemed to have nothing to say from himself! He would assent and echo, but any response was always such as to make her doubt whether she had written plainly, invariably suggesting things of this world and not of the unseen, the world of thought and being. And when she mentioned work he always replied as if she meant an undefined something called *doing good.* He never doubted that the failure of that foolish concert of ladies and gentlemen given to the riff-raff of London, had taught her that whether man be equal in the sight of God or not, any attempt on the part of their natural superiors to treat them as such could not but be disastrous.

—Twenty-Four —

Calamity

One afternoon the post brought a letter from Lord Gartley and two for Mr. and Mrs. Raymount. The one to Mrs. Raymount was written in a strange-looking cramped hand, which she immediately recognized.

"What can Sarah be writing about?" she said, a sudden foreboding of evil crossing her mind.

Hester rose to leave the room. She did not like to read Gartley's letters around her mother—not from shyness, but from shame: she did not want anyone to know how poor her Gartley's utterances were on paper. But before she was six steps away, she heard a cry from her mother and turned.

"Good heavens, what can it be?" said Mrs. Raymount. "Something has happened to him!"

Her face was pale, almost as white as the paper she held.

"Mother, mother! what is it?" Hester asked.

"I knew we were too happy," she moaned. "I knew something was bound to come."

"Let's go to papa," said Hester, frightened but quiet. She took her mother by the hand to lead her. But Mrs. Raymount stood as if fixed to the ground.

In the meantime, Mr. Raymount's letters had been carried to him in the study and one of them had similarly perturbed him. He was pacing up and down the room almost as white as his wife, but his pallor was that of rage.

"The scoundrel!" he cried. "I had the suspicion he was a mean dog! Now all the world will know it—and that he is my son! What have I done that I have given life to a vile hound like this?"

He threw himself in a chair and wept with rage and shame. He had for years been writing of family and social duties, now here was his illustration! His own son! How could he ever show himself again? He would leave the country. Damn the property! The rascal should never succeed to it! Mark would have it—if he lived! And now Hester was going to marry an earl! Not if the truth would prevent it! Her engagement must be broken at once! Lord Gartley would never marry the sister of a thief!

While he was thus raging, a knock came to the door and a maid entered.

"Please, sir," she said, "Miss Raymount says will you come to Mis'ess. She's taken bad!"

This brought him to himself. The horrible fate was hers too! He must go to her. But how could she have heard the vile news? She must have heard it! What else could have made her ill? He followed the maid to where his wife stood in his daughter's arms. He asked no questions, but took her himself, carried her to her room, and laid her on the bed. Then he sat down beside her, hardly caring if she died—the sooner they all died the better! Hester followed them in, and by and by the doctor came.

Hester had picked up the letter, and as her father sat there, she handed it to him. This was what he read:

Dear mistress,

*   It is time to let you know of the goings on here. I never held with bearing tales, and perhaps it's worse to bring tales against Master Cornelius, as is your own flesh and blood, but what am I to do as was left in charge, and to keep the house respectable? He's not been home this three night. And you ought to know as there is a young lady, his cousin from New Zealand, as is come to the house three or four times since you went away, and stayed a long time with him, though it is some time now that I ain't seen her. She is a pretty, modest-looking young lady, though I must say I was ill-pleased when Mr. Cornelius would have her stay all night, and I up and told him if she was his cousin, it wasn't as if she was his sister and it wouldn't do, and I would walk out of the house if he insisted on me making up a bed for her. Then he laughed in my face and told me I was an old fool, and he was only making game of me. But that was after he had done his best to persuade me and I wouldn't be persuaded. I told him if neither he nor the young lady had a character to keep, I had one to lose, and I wouldn't. But I don't think he said anything to her about staying all night, for she come down the stair as innocent-like as any dove, and bid me good night smiling, and they walked away together. And I wouldn't have took upon me to be a spy, nor I wouldn't have mentioned the thing, for it's none of my business so long as nobody doesn't abuse the house as is my charge, but he ain't been home*

149

for three nights, and there is the feelings of a mother! And it's my part to let her know as her son ain't slept in his own bed for three nights, and that's a fact. I hope dear mis'ess it won't kill you to hear it. O why did his father leave him alone in London, with none but an old woman like me, as he always did look down upon, to look after him!

Your humble servant for twenty years,

S.H.

Mrs. Raymount had not read half of Sarah's account. It was enough to learn Cornelius had not been home for three nights. How strange it is that parents with no reasonable ground for believing their children good are yet incredulous when they hear they are going wrong. Helen Raymount concluded her boy had turned into bad ways because he was left in London, although she knew he had never taken to good ways while they were all with him. If he had never gone right, why should she wonder that he had gone wrong?

The doctor was sitting by the bedside, watching the effect of something he had given her. Mr. Raymount rose and led Hester from the room—sternly almost, as if she had been to blame for it all.

Some people when they are angry, speak as if they were angry with the person to whom they are in fact looking for comfort. When in trouble few of us are masters enough of ourselves, because few of us are children enough of our Father in heaven, to behave like gentlemen. But Hester understood and did not resent.

"Is this all your mother knows, Hester?" said her father, pointing to the letter in his hand. She told him her mother had read but the first sentence or two.

He was silent as he returned to the bedside, and stood silent. The life of his dear wife had been suddenly withered at the root, and she had not even yet heard the worst!

His letter was from his wife's brother, in whose bank Cornelius was a clerk. A considerable deficit had been discovered in his accounts. He had not been to the bank for two days, and no trace of him was to be found. His uncle, concerned about the feelings of his sister, had requested the head of his office to be silent. He would wait for his brother-in-law's reply before taking any steps. He feared the misguided youth had reckoned on the forbearance of an uncle, but for the sake of his own future, if for no other reason, this could not be passed over.

"Passed over!" Gerald Raymount would never have considered such a thing. But for his wife's illness, he would already have been on his way to London to repay the missing money!

But something must be done. He must send someone. Who was there to send? There was Hester! She was a favourite with her uncle! And she would not dread the interview, which to him would be an unendurable humiliation. For he had had many arguments with this same brother-in-law concerning the way he brought up his children. They had all turned out well and here was his miserable son a felon, disgracing both families! Yes, let Hester go! There were things a woman could do better than a man! Hester was no child now but a capable woman. While she was gone he could be making up his mind what to do with the wretched boy!

He led Hester again from her mother's room and gave her the letter to read. He watched her as she read—saw her grow pale, then flush, then turn pale again. What she was thinking he could not tell, but he made his proposal at once.

"Hester," he said, "I cannot leave your mother. You must go for me to your uncle and do the best you can. If it were not for your mother, I would have the rascal prosecuted, but it would break her heart."

"Yes, papa," she answered, "I shall be ready to catch the evening train. Am I to say anything to Corney?"

"You have nothing to do with him," he answered sternly. "What is the good of keeping a villain from being as much of a villain as he has within him to be? I will sign you a blank check, which your uncle can fill in with the amount Cornelius has stolen."

On her way to her room Hester met the major. He had just heard of her mother's attack, as he had been out for a long walk.

"But what did it, Hester?" he said. "I can smell in the air that something has gone wrong. What the deuce is it?"

They had met in a dark part of the corridor and had now, at a turn, come opposite a window. Then first the major saw Hester's face. He had never seen her look like that!

"Is your mother in danger?" His tone became gentle, for his heart was, in reality, a most tender one.

"She is very ill. The doctor has been with her now for three hours. I am going to London for papa. He can't leave her."

"Going to London—and by the night train!" said major to himself. "Then there has been bad news! It must be that scoundrel Corney up to some mischief—damn him! I shouldn't be surprised to hear anything bad of him."

But before he had a chance to say anything, he looked up and Hester was gone.

She went to her room, put a few things together, then drank a cup of tea, went to her father to get the check, and was ready by the time the carriage came to the door with a pair of horses. In but a few minutes more she was on her way through the gathering dusk to the railway station.

While the lodge-gate was being opened, she thought she saw someone get up on the box beside the coachman, and fancied it must be a groom going with them. The drive was a rather long and anxious one for Hester. When at last the carriage stopped and the door opened, there was the major in a huge fur coat, holding out his hand to help her down. It was as great a pleasure as a surprise, and she showed both.

"You didn't think I was going to let you travel alone?" he said. "Who knows what wolf might be after my Red Riding Hood!"

Hester told him she was only too glad of his escort. Careful not to seem the least bent on the discovery of the cause of her journey, he seated himself in the farthest corner of the train car, for there was no one else in it, and pretended to go to sleep.

And now Hester began, as a result of the general misery of the family, to contemplate her own situation with a little more honest introspection than before. A mist had slowly been gathering about her, though she had put off looking into it at the undefined forms in the distance. Now these forms slowly began to reveal themselves in shifting yet recognizable reality. The doubts she had tried to ignore when reading Vavasor's letters now at last demanded recognition. Even if this miserable affair with Cornelius should be successfully hushed up, there was yet one who must know of it—she would have to acquaint lord Gartley with what had taken place.

With the realization, one of the shapes in the mist settled into solidity: if the love between them had been an ideal love, she would not have had a moment's anxiety as to how her fiancé would receive the painful news. But she realized she shrank from telling him, for

152

fear of how he might respond. Yet with the insight into her own anxiety came a decision—if he hesitated, that would be enough. His response would involuntarily reveal whether their love was a true one or not. Nothing could make her marry a man who hesitated whether to draw back from her or not. It was impossible.

—Twenty-Five —

In London

Arriving in the city, they went directly to Addison Square. When they had roused Sarah, the major took his leave of Hester, promising to be with her in a few hours, and went to his hotel.

She did not want to rouse speculation at the bank by being recognized as the sister of Cornelius. When the major returned, she asked him to be her messenger to her uncle and tell him that she had come from her father, asking him to inquire where it would be convenient for them to meet. The major undertook the commission at once, and went without asking a question.

Early in the afternoon her uncle came, and behaved to her very kindly. He was chiefly a man of business and, thus, made no particular attempt to show sympathy for the trouble she and her parents were in. Yet sympathy was revealed unconsciously by his manner. He was careful to avoid any remark on the conduct or character of the youth. When she had at last given him her father's check, with the request that he would himself fill it in with the amount Cornelius had stolen, and he with a slight deprecatory smile and shrug had taken it, she ventured to ask what he was going to do with regard to her brother.

"When I take this check," answered her uncle, "it indicates that I treat the matter as a debt paid discharged, and I leave him entirely in your father's hands. He must do as he sees fit. I am sorry for you all, and for you, especially, that you should have had to take an active part in the business. I wish your father could have come."

"I am glad he could not come," said Hester, "for he is so angry with Cornelius that he would probably have insisted that you prosecute him. You never saw such indignation as my father's at any wrong done by one man to another—not to say by one like Cornelius to one like you, Uncle, who have always been so kind to him. It is a terrible blow to him!"

She broke down and wept bitter tears—the first she had shed since learning the news. She wept not only for her family, but for Cornelius as well. How was ever such a child of the darkness to come to love the light? How was one who cared so little for righteousness, one who, in all probability, would only excuse or even justify his crime—if indeed he would trouble himself to do so much—how was one like him to be brought to contrition and rectitude? If the thing were passed over and he was not brought to open shame, he would hold his head as high as ever. And then how would even what regenerative power that might lie in the shame ever be brought to bear upon him?

When her uncle left her, she sat motionless a long time, thinking much but hoping little. The darkness gathered deeper and deeper around her. Some sorrows seem beyond the reach of consolation, in as much as their causes seem beyond setting right. They can at best, as it seems, only be covered over. Forgetfulness alone seems capable of removing their sting, and from that cure every noble mind turns away as unworthy both of itself, and of its Father in heaven. But the human heart has to go through much before it is able to house even a suspicion of the superabounding riches of the creating and saving God. The foolish child thinks there can be nothing where he sees nothing. The human heart feels as if where it cannot devise help, there is none possible to God, as if God, like the heart, must be content to botch the thing up, and make, as we say, the best of it.

But as the heavens are higher than the earth, so are his ways higher than our ways, and his thoughts than our thoughts.

It was a sore and dreary time for Hester, alone in the room where she had spent so many happy hours. She sat in a window seat, looking out upon the leafless trees and the cold, gloomy old statue in the midst of them. Frost was upon every twig. A thin, sad fog filled the comfortless air. There might be warm, happy homes somewhere, but they no longer belonged to her world. The fire was burning cheerfully behind her, but her eyes were fixed on the dreary square. She was hardly thinking—only letting thoughts and feelings come and go. What a thing is life and being, when a soul has become but the room in which ghosts hold their revel, when the man or woman is no longer master of himself, and can no more say to this or that thought, you shall come, and you shall go. That person is a slave to his own existence—he can neither cease to be, nor order his being. He is able only to entangle himself even more in the net he has knotted around him! Such is every soul who is parted from the essential life, who is not one with the Power by which he lives. God is all in all, and he made us out of himself. He who is parted from God is a live discord, an antitruth.

Not such was Hester, and although her thoughts now came and went without her, they did not come and go without God, and a truth from the depths of her own true being was on its way to console her.

How would her fiancé receive the news? That was the agitating question. What would he do?

She would liked to have written at once, but she did not know exactly where he was. But a far stronger reason against writing was that if she wrote, she could not know how he received her sad story. If his mind required making up, which was what she feared, he would have time for it. She must, therefore, communicate the dread message with her own lips. She must see how he took it! If he showed the slightest change toward her, the least tendency to regard the relationship now as an entanglement that he regretted, she could not marry him. If he could not be her earthly refuge in this trouble, she would have none of him. If it should break her heart she would have none of him! But break her heart it would not! There were worse evils than losing a lover! There was losing a true man.

The behaviour of Cornelius had perhaps made her more capable of doubt. Possibly her righteous anger with him inclined her to imagine grounds of anger with another. Probably this feeling of uncertainty regarding her fiancé had been prepared for by things that had passed between them since their engagement, but upon which she had not allowed herself to dwell. Now she was almost in a mood to quarrel with him. Brought to moral bay, she stood with her head high, her soul roused, and every nerve strung to defence. She had not yet cast herself on the care of her Father in heaven. But he was not far from her.

Yet deeper into the brooding fit she sank. Weary with her journey and the sleepless night, her brain seemed to work itself. Then suddenly came the thought that here she was again in the midst of her poor. But how was she to face them and hold her head up among them now? Who was she, of a family of sinners, to speak a word to them? How lightly the poor bore such ills. Even the honest of them would have this cousin or that uncle in jail for so many months, and think no less of him when he was out again. Nothing could degrade them beyond the reach of their sympathies! They had no thought of priding themselves against another because they themselves had not broken the law.

Suddenly Hester felt nearer her poor than ever before, and it comforted her. The bare soul of humanity comforted her. She was not merely of the same flesh and blood with them—not even of the same soul and spirit only, but of the same failing, sinning, blundering breed. Their shame was hers: the son of her mother, the son of her father was a thief! She was and would be more one with them than ever before. If they made less of crime in another, they also made less of innocence from it in themselves! Was it not even better to do wrong, she asked herself, than to think it a great thing not to do it? What merit was there in being what it would be contemptible not to be? The Lord could get nearer to the publican than the Pharisee, to the woman who was a sinner than the self-righteous, honest woman. The Pharisee was a good man, but he thought it a fine thing to be good. The other was humble enough to know what a sad thing it was to be bad. Let her just get among her nice, honest, wicked, poor ones, out of this atmosphere of pretence and appearance, and she would breathe again!

She dropped on her knees and cried to her Father in heaven to make her heart clean altogether, to deliver her from everything mean and faithless, to make her turn from any shadow of evil as thoroughly as she would have her brother repent of the stealing that made them all so ashamed. Like a woman in the wrong, she drew nigh the feet of her master. She too was a sinner. Her heart needed his cleansing as much as any!

And then came another God-given thought. For suddenly she perceived that her self had made her severe and indignant to the son of her own mother, while she was indulgent toward those whose evil did not touch her. If God were to do like her, how many would be redeemed? Corney, whom she had taken care of as a baby—was he not equally to be loved in his sin as the poor who so occupied her heart? But God knew all the difficulties that beset men, and gave them fair play even when sisters did not: he would redeem Corney yet!

True, it seemed impossible that he should ever wake to see how ugly his conduct had been. But there were powers in God's heart that had not yet been brought to bear upon him. Perhaps this was one of them—letting him disgrace himself. If he could but be made ashamed of himself, there would be hope! In the meantime she must get the beam out of her own eye that she might see to take the mote or beam, whichever it might be, out of Corney's! Again she fell upon her knees and prayed God to enable her. Corney was her brother, and must forever be her brother, even if he were the worst thief under the sun! God would see to their honour or disgrace, what she had to do was to be a sister! She rose determined that she would not go home until she had done all she could to find him.

Presently the fact, which at various times cast a dim presence upon her horizon without thoroughly attracting her attention, became plain to her—that she had in part been drawn toward her fiancé because of his social position. Certainly without loving him, she would never have consented to marry him for that, but had she not come the more readily to love him because of it? Had he not been a prospective earl, were there not some things in him which would have possibly repelled her a little more? Would she, for instance, have tried so hard to like the verses he brought her? Clearly, she must take her place with the sinners!

—Twenty-Six —

A Talk With the Major

While she thus meditated, major Marvel made his appearance. He had been watching outside, saw her uncle go, waited another hour, then came to the door and was shown to the room where she still sat, staring out on the frosty trees of the square.

"Why, my child," he said with almost paternal tenderness, "your hand is as cold as ice! Why do you sit so far from the fire?"

She rose and went to the fire with him. He put her in an easy chair and sat down beside her. Common, pudgy, red-faced, bald-headed as he was, she came to him with a sense of refuge. He could scarcely have understood one of her difficulties, would doubtless have judged not a few of her scruples nonsensical. Nevertheless, it was a comfort to her to feel a human soul in a human body near her. For the mere human is divine, though not *the* divine, and to the mere human essential comfort. She was able to look upon the major as a friend in whom she could trust. Unity of opinion is not necessary to confident friendship and warm love.

As they talked, the major could see that she was depressed, and began to tell her some of the more personal parts of his own history. Becoming interested, she began to ask questions and drew from him much that he would never have thought of volunteering. Before their talk was over, she had come to regard the man with a greater respect than she would have imagined possible before. In a high sense the major was a true man. There is nothing shows more how hard it has been for God to redeem the world than the opinions still uttered concerning him and his so-called plans by many who love him and try to obey him: a man may be in possession of the most precious jewels, and yet know so little about them that his

159

description of them would never induce a jeweller to purchase them, but on the contrary make him regard the man as a fool, deceived with bits of coloured glass for rubies and sapphires. Major Marvel knew nothing of the slang of the Pharisees, knew little of the language of either the saints or the prophets. He had, like most Christians, many worldly ways of looking at things, and yet I think our Lord would have said there was no guile in him.

Hester began to question whether she would not be justified in taking the major into her confidence regarding Cornelius. She had received no injunctions to secrecy from her father. She was certain the man would be prudent and keep quiet whatever ought to be kept quiet. Therefore, she told him the whole story, hiding nothing that she knew. The major listened intently, said nothing, betrayed nothing, till she had ended.

"My dear Hester," he said solemnly, after a few moments' pause, "the mysteries of creation are beyond me!"

Hester thought the remark irrelevant, but waited.

"It's such a mixture," he went on. "There is your mother, then Cornelius, then yourself—such differences within the same family! And then little Mark—I will not say too good to live, but too good for any of the common uses of this world! I declare, sometimes he terrifies me!"

"What about him terrifies you?" asked Hester.

"I suppose it's because I'm not made of the stuff of saints—good saints, I mean."

Hester laughed in spite of the gnawing unrest in her heart.

"I think," she said softly, "that one day you will be as good a saint as love can wish you to be."

"Give me time, give me time," replied the major. "But the main cause of my unpopularity—with religious people, you know—was that I hated pretence and humbug—and I do hate humbug, cousin Hester, and shall hate it till I die—and so want to steer clear of it."

"I hate it, I hope almost as much as you do, major Marvel," responded Hester. "But whatever it may be mixed up with, what is true, you know, cannot be false itself."

"Yes, yes! But how is one to know what is true, my dear? There are so many differing claims to the quality! How is one to separate the humbug from the true?"

160

"I have been told, and I believe it," replied Hester, "that the only way to *know* what is true is to *do* what is true."

"But you must *know* what is true before you can begin to *do* what is true."

"Everybody knows something that is true to do—that is, something he ought to lose no time in setting about. The true thing to any man is that which must not be ignored but must be done. It is much easier to know what is true to do than what is true to think. But those who do the one will come to know the other—and none else, I believe."

The major was silent and sat looking thoughtful. At last he rose.

"Is there anything you want me to do in this sad affair, cousin Hester?" he said.

"I want your help to find my brother."

"Why should you want to find him? You cannot do him any good."

"Who can tell that? If Christ came to seek and save his lost, we ought to seek and save our lost."

"But to mix yourself up in his affairs may bring trouble upon yourself."

"Answer me one question, dear major Marvel," said Hester. "Which is in most danger from disease—the healthy or the sick?"

"That's a question for the doctor. But what it has to do with the matter in hand I cannot think."

Hester saw that it was not time to pursue the argument. The idea of a woman like Hester being in any sense defiled by knowing what her Lord knows while she fills up what is left behind of the sufferings of Christ is contemptible. As wrong melts away and vanishes in the heart of Christ, so does the impurity she encounters vanish in the heart of the pure woman. It is there burned up.

"I hardly see what is to be done, regardless," said the major, after a moment's silence. "What do you say to an advertisement in *The Times* to the effect that if C. R. will return to his family, all will be forgiven?"

"That we must not do. There is surely some other way of finding persons without going to the police."

"What do you think your father would like done?"

"I do not know. But as I am Corney's sister, I will venture as a sister may."

"Well, I will do what I can for you—though I greatly fear your brother will never prove worth the trouble."

"People have repented who have gone farther wrong than Corney," said Hester.

"True!" responded the major. "But I don't believe he has character enough to repent of anything. But I will do what I can to find out where he is."

Hester thanked him heartily, and he took his leave.

She had no idea what she would do if she did find Cornelius. if they found him, what would come of it? Was he likely to go home with her? How would he be received if he did go home? and if not, what was she to do with or for him? If want would drive him home, the sooner he came to it the better! We pity the prodigal with his swine, but then first a ray of hope begins to break through the darkness of his fate.

She sat down and wrote to her father, told him what there was to tell, and ending by saying she was doing what a sister was able to do and that major Marvel was doing his best to find him.

The next day she heard from her father that her mother was slowly recovering. On the following day, another letter came saying that her letter had been a great comfort to her mother, but beyond that her father made no remark. Even his silence, however, was something of a relief to Hester.

In the meantime she was not idle. The moment the letter had been sent, she set out to visit her old friends. She went to Mrs. Baldwin's shop and had a little talk with her. Mrs. Baldwin told her that the Frankses had been seen once or twice going about their acrobatics on the street, but she feared they were not getting on. Hester was sorry, but had many more to think of in addition.

There was much rejoicing at her return. There were many changes also—new faces, and not the best news of some who remained. One or two were in prison. Some were getting on better. One man of whom she had been hopeful had disappeared—it was supposed with another man's wife. All the little ones came about her again, but with less confidence, both because she had been away, and because they had grown more than they had improved. But soon things were nearly on the old footing with them.

Every day she went among the poor. Certain of the women were as warmly her friends as before. There was only one who had some experience of the Christian life, but there seemed to be no corresponding influence from this one onto those even who lived in the same house. Who can trace the slow working of leaven?

—Twenty-Seven —

A Scuffle

There was no news of Cornelius—only rumour of a young woman in whose company he had lately been seen, but she, too, had disappeared from sight.

Sarah did her best to make Hester comfortable, and behaved the better that she was humbled by the consciousness of having made a bad job of her caretaking with Cornelius.

It had rained one afternoon, but the sun was now shining and Hester's heart felt lighter as she took deep breaths of the clean-washed air. She went to visit the wife of a bookbinder who had been long laid up with rheumatism. They lived in a large building, much of it in bad repair, occupied by many people much poorer than themselves.

When she knocked at the door, it was opened by the parish doctor.

"We cannot have you come in, Miss Raymount," he said. "We have a bad case of smallpox here. You good ladies must make up your minds to keep away from these parts for a while. Their bodies are in more danger than their souls now. I'm afraid I cannot allow that. You will only carry the infection."

"I will take every precaution."

"While the parish is my responsibility," answered the doctor, "I must object to anything that increases the risk of infection. I know your motives are the best, but I cannot have you going from one house to another. How are we to keep it out of the West End if you ladies carry the seeds of it?"

He turned and closed the door. Hester went back down the stair. Her plan thwarted, she did not know what to do next. Instinctively she sat down on the stairs and began to sing. It was not a wise thing to do, but for the moment she was unable to see its impropriety.

In big cities the children are like flies, gathering swiftly as from out of the unseen. In a moment the stair below Hester was half filled with them. The tenants above opened their doors and came out. Others began to come in from the street to listen, and presently the stair and entrance were filled with people, all shabby and almost all dirty—men and women, young and old, good and bad, listening to the voice of the singing lady, as she was called in the neighbourhood.

By this time the doctor had finished his visit and appeared on the stair above. It was hardly any wonder, when he saw who the singer was, that he should lose his temper. He thought she was deliberately trying to spite his refusal of her request to visit her friends by bringing half the neighbourhood into contact with the infected family. Hurriedly he walked through the crowd and down to where Hester sat. When he reached her he seized her arm from behind and began to raise her and push her down the stair. Some of the faces below grew red with anger. A loud murmur arose and several began to force their way up to rescue her. But the moment Hester saw who it was that had laid hold of her, she rose and began to descend the stair of her own accord, closely followed by the doctor. It was not easy, for many gave a disorderly and, indeed, rather threatening look to the assemblage because of what the doctor had done.

As she reached the door, on the opposite side of the passage, she saw the pale face and glittering eyes of Mr. Blaney, who had already had the pint which, according to his brother-in-law, was more than he could stand.

"Serves you right, miss!" he cried, when he saw who was the center of the commotion. "Serves you right! You turned me out o' your house for singin', an' now you've got no right to come a singin' an' a misbehavin' in ourn!"

The crowd had been gathering from both ends of the passage, for high words draw people yet faster than sweet singing, and the place was so full that it was hardly possible to get out of it. The doctor was almost wishing he had left well enough alone, for he was now a little anxious about Hester. Some of the rougher ones began pushing. The vindictive little man kept up his shouting. All at once Hester spied a face she knew, though it was considerably changed since last she had seen it.

"Now we shall have help!" she said to her companion, making common cause with him despite his antagonism. "Mr. Franks!"

The acrobat was not so far off that she needed to call very loud. He heard and started with eager interest. He knew the voice. With his great muscular arms he parted the crowd right and left, and reached her in a moment.

"Come now! Don't you hurt her!" shouted Mr. Blaney. "She's an old friend o' mine."

"You shut up!" yelled Franks. Then turning to Hester, pulled off his fur cap, made a slight bow, and said briefly,

"Miss Raymount—at your service, miss!"

"I am very glad to see you again, Mr. Franks," said Hester. "Do you think you could get us out of the crowd?"

"Easy, miss. I'll carry you out of it, if you'll let me."

"That will hardly be necessary," returned Hester with a smile.

"Go on before, and make a way for us," said the doctor.

"There is no occasion for you to trouble yourself about me further, doctor," said Hester. "I am perfectly safe with this man. I am sorry to have caused you all this trouble."

She took Franks' arm, and in a minute they were out of the crowd, which speedily made room for them, and onto the street.

But as if everybody she knew was going to appear, who should meet them face-to-face as they turned into Steven's Road, with a fringe of the crowd still at their heels, but lord Gartley! He had written and Mrs. Raymount had let him know that Hester was in London. His lordship went at once to Addison Square, and had just left the house disappointed when he met Hester on Franks' arm.

"Miss Raymount!" he exclaimed.

"My lord!" she returned.

"Who would have expected to see you here?"

"Apparently you did, my lord."

He tried to laugh.

"Come then—I will see you home," he said.

"Thank you. Come, Franks."

As she spoke she looked round, but Franks was gone. Finding she had met one of her own family, as he supposed, he had quietly withdrawn, feeling embarrassed. But he lingered around a corner, to be certain she was going to be taken care of. Seeing them walk away together he was satisfied, and went with a sigh.

—Twenty-Eight —

Gartley and the Major

The two were silent on their way, but for different reasons. Lord Gartley was uneasy at finding Hester in such a position. He had gathered from the looks and words of the following remnants of the crowd that she had been involved in some street-quarrel—trying to calm it no doubt, or to separate the combatants. For a woman of her refinement, she had the strangest proclivity for low company!

Hester was silent, thinking how to begin what she must tell him about Cornelius. Uncomfortable and even slightly irritated at the tone in which his lordship had expressed the surprise he could not help feeling at sight of her so accompanied and attended, she had felt for a moment as if the best thing would be to break with him at once.

It was plain that the relation between them was far from the ideal. Another thing was yet clearer—if he could feel such surprise and annoyance at the circumstances in which he had just met her, it would be well to come to a clearer understanding at once concerning her life-ideal and projects. But she would make up her mind to nothing till she saw how he was going to carry himself now his surprise had had time to pass off. Perhaps it would not be necessary to tell him anything about Corney—they might part upon other grounds!

These thoughts hardly passed logically through her mind; it was filled, rather, with a confused mass of tangled thought and feeling, which tossed about in it like the nets of a fishing fleet rolled together by a storm.

Neither spoke before they reached the house, and Hester began to wonder if he might not already have heard about Cornelius. It was plain he was troubled, plain he was only waiting for the cover of the house to speak. It should be easy, very easy for him to get rid of her.

They entered, and she led the way up the stair. Not a movement of life was audible in the house. The stillness was almost painful.

"Did no one come with you?" he asked.

"No one but major Marvel," she answered, opening the door of the drawing room.

As she closed it, she turned and said, "Forgive me, Gartley. I am in trouble; we are all in trouble. When I have told you about it, I shall be more myself again."

Then without introduction or any attempt to influence the impression of the news, she began her story—telling first of her mother's distress at Sarah's letter, then the contents of that letter, and then those of her uncle's. She could not have done it with greater fairness to her friend—his practiced self-control had opportunity for perfect operation. But the result was more to her satisfaction than she could have dared to hope. He held out his hand with a smile and said, "I am very sorry. What can I do?"

She looked up into his eyes. They were looking down kindly and lovingly.

"Then—then—" she said, "you don't—I mean there's no—I mean, you don't feel differently toward me?"

"Toward you, my angel!" exclaimed Gartley, and held out his arms.

She threw herself into them and clung to him. It was the first time either of them had shown anything like abandonment. Gartley's heart swelled with delight, for till that moment he had been painfully conscious now and then that he played second fiddle. But he was now no longer the second person in the compact.

They sat down and talked the whole thing over.

Now that Hester was at peace, she began to look at it from his point of view.

"I am sorry," she said. "It is very sad you should have to marry into a family so disgraced. What *will* your aunt say?"

"My aunt will treat the affair like the sensible woman she is," replied the earl. "But there is no fear of disgrace. The thing will never be known. Besides, where is the family that hasn't one or more such loose fishes about in its pond?"

From the heaven of her delight Hester almost fell. Was this the way her near-husband looked at these things? But, poor fellow! how could he help looking at them so? This was the way he had been taught from earliest childhood to look at them.

"But we won't think more about it just now," he added. "Let us talk of ourselves!"

"If only we could find him!" returned Hester.

"Depend upon it, he is not where you would like to find him. Men don't come to grief without help! We must just wait till he turns up."

Far as this was from her purpose, Hester was not inclined to argue the point—she could not expect him or anyone out of her own family to be much interested in the fate of Cornelius. They began to talk about other things, and if they were not the things Hester would most readily have talked about, neither were they the things lord Gartley had entered the house intending to talk about. He too had been almost angry, only by nature he was cool and even good-tempered. To find Hester, the moment she came back to London, yielding all over again to her diseased fancy of doing good, to come upon her in the street of a low neighbourhood, followed by a low crowd, and accompanied by a low fellow—well, it was not agreeable! He could not fail to find it annoying, especially with her so near to the prospect of marriage! Something must be done about her habits!

But when he had heard her trouble, he knew this was not the time to say what he had meant to say about it.

He had risen to go and was about to take a loving farewell, when Hester, suddenly remembering, drew back with an almost guilty look.

"Oh," she said, "I should not have let you come near me!"

"What *can* you mean, Hester?" he exclaimed, and would have laid his hand on her arm, but again she drew back.

"There was smallpox in the house I had just left when you met me," she explained.

He started back and stood speechless—showing no more cowardice than anyone in his circle would have justified.

"Has it never occurred to you what you are doing in going to such places, Hester?" he faltered. "It is against all social claim. I am sorry, but—really—I—I—cannot help being a little surprised at you. I thought you had more—more—sense!"

"I am sorry to have frightened you."

"Frightened!" repeated Gartley, with an attempt at a smile, which closed in a yet more anxious look, "—you do indeed frighten me! Don't imagine I am thinking of myself. *You* are the one that is in most danger! And you might carry the infection without getting it yourself!"

"I didn't know it was there when I went to the house—but I would have gone all the same," said Hester. "But I should have had a bath as soon as I got home. Seeing you so suddenly made me forget. I *am* sorry I let you come near me."

"One has no right either to get or carry infection," insisted Lord Gartley. "But there is no time to talk about it now. I hope you will use what preventives you can. It is very wrong to trifle with such things!"

"Indeed it is!" answered Hester. "And I say again I am sorry I forgot. You see how it was—don't you? It was you that made me forget!"

But his lordship was by no means now in a smiling mood. He bade her a rather cold good night, then hesitated, thinking that he must not look too much afraid, and held out his hand. But Hester drew back a third time, saying, "No, no, you must not," and with a solemn bow he turned and went, his mind full of conflicting feelings and perplexing thoughts.

What a glorious creature she was! and how dangerous! What a spirit she had! but what a pity it was so ill-directed! It was horrible to think of her going into such places—and all alone too! How ill she had been trained!—in such utter disregard of social obligation and the laws of nature. It was preposterous! He little thought what risks he ran when he fell in love with *her!* If he got off now without an attack, he would be lucky!

But—good heavens! if she were to take ill herself! "I wonder when she was last vaccinated!" he muttered. "I was last year. I daresay I'm all right! But if she were to die, I should kill myself!" Philanthropy had gone mad! To sympathize with people like that was only to encourage them! Vice was like hysterics—the more kindness you showed, the worse it grew. They took it all as their right! And the more you gave, the more they demanded—never showing any gratitude as far as he knew!

His lordship was scarcely gone when the major came. But Hester was not to be seen at the moment, for she had already begun her bath, taking what measures seemed advisable for her protection and those about her. But she had no fear, for she did not believe in chance. The same and only faith that would have enabled him to face the man-eating tiger enabled her to face the smallpox. If she did die by going into such places, it was all right.

The major sat down and waited.

"I am at my wits' end!" he said when at length she entered the room. "I can't find the fellow. I've had a detective on it, but he hasn't got a trace of him yet. Don't you think you had better go home? I will do what can be done, you may be sure of that."

"I *am* sure," answered Hester, "but I would rather be here than have Papa leave mama. And he won't as long as I stay."

"But it must be dreary for you."

"I go about among my people," she said.

"Ah," he returned. "Then I hope you will be careful what houses you go into, for I hear smallpox is in the neighbourhood."

"I have just come from such a house," she replied. The major rose in haste. "But," she went on, "I have changed all my clothes and had a bath since."

The major sat down again.

"My dear young lady!" he said, the roses a little ashy on his cheekbones, "do you know what you are about?"

"I hope I do—I *think* I do," she answered.

"Hope! Think!" repeated the major.

"Well, *believe*," said Hester.

"Come! come!" he rejoined almost rudely, "you may hope or think or believe what you like, but you have no business to act but on what you *know*."

"I suppose *you* never act where you do not know the outcome!" returned Hester. "You always *know* you will win the battle, kill the tiger, beat the smallpox."

"It's all very well for you to laugh!" returned the major, "but what is to become of us if you catch it? Why, my dear cousin, you might lose every scrap of your good looks! Really, this is most imprudent! It is your life, not your beauty only you are imperiling!"

"Is the smallpox worse than a man-eating tiger?" she asked.

"Ten times worse," he answered. "You can fight the tiger, but you can't fight the smallpox. You really ought not to run such fearful risks."

"How are they to be avoided? Every time you send for the doctor you run a risk! You can't order a clean doctor every time!"

"But it is our duty to take care of ourselves."

"One word, dear major Marvel, if you do not mind—did God take care of Jesus?"

"Of course! of course! But he wasn't like other men, you know."

"I don't want to fare better. That is, I don't want to have more of God's care than he had."

"I don't understand you. I should think if we were sure God took as good care of us as of him—"

But there he stopped, for he began to have a glimmer of where she was leading him.

"Did he keep him what you call safe?" said Hester. "Did he not allow the worst man could do to overtake him? Was it not the very consequence of his obedience?"

"Then you have made up your mind to die of the small-pox?—In that case——"

"Only if it be God's will," interrupted Hester. "If I die of the small-pox, it will not be because it could not be helped, or because I caught it by chance, it will be because God allowed it as best for me and for us all. It will not be a punishment for breaking his laws. Of course all that sounds nonsense to anyone who does not understand it."

"That's me, your humble servant," said the major. "I don't doubt you mean well, and that you are a most courageous and indeed heroic young woman. Yet it is time your friends interfered, and I am going to write by the next post to let your father know how you are misbehaving yourself."

"They will not believe me quite so bad as I fear you will represent me."

"I don't know. I must write anyhow."

"That they may order me home to give them the small-pox? Wouldn't it be better to wait and be sure I had not taken it already? Your letter, too, might carry the infection. I think you had better not write."

"You persist in making fun of it! I say again it is not a thing to be joked about," said the major.

"I think," returned Hester, "that whoever lives in constant fear of infection might just as well catch it and have done with it. I know I would rather die than live in the fear of death. What we've got to do we must just go and do without thinking about the danger. I believe it is often the best wisdom to be blind and let God be our eyes as well as our shield. God took complete care of Jesus. And yet he allowed the worst man could do to overtake him. That was the consequence of his obedience. I don't want my obedience to be any less in the work God has called me to do."

She held out her hand to him.

"You should not needlessly put yourself in danger," she said. "You must not come to me except I send for you. If you hear anything of Corney, write, please."

"You don't imagine," rejoined the major, "that I am going to turn tail where you advance? I'm not going to run from the small-pox any more than you. So long as he doesn't get on my back to hunt other people, I don't care. By George! you women have more courage ten times than we men!"

"What we've got to do we just go and do, without thinking about danger. I believe it is often the best wisdom to be blind and let God be our eyes as well as our shield."

"You're fit for a field-marshal, my dear!" said the major enthusiastically—adding, as he kissed her hand, "I will think over what you have said, and at least not betray you without warning."

"That is enough for the present," returned Hester, shaking hands with him warmly.

The major left filled with admiration for "Cousin Helen's girl."

"By Jove!" he said to himself, "it's a good thing I didn't marry Helen. She would never have had a girl like that if I had! Things always work out for the best. The world needs a few such in it—even if they be fools—though I suspect they will turn out the wise ones, and we the fools for taking such care of our precious selves!"

But the major was by no means a selfish man. He was pretty much mixed, like the rest of us. Only, if we do not make up our minds not to be mixed with the one thing, we shall by and by be but little mixed with the other.

That same evening the major sent her word that one answering the description of Cornelius had been seen in the neighbourhood of Addison Square.

—Twenty-Nine —

Further Down

The Frankses had at last reached the point of being unable to pay for their lodging. They were two weeks' rent behind. Their landlady did not want to be too hard on them, but what could a poor woman do? she said. Thus, the day finally came when they had to go forth like Abraham without a home. The weakly wife had to carry the sickly baby who, with many ups and downs, had been slowly wasting away. The father went laden with the larger portion of the goods yet remaining to them, leading the boys bearing the small stock of implements belonging to their art.

They had delayed their departure till after dusk, for Franks could not help a vague feeling of blame for the condition of his family, and shrank from being seen by men's eyes. The world was like a sea before them—a prospect of ceaseless motion through the night, with the hope of an occasional rest on a doorstep or the edge of the curbstone when the policeman's back was turned. They set out with no place to go—to tramp on and on with no goal before them.

At length as they wandered they came to an area where there seemed to be only small houses and mews. Presently they found themselves in a little lane with no street, at the back of some stables, and had to return along the rough-paved, neglected way. It was such a quiet and secluded spot that Franks thought they should find its most sheltered corner to sit down and rest, and possibly sleep. But nearly the same moment he heard the measured step of a policeman on the other side of the stables. Instinctively, hurriedly, they looked around for some place of concealment, and saw, at the end of a blank wall, belonging apparently to some kind of warehouse, a narrow path between that and the wall of the next property. Taking no thought to where it led, anxious only to escape the policeman, they turned quickly into it. Scarcely had they done so when little Moxy, whose hand his father had let go, disappeared with a little cry, and then a little whimper came up from somewhere through the darkness.

"Hold your noise, you rascal!" said his father sharply but under his breath. "The bobby will hear you and have us all in the lock-up!"

Not a sound more was heard, and the boy did not reappear. "Good heavens, John!" cried the mother in an agonized whisper, "the child has fallen down a sewer!"

"Hold your noise," said Franks again.

"'Tain't a bad place," cried a little voice in a whisper broken with repressed sobs. "I don't think, only I've broken one o' my two legs— it won't move."

"Thank God, the child's alive!" cried the mother.

By this time the steps of the policeman were fading in the distance. Franks turned and climbed down a few steps into the opening through which Moxy had fallen. When he found him he lifted him, but the child gave a low cry of pain. It was impossible to see where or how much he was hurt. The father sat down and took him on his knees.

"You'd better come down an' sit here, wife," he said in a low dull voice. "The boy's hurt, an' down here you'll be out o' the wind at least."

They all got as far down the stair as its room would permit—the elder boys with their heads hardly below the level of the wind. But by and by one of them crept down past his mother, and began to feel what sort of place they were in.

"Here's a door, father!" he said.

"Well, 'tain't no door open to the likes o' us. 'Tain't no door open for the likes o' us but the door o' the grave."

The boy's hand came upon a latch. He lifted it and pushed.

"Father," he cried, "it *is* open!"

"Get in then," said his father.

"I daren't. It's so dark!" he answered.

"Here, you come an' take Moxy," said the father with faintly reviving hope, "an' I'll see what sort of place it is. If it's any place at all, it's better than bein' in the air all night at this freezin' time."

So saying he gave Moxy to his bigger brother and went to learn what kind of place they had stumbled into. Feeling with foot and hand, he went in. The floor was earthen and the place had a musty smell. It might be a church vault, he thought. In and in he went, sliding his foot on the soundless floor, and sliding his hand along the cold wall—on around two corners, past a closed door, and back to that by which he had entered, where the family sat waiting his return.

"Wife," he said, "we can't do better than to take the only thing that's offered. The floor's firm an' it's out o' the air. It's some sort of a cellar—perhaps at the bottom of a church. It did look as if it was left open just for us!"

He took her by the hand and led the way into the darkness, the boys following, one of them with a hold of his mother, and his arm round the other, who was carrying Moxy. Franks closed the door behind them. They had gained a refuge. Feeling about, one of the boys came upon a large packing case. Franks laid it down against the inner wall, sat down, and made his wife lie upon it with her head on his knees, and took Moxy again in his arms, wrapped in one of their three thin blankets. The boys stretched themselves on the ground and were soon fast asleep. The baby moaned by fits all night long.

In about an hour Franks, who did not fall asleep for some time, heard the door open softly and stealthily, and seemed aware of a presence beside themselves in the place. He concluded some other poor creature had discovered the same shelter, or, if they had got into a church vault, it might be some wandering ghost. But he was too weary for further speculation, or any uneasiness. However, when the slow light crept through the chinks of the door, he found they were quite alone.

It was a large dry cellar, empty except for the old packing case. They would have to use great caution, and do their best to keep their hold of this last retreat! Misfortune had driven them into the earth; it would be fortune to stay there.

When his wife woke he told her what he had been thinking. He and the boys would creep out before it was light and return after dark. She must not even put a finger out of the cellar door all day.

He laid Moxy down beside her, woke the two elder boys, and went out with them.

They were so careful that for many days they continued undiscovered. Franks and the boys went and returned, and gained bread enough to keep them alive, but it may well seem a wonder they did not perish with cold. It is amazing what even the delicate can sometimes go through when survival is at stake.

—Thirty —

Differences

About noon the next day lord Gartley called. Whether he had got over his fright, thought the danger now less imminent, or was vexed with himself that he had *appeared* to be afraid, I do not know. Hester was very glad to see him again.

"I think I am a safe companion today," she said. "I have not been out of the house yet. But till the bad time is over among my people, I think we had better be content not to meet."

Lord Gartley mentally gasped. He stood for a moment speechless, gathering his thoughts, which almost refused to be gathered.

"Do I understand you, Hester?" he said. "It would trouble me more than I can tell you to find I do. You don't mean to say you are going out—again!"

"Is it possible you thought I would abandon my friends to the smallpox, as a hireling his sheep to the wolf?"

"There are those whose business it is to look after them."

"I am one of those," returned Hester.

"Well," answered his lordship, "for the sake of argument, we will allow it *has* been your business up till now. But how can you imagine it is your business any longer?"

The fire of Hester's indignation burst into flame and she spoke as lord Gartley had never heard her speak before.

"I am aware, my lord," she said, "that eventually I would have new duties to perform, but I never imagined that they would displace the old. The claims of love surely cannot obliterate those of friendship! The new should make the old better, not sweep it away!"

"But, my dear girl, the thing is preposterous!" exclaimed his lordship. "Don't you see you will enter on a new life! The duties of a wife are altogether distinct from those of an unmarried woman."

"But if the position of a wife is the higher, then it must enable her to do yet better those things that were her duty before."

"Not if it be impossible she should do the same things."

"Of course not if they are impossible—I trust I shall never attempt the impossible.

"You have begun to attempt it now."

"I do not understand you."

"It is impossible to perform the duties of the station you are about to occupy as wife of a lord, and continue to do as you are doing now. The attempt would be absurd."

"How shall I know if it is impossible for me—I have not tried it yet."

"But I know what your duties will be, and I assure you, my dear Hester, you will find the thing cannot be done."

"You have given me more than I can manage all at once," she replied in a troubled voice. "It seems as if you are saying that the portion of society that is healthy and wealthy would have a stronger claim on my attention than the portion that is poor and sick. I must think."

Lord Gartley was for a moment bewildered—not from any feeling of the force of what she said, but from inability to take it in. He had to turn himself about two or three times mentally before he could bring himself to believe she actually meant that those to whom she alluded were to be regarded as a portion of the same society that ruled his life. He thought another moment, then said:

"There are sick in every class. You would have those of your own to visit. Why not leave others to visit those of theirs?"

"Then of course you would have no objection to my visiting a duchess who had smallpox?"

Lord Gartley was on the point of saying that duchesses never got smallpox, but he did not, afraid that Hester might know something to the contrary.

"There could be no occasion for that," he said. "She would have everything she could want."

"And the others do not. To desert them would be to desert the Lord. He will count it so."

"And to help them, you would be careless of those of your own class to whom you might spread the disease!"

"Don't imagine that because I trust in God I have no fear of what the smallpox can do to me and that I would therefore neglect any necessary preventive. That would be to tempt God."

"But you will not keep away?"

"You know I was taken unprepared yesterday."

"Is it possible you truly mean to give up society for the sake of nursing the poor?"

"Only if occasion should demand it."

"And how should I account for it."

It was to Hester as if a wall rose suddenly across the path between them. It became all but clear that he and she had been going on without any real understanding of each other's views in life. Her expectations tumbled about her like a house of cards. If he wanted to marry her, full of designs and aims in which she did not share, and she was going to marry him, expecting sympathies and helps which he had not the slightest inclination to give her, where was the hope for either of them of anything worth calling success?

She sat silent. She wanted to be alone that she might think. It would be easier to write than to talk further. But she must know more clearly what was in his mind.

"Do you mean, then, Gartley," she said, "that when I am your wife, if ever I am, that I shall have to give up all the friendships to which I have devoted so much of my life?"

Her tone was dominated by the desire to be calm, to get at his real feeling. Gartley mistook it, and supposed her at last yielding to his influence. He concluded that now he had only to be firm so as to put future discussion of the matter to rest forever.

"I would not for a moment act the tyrant, or say you must never go into such houses again. Your own good sense, the innumerable engagements you will have, the endless calls upon your time and accomplishments, will guide you as to what attention you can spare to the claims of benevolence. But in the circle to which you will in the future belong, nothing is considered more out of place than to speak of these persons, whatever regard you may have for their spiritual welfare, as your *friends.* You know well enough that such persons cannot be your friends."

This was more than Hester could bear. She broke out with a passion for which she was afterward sorry, though by no means ashamed.

"They *are* my friends. There are twenty of them who would do more for me than you would!"

Lord Gartley rose. He was hurt. "Hester, you think so little of me or my anxiety for your best interests that I cannot but suppose it will be a relief to you if I go."

She answered not a word—did not even look up, and his lordship walked gently but unhesitatingly from the room.

"It will bring her to her senses!" he told himself.

Long after he was gone, Hester sat motionless, thinking. What she had vaguely foreboded—she knew now that she had foreboded it all along—had come! They were not, never had been, never could be at one about anything! He was a mere man of this world, without relation to the world of truth. And yet she loved him—would gladly do anything for him, if by so doing he could be saved from himself and given to God instead. But she could not marry him! That would be to swell his worldly triumphs, help gild the chains of his slavery. It was one thing to die that a fellow creature might have all things good—another to live a living death that he might persist in the pride of life! She could not throw God's life to the service of Satan!

Was it then all over between them? Might he not come again and say he was sorry he had left her? He might indeed. But would that make any difference to her? Had he not beyond a doubt disclosed his real way of thinking and feeling? If he could speak as he had now, after they had talked so much, what spark of hope was there in marriage?

To forget her friends that she might go into *society* as a countess! The very thought was contemptible. She would leave such ambition to women that devoured novels and studied the peerage! One loving look from human eyes was more to her than the admiration of the world. If only the house were her own. Then she might turn it into a hospital! She would make it a hope to which anyone sick or sad, any outcast of the world might flee for shelter! She would be more than ever the sister and helper of her own, cling tighter than ever to the skirts of the Lord's garment, that the virtue going out of him might flow through her to them!

How easy is it, in certain moods, to think thoughts of unselfish devotion. But how hard is the doing of the thought in the face of a thousand unlovely difficulties! Hester knew this, but, God helping, was determined not to withdraw hand or foot or heart. She rose and, having prepared herself, set out to visit her people. First of all she would go to the bookbinder's and see how his wife was attended to.

The doctor was not there and she was readily admitted. The poor husband, unable to help, sat by the scanty fire, a picture of misery. A neighbour, not yet quite recovered from the disease herself, had taken upon herself the duties of nurse. Hester gave her what instructions she thought she might carry out, told her to send for anything she wanted, then rose to leave.

"Won't you sing to her a bit, miss, before you go?" said the husband. "It'll do her more good than all the doctor's stuff."

"I don't think she's well enough," said Hester.

"Not to get all the good out of it, I daresay," rejoined the man, "but she'll hear it like in a dream, an' she'll think it's the angels a singin'. An' that'll do her good, for she do like all them creatures!"

Hester yielded and sang, thinking all the time how the ways of the open-eyed God look to us like things in a dream, because we are only in the night of his great day, asleep before the brightness of his great waking thoughts. The woman had been tossing and moaning in discomfort, but as Hester sang she grew still, and when she ceased lay as if asleep.

"Thank you, miss," said the man. "You can do more than the doctor, as I told you! When he comes, he always wakes her up. You make her sleep true!"

—Thirty-One —

Deep Calleth Unto Deep

In the meantime, yet worse trouble had come upon the poor Frankses. About a week after they had taken possession of the cellar, little Moxy, who had been weak ever since his fall down the steps, became seriously ill and grew worse and worse. For some days they were not much alarmed, for the child had often been ailing—oftener lately since they had not been faring so well. And even when they were better off they dared not get a doctor to look at him for fear of being turned out and having to go to the workhouse.

By this time they had managed to make the cellar a little more comfortable. They got some straw and with two or three old sacks made a bed for the mother, the baby, and Moxy on the packing case. By the exercise of their art they had gained enough money to keep them in food, but never enough to pay for even the poorest room.

The parents loved Moxy more tenderly than either of his brothers, and it was with sore hearts they saw him getting worse. The sickness was a mild smallpox—so mild that they did not recognize it, yet more than Moxy could bear, and he was gradually sinking. When this became clear to the mother, then indeed she felt the hand of God heavy upon her.

Religiously brought up, she had through the ordinary troubles of a married life sought help from the God in whom her mother had believed. Our mothers and fathers, if at all decent parents, are our first mediators with the great father, whom we can worse spare than any baby his mother. But with every fresh attack of misery, every step further down on the stair of life, she thought she had lost her last remnant of hope. No man, however little he may recognize the hope in him, knows what it would be to be altogether hopeless.

Now Moxy was about to be taken from them. No deeper misery seemed possible! Nothing seemed left them—not even the desire of deliverance. How little hope there is in the commoner phases of religion! The message grounded on the uprising of the crucified man, has as yet yielded but little victory over the sorrows of the grave, and but small anticipation of the world to come—perhaps a little hope of deliverance from hell, but scarce a foretaste of a blessed time at hand when the heart shall exult and the flesh be glad. In general there is at best but a sad looking forward to a region scarcely less shadowy and far more dreary than that of the pagan poets. When Christ cometh, shall he find faith in the earth—even among those who think they believe that he is risen indeed? Margaret Franks, in the cellar of her poverty, the grave yawning below it for her Moxy, felt as if there was no heaven at all, only a sky.

But a strange necessity now compelled her to rouse afresh all the latent hope and faith and prayer that were in her.

By an inexplicable insight, the child seemed to know that he was dying. For one morning, after having tossed about all night long, he suddenly cried out in the most pitiful tone,

"Mother, don't put me in a hole!"

As far as any of them knew he had never seen a funeral—at least to know what it was—and had never heard anything about death or burial. His father had a horror of the subject.

The words went like a knife to the heart of the mother.

Again came the pitiful cry,

"Mother, don't put me in a hole!"

Most mothers would have sought to soothe the child, their own hearts breaking all the while, with the assurance that no one would put him into any hole or anywhere he did not want to go. But this mother could not lie in the face of death, and before she could answer, a third time came the cry, this time in despairing though supressed agony—

"Mother, don't let them put me in a hole!"

The mother gave a cry like the child's and her heart melted.

"Oh, God!" she gasped, and could say no more.

But with the prayer—for what is a prayer but a calling on the name of the Lord—came a little calm, and she was able to speak. She bent over and kissed him on the forehead.

"My darling Moxy, mother loves you," she said.

What that had to do with it she did not ask herself. The child looked up in her face with dim eyes.

"Pray to the heavenly father, Moxy," she went on—and there stopped, thinking what she should tell him to ask for. "Tell him," she resumed, "that you don't want to be put in a hole, and tell him that Mother does not want you to be put in a hole, for she loves you with all her heart."

"Don't put me in the hole," said Moxy.

"Jesus Christ was put in the hole," said the voice of the next older boy from behind his mother. He had just come in softly. It was Sunday, and he had strolled into a church somewhere and had heard the wonderful story of hope. It was remarkable that he had taken it in as he did, for he went on to add, "but he didn't mind much, and soon got out again."

"Ah, yes, Moxy!" said the poor mother, "Jesus died for our sins, and you must ask him to take you up to heaven."

But Moxy did not know anything about sins, and just as little about heaven. What he wanted was an assurance that he would not be put into the hole. And the mother, now a little calmer, thought she saw what she ought to say.

"It isn't your soul, it's only your body, Moxy, that they put in the hole," she said.

"I don't want to be put in the hole," Moxy almost screamed.

The poor mother was at her wits' end. But here the child fell into a troubled sleep, and for some hours a grave-like silence filled the dreary cellar.

—Thirty-Two —

Deliverance

On this same particular Sunday Hester had been to church, and had then visited some of her people, carrying them words of comfort and hope. They received them from her, but none of them, had they gone, would have found them at church. How seldom is the man in the pulpit able to make people feel that the things he is talking about are relevant to them! Neither when the heavens are black with clouds and rain, nor when the sun rises glorious in a blue perfection, do many care to sit down and be taught astronomy! But Hester was a live gospel to them—most of all when she sang. Even the name of the Saviour uttered in her singing tone and with the expression she gave it, came nearer to them than when she spoke it.

How many things there are in the world in which the wisest of us can hardly perceive the hand of God! Who not knowing could ready the lily in its bulb, the great oak in the pebble-like acorn? God's beginnings do not *look* like his endings, but they *are*. The oak *is* the acorn, though we cannot see it.

The ranting preacher, uttering huge untruths, may yet wake vital truths in chaotic minds—convey to a heart some saving fact, rudely wrapped in husks of lies even against God himself.

Mr. Christopher, thrown at one time into daily relations with a good sort of man, had tried all he could to rouse him to a sense of his higher duties and spiritual privileges, but entirely without success. A preacher came round, whose gospel was largely composed of hell-fire and malediction, with frequent allusion to the love of a most unlovely God, as represented by him.

This preacher woke up the man. "And then," said Christopher, "I was able to be of service to him, and get him on. He speedily outgrew the lies his prophet had taught him, and became a devout Christian, while the man who had been the means of rousing him was tried for bigamy, convicted and punished.

This Sunday, in her dejection and sadness about Gartley, over whom—not her loss of him—she mourned deeply, Hester felt more than ever how little she was able to touch her people. There came upon her a hopelessness that sank into the very roots of her life. She was having to learn that even in all dreariness, of the flesh and of the spirit, the refuge is the same—he who is at once the root and crown of life.

The day was an oppressive, foggy, cold, dreary day. The service at church had not seemed interesting. She laid the blame on herself, not on the prayers, the lessons, or the preacher, though in truth some of these could have been better. The heart seemed to have gone out of the world—as if God had gone to sleep and his children had waked before him and found the dismal gray of the world's morning. She tried her New Testament, but Jesus, too, seemed far away. She tried some of her favourite poems, but all were infected with the same disease—with commonplace nothingness. Everything seemed mere words! words! words! Nothing was left her in the valley but the last weapon—prayer. She fell upon her knees and cried to God for life. "My heart is dead within me," she said, and poured out her lack into the hearing of him from whom she had come.

It is perhaps out of such seasons that emerges the final victory of faith. Faith, in such circumstances, must be of the purest, and may be of the strongest. In few other circumstances can it have such an opportunity—can it rise to equal height. It may be its final lesson, and deepest. God is in it just in his seeming to be not in it—that we may choose him in the darkness of the feeling, stretch out the hand to him when we cannot see him, verify him in the vagueness of the dream, call to him in the absence of impulse, obey him in the weakness of the will.

But even in her prayers Hester could not get near him. It seemed as if his ear was turned away from her cry, and she sank into a kind of lethargic stupor.

There are times, in order to give us the spiritual help we need, when it is necessary for God to cast us into a sort of mental quiescence, that the noises of winds and waters of the questioning

189

intellect and roused feelings may not interfere with the impression the master would make upon us. But Hester's lethargy lasted long, and was not so removed. She rose from her knees in a kind of despair she had never known.

It had been dark for hours, but she lit no candle, sitting in bodily as well as spiritual darkness. She was in her bedroom, which was on the second floor, at the back of the house, looking out on the top of the gallery that led to the great room. She had no fire. One was burning away unheeded in the drawing room below. She was too miserable to care whether she was cold or warm. When she had got some light in her body, then she would go and get warm!

She did not know what time it was. She had been summoned to the last meal of the day, but had forgotten the summons. It must have been about ten o'clock. The streets were silent, the square deserted—as usual. The evening was raw and cold, one to drive everybody indoors that had doors to go in.

Through the cold and darkness came a shriek that chilled her with horror. Yet it seemed as if she had been expecting it—as if the cloud of misery that had all day been gathering deeper and deeper above and around her had at length reached its fullness and burst forth. It was followed by another and yet another. She could not tell where they came from. Certainly not from the street, for all outside was still. And there was a certain something in the sound of them that made her sure they rose from within the house. Was Sarah being murdered? She was halfway down the stairs before the thought became plain in her mind.

The house seemed unnaturally still. At the top of the kitchen stairs she called aloud to Sarah—as loud, that is, as a certain tremor in her throat would permit. There came no reply. Down she went to face the worst: she was a woman of true courage—that is, a woman whom no amount of apprehension could deter when she knew she ought to seek the danger.

In the kitchen stood Sarah, motionless, frozen with fear. A candle was in her hand, just lighted. Hester's voice seemed to break her trance.

She started, stared, and began trembling. Hester made her drink some water, and then she came to herself.

"It's in the coal cellar, miss!" she gasped. "I was that minute going to fetch a scuttleful! There's something buried in them coals as sure as my name's Sarah!"

"Nonsense! Who could scream like that from under the coals? Come. We'll go and see what it is."

"Laws, miss, don't you go near it now! It's too late to do anything. Either it's the woman's spirit as they say was murdered there, or it's a new one."

"And you would let her be killed without interfering?"

"Oh, miss, all's over by this time!" persisted Sarah with trembling white lips.

"Then you are ready to go to bed with a murderer in the house?"

"He's done his business now, an' 'll go away."

"Give me the candle. I will go alone."

"You'll be murdered, miss—as sure's you're alive!"

Hester took the light from her and went toward the coal cellar. The old woman sank on a chair.

I have already alluded to the subterranean portion of the house, which extended under the great room. A long vault, corresponding to the gallery above, led to these cellars. It was a rather frightful place to go into in search of the source of a shriek. Its darkness was scarcely affected by the candle she carried—it seemed only to blind her own eyes. The black tunnel stretched on and on, like a tunnel in a feverish dream, before the cellars began to open from it. She walked on, I cannot say fearless, but therefore only the more brave. At last she reached the coal cellar, the first that opened from the passage, and looked in. The coal pile was low and the place looked large and black—she could see nothing. She went in and moved about until she had thrown light into every corner, but no one was there. She was about to return when she remembered that there were other cellars—one the wine cellar, which was locked. She would go ask Sarah if she knew where the key to it was. But just as she left the coal cellar, she heard a moan followed by several low sobs. Her heart began to beat violently, but she stopped to listen.

The light from her candle fell upon another door, a step or two from where she stood. She went to it, laid her ear against it and listened. The sobs continued a while, ceased, and all became silent again. Then clear and sweet, but strange and wild, as if from some unearthly region, came the voice of a child:

"Mother," it rang out, "you *may* put me in the hole."

Then the silence fell deep as before.

Hester stood for a moment horrified. Her excited imagination suggested some deed of superstitious cruelty in the garden of the adjoining house. And the sobs and cries lent themselves all the more toward something in that direction. She recovered herself instantly and ran back to the kitchen.

"Do you have the keys of the cellars, Sarah?"

"Yes, miss, I think so."

"Where does the door beyond the coal cellar lead to?"

"Not to nowhere, miss. That's a large cellar as we never use. I ain't been into it since the first day when they put some of the packing cases there."

"Give me the key," said Hester. "Something is going on there we ought to know about."

"Then pray send for the police, miss!" answered Sarah, trembling. "It ain't for you to go into such places!"

"What! Not in our own house?"

"It's the police's business, miss!"

"Then the police are their brothers' keepers, and not you and me, Sarah?"

"It's the wicked as is in it, I fear, miss."

"It's those that weep anyhow, and they're our business. Quick! Show me which is the key."

Sarah sought the key in the bunch, and noting the coolness with which her young mistress took it, gathered a little courage from hers to follow, a bit behind.

When Hester reached the door, she carefully examined it, so she would be able to do what she had to do as quickly as possible. There were bolts and bars upon it, but not one of them was fastened—it was secured only by the bolt of the lock. She set the candle on the floor and inserted the key as quietly as she could. It turned without much difficulty, and the door fell partly open with a groan of the rusted hinge. She grabbed the light and went in.

It was a large, empty place. For a few moments she could see nothing. But presently she saw, somewhere in the dark, a group of faces, looking white through the surrounding blackness, the eyes of them fixed in amazement—if not terror—upon herself. Advancing toward them, she almost immediately recognized one of them—then another. But what with the dimness, the ghostliness, and the strangeness of it all, felt as if surrounded by the veiled shadows of a dream. But whose was that pallid little face whose eyes were not upon her with the rest? It stared straight ahead into the dark, as if it had no more to do with the light! She drew nearer to it. The eyes of the other faces followed her.

When the eyes of the mother saw the face of her Moxy, who had died in the dark, she threw herself into a passion of tears and cries. When Hester turned in pain from the agony of the mother, she saw the man kneeling with uplifted hands of supplication at her feet. A torrent of divine love and compassion filled her heart, breaking from its deepest God-haunted caves. She stooped and kissed the man on his forehead.

Many are called but few chosen. Hester was the disciple of him who could have cured the leper with a word, but for reasons of his own, not far to seek by such souls as Hester's, laid his hands upon him, sorely defiling himself in the eyes of the self-respecting bystanders. The leper himself would never have dreamed of his touching him.

Franks burst out crying like a child. All at once in the depths of hell, the wings of a great angel were spread out over him and his! No more starvation and cold for his poor wife and the baby! The boys would have plenty now! If only Moxy—but he was gone where the angels came from. Theirs was a hard life! Surely the God his wife talked about must have sent her to them! Did he think they had borne enough now? Only he had borne it so poorly! So thought Franks, in dislocated fashion, as he remained kneeling.

Hester was now kneeling also, with her arms around the mother who held the body of her child. She did not speak to her, did not attempt a word of comfort, but wept with her. She, too, had loved little Moxy! She, too, had heard his dying words. In the midst of her own loneliness and seeming desertion, God had these people already in the house for her to help! The back door of every tomb opens on a hilltop.

With awestruck faces the boys looked on. They, too, could not see Moxy's face. They had loved Moxy—loved him more than they knew yet.

The woman at length raised her head and looked at Hester.

"Oh, miss, it's Moxy!" she said, bursting into a new passion of grief.

"The dear child!" said Hester.

"Oh, miss, who's to look after him now?"

"There will be plenty to look after him. You don't think he who provided a woman like you for his mother before he sent him here would send him there without having somebody ready to look after him?"

"Well, miss, it wouldn't be like him—I don't think!"

"It would *not* be like him," responded Hester.

Then she asked them a few questions about their history since she last saw them, and how it was they had sunk so low. The answers she received were more satisfactory than her knowledge had allowed her to hope.

"But oh, miss!" exclaimed Mrs. Franks, "you ought not to ha' been here so long. The little angel there died o' the smallpox, as I know too well, an' it's no end o' catching!"

"Never mind me," replied Hester. "I'm not afraid. But," she added, rising, "we must get you out of this place immediately."

"Oh, miss! where would you send us?" said Mrs. Franks in alarm. "There's nobody as'll take us in! An' it would break both our two hearts to be parted at such a moment, when us two's the father an' mother o' Moxy. An' they'd take Moxy from us, an' put him in the hole he was so a feared of!"

"You don't think I would leave my own flesh and blood in the cellar!" answer Hester. "I will go and make arrangement for you above, and be back presently."

"Oh, thank you, miss!" said the woman as Hester set the candle down beside them. "I do want to look on the face of my blessed boy as long as I can. He will be taken from me altogether soon."

"Mrs. Franks," rejoined Hester, "you mustn't talk like a heathen."

"I didn't know I was saying anything wrong, miss!"

"Don't you know," said Hester, smiling through her tears, "that Jesus died and rose again that we might be delivered from death?

194

Don't you know that it's *he* and not death that has got your Moxy? He will take care of him for you until you are ready to have him again. Both you and Moxy were born of God's own soul. If you know how to love, he loves ten times more."

"The Lord love you, miss! An angel o' mercy you been to me an' mine."

"Goodbye then for a few minutes," said Hester. "I am only going to prepare a place for you."

Only as she said the words did she remember who had said them before her. And as she went through the dark tunnel, she sang with a voice that seemed to beat at the gates of heaven, "Thou didst not leave his soul in hell."

Mrs. Franks threw herself again beside her child, but her tears were not so bitter now.

"She'll come again for us," she murmured. "An' Christ'll receive my poor Moxy to himself! If he wasn't, as they say, a Christian, it was only as he hadn't time—so young, an' all the hard work he had to do—with his precious face a grinnin' like an angel between the feet of him, a helpin' his father to make a livin' for us all! If ever there was a child o' God's makin' it, it was that child!"

Thoughts like these kept flowing through the mind of the bereaved mother as she lay with her arm over the body of her child—now more lovely to her than ever. The smallpox had not been severe—only severe enough to take a feeble life from the midst of privation. He lay like a sacrifice that sealed a new covenant between his mother and her Father in heaven.

We have yet learned but little of the blessed power of death. We call it an evil, but it is a holy, friendly thing. We are not left shivering all the world's night in a stately portico with no house behind it. Death is the door to the temple-house, whose God is not seated aloft in motionless state, but walks about among his children, receiving his pilgrim sons in his arms, and washing the sore feet of the weary ones. Either God is altogether like Christ, or the Christian religion is a lie.

Not a word passed between husband and wife. Their hearts were too full for speech, but their hands found and held each other's. It was the strangest concurrence of sorrow and relief! The two boys sat on the ground with their arms about each other. So they waited.

—Thirty-Three —

On the Way Up

Hearing only the sounds of a peaceful talk, Sarah had ventured near enough to the door to hear something of what was said. Her mind was set to rest by finding that the cause of her terror was but a poor family that had sought refuge in the cellar. She woke up to the situation and was ready to help. More than sufficiently afraid of robbers and murderers, she was not afraid of infection. "How could an old woman like me get the smallpox! I've had it bad enough once already!" She was rather staggered, however, when she found what Hester's plan for the intruders was.

Since the night of the concert, nothing more had been done to make the great room habitable by the family. It had been well cleaned out and that was all. But what better place, thought Hester, could there be for a smallpox ward!

She told Sarah to light a big fire as quickly as possible, while she settled what could be done about beds. Almost all in the house were old-fashioned wooden ones, hard to take down, heavy to move, and hard to put up again. With only her and Sarah it would take a long time! For safety, too, it would be better to use iron beds which could be easily purified—only it was Sunday night, and late! But she knew the merchant in Steven's Road. She would go to him and see if he had any beds and if he would help her put them up at once.

The raw night made her rejoice all the more that she had got hold of the poor creatures drowning in the social swamp. It was a consolation against her own sorrows to know that virtue was going out of her for rescue and redemption.

She had to ring the bell many times before the door opened, for it was now past eleven o'clock. The man was not pleased at being taken from his warm bed to go out and work—on such a night, too!

196

He made what objections he thought he could, to no avail. She told him it was for some who had nowhere to lay their heads, and in her turn more than hinted that he could hardly know what Sunday meant if he did not think it right to do any number of good deeds on it. Finally assenting to Hester's arguments, he went to find the beds she wanted. Having got the two beds extracted piecemeal from the disorganized heaps in his back shop, he and Hester proceeded to carry them home—and I cannot help wishing lord Gartley had come upon her at the work—no easy job, for she made three trips back and forth and they were heavy. It was long after midnight before the beds were ready—and a meal of coffee, toast, bread and butter was spread in the great room. Then, at last, Hester went back to the cellar.

"Now, come," she said, taking up the baby, which had just weight enough to lie and let her know how light it was, and led the way.

Franks rose from the edge of the packing case, on which the body of Moxy still lay, with his mother yet kneeling beside it, and put his arm round his wife to raise her. She yielded, and he led her away after their hostess, the boys following hand in hand. But when they reached the cellar door, the mother gave a heartbroken cry, and, turning, ran and threw herself again beside her child.

"I can't! I can't!" she said. "I can't leave my Moxy lyin' here all alone! He ain't used to it. He never once slept alone since he was born!"

"He is not alone," said Hester. "The darkness may be full of eyes. And the night itself is only the black pupil of the Father's eye.—But we're not going to leave the darling here. We'll take him too, of course, and find him a good place to lie in."

The mother was satisfied, and the little procession passed through the dark passage and up the stair.

The boys looked pleased at sight of the comforts that waited them, but a little awed with the great lofty room. And over the face of Franks passed a gleam of joy mingled with gratitude. Much had not yet begun to be set to rights between him and the high government above. But the mother's heart was with the little boy lying alone in the cellar. Suddenly with a wild gesture she made for the door.

"Stop! stop, dear Mrs. Franks!" cried Hester. "Here, take the baby. Sarah and I are going immediately to bring him out of the cellar, and lay him where you can see him when you please."

Again she was satisfied. She took the baby and sat down beside her husband.

I have mentioned a room with a low ceiling under the great one. In this Hester had told Sarah to place a table covered with white. They would lay the body there in such a way as would be a sweet remembrance to the mother.

As they went, Hester asked, "But how can the Frankses have got into the place?"

"There is a back door to it," answered Sarah. "The first load of coals came in that way, but master wouldn't have it used. He didn't like a door to his house he never set eyes on, he said."

"But how could it have been open to let them in?" said Hester.

When they reached the cellar, she took the candle and went to look at the door. It was pushed closed, but not locked, and had no fastening upon it except the lock, in which was the key. She turned the key, took it out, and put it in her pocket.

Then they carried up the little body, washed it, dressed it in white, and laid it, as a symbol of a peace more profound, on the table. They lighted six candles, three at the head and three at the feet, that the mother might see the face of her child, and because light not darkness befits death. Then they went to fetch the mother.

She was washing the things they had used for supper. The boys were already in bed. Franks was staring into the fire. The poor fellow had not even looked at such warmth for some time. Hester asked them to go and see where she had laid Moxy, and they went with her. The beauty of death's courtly state comforted them.

"But I can't leave him alone!" said the mother "—all night too!— he wouldn't like it! I know he won't wake up no more. Only, you know, miss—"

"Yes, I know very well," replied Hester.

"I'm ready," said Franks.

"No, no!" returned Hester. "You are worn out and must go to bed, both of you. I will stay with him tonight and see that no harm comes to him."

After some persuasion the mother consented, and in a little while the house was quiet. Hester threw a fur cloak around herself and sat down in the chair Sarah had placed for her beside the dead boy.

She prayed to the Father, awake with her in the stillness, and then she began to think about the dead Christ. What would it have been like to sit beside that body all the night long! Oh, to have seen it come to life! To see it move and wake and rise with the informing God! Every dead thing belonged to Christ, not to something called *Death!* This dead thing was his! It was dead as he had been dead, and not otherwise. There was no reason for the fear which had begun to steal over her. There was nothing dreadful here, any more than in sitting beside the cradle of a child yet unborn! In the name of Christ she would fear nothing! He had abolished death!

Thus thinking, she lay back in her chair, closed her eyes, and thanking God for having sent her relief through helping his children, fell fast asleep.

She started suddenly awake, seeming to have been roused by the opening of a door. The fringe of a departing dream lay yet upon her eyes. Was the door of the tomb in which she had lain so long burst from its hinges? Was the day of the great resurrection come? Swiftly her senses settled themselves, and she saw plainly and remembered clearly. Yet could she be really awake? For in the wall opposite stood the form of a man!

She neither cried out nor fainted, but sat gazing. She was not even afraid, only dumbstruck with wonder. The man did not look fearful. A smile she seemed to have seen before broke gradually from his lips and spread over his face. The next moment he stepped from the wall and came toward her.

Then sight and memory came together—in that wall was a door, said to lead into the next house. For the first time she saw it open!

The man came nearer and nearer. It was Mr. Christopher! She rose and held out her hand.

"You are surprised to see me!" he said, "—and well you may be. Am I in your house? And what does this all mean? I seem to recognize the sweet face on the table. I must have seen you and it together before! Yes! it is Moxy!"

"You are right, Mr. Christopher," she answered. "Dear little Moxy died of the smallpox in our cellar. He was just gone when I found them there."

"Is it wise of you to expose yourself so much to the infection?" he said.

"We have our work to do—life or death is the care of him who sets the work. But tell me how you came to be here. It almost looked to my sleepy eyes as if an angel had melted his own door through the wall!"

"No, I came here in the simplest way in the world," he replied, "though I am no less surprised than you to find myself in your presence. I was called to see a patient. When I went to return as I came, I found the door by which I had entered locked. Then I remembered passing a door on the stair and went back to try it. It was bolted on the side to the stair. I withdrew the bolts, opened the door gently, and beheld the wonderful sight of you sitting beside the white body of Moxy. I saw only the up-turned face of the dead, and the down-turned face of the sleeping! I seemed to look into the heart of things, and see the whole waste universe waiting for the sonship, for the redemption of the body, the visible life of men! I saw that love, trying to watch by death, had failed, because the thing that is not needs not to be watched. I think I must have unconsciously pushed the door against the wall, for somehow I made a noise with it and you woke."

Christopher stood silent. Hester could not ask him to sit down, but she must understand how he had gotten into the house. Where was his patient? In the next house? The thing certainly must be looked into! That door must be secured on their side. Their next midnight visitor might not be so welcome as this, whose heart burned to the same labour as her own!

"I never saw that door open before," she said, "and none of us knew where it led. We took it for granted it was into the next house, but the old lady was so cross—"

Here she checked herself, for if Mr. Christopher had just come from that house, he might be a friend of the old lady's.

"It goes into no lady's house, so far as I understand," said Christopher. "The stair leads to an attic—I should fancy over our heads here—much higher up though."

"Would you show me how you came in?" said Hester.

"With pleasure," he answered, and taking one of the candles, led the way.

"I would not let the young woman leave her husband to show me out," he went on. "When I found myself a prisoner, I thought I would try this door before interrupting the sleep of a patient with smallpox. You seem to have it all around you here!"

Through the door so long mysterious Hester stepped on a narrow, steep stair. Christopher turned downward and trod softly. At the bottom he passed through a door admitting them to a small cellar, a mere recess. From there they came into that which the Frankses had occupied. Christopher went to the door Hester had locked and said, "There is where I came in. I suppose one of your people must have locked it."

"I locked it myself," replied Hester, and told him briefly the story of the evening.

"I see!" said Christopher. "We must have passed through just after you had taken them away."

"And now the question remains," said Hester, "—who can be in our house without our knowledge? The stair is plainly in our house."

"Beyond a doubt, but how strange it is you should know your own house so imperfectly! I fancy the young couple, having gotten into some difficulty, found entrance the same way the Frankses did, only they went farther and fared better!—to the top of the house, I mean. They've managed to make themselves pretty comfortable too! There is something peculiar about them—I can hardly say what."

"Could I not go up with you tomorrow and see them?" said Hester.

"That would hardly do. I could be of no further use to them if they were to think I betrayed them. You have a perfect right to know what is going on in your house, but I would rather not appear in the discovery. One thing is plain, you must either go to them or unlock the cellar door. You will like the young woman. She is a capable person—an excellent nurse. Shall I go out this way?"

"Will you come tomorrow? I am alone and cannot ask anybody to help me because of the smallpox. And I shall need some help for the funeral. You do not think me troublesome?"

"Not in the least. It is all part of my business. I will manage it for you."

"Come then, I will show you the way out. This is No. 18, Addison Square. You need not come in the cellar way next time."

"If I were you," said Christopher, stopping at the foot of the kitchen stair, "I would leave the key in that cellar door. The poor young woman would be terrified to find they were prisoners."

She turned immediately and went back. He followed and replaced the key.

"Now let us fasten up that door I came in by," said Christopher.

This was soon done, and he left.

What a strange night it had been for Hester! For the time she had forgotten her own troubles! Ah, if she had been of one mind with lord Gartley, where would those poor creatures be now? Woe for the wife whose husband has no regard to her deepest desires, her highest aspirations!—who loves her so that he would be the god of her idolatry, not the friend and helper of her heart, soul, and mind! Many of Hester's own thoughts were revealed to her that night by the side of the dead child. It became clear to her that she had been led astray, in part by the desire to rescue one to whom God had not sent her, in part by the pleasure of being loved, and in part by worldly ambition.

Marriage might be the absorbing duty of some women, but was it necessarily hers? Certainly not with such a man. Might not the duties of some callings be incompatible with marriage? Did not the providence of the world ordain that not a few should go unmarried? Was a husband to take the place of Christ and order her life for her? Was man enough for woman? Did she not need God? It came to that! Was he or God to be her master? It grew clearer and clearer. There was, there could be, no relation of life over which the Lord was not supreme!

When the morning came and she heard Sarah stirring, she sent her to take her place, and went to get a little rest.

—Thirty-Four —

The Attic Room

But Hester could not sleep. She rose, went back to the room where Moxy lay, and sent Sarah to get breakfast ready. An urgent desire came upon her to know the people who had come, like swallows, to tenant in the space overhead. She opened the door through which the doctor had come when she first saw him the night before, and stole gently up the stair—steep, narrow, and straight—which ran the height of the two rooms between the walls. A long way up she came to another door and, peeping through a chink in it, saw that it opened to the small orchestra high in the end-wall of the great room. Probably, at one time, the stair had been an arrangement for the musicians.

Going higher yet, till she all but reached the roof, the stair brought her to a door. She knocked. No sound of approaching footsteps followed, but after some little delay it was opened by a young woman, with a finger on her lip and a scared look in her eye. She had expected to see the doctor, and was startled to see Hester instead. There was little light where she stood, but Hester could not help feeling as if she had seen her somewhere before. She came out on the landing and shut the door behind her.

"He is very ill," she said. "He hears a strange voice even in his sleep. It is dreadful to him."

Her voice was not strange, and the moment she spoke it seemed to light up her face. With a pang she could scarcely account for, Hester recognized Amy Amber.

"Amy!" she said.

"Oh, Miss Raymount!" cried Amy joyfully, "is it indeed you? Have you come at last? I thought I was never to see you anymore!"

"Amy," said Hester, "I am bewildered. How do you come to be here? I don't understand."

"*He* brought me here."

"*Who* brought you here?"

"Why, miss!" exclaimed Amy, as if hearing the most unexpected of questions, "who else should it be?"

"I have not the slightest idea," returned Hester.

But the same instant a feeling strangely mingled of alarm, discomfort, indignation, and relief crossed her mind.

Through her palour Amy turned whiter still, and then turned a little away, like a person offended.

"There is but one, miss," she said. "Who should it be but him?"

"Speak his name," said Hester almost sternly. "This is no time for hide-and-seek. Tell me whom you mean."

"Are you angry with me?" faltered Amy. "Oh, Miss Raymount, I don't think I deserve it!"

"Speak out, child! Why should I be angry with you?"

"Do you know what it is?—Oh, I hardly know what I am saying! He is dying! He is dying!"

She sank on the floor and covered her face with her hands. Hester stood a moment and looked at her weeping, her heart filled with sad dismay. Then softly and quickly she opened the door of the room and went in.

Amy jumped to her feet, but too late to prevent her, and followed trembling, afraid to speak, but relieved to find that Hester moved so noiselessly.

It was a large room, but the roof came down to the floor nearly all around. It was lighted only with a skylight. In the farthest corner was a screen. Hester crept gently toward it, and Amy after her, not attempting to stop her. She came to the screen and looked behind it. There lay a young man in a troubled sleep, his face swollen and red and blotched with the smallpox, but through the disfigurement she recognized her brother. Her eyes filled with tears. She turned away and stole out again as softly as she came in. Amy had been looking at her anxiously, and when she saw the tenderness of her look, she gathered courage and followed her. Outside, Hester stopped, and Amy again closed the door.

"You *will* forgive him, won't you, miss?" she said pitifully.

"What do you want me to forgive him for, Amy?" asked Hester, suppressing her tears.

"I don't know, miss. You seemed angry with him. I don't know what to make of it. Sometimes I feel certain it must have been his illness coming on that made him weak in his head and talk foolishness. Sometimes I wonder whether he has really been doing anything wrong."

"He must have been doing something wrong. Otherwise, how should *you* be here, Amy?" said Hester with hasty judgment.

"He never told me, miss, or of course I would have done what I could to prevent it," answered Amy, bewildered. "We were so happy, miss, till then! And we've never had a moment's peace since! That's why we came here—to be where nobody would find us. I wonder how he came to know the place!"

"Then do *you* not know where you are, Amy?"

"No, miss, not in the least. I only know where to buy the things we need. He has not been out once since we came."

"You are in our house, Amy. What will my father say! How long have you—have you been—"

Something in her heart or her throat prevented Hester from finishing the sentence.

"How long have I been married to him, miss? You surely know that as well as I do, miss!"

"My poor Amy! Did he make you believe we knew about it?"

Amy gave a little cry.

"Alas!" said Hester, "I fear he has been more wicked than we know! But, Amy, he has done something else very wrong."

Amy covered her face with her apron, through which Hester could see her soundless sobs.

"I have been doing what I could to find him," continued Hester, "and here he was close to me all the time! But it adds greatly to my misery to find you with him, Amy!"

"Indeed, miss, how was I to suspect he was not telling me the truth? I loved him too much for that! I told him I would not marry him unless he had his father's permission. And he pretended he had got it, and read me such a beautiful letter from his mother! Oh, miss, it breaks my heart to think of it!"

Suddenly a new fear came upon Hester—had he also deceived the poor girl with a pretended marriage? What her father would say to a marriage was hard to think. What he would say to a deception, she knew!

Such thoughts passed swiftly through her mind as she stood half turned from Amy, looking down the steep stair that sank like a precipice before her. She heard nothing, but Amy started and turned to the door. She was following her when Amy said, in a voice almost of terror, "Please, miss, do not let him see you till I have told him you are here."

"Certainly not," answered Hester, and drew back, "—if you think the sight of me would hurt him!"

"Thank you, miss; I am sure it would," whispered Amy. "He is frightened of you."

"Frightened of me!" said Hester to herself, when Amy had gone in. "I thought he only disliked me. I wonder if he would have loved me a little if he had not been afraid of me! Perhaps I could have made him love me if I had tried. It is easier to arouse fear than love."

It may be very well for a nature like Corney's to fear a father. Fear does come in for some good where love is in short supply, but I doubt if fear of a sister can do any good.

Then first it began to dawn upon Hester that there was in her a certain hardness of character distinct in its nature from that unbending devotion to the right, which is imperative—belonging, in truth, to the region of her weakness—that self which fears for itself, and is of death, not of life. But she was one of those who, when they discover a thing in them that is wrong, take refuge in the immediate attempt to set it right—with the conviction that God is on their side to help them.

She went down to the house to get everything she could think of to make the place more comfortable. It would be a long time before the patient could be moved. Poor Amy! She was but the shadow of her former self, but a shadow very pretty and pleasant to look at. Hester's heart was sore to think of such a bright, good, honest creature married to a man like her brother. She was sure Amy could have done nothing to be ashamed of. Where there was blame, it must be Corney's.

It was with feelings still strangely mingled of hope and dismay that, having carried everything she could for the time up to Amy, she gave herself to the comfort of her other guests.

Left alone in London, Corney had gone idly roaming about the house when another man would have been reading or doing something with his hands. Eventually he discovered the door in the wainscot of the low room and the room to which it led. Contriving often to meet Amy, he had grown rapidly more and more fond of her—became indeed as much in love with her as was possible to him. Without a notion of denying himself anything he desired and could possibly have, he determined she should be his, but from fear as well as the deceit so natural to his being, he avoided the direct way of winning her. He judged that the straight line would not be the shortest: his father would never consent to his marriage with a girl like Amy. Ultimately he contrived to persuade her to a private marriage—contrived also to prevent her from communicating with his sister.

His desire to please her, and his passion for showing off, soon brought him into straits for money. He could not ask his father for any; he would have insisted on knowing how it was that he suddenly found his salary so insufficient. He went on and on, changing nothing of his habits, until he was positively without a shilling. Then he borrowed, and went on borrowing small sums from those about him, till he was ashamed to borrow more. The next thing was to *borrow* a trifle of what was passing through his hands in the bank. He was only borrowing, and from his own uncle. After all, his uncle had so much, and he was in such straits! It was the height of injustice! Of course he would replace it long before anyone knew!

Thus, by degrees, the poor weak creature, deluding himself with excuses, slipped into the consciousness of being a thief. There are some, I suspect, who fall into vice from being so satisfied with themselves that they scorn to think it possible they should ever do wrong.

He went on taking and taking, until, at last, he was obliged to confess to himself that there was no possibility of making restoration before the time came when his *borrowing* was discovered as out-and-out embezzlement. Then, in a kind of cold despair, he grabbed a large sum and left the bank an unconvicted felon. What story he told Amy, who was now his wife, I do not know. But once convinced of the necessity for concealment, she was as careful as he. He brought her to their refuge by the back way. She came and went only through the cellar, and knew no other entrance. When they found that, through Amy's leaving the door unlocked when she went out to shop, others had taken refuge in the cellar, they dared not, for fear of attracting attention to themselves, warn them off the premises.

—Thirty-Five —

Amy and Corney

The Frankses remained at rest until the funeral was over, and then Hester encouraged the father and sons to go out and follow their calling while she and the mother did what could be done for the ailing baby, who could not linger long behind Moxy. And the very first day, though they went out with heavy hearts and could hardly have played with much spirit, they brought home more money than any day for weeks before.

The same day lord Gartley called, but was informed by Sarah, who opened the door but a crack, that the smallpox was in the house and that she could admit no one but the doctor. She said that her young mistress was perfectly well, but was in attendance upon the sick and could and would see nobody. So his lordship was compelled to go without seeing her, not without a haunting doubt that she did not want to see him.

The major also made his appearance that day. Sarah gave him the same answer, adding by her mistress's directions that in the meantime there was no occasion to make further inquiry about Mr. Cornelius. It was all—as Sarah put it—explained, and her mistress would write to him.

But what was Hester to tell her father and mother? Until she knew with certainty the fact of her marriage, she shrank from mentioning Amy, and for the present it was impossible to find out anything from Cornelius. She decided to simply write that she had found him, but very ill, that she would take the best care of him she could, and as soon as he was able to be moved, she would bring him home.

The big room was, for the time, given over to the Frankses. The wife kept everything tidy, and they managed things their own way. Hester inquired about their needs now and then, to be sure they had everything necessary, but left them to provide for themselves.

She did her best to help Amy without letting her brother suspect her presence, and gradually she made the room more comfortable for them. Corney had indeed taken a good many things from the house, but had been careful not to take anything Sarah would miss.

He was covered with the terrible infection, and if he survived, which often seemed doubtful, would probably be much changed in appearance, for Amy could not keep his hands from his face. In small trifles is the lack of self-control manifested, and its consequences are sometimes grievous.

He began at last to recover, but it was long before he could be treated in any way other than as a child—he was so feeble and unreasonable. The first time he saw and knew Hester, he closed his eyes and turned his head away as if he would have no more of such an apparition. She left, but watched to see him, in his own sly way, looking through half-closed lids to know whether she was gone. When he saw Amy where Hester had stood, his face beamed. "Amy," he said, "come here." When she came, he took her hand and laid it on his cheek, little knowing what a disfigured cheek it was.

"Thank God!" thought Hester. She had never seen him look so loving toward anyone, despite his disfigurement.

She took care not to show herself again till he was more accustomed to the idea of her presence.

The more she saw of Amy the better she liked her. She treated her patient with good sense, and was so carefully obedient to Hester and the doctor that she rose every day in Hester's opinion, as well as found a yet deeper place in her heart.

His lordship wrote, making apology for anything he had said, from anxiety about one he loved. He would gladly talk the whole matter over with her as soon as she would allow him to. For his part, he had no doubt that her good sense would eventually convince her of the reasonableness of all he had sought to urge upon her. As soon as she was able, and judged it safe to admit a visitor, his aunt would be happy to call upon her. For the present, as he knew she would not admit him, he would content himself with frequent and most anxious inquiries after her, reserving discussion for a happier, and, he hoped, not very distant time.

Hester smiled a curious smile at the prospect of a call from Miss Vavasor. Was she actually going to plead her nephew's cause?

As her brother grew better and things became a little easier, the thought of lord Gartley came oftener, with something of the old feeling for the man himself, but mingled with sadness and a strange pity. She would never have been able to do anything for him!

If God cannot save a man by all his good gifts, a woman's giving of herself as a slave to his lower nature can only make him all the more unredeemable. But the withholding of herself *may* do something—may at least, as the years go on, wake in him some sense of what a fool he had been. The man who would go to the dogs for lack of the woman he fancies will go to the dogs when he has her too—and may possibly drag her to the dogs with him.

Hester at last began to see something of this. She recalled how she had never once gained from him a worthwhile reply to anything she had said. She had, in her foolishness, supplied from her own imagination the defective echoes of his response! She saw many things otherwise than before. She loved the man enough to die for him, but it was quite another thing to marry him, And now that her spirit was awakened toward the truer nature of things, it was Cornelius, no longer Vavasor, who occupied her thoughts. His dear, good little wife was doing all she could for him, but it would take sister and mother and all to save him! She could not do so much for him as Amy now, but by and by there would be his father to meditate with—to that she would give her energy!

But his poor mother! Would she even recognize him—so terribly scarred and changed? He was young, and might in time grow more like his old self, but for now he was anything but pleasant to look at. Corney had always been one who took pleasure in his own looks, regarding himself as superior on most grounds, and particularly on that of good looks. But now he could not but admit that he was anything but handsome to behold. It was a pain that in itself could do little to cast out the evil spirit that possessed him. But it was something that the evil spirit, while it remained in him, should be deprived of one source of its nourishment. It was a good thing that from any cause, the transgressor should find his ways hard. After his first look at himself, he threw the mirror from him and burst into tears, which he did not even try to conceal.

It was notable that from that time he was more dejected and less peevish. Still Hester found it difficult to bear with his remaining peevishness and bad temper, knowing what he had made of himself, and that he knew she must know it. But at such hard moments she had the good sense to leave him to the soothing ministrations of his wife. Amy never set herself against him. First of all she would show him that she understood what was troubling him, then would say something sympathetic or coaxing, and always had her way with him. She had the great advantage that he had not yet once quarrelled with her.

That gave a ground of hope for her influence with him that his sister had long lost. God had made Amy so that she had less trouble from selfishness than most people. Hester had far more trouble than Amy in conquering her self-assertiveness. In Hester it was, no doubt, associated with a loftier nature, and the harder victory would have its greater reward, but until finally conquered it would continue to hinder her walk in the true way. So Hester learned from the sweetness of Amy, as Amy from the unbending principles of Hester.

She at last made up her mind that she would take Cornelius home without giving her father the opportunity of saying he should not come. She would presume that he must go home after such an illness. The result she would let take care of itself, even though the first meeting between father and son could in no case be a happy one.

With gentle watchfulness she regarded Amy, and was more and more satisfied that she could have had no hand in the wrongdoing. But she could not believe that had Amy known before she married him what kind of person Cornelius was, she would have given herself to him. It hardly occurred to her how nearly the man she had once accepted stood on the same level of manhood. But Amy was the wife of Cornelius, and that made an eternal difference. Her duty was as plain as Hester's—and the same—to do the best for him!

When he was able to be moved, Hester brought them into the house, and placed them in a comfortable room. She then moved the Frankses into the room they had left, giving it over to them, for a time at least. With their own entrance through the cellar, they would be able to live there as they wished. Hester's only stipulation was that they were to let her know if they found themselves in any difficulty. And now, for the first time in her life, Hester wished she had some financial resources of her own so she might act with freedom.

—Thirty-Six —

Miss Vavasor

About three weeks after lord Gartley's call, during which he had left a good many of his calling cards in Addison Square, Hester received the following letter from Miss Vavasor:

My dear Miss Raymount:
I am very anxious to see you, but fear it is hardly safe to call upon you yet. I do not want to willingly be the bearer of infection into my own circle, but I must communicate with you somehow, for your own sake as well as Gartley's, who is pining away for lack of the sunlight of your eyes. I will leave the matter entirely in your judgment. If you tell me you consider yourself out of quarantine, I will come to you at once. If you do not, will you propose something, for we must meet.

Hester pondered the matter well before returning an answer. She replied that it was impossible to say there was no danger, for her brother, who had been ill, was still in the house, too weak for the journey to Yrndale. She would rather suggest that they meet in some quiet corner of one of the parks. She need hardly add that she would take every precaution against carrying infection.

The proposal proved acceptable to Miss Vavasor. She wrote suggesting a time and place. Hester agreed, and they met.

Hester appeared on foot. Miss Vavasor, who had remained seated in her carriage, got down as soon as she saw her, and advanced to meet her with a smile. She was perfect in surface hospitality.

"How long is it now," she began, "since you saw Gartley?"

"Three weeks or a month," replied Hester.

"I am sadly afraid you cannot be much of a lover, not to have seen him for so long and still look so contented," smiled Miss Vavasor, with gently implied reproach.

"When one has one's work to do—" Hester began.

"Ah, yes!" returned Miss Vavasor, not waiting for the rest of the sentence. "I understand you have some peculiar ideas about work. That kind of thing is spreading very much in our circle, too. I know many ladies who visit the poor. The custom came in with these women's-rights people. I fear they will upset everything before long. No one can tell where such things will end."

"No," replied Hester. "Nothing has ever stopped yet. We know nothing about the ends of things—only the beginnings."

"You and Gartley had a small misunderstanding, he tells me, the last time you met," said Miss Vavasor after a short pause.

"I think not," answered Hester, "at least I think I understood him very well."

"My dear Miss Raymount, you must not be offended with me. I am an old woman, and have had to soothe over differences that had got in the way of the happiness of many couples. I am not boasting when I say I have had considerable experience in that sort of thing."

"I do not doubt it," said Hester. "What I do doubt is that you have had any experience of the sort necessary to set things right between lord Gartley and myself. The fact is, for I will be perfectly open with you, that I saw then—for the first time plainly—that to marry him would be to lose my liberty."

"Not more than every woman does who marries, my dear."

"Except that he would expect me to turn away from obeying a higher calling even than the natural calling of a woman to marriage."

"I am not aware of any higher calling."

"I am. God has given me gifts to use for my fellow-man, and use them I must until he, not man, stops me. That is my calling."

"But you know that of necessity a woman must give up many things when she accepts the position of a wife, and possibly the duties of a mother."

"I would heartily acknowledge the natural claims upon a wife or mother."

"But one of the duties of a wife is the claim society has upon her."

"I could never subject myself to a code of laws assumed by society, not merely opposed to the work for which I was made, but to the laws of all human relations."

"I do not quite understand you," said Miss Vavasor.

"Well, for instance," returned Hester, "a mother in your class often considers the duties she owes to society paramount even to those of a mother. Because of them, she entrusts her children in the nursery to the care of other women, not always of the highest intelligence or character."

"Not knowingly," said Miss Vavasor. "We are all liable to mistakes."

"But God has given the charge of children to mothers and fathers, not hirelings."

Miss Vavasor began to think it scarcely desirable to bring a woman of such levelling opinions into their quiet circle. She would be preaching next that women were wicked who did not nurse their own brats! But she would be faithful to Gartley!

"To set up as reformers would be to have the whole hive about our ears," she said.

"That may be," replied Hester, "but it does not apply to me. I keep the beam out of my own eye which I have no hope of pulling out of my neighhour's. I do not belong to your set."

"But you are about to belong to it, I hope."

"I hope not."

"You are engaged to marry my nephew."

"Not irrevocably, I trust."

"You should have thought of all that before you gave your consent. Gartley thought you understood. Certainly our circle is not one for saints."

"I thought I had done and said more than was necessary to make Gartley understand my ideas of what was required of me in life. I thought he sympathized with me and even that he would be what help to me he could. Now I find instead that he never believed I meant what I said, but all the time intended to put a stop to the aspiration of my life—ministry to the poor—the moment he had it in his power to do so."

"Ah, my dear young lady, you do not know what love is!" said Miss Vavasor, as if *she* knew what love was. "A woman really in love," she went on, "is ready to give up everything, yes, my dear, *everything*, for the man she loves. She who is not equal to that does not know what love is."

"Suppose he should prove unworthy of her?"

"That would be nothing, positively nothing. If she had once learned to love him, she would see no fault in him."

"*Whatever* faults he might have?"

"Whatever faults. Love has no second thoughts. A woman who loves gives herself to her husband to be moulded by him."

"I fear that is the way men think of us," said Hester sadly. "With all my heart I say a woman ought to be ready to die for the man she loves—she cannot really love him if she would not. But that she should agree with all his thoughts, feelings, and judgments, even those that she would despise in others, is to me something no true woman could do who had not first lost her reason."

"I see," Miss Vavasor concluded inwardly, "she is one of the strong-minded who think themselves superior to any man. Gartley will be well rid of her—that is my conviction! I think I have done nearly all he could require of me."

"I tell you honestly," continued Hester, "I love lord Gartley so much that I would gladly yield my life to do him any worthy good. Of course I would do that to redeem any human creature from the misery of living without God. Perhaps I would even marry lord Gartley if only I knew that he would not try to prevent me from being the woman I ought to be and have to be. But I could never marry one who opposed my being what I ought to be, what I desire, determine, and with God's help will be! Certainly a wife must love her husband grandly—passionately. But there is one to be loved immeasurably more grandly, even *passionately*—he whose love creates all other loves."

"Heavens!" exclaimed Miss Vavasor to herself, "what an extravagant young woman! She won't do for us!"

But what she said to Hester was, "Don't you think, my dear, all that sounds a little—just a little extravagant? You know as well as I do that that kind of thinking is out-of-date—does not belong to today's world. Nothing will ever bring in that kind of thing again. It is all very well to go to church, but really it seems to me that such extravagant notions about religion must have a great deal to do with the present sad state of affairs."

"What do you take God for, a priest?" said Hester. "Was Jesus Christ a priest. What did he mean when he said that whoever loved anyone else more than him was not worthy of him? Or do you confess the ideas of 'religion,' as you call it, true—but then say they are of no consequence? If you do not care about what God wants of you, I can simply say that I care about nothing else. And if ever I should change, I hope he will soon teach me better—whatever sorrow may be necessary for me to that end. I desire not to care a straw about anything he does not care about."

"It is very plain at least," said Miss Vavasor, "that you do not love my nephew as he deserves to be loved. You have very different ideas from such as were taught in my girlhood concerning the duties of wives. A woman, I used to be told, was to fashion herself for her husband, fit her life to his life, her thoughts to his thoughts, her tastes to his tastes."

The idea would have seemed absurd, to anyone really knowing the two, of a woman like Hester fitting herself into the mould of a man like lord Gartley. For what would be done with the quantity of her that would be left after his lordship's small mould was filled! Instead of walking on together in simple equality, in mutual honour and devotion, each helping the other to be better still, the ludicrous notion that Miss Vavasor held would have the woman—large and noble though she may be—come cowering after her husband— spiritual pigmy though he might be—as if he were the god of her life. Not the less if the woman be married to such a man, will it be her highest glory, by the patience of Christ, by the sacrifice of self, yea of everything save the will of God, to win the man, if he may by any means be won, from the misery of his self-seeking to a noble shame of what he now delights in.

"You are right," said Hester. "I do not love lord Gartley sufficiently for that. Thank you, Miss Vavasor. You have helped me come to the thorough conviction that there could never have been any real union between us. Can a woman love with the truest love a man who does not care that she should attain to the perfect growth of her nature? *He* would have been quite content that I should remain forever the poor creature I am. He would not have sought to raise me above myself. The man I shall love as I could love must be a greater man than that. No! I will be a woman and not a countess!— I wish you good morning, Miss Vavasor."

She held out her hand. Miss Vavasor drew herself up and looked with cold annihilation into her eyes. The warm blood rose from Hester's heart to her brain, but she quietly returned her gaze. It seemed minutes where only seconds passed. Hester smiled at last and said,

"I am glad you are not going to be my aunt, Miss Vavasor. I am afraid I would cause you nothing but grief."

"Thank goodness, no!" cried Miss Vavasor, with a slightly hysterical laugh. Unused to having such a strong, full, pure look fixed fearlessly upon her without defiance, it had unnerved her. Notwithstanding her educated self-command, she felt cowed before the majesty of Hester. She now had to go back to her nephew and confess that she had utterly failed where she had expected an easy victory. She had to tell him that his lady was the most peculiar, most unreasonable young woman she had ever had to deal with, and that she was not only unsuited to him, but quite unworthy of him.

She turned and walked away, attempting a show of dignity but showing only haughtiness—an adornment only the possessor does not recognize as counterfeit. Then Hester turned and walked in the opposite direction, feeling that one portion of her history was at an end.

She did not know that she was constantly attended at some distance by a tall, portly gentleman of ruddy complexion and military bearing. He had seen her interview with Miss Vavasor and had beheld with delight the unmistakable signs of serious difference that culminated in their parting.

Since coming to London with Hester he had, as far as possible, kept guard over her, and had known a good deal more of her goings and comings than she was aware of—all with completely unselfish devotion. He was willing to follow at a distance, ready to intervene at any moment when intervention may have proved desirable. She had let him know that she had found her brother, that he was very ill, and that she was helping to nurse him, but she had not yet asked his help. As if in obedience to orders, therefore, he did not even now call on her. But the next day he found a summons waiting for him at his club.

Thinking it better to prepare him for what she was about to ask of him, Hester mentioned in her note that in a day or two she was going to Yrndale with her brother and his wife.

"Marriage and embezzlement!" exclaimed the major when he read it. "This complicates matters. Poor devil! If he were not such a confounded ape, I should pity him! But the smallpox and a wife may perhaps do something for him!"

When he reached the house Hester received him warmly, and at once made her request that he would go with them. He agreed immediately, but thought she had better not say he was coming, as under the circumstances he would not receive a proper welcome.

—Thirty-Seven —

Mr. Christopher

On the last Sunday evening before she was to leave for Yrndale, Hester had gone to see a poor woman in a house she had not been in before. Walking up the dismal stair, dark and dirty, she heard a moaning from a room the door of which was a little open. She peeped in, and saw on a low bed a poor woman, old, yellow, and wrinkled, apparently at the point of death. Her throat was bare, and she saw the muscles of it knotted in the struggle for life.—Is not death the victorious struggle for life?

She was not alone—a man knelt by her bedside, his arm under the pillow to hold her head higher, and his other hand clasping hers.

"The darkness! the darkness!" moaned the woman.

"Are you lonely?" said the voice of the man, low and broken with sympathy.

"All, all alone," sighed the woman.

"I can do nothing for you. I can only love you."

"Yes, yes," said the woman hopelessly.

"You are slipping away from me, but my master is stronger than me and can help you yet. He is not far from you, though you can't see him. He loves you too, and only wants you to ask him to help you. He can cure death as easy as any other disease."

No reply came for a moment. Then came the cry,

"Oh, Christ, save me!"

Suddenly Hester was seized with a sudden impulse—she thought afterwards the feeling of it might be like what men and women of old had when the Spirit of God came upon them. It seemed she had not intended song when the sounds coming from her mouth entered her ears. The words she uttered were those and no more, over and over again, which the poor dying woman had just spoken: "O Christ, save me!" But the song-sounds in which they were lapt and with which they came winged from her lips, were as an outpouring of her whole soul. They seemed to rise from some eternal deep within her, yet not to be of her making. She was as in the immediate presence of Christ, pleading with him for the consolation and strength which his poor dying creature so sorely needed.

The holy possession lasted but a minute or so and left her without further words. She turned away and continued up the stairs.

"The angels! the angels! I'm going now!" said the woman feebly.

"The angel was praying to Christ for you," said Christopher. "Oh, living brother, save our dying sister."

"Oh, Christ, save me!" she murmured again, and they were her last words.

Christopher laid the body gently back on the pillow. A sigh of relief passed from his lips and he went from the room to give notice of the death. He must go on to help the living!

Such may seem nothing but empty religious sentiment to the man of this world. But when the inevitable Death has him by the throat, when he lies like that poor woman, lonely in the shadow, though his room be crowded with friends and possessions, whatever his theories about the afterlife, it may be an awful hour in which no one but Christ will be able to comfort him.

Hester's heart was full when she found the woman she went to see, and she was able to speak as she had never spoken before. She never troubled her poor with any of the theories of salvation, which, right or wrong, are not the things to be presented for men's reception—now any more than in the days of the first teachers who knew nothing of them. They serve but to obscure the vision of the live brother in whom men must believe to be lifted out of their evil and brought into the air of truth and the room for growing deliverance.

Hester spoke of Christ, the friend of men, who came to save every one by giving him back to God, as one gives back to a mother the stray child who has run from her to escape obeying her.

The woman at least listened. And then she sang to her. But she could not sing as she had sung a little while before. One cannot have

222

or give the best always—not at least until the soul shall be always in its highest and best moods—a condition which may perhaps be on the way to us, though I am doubtful whether the created will ever stand continuously on the apex of conscious existence. Perhaps we may be full of God always and yet not always full of the ecstasy of good, or always able to make it pass in sweet splendours from heart to heart.

Hester was walking home when, passing through a court on her way, she heard the voice of a man, which she again recognized as that of Mr. Christopher. Glancing about her she discovered that it came from a room half under ground. She went to the door. A little crowd of dirty children was making noise around it, and she could not hear all of what was going on, but she did hear enough to tell that the doctor was speaking to a small group of the poor, pleading with his fellows not to sink in misery but to live and rejoice, even in their present state. She went in.

It was a low room, and though the crowd was not large, the air was stifling. The doctor stood at the far end. Some of his congregation were decently dressed, but most wore their ordinary clothes. Only a handful seemed to be listening to him. That the speaker was in earnest there could be no doubt. His eyes were glowing, his face was gleaming with a light of its own, and his gestures were full of meaning The whole rough appearance of the man was elevated into dignity. Simplicity and forgetfulness of himself were manifest in both carriage and speech, and he kept saying the simplest things to them about God's desire to love them. He told them that they were like orphan children, hungry in the street, raking the gutter for what they could get, while behind them stood a grand, beautiful house where their father lived, waiting for any one of them to turn and run in to him.

"You may say, why does he not send them a message," he was saying, "to tell them he is there waiting for them. But that is just what he does do. He is constantly sending out messengers to tell them to come in," he went on. "But they mostly laugh at them. 'It's not likely,' they say, 'a man like that would trouble his head about such as us, even if we were his children!' And are some of you thinking inside now, '*We* wouldn't do that! We should be only too glad to believe it'? But there's the rub. These children who won't go into the house are just like you—they won't do anything about it. Why, here I am, sent to you with this very message, and you fancy I am only talking without meaning. I am one of those who have been in the house and have found my father to be oh so grand! And I have come out again to tell you that if you go in, you will have the same kindness that I have had. All the servants of the house will rejoice over you with music and dancing—so glad that you have come home. But you will not take the trouble to go.

"There are certain things required of you when you go," he went on. "Perhaps you are too lazy or dirty in your habits to want to do such things. I have known some to refuse to scrape their shoes when they went in, and then complain loudly that they were refused admittance. A fine house it would be if they were allowed to run in and out as they pleased! In a few months the grand beautiful house would be as wretched and dirty as the houses they live in now. Those are the people that keep grumbling about not being rich. They want to loaf about and drink and be a nuisance to everybody. They think it hard they should not be able to do just as they please with everything that takes their fancy, when they would do nothing but break and spoil it, and make it no good to anybody. Their father, who can do whatever he sees fit, is not one to let such disagreeable children work what mischief they like! He is a better father than that. And the day is coming when, if he can't get them to mind him any other way, he will put them where they will be ten times more miserable than ever they were at the worst time of their lives, and make them mind. Out of the same door whence came the messengers to ask them in, he will send dogs and bears and lions and tigers and wild cats out upon them.

"I daresay, some of you will say, 'But that's not the sort of thing we care about. We know you're just dressing up religion in your little fable about the beautiful house, and we don't need it.' I know this is not the kind of thing some of you care for. I know the kind of thing you *do* care for—low, dirty things. You are like a child that prefers mud and the gutter to all the beautiful toys in a grand shop. But though these things are not the things you want, they are the things you need. And the time will come when you will say, 'Ah, what a fool I was not to look at the precious things and take them when they were offered me!'"

After about twenty minutes he ceased. Then he read a short hymn, repeating each verse before they sang it, for there was no other hymn-book than his own. It was the simplest hymn, Hester thought, she had ever heard. He began the singing himself to a well-known tune, but when he heard the voice of Hester take it up, he left the leading to her, and taking himself to the bass, did his part there. When they heard her voice the people all turned to look, and some began to whisper, but presently resumed the hymn.

When it was ended, he prayed for two or three minutes, not more, and sent them away. Being near the door, Hester went out with the first ones, and walked home, filled with pleasure in the thought of such preaching. She did not yet know that Christopher taught them there every Sunday, and that this sermon, if such it could be called, was but one wave in the flow of a great river.

As she thought, Hester, like the true soul she was, turned to the questioning of herself—how much of her own self was awake? Had she been obedient only to that she had been taught, or obedient to the God himself? Of one thing she could be sure—that she had but the faintest knowledge of him whom to know is life eternal.

She was near the turning that led to the square when she heard a quick footstep behind her, and was presently overtaken by Mr. Christopher.

"I was so glad to see you come in!" he said. "It made me able to speak all the better, for I was then sure of some sympathy in the spiritual air. It is not easy to go on when you feel all the time a doubt whether anyone is hearing your words."

"I do not see," said Hester, "how anyone could misunderstand what you were saying."

"Ah!" he returned, "the one incomprehensible thing is ignorance. To understand why another does not understand seems to me beyond the power of our humanity. I have been trying now for a good many months to teach these people, but I am not sure a single thought has passed from my mind to theirs. I sometimes wonder if I am just beating the air. But I must tell you how your singing comforted the poor woman at whose door you stopped this afternoon. I saw it in her face. She thought it was the angels. And it was one angel, for did not God send you? She died just a minute or two later."

They walked some distance before either spoke again.

"I was surprised," said Hester at length, "to find you taking the clergyman's part as well as the doctor's."

"I hope I took no clergyman's part," returned Christopher. "I took but the part of a human being, bound to share with his fellows. What could make you think so? Did I preach like a clergyman?"

"Not very," she answered.

"I am glad of that," he returned. "Our Lord was a layman. My experience with most of society's clergy has resulted in mere and simple contempt. I have another master."

"But if anybody and everybody should be at liberty to preach, how are we to have any assurance what kind of doctrine will be preached?"

"We must go without it.—I am aware that there are many uneducated preachers who move the classes the clergy cannot touch. Their preaching has far more visible effect, I know, than mine."

"Why do you not then preach like them?"

"I would not if I could, and could not if I would. I do not believe one half the things either the clergy or these lay-preachers say."

"But you imply they are doing more good. How can they do good if what they say is not true?"

"I did not say they did good—about that I cannot tell. That may need centuries to determine. I said they moved people more than many of the clergy. The fundamental element of what they say is mostly true, only the forms they express it in contain much that is false, which is true of all preachers in all churches, lay and clergy. For myself, I cannot preach many of the accepted doctrines because I do not believe them. If I did believe them they would take from me the heart to preach."

"Can it be," said Hester, "that falsehood is more powerful than truth—and for truth too?"

"By no means, though it may *move* people more visibly. Many false doctrines work powerfully on the emotions.. But a falsehood has in itself no power but for evil. It is the spiritual truth clothed in the partially false form that is powerful. Clearer truth will follow in the wake of it, and cast the false forms out—they serve but to make a place of seeming understanding in ignorant minds, wherein the truths themselves may lie and work with their own might. But if what I teach be nearer the truth, even if it be harder to get in, it will in the end work more truth. In the meantime I say God-speed to every man who honestly teaches what he honestly believes. Paul was grand when he said he would rejoice that Christ was preached, from whatever motive he might be preached. If you say those people, though contentious, may have preached good doctrine, I answer— Possibly, for they could not have preached much of what is called doctrine now-a-days. If they preached theories of their own, they were teachers of lies, for they were not true men, and the theories of an untrue man cannot be true. But they told something about Christ, and of that Paul was glad."

Some may wonder that Hester, having got so far as she had, should need to be told such things. But she had never had occasion to think about them before, though the truth wrought out in her life had rendered her capable of seeing them the moment they were put before her.

"I am very interested," she said. "Your profession has to do with the bodies of men, but you seem to care more for their souls."

"I began to study medicine that I might have a good, ostensible reason for going about among the poor. It was not primarily from the desire to alleviate their sufferings, but in the hope of starting them on the way toward victory over all evil. I saw that the man who brought them physical help had a chance with them such as no clergyman ever would.

"I fear I have not done much. I say to myself that perhaps I may have done something. So I will try on, helping God as the children help the father.—You know that grand picture, on the ceiling of the pope's chapel, of the making of Adam?"

"Michaelngelo's?—Yes."

"You must have noticed then how the Father is accompanied by a crowd of young ones—come to help him to make Adam, I always think. The poet has there, consciously or not, hit upon a great truth—it is the majesty of God's great-heartedness, and the majesty of man's destiny, that every man must be a fellow-worker with God. I want to help God with my poor brothers."

"How well I understand you!" said Hester. "But would you mind telling me how you first began? I started thinking of these things because I saw how miserable so many people were, and longed to do something to make life better for them."

"That was not quite the way with me," replied Christopher. "In the first place, you may suppose I could not have followed my wishes if I did not have money. I did have a good deal—left me by my grandfather. My father died when I was a child, I am glad to say."

"Glad to say!" repeated Hester in surprise.

"Yes. If he had lived, he may have followed in my grandfather's footsteps. Not that my grandfather was considered a bad man. On the contrary, he stood high in the world's opinion. When he died and left me his money, it was necessary that I look into his business affairs, for it was my mother's wish that I should follow it. In the course of my investigation I came across things which I considered to be dishonest in the way the business had been run. And where there had been wrong, I felt there must be atonement, restitution. I could not look on the money that had been left me as mine, for part of it at least, I cannot say how much, ought not to be mine at all.

"Gradually it grew clearer to me that there could be no real good but oneness with the will of God—that man's good lay in becoming what the inventor of him meant in the inventing of him—to speak after the fashion of man's making. Continuing to think about it all, and reading my New Testament, I came to see that, if the story of Christ was true, the God that made me was inconceivably lovely, and that the perfection, the very flower of existence, must be to live the heir of all things, at home with the Father.

"Next, mingled inextricably with my resolve about the money, came the perception that my fellow-beings, my brothers and sisters of the same father, must be, next to the father himself, the very atmosphere of life, and that perfect misery must be to care only for one's self. With that there woke in me such a love and pity for my people, my own race, my human beings, my brothers and sisters, whoever could hear the word of the father of men, that I felt the only thing worth giving the energy of a life to, was the work that Christ gave himself to—the delivery of men out of their lonely and mean devotion to themselves, into the glorious liberty of the sons of God, whose joy and rejoicing is the rest of the family.

"Then I saw that here the claim upon my honesty, and the highest calling of man met. I saw that were I as free to do with my grandfather's money as it was possible for man to be, I could in no other way use it altogether worthily than in aiding to give outcome, shape and operation to the sonship and brotherhood in me. I have not yet found how best to use it all, and I will do nothing in haste, which is the very opposite of divine, and sure to lead astray. But I keep thinking in order to find out, and it will continue to be revealed to me. God who has laid the burden on me will enable me to bear it until he shows me how to unpack and disperse it.

"Therefore, I spent a portion in further study, and especially the study of medicine. I could not work miracles; I had not the faith necessary to that, if such is now to be had, but God might be pleased I should heal a little by the doctor's art. So doing I should do yet better, and learn how, to spend the money upon humanity itself, repaying to the race what had been wrongfully taken from its individuals to whom it was impossible to restore it, and should while so doing at the same time fill up what was left behind for me of the labours of the Master.

"That is my story. I now try to work steadily, without haste, and have this very day gotten a new idea that may have some true possibilities in it."

"Will you tell me what it is?" said Hester.

"I don't like talking about things before they are begun," answered Christopher.

"I know what I would do if I had money!" said Hester.

"You have given me the right to ask what—though perhaps not the right to an answer."

"I would have a house of refuge to which anyone might run for shelter or rest or warmth or food or medicine or whatever he needed. It should have no society or subscription or committee, but would be my own to use as God enabled me. It should be a refuge for the needy, those out of work, to the child with a cut finger. I would not take in drunkards or ruined speculators—at least not before they were very miserable indeed. The suffering of such is the only desirable consequence of their doing, and to save them from it would be to take from them their last chance."

"It is a lovely idea," said Christopher heartily. "One of my hopes is to build a small hospital for children in some lovely place, near some sad, ugly one. But I am in no hurry. Nothing worth calling good can or ever will be started full grown. The essential of any good is life, and the very body of created life, and essential to it, is growth. Small beginnings with slow growings need time to root themselves thoroughly—I do not mean in place nor yet in social regard, but in wisdom. Such even prosper by failures, for their failures are not too great to be rectified. God's beginnings are imperceptible, whether in the region of soul or of matter.

"Besides, I believe in no good done except in people—by personal operative presence of soul, body and spirit. God is the one only person, and it is our personality alone, so far as we have any, that can work with God's perfect personality. God can use us as tools, but to be a tool of, is not to be a fellow-worker with. How the devil would have laughed at the idea of a society for saving the world! But when he saw one take it in hand, one who was in no haste even to do that, one who would only do the will of God with all his heart and soul, and cared for nothing else, then indeed he might tremble for his kingdom!

"It is the individual Christians forming the church by their obedient individuality, that have done all the good done since men for the love of Christ began to gather together. It is individual fervour alone that can combine into larger flame. There is no true power but that which has individual roots. Neither custom nor habit nor law nor foundation is a root. The real roots are individual conscience that hates evil, individual faith that loves and obeys God, individual heart with its kiss of charity."

"I think I understand you. I am sure I do in part, at least," said Hester

They had unconsciously walked twice around the square as they talked, and had now a third time reached the house. He went in with her and saw his patient, then went home to an evening with his Greek New Testament.

—Thirty-Eight—

An Arrangement

Second causes are God's as much as first, and Christ made use of them as his father's way. It would be a sad world indeed if God's only means of making his presence known was interference, that is, miracle. The roundabout common ways of things are just as much his as the straight, miraculous ones—I incline to think *more* his, in the sense that they are plainly the ways he prefers. In all things that are, he is present—even in the evil we bring into the world, to foil it and bring good out of it. We are always disbelieving in him because things do not go as we intend and desire them to go. We forget that God has larger ends, even for us, than we can see, so his plans do not fit ours. If God were not only to hear our prayers, as he does ever and always, but to answer them as we want them answered, he would not be God our Saviour, but the ministering genius of our destruction.

Since her homecoming, Hester had not yet been to see Miss Dasomma because of the smallpox danger. But now she thought she might visit her friend. After telling her of herself and lord Gartley, Hester told her teacher that her brother Cornelius had been behaving very badly, and had married a young woman without letting them know. Her father and mother were yet unaware of the fact and she dreaded having to tell them of it. He had been very ill with smallpox and she was now planning to take them home. But she did not know what to do with his wife until after she had broken the matter to them since she knew her father would be very angry.

"Could I see the young lady?" asked Miss Dasomma thoughtfully.

"Surely, any time," replied Hester, "now that Corney is so much better."

Miss Dasomma called, and was so charmed with Amy that she proposed to Hester that Amy should stay with her.

Now came the painful necessity of breaking to the young wife that her husband had deceived her, and that, as a result, she must be parted from him for a while.

Had Cornelius not been ill and helpless, he would probably have refused to go home. But he did not venture a word of opposition to Hester's determination. Notwithstanding his idiotic pretence of superiority, he had a kind of thorough confidence in Hester. In his sickness something of the old childish feeling about her as a refuge from evil had returned to him, and he was now nearly ready to do whatever she pleased, trusting her to get him out of the scrape he was in.

"But now tell me, on your word of honour," she said to him that same night when she was alone with him, "are you really and truly married to Amy?"

She was delighted to see him blaze up in anger.

"Hester, you insult us both!" he said

"No, Cornelius," returned Hester, "I have a right to distrust you because of all that has happened. But I do not distrust Amy in any way."

At this Cornelius swore a solemn oath that Amy was as much his lawful wife as he knew how to make her.

"Then what is to be done with her when you go home? You cannot expect that she will be welcomed. I have not dared tell them of your marriage—only of your illness."

"I don't know. How should *I* know!" answered Cornelius with a return of his old manner. "I thought you would manage it for me! This cursed illness—"

"Cornelius!" said Hester, "this illness is the greatest kindness God could have shown you."

"Well, we won't argue about that!—Sis, you must get me out of this scrape!"

Hester's heart swelled at the sound of the old loving nursery word. She turned to him and kissed him.

"I will do what I honestly can, Cornelius," she said.

"All right!" replied Corney. "What do you mean to do?"

"Not to take Amy with us. She must wait till they know."

"Then my wife is only to be received on sufferance!"

"After what you have done, it is hardly any wonder that our father should be angry with you. It is possible he may refuse even to see you."

"Then I'm not going! Better stay here and starve if they won't receive my wife!"

"If so, I must at once tell Amy what you have done. She will have to know everything someday, but it ought to come from you, not me. You will never be fit for honest company till you have told your wife how you have deceived both her and your family."

Hester thought she must not let him fancy that things would now go back into the old grooves—that his crime would become a thing of no consequence and pass by, ignored and forgotten. Evil cannot be destroyed without repentance.

He was silent as one who had nothing to answer.

"So now," said Hester, "will you, or must I, tell Amy that she cannot go home with us, and why?"

He thought for a moment.

"I will," he said.

Hester left him and sent Amy to him. In a few minutes she returned. She had been weeping, but now looked quite in control of herself.

"Please, miss," she said—but Hester interrupted her.

"You must not call me *miss,* Amy," she corrected. "You must call me *Hester.* Am I not your sister?"

A gleam of joy shone from the girl's eyes, like the sun through red clouds.

"Then you have forgiven me!" she cried.

"No, Amy. I had nothing to forgive you of. You may have been foolish, but everybody can't always be wise. And now we must have time to set things straighter without doing more mischief, and you mustn't mind staying a little while with Miss Dasomma."

"You won't be too hard on him when he hasn't me to comfort him—will you, Hester?"

"I will think of my new sister who loves him," replied Hester. "But I love him too, Amy. Oh, Amy! you must be very careful over him. You must help him to become good, for that is the highest duty of everyone toward a neighbour, particularly of a wife toward a husband."

Amy was crying afresh, but there was no shadow of resentment in her weeping.

—Thirty-Nine —

Things at Yrndale

In the meantime things had been very gloomy at Yrndale. Mrs. Raymount was better in health but hardly more cheerful. She could not get over the sadness of what her boy had become. But the thing that most oppressed her was to see the heart of his father so turned from the youth. Cornelius had not been pleasant since he first began to come within sight of manhood. But she had always looked to the time when growing sense would prevail, and now this was the outcome of her hopes and prayers for him! Her husband went about sullen and listless. He wrote no more. How could one thus disgraced in his family presume to teach the world anything? How could he any longer hold his head up? Cornelius's very being cast doubt on all he had ever said or done!

He had been proud of his children. But now all was falling into ruin around him. For hours he would sit with his hands in his pockets, scarcely daring to think, for the misery of the thoughts that came crowding out the moment the smallest chink was opened in their cage. He had become short, I do not say rough, in his speech to his wife. He would break into sudden angry complaints against Hester for not coming home. The sight of the children was a pain to him. Though he had been told nothing of the cause of his parents' misery, Mark had sympathy and insight enough to perceive that something was badly amiss. He would sometimes stand and gaze at his father, but the solemn, far-off, starry look of the boy's eyes never seemed to disturb him. He loved his father as few boys love, and yet had a certain dread of him and discomfort in his presence, which he could not have accounted for, and which would vanish at once when he spoke to him.

He had never quite recovered from the effects of his near drowning. He had grown thinner and his food did not seem to nourish him. His being seemed slowly slipping away from its hold on the world. He was full of dreams and fancies, all of the higher order of things where love is the law. He spent many happy hours alone, seeming to the ordinary eye to be doing nothing, because his doing was with the unseen. When such as Mark die, we may well imagine them wanted for a special work in the world to which they go. Some of us may one day be ashamed of our outcry after our dead when we discover why they were called.

The mother looked at the child, but said nothing. Sorrow was now the element of her soul. Cornelius had destroyed the family heart.

Mark seldom talked about his brother. Before he went away he had begun to shrink from him a little, as with some instinct of an inward separation. He would stand a little way off and look at him as if he were a stranger in whom he was interested, and as if he himself were trying to determine what attitude to assume toward him. When he heard that he was seriously ill, the tears came into his eyes, but he did not speak.

To the mother, it seemed that the boy must be looking toward a region to which she herself had begun to look with longing. The way her husband took their grief made them no more a family, but a mere household. He brooded alone and said nothing. They did not share sorrow as they had shared joy.

At last came a letter from Hester saying that in two days she hoped to start with Corney to bring him home. The mother read the letter, and with a faded gleam of joy on her countenance, passed it to her husband. He took it, glanced at it, threw it from him, rose, and left the room. For an hour his wife heard him pacing up and down his study; then he took his hat and stick and went out. What he might have resolved to do had Corney been returning in good health, I do not know—possibly kick him out of the house for his impudence in daring to show his face there. But even this wrathful father could hardly turn from his sickly child—even if he was the greatest scoundrel under the sun. But that still could not make him acknowledge him! Swine were the natural companions of the prodigal, and the sooner he was with them the better! Truly the heart of the father had turned from his son. The Messiah came to turn the hearts of the fathers to their children. Strange it should have ever needed doing! But it needs doing still.

Gerald Raymount went walking through the pine woods on his hills, but there was now little satisfaction to be found in his land. He had taken honesty as a matter of course in his family. Were they not *his* children? Yet he had never known anything of what was going on in the mind of his son. He had never asked himself if his boy loved the truth. And now he was astonished to find *his* boy no better than the common sort of human animal!

But often an act of open disgrace is the quickest road toward repentance. There is little hope of the repentance and redemption of some until they have committed one or another of the many wrong things of which they are daily, through a course of unrestrained selfishness, becoming more and more capable.

Few seem to understand that the true end is not to keep their children from doing what is wrong, though that is on the way to it, but to render them incapable of doing wrong. While one is capable of doing wrong, he is no nearer right than if that wrong were done—not so near as if the wrong were done and repented of. Some minds are never roused to the true nature of their selfishness until having done some patent wrong, the eyes of the collective human conscience are fixed upon them. Doubtless in the disapproving crowd are many just as capable of the wrong as they, but the deeper nature in them, God's and not yet theirs shouts its disapproval, and the culprit feels it.

Happy is he if then at last he begins to turn from the evil itself, and thus repent! This Cornelius had not begun to do yet, but his illness, while perhaps it delayed the time when the thought of repentance should present itself, made it more likely the thought would be entertained when it did present itself.

The father came back from his lonely walk in no better frame of mind—just as determined that his son should no more be treated as a son. He could not refuse him shelter in his house for a time, but it should be on sufferance and from no right of sonship!

The heart of the mother, however, was longing after her boy, like a human hen whose chick has run from under her wing and come to grief. He had sinned, he had suffered, and was in disgrace.

The very things that made his father feel he could not speak to him again worked in the deeper nature of the mother in the opposite fashion. Was he unlovely?—she must love him the more! Was he selfish and repellent?—she must get the nearer to him! Everything was reason to her for love and more love. She would clasp him so close that evil should not touch him! Satan himself could not get at him with her whole mother-being folded round him! Now that sickness and shame had cast down his proud spirit, love would have room to enter and minister! The good of all evil is to make a way for love, which is essential good. Therefore evil exists, and will exist, until love destroys and casts it out.

Corney could not keep his mother out of his heart now! She thought there were ten things she could do for him now to one she could have done for him before! When, oh when would he appear, that her heart might go out to meet him!

—Forty —

The Return

The day came. It was fine in London. The invalid was carefully wrapped up for the journey. Hester, the major and Miss Dasomma followed the young couple to the station. There the latter received the poor little wife, and when the train was out of sight, took her home with her.

The major who got into the next carriage, at every stop ran to see if anything was wanted. When they reached the station, he got on the box of the carriage the mother had sent to meet them.

Thus Hester bore her lost sheep home—in little triumph and much anxiety. When they stopped at the door no one was on the outlook for them. The hall was not lighted and the door was locked.

The major rang the bell. Before the door was opened Hester had got down and stood waiting. The major took the youth in his arms and carried him into the dining-room, so weary that he could scarcely open his eyes. There seemed no light in the house, except the candle the man brought when he came to open the door.

Corney begged to be put to bed. "I wish Amy was here!" he murmured. Hester and the major were talking together.

Hester hurried from room to room and returned in a moment.

"I was sure of it," she whispered to the major. "There is a glorious fire in his room and everything is ready for him. The house is my father, but the room is my mother."

The major carried him easily up the stair—he had become so thin and light. The moment they were past the door of her room, out came the mother into the corridor, gliding pale and noiselessly after them. Hester looked around and saw her, but her mother laid a finger on her lips, and continued to follow without a word.

When they were in Corney's room, she came to the door, looked in, and watched them, but did not enter. Cornelius did not open his eyes. The major laid him down on the sofa near the fire. A gleam of it fell on his face. The mother drew a sharp quick breath and pressed her hands against her heart—there was his sin upon his face, branding him that men might know him.

But therewith came a fresh rush from the inexhaustible fountain of mother-love. She would have taken him into her anew, with all his sin and pain and sorrow, to clear away in herself brand and pollution, and bear him anew—even as God bears our griefs, and carries our sorrows, destroys our wrongs, taking their consequences on himself, and gives us the new birth from above. Her whole wounded heart seemed to go out to him in one trembling sigh, as she turned to go back to the room where her husband sat with hopeless gaze fixed on the fire.

She had but strength to reach the side of the bed, and fell senseless upon it. He started up with a sting of self-accusation—he had killed her, exacting from her a promise that by no word would she welcome the wanderer that night. For she would not have her husband imagine in his bitterness that she loved the erring son more than the father whose heart he had all but broken, and had promised. She was, in truth, nearly as anxious about the one as the other, for was not the unforgivingness of the one as bad—was it not even worse than the theft of the other.

Her husband lifted her, laid her on the bed, and proceeded to administer the restoratives he now knew better than any other how to employ. In a little while he was relieved, her eyelids began to tremble. "My baby!" she murmured, and the tears began to flow.

"Thank God!" said Mr. Raymount, and got her to bed.

But strange to say, for all his stern fulfilment of duty, he did not feel fit to lie down beside his wife. He would watch. She might have another bad turn!

From the exhaustion that followed excess of feeling, she slept. He sat watchful by the fire. She was his only friend, he said, and now she and he were no more of one mind! Never until now had they had difference!

Hester and the major got Corney to bed, and instantly he was fast asleep. The major arranged himself to pass the night by the fire;

Hester went to the adjoining room where she, too, was presently fast asleep. There was no gnawing worm of duty undone or wrong unpardoned in her bosom to keep her awake.

The night began differently with the two watchers. The major was troubled in his mind at what seemed the hardheartedness of the mother, for he loved her with a true brotherly affection. He had not seen her looking in at the door. He did not know the cause of her appearing so withdrawn.

He brooded long over the thing, but by degrees forgot her and fell to thinking about his own mother.

As the major sat thinking, the story came back to him which she had told him and his brothers, all now gone but himself, as they sat around her one Sunday evening in their room, about the boy who was tired of being at home, and asked his father for money to go away, and how his father gave it him, thinking it better he should go than grumble at the best he could give him. The boy grew naughty and spent his money in buying things that were not worth having, and in eating and drinking with greedy, coarse people till at last he had nothing left to buy food with and had to feed swine to earn something, and how at last he fell to thinking about going home.

It all came back to the major's mind just as his mother used to tell it—how the poor prodigal, ragged and dirty and hungry, had set out for home, and how his father had seen him coming a great way off and knew him at once, and ran out to meet him, and welcomed him and kissed him. True, the prodigal came home repentant, but the father did not wait to know that, but ran to meet him without condition.

As the major thus reflected, he kept coming nearer and nearer to the Individual lurking at the keyhole of every story. Only he had to go home. Otherwise, how was his father to receive him?

"I wonder," he said, "if when a man dies, that is counted as going home. I hardly think so, for that is something no man can help. I should find myself no better off than this young rascal when he goes home because he can't help it!"

The end of it was that the major, there in the middle of the night, got down on his knees and tried, as he had not done in years, to say the prayers his mother had taught him—speaking from his heart as if one was listening, one who, in the dead of the night, did not sleep, but kept wide awake lest one of his children should cry.

In his wife's room, Gerald Raymount sat on into the dead of the night. At last, as his wife continued to sleep soundly, he thought he would go down to his study and find something to turn his thoughts from his misery. None such had come to him as to his friend. He had been much more of a religious man than the major, but it was the *idea* of religion, and the thousand ideas it broods, more than the practice of it daily, that was his delight. He philosophized and philosophized well of the relations between man and his maker, of the necessity to human nature of a belief in a God, of the disastrous consequences of having none, and such like things. But having an interest is a very different thing from being in such a close relation with the father that the thought of him is an immediate and ever-returning joy and strength. He did not rejoice in the thought of the inheritance of the saints in light, as the inheriting of the nature of God, the being made partaker of the father's essential blessedness: he was far yet from that. He was so busy understanding with his intellect that he missed the better understanding of heart and imagination. He was always so pleased with the thought of a thing that he missed the thing itself—whose *possession,* not its thought, is essential. Thus when the trial came, it found him no true parent.

The youth of course could not be received either as clean-handed or as repentant. But love is at the heart of every right way, and essential forgiveness at the heart of every true treatment of the sinner. That the father should not have longed above all things for his son's repentance, that he should not have met even a seeming return, that he should have nourished resentment because the youth had sinned against his family, that he should think how to make him feel his scorn most keenly—this made the father a kind of paternal Satan who sat watching by the repose of the most Christian, because most loving, most forgiving, most self-forgetting mother. While she slept in the peace of a mother's love, he sat stirring up in himself fresh whirlwinds of indignation.

He rose, and treading softly, left the room and went to his study. The fire was not yet out. He stirred it and made it blaze, lighted his candles, took a book from a shelf, sat down, and tried to read. But it was no use. His thoughts were such that they could hold no

242

company with other thoughts. The world of his kind was shut out; he was a man alone because he was unforgiving and unforgiven. His soul slid into the old groove of misery, and so the night slid away.

The nominal morning, if not the dawn was near, when the door of the old library opened so softly that he heard nothing, and before he was aware of it, a child in a long white gown stood by his side. He started violently. It was Mark—but asleep. He had seen his mother and father more than usually troubled all day and their trouble had haunted him in his sleep. It had roused him without waking him from his dreams, and the Spirit of love had directed him to the presence of his father. He stood a little way from him, his face white as his dress, not a word coming from his mouth, silent, haunted by a smile of intense quiet, as of one who, being comforted, would comfort. There was also in the look a slight something like idiocy, for his soul was not precisely with his body. His thoughts, though concerning his father, were elsewhere. The circumstances of his soul and of his body were not the same, and so, being twinned, that is, divided, he was as one beside himself. His eyes, although open, evidently saw nothing, and thus he stood for a little time.

There had never been tender relations between Mark and his father like those between the boy and his mother and sister. His father was always kind to him, but between him and his boys he had let grow a kind of hard skin. Even when as tiniest children they came to be kissed before going to bed, he did not like the contact of their faces with his. No woman, and perhaps not many men will understand this, but it was always a relief to Mr. Raymount to have the nightly ceremony over. He thought there was nothing he would not do for their good, and I think his heart must in the main have been right toward them. But the clothes of his affections somehow did not sit easy on him, and there was a good deal in his behaviour to Cornelius that had operated unfavourably on the mind of the youth. Even Mark, although, as I have said, he loved him dearly, was yet a little afraid of him—never went to him with a confidence, never snuggled close to him, never sat down by his side to read his book in a heaven of twilight peace, as he would with his mother. He would never have gone to his father's room for refuge from sleeplessness.

Not recognizing his condition, his father was surprised and even annoyed, as well as startled: he was in no mood for such a visit. He felt also strangely afraid of the child, but could not have told why. Wretched about one son, he was dismayed at the nocturnal visit of the other. The cause was of course his wrong condition of mind. Lack of truth and its harmony in ourselves alone can make us miserable. There is a cure for everything when that is cured. No ill in our neighbours, if we be right in ourselves, will ever seem hopeless to us. But while we stand wrapped in our own selfishness, our neighbour may well seem incurable, for not only is there nothing in us to help their redemption, but there is that in ourselves, and cherished in us, which cannot be forgiven, but must be utterly destroyed.

There was an unnatural look, at the same time pitiful and lovely, about the boy as the father sat staring in gathering dread. He had nearly imagined him an angel of some doom.

Suddenly the child stretched out his hands to him and came close to his knee. Remembering how once before, when a tiny child, he had gone into a kind of fit when awakened suddenly, and anxious to avoid anything of the kind again, the father took the child softly in his arms, lifted him to his knees, and held him. An expression of supreme delight came over the boy's face—a look of absolute contentment mingled with hope. He put his thin hands together as if saying his prayers, but lifted his look to that of his father. How could his earthly father know that in his dreams, the boy thought he was sitting in the lap of his heavenly Father? And now his lips began to move, and a murmur came from them, which grew into barely audible words. He was indeed praying to his father, but a father closer to him even than the one upon whose knees he sat.

"Dear God," said the child, "I don't know what to do for papa and Corney. I am afraid they are both naughty. I would not say so to anybody but you, God, for papa is your little boy as I am his little boy, and you know all about it. I don't know what it is, and I think Corney must be more to blame than my dear papa, but when he came home to-night he did not go to papa, and papa did not go to him. They never said How do you do, or Good night to the other— and Corney very ill too. Oh, God, you are our big papa! Please put it all right. Please, dear God, make papa and Corney good. You know they must love each other. I will not pray a word more, for I know you will do just what I want. Goodbye, God. I'm going to bed now—down there. I'll come again soon."

With that he slipped from his father's knee, who did not dare to detain him, and walked from the room with slow, stately step.

By now the heart of the strong, hard man was swelling with the love that was at last coming awake. He could not weep, but felt dry, torturing sobs welling up from within him that seemed as if they would kill him. He rose to see the boy safely in bed.

In the corridor he breathed more freely. Through an old window, the bright moon, shining in peace with no one to see, cast a shadow in the shape of a cross, partly on the wall and partly on the floor. Severe Protestant as Gerald Raymount was, he found himself on his knees in the passage in front of the shadow—not praying, not doing anything he knew, but under some spiritual influence known only to God.

When the something had reached its height and the passion was over and his soul was clearing of the storm that had swept through it, he rose from his knees and went up to Mark's room, two stories higher. The moonlight was there too, and the father saw the child's white bed glimmering like a tomb.

He drew near, but through the gray darkness it was some seconds before he could rightly see the face of his boy. For a moment—I wonder how brief a moment is enough for a death-pang to feel eternal!—for an awful moment he felt as if he had lost him, that when he left the study he had been lifted straight to the bosom of the Father to whom he had prayed!

Slow through the dusk dawned his face. He had not then been taken bodily!—yet not the less was he gone! It was assuredly a dead face! But as he gazed in a fascination of fear, his eyes grew abler to distinguish, and he saw that he breathed.

The boy seemed in his usual health, and was sleeping peacefully—dreaming pleasantly, for the ghost of a smile glinted about his just parted lips. Then upon the father—who was not, with all his hardness, devoid of imagination—came the wonder of watching a dreamer. What might be going on within that brain? Splendid visions might be gliding through the soul of the sleeper—

his child, born of his body and his soul—and not one of them was open to him!

But how much nearer to him in reality was the child when awake and about the house? Even then, how much did he know of the thoughts, the loves, the imaginations, the desires, the aspirations that moved in the heart and the brain of the child? The boy was sickly—he might be taken from him before he had made any true acquaintance with him! He was just the sort of child to die young! Certainly he might see him in the other world, but the boy would have so few memories of him, so few associations with him, that it would be hard to tie the new to the old!

He turned away and went back to his room. There, with a sense of loneliness deeper than he had ever felt before, he went down on his knees to beg the company of God whose existence he had so often defended as if it were in danger from his creatures, but whom he had so little regarded as actually existent that he had not yet sought refuge with him. All the house was asleep—the major had long ended his prayers and was slumbering by the fire—when Raymount knelt before the living source of his life, and rose from his knees a humbler man.

—Forty-One —

A Sad Beginning

Toward morning Gerald Raymount went to bed and slept late. Alas, when he woke the old feeling had returned! How *could* he forgive the son that had so disgraced him!

Instead of going once again to the living strength, he began to try to persuade himself on philosophical grounds that the best thing would be to forgive his son, that it was the part of the wise man to abstain from harshness. But he had little success with himself. Anger and pride were too much for him. His breakfast was taken to him in the study, and there Hester found him an hour later, his food still untouched. He submitted to her embrace, but scarcely spoke and asked nothing about Corney. Hester felt sadly chilled and hopeless.

But she had begun to learn that one of the principal parts of faith is patience, and that the setting of wrong things right is so far from easy that not even God does it all at once. Time is nothing to him who sees the end from the beginning. He does not grudge thousands of years of labor. The things he cares to do for us require our co-operation, and that makes the great difficulty—we are such poor fellow-workers with him! All that seems to deny his presence and labour only, necessitates a larger theory of that presence and labour. Yet time lies heavy on the young especially, and Hester left the room with a heavy heart.

The only way in such stubbornnesses of the spirit, when we cannot feel that we are wrong, is to open our hearts, in silence and loneliness and prayer, to the influences from above—stronger for the right than any for the wrong, to seek the sweet enablings of the living light to see things as they are—as God sees them, who never is wrong because he has no selfishness. To rise humbly glorious above our low self, to choose the yet infant self that is one with Christ, who sought never his own but the things of his father and brother, is the redemption begun, and the inheritance will follow.

Mr. Raymount, like most of us, was a long way indeed from this yet. He strove hard to reconcile the memories of the night with the feelings of the morning—strove to realize a state of mind in which a measure of forgiveness to his son blended with a measure of satisfaction to the wounded pride he called paternal dignity.

How could he take his son to his bosom as he was? he asked—-but did not ask how he was to draw him to repentance! He did not think of the tender entreaty with which, by the mouths of his prophets, God pleads with his people to come back to him. If the father, instead of holding out his arms to the child he would entice to his bosom, folds them on that bosom and turns his back—expectant it may be, but giving no sign of expectancy, the child will hardly suppose him longing to be reconciled. No doubt there are times when and children with whom any show of affection is not only useless but injurious, tending merely to increase their self-importance. In such case the child should not see the parent at all. But it was the opposite reason that made it better Cornelius should not yet see his father—he would have treated him so that he would only have hated him.

For a father not to forgive is in truth far worse than for a son to need forgiveness. Such a father, as well as the son, will of course go from bad to worse unless he repents. The shifty, ungenerous spirit of compromise awoke in Raymount. He would be very good, very gentle, very kind to everyone else in the house. He would walk softly—he was not ready to walk uprightly—but he would postpone his forgiveness. He knew his feelings toward Corney were wearing out the heart of his wife—but he would not yield. There was little Mark, however. He would make more of him, know him better, and make the child know him better.

He went to see how his wife was. Finding that she was a trifle better, he found himself annoyed. In the selfishness of his misery, he looked upon her happiness at having her worthless son home as a lack of sympathy with himself. He did not allude to Cornelius, but said he was going for a walk, and went to find Mark—with a vague hope of consolation in the child who had clung to him so confidently in the night. He had forgotten it was not to him that the boy's soul had clung, but to the father of both of them.

Mark was in the nursery, as the children's room was still called. When Mark heard his father's step, he bounded to meet him. When his sweet moonlit rather than sunshiny face appeared at the door, the gloom on his father's yielded a little. The gleam of a momentary smile broke over it, and he said kindly:

"Come, Mark, I want you to go for a walk with me."

He was not doing the right thing in taking him out, but he was not thinking of that just now. He ought to have known that the boy was still too weak for anything to be called a walk. Neither was the weather fit for his going out. But absorbed in his own trouble, the father did not think of his weakness, and Hester was not there to object. So away they went. Mark was delighted to be his father's companion, never doubting all was right, and forgot his weakness as entirely as his father did.

With his heart in such a state, the father naturally had next to nothing to say to the boy, and they walked on in silence. But that did not affect Mark—he was satisfied to be with his father whether or not he spoke to him. From God he had learned not to dislike silence. Without knowing it, he was growing tired as they walked. When weariness at last became conscious, it came upon him all at once and poor Mark found he could scarcely put one leg in front of the other.

The sun had been shining when they started—a beautiful but not very warm spring sun. But now it had grown cloudy and rain threatened. They were in the middle of a bare, lonely moor, easily reached from the house but of considerable size in all directions, and the wind had begun to blow cold. Sunk in his miserable thoughts, all the more miserable now that he had relapsed into unforgiving unforgiveness, the father saw nothing of his child's failing strength, and kept trudging on. All at once he became aware that the boy was not by his side. He looked around, but he was nowhere to be seen. Alarmed, he stopped, turned, and called his name. The wind was blowing the other way and at first he heard no reply. He called again and this time thought he heard a feeble response. He retraced his steps rapidly.

Some four or five hundred yards back, he came to a hollow where Mark sat on a tuft of brown heather, looking as white as the moon in daylight.

His anxiety relieved, the father felt annoyed, and berated the little fellow for stopping.

"I wasn't able to keep up, papa," replied Mark. "So I thought I would rest a while, and meet you as you came back."

"You ought to have told me. I wouldn't have brought you if I had known you would behave so. Come, get up, we must go home."

"I'm very sorry, papa, but I don't think I can."

"Nonsense!"

"There's something wrong with my knee."

"Try," said his father, growing frightened again.

He obeyed and rose, but with a little cry dropped on the ground. He had somehow injured his knee and could not walk a step.

His father stooped to lift him.

"I'll carry you, Markie," he said.

"Oh, no, you must not papa! It will tire you!"

His father was already walking homeward with him.

The next moment Mark saw the waving of a dress.

"Oh!" he cried, "there's Hessie! She will carry me!"

"You little goose!" said his father tenderly. "Can she carry you better than I?"

"She is not stronger than you, papa, because you are a big man. But I think Hessie has more carry in her. She has such strong arms!"

Hester was running, and quite out of breath when she came near.

She had feared how it would be when she found her father had taken Mark for a walk. Her first feeling was of anger, for she had inherited not a little of her father's spirit. Indirectly the black sheep had roused evils in the flock unknown before. However, when she saw the boy's arms around his father's neck and his cheek laid against his, her anger left her and she was sorry and ashamed, even though from his face she could tell that Mark was suffering greatly.

"Let me take him, papa," she said.

But the father had no intention of giving up the child. Before he knew it, however, the boy had stretched out his arms to Hester and was out of his and into hers, and he was left to follow in distressed humiliation.

"He is too heavy for you, Hester," he said. "Surely it is my fault. I ought to bear the penalty!"

"It is no penalty—is it, Markie?" said Hester merrily.

"No, Hessie," replied Mark. "You don't know how strong Hessie is, papa!"

But by and by Hester found, with all her goodwill, that her strength was not quite up to it, and was obliged to yield him to her father. It was much to his relief, for a sense of moral weakness had invaded him as he followed his children—he was rejected by his family and had become a nobody in it.

When at length they reached home, Mark was put to bed and the doctor sent for.

—Forty-Two —

Mother and Son

In the meantime Cornelius kept his bed. The moment her husband was gone, his mother rose and hastened to her son! She tottered across his floor, threw herself on the bed beside him, and took him to her bosom.

With his mother Corney had never pretended to the same degree as with other people, and his behaviour to her was now more genuine than to any but his wife. He clung to her as he had never clung since his infancy. He felt that, let his father behave to him as he might, he had yet a home. All the morning he had been fretting, in the midst of Hester's kindest attentions, that he did not have his wife to do things for him as he liked them done. But now that Cornelius had his mother, he was more content, or rather less discontented—more agreeable in truth than she had known him since first he went to business. She felt greatly consoled, and he so happy with her that he began to wish that he had not a secret from her—for the first time in his life to be sorry that he was in possession of one. He grew even anxious that she should know it, but none the less anxious that he should not have to tell it.

A great part of the time when her husband supposed her asleep, she had been lying wide awake, thinking of the Corney she had lost, and the Corney that had come home to her instead. She was miserable over the altered looks of her disfigured child. The truest of mothers, with all her love for the real and indifference to outsides, can hardly be expected to reconcile herself with ease to a new face on her child—she has loved him in one shape, and now has to love him in another! It was almost as if she had received again another child—her own indeed, but taken from her the instant he was born and never seen by her since—whom, now she saw him, she had to learn to love in a shape different from that in which she had been accustomed to imagine him.

His sad, pock-marked face had a torturing fascination for her. It was almost pure pain, yet she could not turn her eyes from it. She reproached herself that it gave her pain, yet was almost indignant with the face she saw for usurping the place of her boy's beauty. At the same time very pity made her love with a new and deeper tenderness the poor spoilt visage, pathetic in its ugliness.

Not a word did she utter of reproach. His father was doing enough for both in that way! Every few minutes she would gaze intently in his face for a moment, and then clasp him to her heart as if seeking a shorter way to his presence than through the ruined door of his countenance.

Hester, who had never received from her half so much show of tenderness, could not help, like the elder brother in the divine tale, a little choking at the sight, but she soon consoled herself that the less poor Corney deserved it the more he needed it. The worst of it to Hester was that she could not with any confidence look on the prodigal as a repentant one. And if he was not, all this tenderness, she feared and with reason, would but blind him to his moral condition. But she thought also that God would do what he could to keep the love of such a mother from hurting, and it was not long before she was encouraged by a softness in Corney's look, and a humid expression in his eyes which she had never seen before.

Doubtless had he been as in former days, he would have turned from such over flow of love as womanish gush. But disgraced, worn out, and even to his own eyes an unpleasant object, he was not so much inclined to repel the love of the only one knowing his story who did not feel for him more or less contempt. Sometimes in those terrible half-dreams in the dark of early morning when suddenly waked by conscience to hold a tete-a-tete with her, he would imagine himself walking into the bank, and encountering the eyes of all the men on his way to his uncle, whom next to his father he feared—then find himself running for refuge to the bosom of his mother. She was true to him yet!

Slowly, slowly, something was working on him—now in the imagined judgment of others, now in the thought of his wife, now in the devotion of his mother. Little result was there for earthly eye, but the mother's perceived or imagined a difference in him. If only she could perceive something plain to tell her husband! If the ice that froze up the spring of his love would but begin to melt!

For to whom are we to go for refuge from ourselves if not to those through whom we were born into the world, and who are to blame for more or less of our unfitness for a true life?—"His father must forgive him!" she said to herself. She would go down on her knees to him. Their boy should not be left out in the cold! If he had been guilty, what was that to the cruel world so ready to punish, so ready to do worse! The mother still carried in her soul the child born of her body, preparing for him the new and better, the all-lovely birth of repentance unto life.

Hester had not yet said a word about her own affairs. No one but the major knew that the engagement to lord Gartley was broken. She did not want to add still another element of perturbance to the overcharged atmosphere. She would not add disappointment to grief.

In the afternoon the major, who was staying in the village two miles off, made his appearance. No sooner did he learn of Mark's condition than he insisted on taking charge of him. Hester could not but be pleased with the proposal, for she had so much else to see to. So the major took the position of head nurse, with Saffy for his aide and one of the servants for an orderly.

Hester's mind was almost constantly occupied with wondering how to let her father and mother know what they must know soon, and ought to know as soon as possible. She would tell her father first. Her mother should not know till he did. But she could not see how to begin. Everything seemed at a standstill.

So she waited, as she should. For much harm comes of the impatience that outstrips guidance. People are too ready to think *something* must be done, and forget that the time for action may not have arrived, that there is seldom more than one thing fit to be done, and that doing the wrong thing before that one right thing is revealed is always worse than doing nothing.

Cornelius gradually grew better and at last was able to go downstairs. But the weather continued so unfavourable that he could not go outside. He had not yet seen his father, and his dread of seeing him grew to a terror. He never left his room unless he knew his father was not in the house, and, even then, would sit at some window that commanded a view of the door by which he was most likely to enter. He enticed Saffy to be his scout and bring him word in what direction his father went. The father was just as anxious to avoid him, fully intending, if he met him, to turn his back upon him. But it was a rambling and roomy old house, and there was plenty of space for both. A whole week passed and they had not met—to Hester's disappointment, who cherished some hope in a chance encounter.

She had just one consolation. Ever since Cornelius had been safe under her wing, their mother had been noticeably improving. But even this was a source of irritation to the father's brooding selfishness. He thought to himself, "Here I have been nursing her through the illness in vain, and the moment she gets the rascal back, she begins to improve! She would be perfectly happy with him if she never saw me again!"

The two brothers had not yet met. For one thing, Corney disliked the major, and for another, the major objected to an interview. He felt certain the disfigurement of Corney would distress Mark too much, and retard the possible recovery of which he was already in great doubt.

—Forty-Three —

Miss Dasomma and Amy

Miss Dasomma was quite as pleased with Amy as she had expected to be. Her teachableness was indeed a remarkable point in her character.

She began at once to teach her music. She understood quickly, but the doing of what she understood she found very hard—the more so that her spirit was still ill at ease. Corney had deceived her, and had done something very wrong besides. Now she was parted from him.

All was very different from what she had expected in marrying her Corney. Also, from her weariness and anxiety in nursing him, and from other causes as well, her health was not what it had been. Then Hester's letters were a little stiff. She felt it without knowing what she felt or why they made her uncomfortable. It was from no pride or lack of love they were such, but from Hester's uncertainty— the discomfort of knowing they were no nearer a solution of their difficulty than when they parted at the station. She still did not know what she was going to do in the matter! This prevented all free flow of communication. Hester was unable to say what she would have liked to say, and unwilling to tell the uncomfortable condition of things, and thus there grew a gulf between her and her sister.

Amy naturally surmised that the family was not willing to receive her, and that the same unwillingness, though she was too good to yield to it, was in Hester also. But in fact, Hester knew that the main hope for her brother lay in his love for Amy and her devotion to him—in her common sense, her true, honest, bright nature. She was only far too good for Corney!

Then again Amy noted, for love and anxiety made her very sharp, that Miss Dasomma did not read to her every word of Hester's letters. Once she stopped suddenly in the middle of a sentence, and after a pause went on with another. There must have been something she was not to know! Something must not be going right with her husband! Was he worse and they were afraid to tell her? Perhaps they were treating him as her aunts treated her—making his life miserable—and she was not with him to help him bear it!

She brooded over the matter, but not for long. At last she threw herself on her knees and begged her friend to tell her all that her sister's letter had said.

"But, my dear," said Miss Dasomma, "Hester and I have been friends for many years, and we may well have things to say to each other we should not care that even one we love as much as you to hear. A lady must not be inquisitive, you know."

"I know, and I would never pry into other people's affairs. But just tell me it was nothing about my husband and I shall be quite content."

"But think a moment, Amy," returned Miss Dasomma, who began to find herself in the midst of a difficulty, "there might be things between his family and him which they are not quite prepared to tell you until they know you better. Some people in the way they treated you would have been very different from that angel sister of yours! There is nobody like her that I know!"

"I love her with my whole heart," replied Amy sobbing. "But even she must not come between Cornelius and me. If it is anything affecting him, his wife has a right to know about it—a greater right than any one else. No one has a right to conceal it from her!"

"Why do you think that?" Miss Dasomma was anxious to shift the track of the conversation, for she did not see how to answer Amy's appeal. She could not lie, but neither did she feel at liberty to tell her the truth of Corney's involvement with his uncle, and if she continued to evade her question, the poor child might imagine something even more dreadful.

"Why, miss, I have to do what I can for him, and I have a right to know what there is to be done."

"But can you not trust his own family?"

"Yes, surely," replied Amy, "if they were not angry with him. But he's mine, miss! And I've got to look after him. If anybody's not doing right by him, I ought to be there to see him through it!"

Here Miss Dasomma's prudence left her for a moment.

"That's all you know, Amy!" she blurted out—and bit her lip almost the same moment, angry with herself for her hasty remark.

"What is it?" Amy cried. "I *must* know what it is! You *shall* not keep me in the dark! I *must* do my duty to my husband! If you do not tell me, I will go to him."

In terror at what might be the result of her hasty remark, Miss Dasomma faltered, reddened, and betrayed considerable embarrassment. A prudent person, lapsing into a dilemma, is specially discomfitted. She had committed no offence against love, had been guilty of no selfishness or meanness, yet was in a miserable predicament. Amy saw, and was all the more convinced and determined. She persisted, and Miss Dasomma knew that she would not give up.

"How can you wonder," she said with confused vagueness, "when you know he deceived you and never told them he was going to marry you? How can you wonder that one who could behave like that would be only too likely to do other things?"

"Then there *is* something more—something I know nothing about!" exclaimed Amy. "I suspected it from Hester's face. I *must* know what it is! I may be young and silly, but I know what a wife owes to her husband! It is my business."

Miss Dasomma was silent. She had awakened a small volcano, which, though without intending harm against vineyards and villages, would go to its ends regardless of them. She must either answer her questions or persuade her not to ask any.

"I beg you," she said, "not to do anything rash. Can you not trust friends who have proved themselves faithful?"

"Yes, for myself," answered Amy. "But it is my *husband!*"—she almost screamed the word—"And I will trust nobody to take care of *him*. They can't know how to treat him or he would love—"

She did not finish the sentence, for the postman's knock came to the door. She bounded off to see what he had brought. She returned with a look of triumph—a look so wildly exultant that her hostess was momentarily alarmed, thinking that she may have appropriated a letter not addressed to her.

"Now I shall know the truth!" she declared. "This is from *him!*"

And with that she flew to her room. Miss Dasomma should not hear a word of it! How dared she keep from her what she knew about her husband!

It was Corney's first letter to her. It was filled, not with direct complaints, but a general grumble. Here is a part of it.

> I do wish you were here, Amy, my own dearest! I love nobody like you—I love nobody but you. If I did wrong in telling you a few diddle-daddies, it was because I loved you so I could not do without you. And what comforts me for any wrong I have done is that I have you. That would make up to a man for anything short of being hanged! You little witch, how did you contrive to make a fool of a man like me! I should have been in none of this scrape but for you! My mother is very kind to me, of course—ever so much better company than Hester! she never looks as if a fellow had to be put up with, or forgiven, or anything of that sort, in her high and mighty way. But you do get tired of a mother always keeping on telling you how much she loves you. You can't help thinking there must be something behind it all. Depend upon it she wants something of you—wants you to be good, I daresay—to repent, don't you know, as they call it! They're all right, I suppose, but it ain't nice for all that. And that Hester has never told my father yet.
>
> I haven't even seen my father. He has not come near me once! Saffy wouldn't look at me for a long time—that's the last of the litter, you know. She shrieked when they called to her to come to me, and cried, "That's ugly Corney! I won't have ugly Corney!" So you may see how I am used! But I've got her under my thumb at last, and she's useful. Then there's that prig Mark! I always liked the little wretch, though he is such a precious humbug! He's in bed—put out his knee, or something. He never had any stamina in him! Scrofulous, don't you know! They won't let me go near him—for fear of frightening him! But that's that braggart, major Marvel—and a marvel he is, I can tell you! He comes to me sometimes, and makes me hate him—talks as if I wasn't as good as he,—as if I wasn't even a gentleman! Many's the time I long to be back in the garret—horrid place! alone with my little Amy!

So went the letter.

When Amy next appeared she was in another mood. Her eyes were red and her hair was in disorder. She had been lying now on the bed, now on the floor, pulling at her hair, and stuffing her handkerchief in her mouth.

"Well, what is the news?" asked Miss Dasomma, as kindly as she could speak, and as if she saw nothing peculiar in her appearance.

"You must excuse me," replied Amy, with the stiffness of a woman of the world resenting intrusion. "Do not think me unkind, but there is positively nothing in the letter that would interest anyone but me."

Miss Dasomma said nothing more. Perhaps she was going to escape without further questioning! And though she was anxious about what the letter might have contained to have put the poor girl in such a state, she would not risk the asking of a single question more.

The solemn fact was that his letter, in conjunction with the word Miss Dasomma let slip, had at last begun to open Amy's eyes a little to the real character of her husband. She herself had seen a good deal of his family, and found it hard to believe they would treat him unkindly. Something must be at the root of it all, something she did not know about, the same thing that made him take to the garret and hide there! The more she thought about it, the more convinced she was that he had done something hideously wrong.

From the first glimmer of certainty as to the uncertain facts, she saw with absolute clearness what she must do. There was that in the tone of the letter also, which, while it distressed her more than she was willing to allow, strengthened her determination—especially the way in which he spoke of his mother, for she not only remembered her kindness at Burcliff, but loved the memory of her own mother with her whole bright soul. But what troubled her most of all was that he should be so careless about the wrong he had done, whatever it was. "I must know all about it!" she said to herself, "or how am I to help him?" It seemed to her the most natural thing that when one has done a wrong, he should confess it—thus having done with it, disowning and casting away the cursed thing. But this Cornelius did not seem inclined to do! She was bound to learn the truth of the thing.

By degrees her mind grew calm in settled resolve. Should she tell Miss Dasomma what was in her thoughts? Neither she nor Hester had trusted her with what they knew. Need she trust them? She must take her own way in silence, for they would be certain to oppose it. Could they be trying to keep her and Corney apart?

All the indignant strength and unalterable determination of the little woman rose in arms. She would see who could keep them apart now that she had made up her mind! She had money of her own— and there was the jewellry Corney had given her! It must be valuable, for Corney hated fake things. She would walk her way, work her way, or beg her way if necessary, but nothing would keep her from Corney!

Not a word more concerning their differences passed between her and Miss Dasomma. They talked cheerfully and kissed as usual when parting for the night.

The moment she was in her room, Amy began to pack a small carpetbag. When that was done she made a bundle of her cloak and shawl and then lay down in her clothes. Long before dawn she crept softly down the stairs, and sneaked out.

Thus for the second time she was a fugitive—the first time *from*, now *to*.

When Miss Dasomma had been up for some time the next morning, she went up to see why Amy was making no appearance. One glance around the room told her that she was gone. At first she was dreadfully anxious, not suspecting where she had gone, thinking that perhaps the letter which had made her so miserable contained the announcement that their marriage was not a genuine one. If so, then in the dignity of her true heart, she must have at once forever taken her leave of Cornelius.

She wrote to Hester, but the post did not leave before evening, and would not arrive until the afternoon of the next day.

When Amy got to the station she found she was in time for the first train of the day. There was no third class on it, but she found she had enough money for a second-class ticket, and without a moment's hesitation, though it left her almost penniless, she took one.

—Forty-Four —

The Sick Room

At Yrndale things went on in the same dull way, anger burrowing like a devil-mole in the bosom of the father, a dreary spiritual fog hanging over all the souls, and the mother wearying for some glimmer of a heavenly dawn. Hester felt as if she could not endure it much longer.

But there was one bright spot in the house yet—Mark's room, where the major sat by the bedside of the boy, reading, telling him stories, or now and then listening to him as he spoke childlike wisdom in childish words. Saffy came and went, by no means so merry now. In Mark's room she would at times be her old self again, but nowhere else. Infected by Corney, she had begun to be afraid of her father, and like him watched to keep out of his way. What seemed to add to the misery, though in reality it operated the other way, was that the weather had again put on a wintry temper. Sleet and hail, and even snow fell, alternated with rain and wind, day after day for a week.

One afternoon the wind rose almost to a tempest. The rain drove in sheets, beating unmercifully against the windows of Mark's room. His was a cheerful room, though low-pitched and very old, with a great beam across the middle of it. There were coloured prints, mostly of Scripture subjects, on the walls; and the beautiful fire burning in the grate shone on them and reflected from the polished floor. The major sat by it in his easy chair. A bedroom had been prepared for him next to the boy's, and Mark had a string close to his hand whose slightest pull rang a little bell that woke the major like a cannon on the field of battle.

This afternoon, with the rain-charged wind rushing in fierce gusts against the windows, and twilight coming on all the sooner because the world was wrapped in blankets of wet clouds, the major was reading, but soon grew sleepy. A moment more and he was far away, following an imaginary tiger, when Mark woke him with the question:

"Are you ever afraid, Majie? Does the thunder and rain frighten you?"

The major sat bolt upright, rubbed his eyes, stretched himself, but quietly enough that Mark might not know he had waked him, and gave a *hem* as if pondering deeply instead of trying hard to gather wits enough to understand the question. When he trusted his voice not to betray him, he answered:

"Well, Mark, I can't say I would like to be out in it."

"I'm not afraid," said Mark. "A day like this makes me feel ever so safe! For you know if God were to go to sleep and forget his little Mark, then he would forget that he was God, and would not wake again, and that could not be! He can't forget me or you, majie, more than any one of the sparrows. Jesus said so. And what Jesus said, lasts forever. His words never wear out, or need to be made over again.— Majie, I do wish everybody was as good as Jesus! He won't be pleased till we all are. Isn't it glad! That's why I feel so safe that I like to hear the wind roaring. If I did not know that he knows all about the wind, and that it is not the bad man's wind, but the good man's wind, I should be unhappy, for it might hurt somebody, and now it cannot. If I thought he did not care whether everybody was good or not, it would make me so miserable that I should like to die and never come to life again!—He will make Corney good—won't he, majie?"

"Well, I hope so."

"But don't you think we ought to do something to help make Corney good? I don't think we ought to leave Corney to mother all alone. It's too hard for her! Corney never was willing to be good! I can't understand that! Why doesn't he like to be good? It's surely good to be good."

"Yes, Mark, but some people like their own way even when it's selfish, better than God's way when it's nice."

"But God must be able to let them know what foolish creatures they are, majie!"

Being so much with the boy, the major was unconsciously growing quite knowing in the lovely childlikeness that is like the Ancient of days. Some foolishly object that the master taught what others had taught before him, as if he should not be the wise householder with his old things as well as new. They recognize the old things—the new they do not understand. Who first taught that the mighty God, the Lord, the maker of heaven and earth, was like a child! Who first said, "Love one another as I have loved you"?

"It just won't do for you and me to be so safe from all the storm and wind," Mark went on, "wrapped in God's cloak, and poor Corney out in the wind and rain. You may say it's his own fault—it's because he won't let God take up and carry him. That's very true, but then that's just the pity of it! It is all so dreadful! I can't understand it!"

The boy could understand good, but was perplexed with evil.

While they talked in their comfortable nest, there was one out in the wind and rain, all but exhausted, who hastened with what poor remaining strength she had to do His will. Amy, left at the station with an empty purse, had set out to walk through the wet darkness, up hill and down dale to find her husband—the man God had given her to look after.

—Forty-Five —

Vengeance is Mine

That same morning, Mr. Raymount had found it, or had chosen to imagine it necessary, to start early in the day for the county town on something he called business, and was not expected home before the next day. In his absence Cornelius went freely wandering about the house, lunching with his mother, Hester and Saffy like one of the family.

His mother, wisely or not, did her best to prevent his feeling different from old times. Their conversation at the table was neither very interesting nor very satisfactory. How could it be? A child of Satan might just as well be happy in the house of God, as the unrepentant Cornelius in the house of his mother, even in the absence of his father. Their talk was poor and intermittent. Well might the youth long for his garret and the company of the wife who had nothing for him but smiles and sweetest attentions!

After dinner he sat alone for a while at the table. He had been ordered wine during his recovery and was already in danger of adding a fondness for it to his other weaknesses. But the mother, wise and aware of the danger, had kept the administration of the medicine in her own hands. Today, however, she had been called from the room and had not put away the decanter. Thus Cornelius had filled his glass repeatedly without interruption. When his mother reentered the room, she noticed the nearly empty decanter, but thought it better to say nothing.

Cornelius tried to conceal the effects of the wine as he left the room, sauntering into the library and then into the study, where his father's collection of books was kept. He lit a lamp, took down a volume of poetry, threw himself into his father's chair, and began to read. He had never been able to read long without weariness, and from the wine he had drunk and his weakness, he was presently overcome with sleep. His mother came and went, but would not disturb him. I fear that her satisfaction in having him under her roof was beginning to wane from the constant stress of a presence that showed no more signs of growth than a dead man. But her faith was strong and she waited in hope.

The night was now very dark. Above, the major and the boy talked of sweet, heavenly things. Down below, the youth lay snoring, where, had his father been at home, he would not have dared show himself. The mother was in her own room, and Hester in the drawing room—where, in the oppression of the times, she never now played her piano. The house was quiet except for the noise of the wind and the rain, and those Cornelius did not hear.

Suddenly he started awake and sat up in terror. A hand was on his shoulder, gripping him like a metal instrument, not a thing of flesh and blood. The face of his father was staring at him through the lingering vapours of his stuporous sleep.

Mr. Raymount had started out in the morning with a certain foolish pleasure in the prospect of getting wet through and through and being generally ill-used by the atrocious weather, as he called it. Thinking to shorten the way, he took a certain shortcut he knew, but found the road very bad. The mud drew off one of his horse's shoes, but he did not discover it for a long way—not until he came to a piece of newly mended road where the poor animal fell suddenly lame. He dismounted and made for an inn a mile or two farther on, where he stayed and had some refreshment while his horse was being attended to by a local smithy. By the time he was again mounted, the weather was worse than ever and it was so late that he could not have hoped to reach the town in time to do his business. He, therefore, gave up his intended journey, and turning aside to see a friend in the neighbourhood, resolved to go home again that same night.

His feelings when he saw his son asleep in his chair, were not like those of the father in that one story of all the world. He had been giving place to the devil for so long, that the devil was now able to do with him as he would—for a season at least. Nor would the possessed ever have been able to recognize the presence of the devil, had he not a minute or two of his full will with them? Or is it that the miserable possessed goes farther than the devil means him to go? I doubt if he cares that we should murder—I fancy he is satisfied if only we hate well. Murder tends a little to repentance, and he does not want that. Anyhow, we cherish the devil like a spoiled child, till he gets too bad and we find him unendurable. Departing then, he takes a piece of the house with him, and the tenant is not so likely to mistake him when he comes again.

He was annoyed, even angry, to see this unpleasant son of his asleep in *his* chair!

"The sneak!" he said! "he dares not show his face when I'm at home, but the minute he thinks me safe, gets into my room and lies in my chair! Drunk, too, by Jove!" he added, as a fume from the sleeper's breath reached the nostrils beginning to dilate with wrath. "What can that wife of mine be about, letting the rascal go on like this! She is faultless except in giving me such a son—and then helping him to fool me!"

He forgot the old forger of a bygone century! His side of the house had, I should say, a good deal more to do with what was unsatisfactory in the lad's character than his wife's.

The devil saw his chance, sprang up, and mastered the father.

"The snoring idiot!" he growled, and seizing his boy by the shoulder and neck he roughly shook him awake.

The father had been drinking, not what would some have considered too much, but enough to add to the fierceness of his wrath. He had come into the study straight from the stable, and when the poor creature looked up half awake and saw his father standing over him with a heavy whip in his hand, he was filled with a terror that nearly paralyzed him. He sat and stared with white, trembling lips and red eyes, and a look that confirmed the belief of the father that he was drunk.

"Get out of there, you dog!" cried his father, and with one sweep of his powerful arm, half dragged, half hurled him from the chair. He fell on the floor, and in weakness mixed with cowardice lay where he fell. The devil—I am sorry to have to refer to him so often, but he played a notable part in the affair, and I should be more sorry not to acknowledge his part in it—rushed at once into the brain and heart and limbs of the father's abandoned house.

When Raymount saw the creature who had turned his previously happy life to shame lying at his feet, he became instantly conscious of the whip in his hand. Without a moment's pause of hesitation, he raised his arm high over him and brought it down with a fierce lash on the quivering flesh of his son. The boy richly deserved the punishment, but God would not have struck him that way. There was the poison of hate, not the leaven of love, in the blow. He again raised his arm aloft, but as it descended, the piercing shriek that broke from Corney's lips startled even the possessing demon, and the violence of the blow was broken. But the lash of the whip found his face and marked it for a time worse than the smallpox.

What the father would have done next I do not know. While the cry of his son yet sounded in his ears, another cry—almost an echo from another world—rang ghastly through the storm like the cry of a banshee. It seemed to come from far away, but the next instant a spectral face flitted swift as a bird up to the window and laid itself close to the glass of the French window. A moment more and it burst open with a great clang and clash and tinkle of shattering glass, and a small figure leaped into the room with a second cry that sounded like a curse in the ears of the father.

She threw herself on the prostrate youth, and covered his body with hers, then turned her head and looked up at the father with indignant defiance in her flashing eye. Cowed with terror and smarting with keenest pain, the youth took his wife in his arms and sobbed like the beaten thing he was.

Amy's eye gleamed—protection grew fierce and fanned the burning sense of wrong. The father stood over them like a fury rather than a fate—stood as the shock of Amy's cry and her stormy entrance, like that of an avenging angel, had fixed him.

But presently he began to recover his senses, jumping to the conclusion that this worthless girl had drawn Cornelius into her evil ways and was the cause of ruining him and his family forever!

The thought set the geyser of his rage roaring and spouting in the face of heaven. He heaved his whip and a punishing blow fell upon her. But instead of another shriek following the lash, nothing came but a shudder and a silence, and the unquailing eye of the girl fixed itself like a spectre upon her assailant.

He struck her again. Again came the shivering shudder and the silence. Cry she would not, even if he killed her!

The sense that she had kept the blows from falling upon Corney upheld the brave creature. She once drew in her breath sharply, but never took her eyes from the man's face. Then, suddenly, the light in them began to fade and went quickly out. Her head dropped like a stone upon the breast of her cowardly husband. Now, even mute defiance was gone.

What if he had killed the woman, thought Raymount, as he stood with subsiding passion looking down on the miserable pair.

Amy had walked all the long distance from the station and had lost her way and had to ask directions several times. Again and again she had all but lain down to die on the moorland waste onto which she had wandered. Then the thought of Corney and his need roused her again. Wet all the way through, blown about by the wind so that she could hardly breathe, and faint with hunger and cold, she struggled on. When at last she got to the lodge gate, the woman in charge of it took her for a common beggar and could hardly be persuaded to let her pass. But then she heard her husband's cry. She saw the lighted window, ran into the grounds and straight toward it, dashed it open and entered. It was the last expiring effort of the poor remnant of her strength. She had not life enough left to resist the shock of her father-in-law's blows.

While the father was still looking down on his children, the door opened softly and the mother entered. She did not even know that her husband had returned and had come in merely to know how her unlovely but beloved child was faring in his sleep. She stood still. She saw what looked like a murdered heap on the floor, and her husband standing over it. Behind her came Hester, who looked over her shoulder and understood at once.

She nearly pushed her mother aside as she sprang to help. Her father tried to prevent her. "No, father!" she said. "It is time to disobey!"

All was clear to her! Amy had come, and died defending her husband from her father! Hester put her strong arms around the dainty little figure and lifted it limp, its long wet hair and helpless head hanging over the crook of her arm. She gave a great sob. Was this what Amy's lovely, brave womanhood had brought her to! What creatures men were! She glanced down and saw on Amy's neck a frightful swollen welt.

She looked to her father. There was the whip in his hand.

"Oh, papa!" she screamed. She could not look him in the face. As she dropped her eyes, she saw the terrified face of Cornelius open its eyes.

"Oh, Corney!" said Hester, in the tone of an accusing angel, and ran from the room with Amy in her arms.

The mother darted to her son.

But the wrath of the father rose afresh at the sight.

"Let the hound lie!" he said, stepping between them. "What right has he to walk the earth like a man?"

"You've killed him, Gerald!—your own son!" said the mother with a cold, still voice.

She saw the dreadful mark on his face, began to stagger, and would have fallen. But the arm that, through her son, had struck her heart caught and supported her. The husband bore his wife once more to her room, and the foolish son was left alone on the floor, smarting in pain, ashamed, and full of fear for his wife, yet in ignorance that his father had so violently whipped her.

A moment more and he rose. As he did, all at once he realized that the terror of his father was gone. They had met, and his father had put himself in the wrong. He was no more afraid of him. It was not hate that had cast out fear. I do not say that he felt no resentment. Cornelius was not quite so noble as that. But it consoled him that he had been hardly used by his father. He had been accustomed to look vaguely up to his father as a sort of rigid but righteous divinity. In a disobedient, self-indulgent, poverty-stricken nature like his, reverence could only take the form of fear. And now that he had seen his father in a rage, the feeling of reverence, such as it was, had begun to give way, and with it the fear. They were more upon a level. And too, his father's unmerciful use of the whip to him seemed a sort of settling of scores, thence in a measure, a breaking down of the wall between them. A weight as of a rock was lifted from his mind by this violent blowing up of the horrible negation that had been between them so long. He felt—as when punished in boyhood—as if the storm had passed, and the sun had begun to appear. He did not yet know to what a state his wife was brought. He knew she was safe with Hester.

He listened, and finding all quiet, stole, smarting and aching, slowly to his room and there tumbled into bed, longing for Amy to come to him. He was an invalid, after all, and could not go about looking for her! It was her part to find him! In a few minutes he was fast asleep once more, and forgot everything in dreams of the garret with Amy.

When Mrs. Raymount came to herself, she looked up at her husband. He stood expecting such reproaches as never yet in their married life she had given him. But she stretched out her arms to him and drew him to her. Her pity for the misery that could have led him to behave so horribly joined to her sympathy in the distressing repentance she did not doubt must have already begun.

It went deep to the man's heart. His wife's embrace was like balm to the stinging wound of the deep sense of degradation that had seized him—not for striking his son, who, he continued to say, entirely deserved it, but for striking a woman, whoever she might be. But it was only when, through Hester's behaviour to her and the words that fell from her, he came to know who she was, that the iron, the beneficient spearhead of remorse, entered his soul.

Strange that the mere fact of our knowing *who a person is* should make such a difference in the way we think of and behave to that person! A person is a person just the same, whether one of the few of our acquaintances or not, and his claim on us for all kinds of human compassion just the same. Our knowledge of anyone is a mere accident, and should at most only make us feel it more.

But recognition of Amy showed his crime all the more heinous. It brought back to Mr. Raymount's mind the vision of the bright girl he used to watch in her cheerful service at Burcliff, and with that vision came the conviction that not she but Corney must be primarily to blame. He had twice struck the woman his son had wronged!

He pronounced himself the most despicable and wretched of men. He had lifted his hand against a woman that had been but in her right in following his son, and had shown herself ready to die in his defence! His wife's tenderness confirmed these feelings, and he lay down in his own room a few moments later a humbler man than he had ever been in his life.

—Forty-Six—

Father and Daughter-in-Law

Hester carried poor little Amy to her own room, laid her on her own bed, and did for her all she could. With hands tender as a mother's, and weeping eyes, she undressed her, put her in a warm bath, then got her into bed, using every enticement to induce her to take some nourishment.

She had poor success, however, for the heart seemed to have gone out of her. She lay like one dead and seemed to care for nothing. She scarcely answered when Hester spoke, though she tried to smile. It was the most pitiful smile Hester had ever seen. Her brain was haunted with the presence of Corney's father, who seemed ever and always standing over her and Corney with his terrible whip. The only thing she could think of was how to get her husband away from the frightful place. Hester did her best to reassure her, telling her Corney was fast asleep and little the worse, and finally, shortly after midnight, was successful in getting the exhausted girl to sleep. Then she herself lay down on the sofa beside her.

In the gray of the morning Mr. Raymount awoke. He was aware of a great silence about him. He looked out the window and saw in the east the first glimmer of a lovely spring day. The stillness awed, almost frightened him. His very soul seemed hushed, as if in his sleep a Voice had said, "Peace! Be still!"

He felt like a naughty child, who, having slept, seems to have slept away his naughtiness. Yesterday seemed far away—only the shudder of it was left. But he knew if he began to think it would be back with its agony. Had some angel been by his bedside to soothe him? A demon had surely possessed him! Had it been but hinted as within the bounds of possibility that he should behave to a woman as he had behaved, he would have laughed the idea to scorn!

He had always thought himself a chivalrous gentleman! This was the end of his faith in himself! His grand Hester would not feel herself safe from him! Truly a demon had possessed him—might not an angel indeed have been by him as he slept?

Then rose in his mind's eye the face of Amy Amber. What had become of the poor girl? Surely his wife and daughter would be taking care of her. But still he must do something for her, and somehow make atonement for treating her so brutally.

Hope dawned feebly on his murky horizon. He would be good to her. There was something to be done for everybody. If she had gone back out into the night, he would spend every penny he had to find her!

Cornelius would know where she was. He must see him! And he would tell him he was sorry he had struck him, too. What could have gotten into him that he had whipped his own son!

In the still, dark gray of the morning he went to his son's room.

When he reached the door he saw it was open a little. The next instant he heard a soft voice inside speaking persuadingly. He went closer and listened. It was Amy Amber's voice!—in his house! in his son's room!

And after the lesson he had given them the night before!

He looked in quietly. The dainty little figure was half lying on the bed, with an arm thrown around his son. He could not see her face, but he could clearly hear her words through the dusk.

"Corney darling, you must get up. You must come away. I have come to take you away from them. I knew they were not treating you well. That was what made me come. I know you have done something very wrong to make your father so angry with you. It doesn't matter to me. I am your own. But you cannot have said you were sorry or he would have forgiven you. He can't be a bad man—though he did hurt me dreadfully!"

"He is a very good man!" muttered Corney from the pillow.

"But I'm afraid," continued Amy, "if he hasn't been able to make you sorry before, he will never be able now! To beat you as he did last night will never make you repent."

"Oh, he didn't hurt me much! You don't think a fellow would mind that sort of thing from his own father—when he was in a passion, don't you know? Besides, Amy—to you I will confess it—I gave him good reason."

"Come, then, come. We will go somewhere. I want to make you think the right way about the thing, and when you are sorry, we will come back and tell him so. Then perhaps he will forgive me and we shall be all happy again."

What was this he heard! thought Raymount. The cunning creature! This was her trick to entice him from his home!—And just as the poor boy was beginning to repent too! She knew her trade! She would fall in with his better mood and pretend goodness! She would help him to do what he ought! She would be his teacher in righteousness! Deep, deep she was—beyond anything he had dreamed possible! No doubt the fellow was just as bad as she, but not the less must he do what little he yet might for the redemption of his son!

But as he thought thus, his conscience smote him that Cornelius could not but prefer going with one who loved him and talked to him like that, whatever she was, to staying with a father who treated him as he had been doing ever since he came home? He would behave to him very differently after this. He, too, would repent! But first he must interfere now with the wicked girl's schemes. What else was a father for?

He pushed the door wide open and went in.

Amy heard him and raised herself from the bed to face him. There was just enough light to see that it was the father, and the horrid idea shot through her mind that he had come to lash his son again. She roused every fevered nerve to do battle with the strong man for his son. Clenching her little hand hard, she stood like a small David between the bed and the approaching Goliath.

"Get out of this room!" he said with the sternness of rising wrath.

"I came to take him away," said Amy, who had begun to tremble from head to foot. "It is my business to take care of him."

"Your business! When he has his own family? His own mother!"

"If a man is to leave father and mother and cleave to his wife," answered Amy, "it's the least thing the wife can do to take care of him from his father!"

Mr. Raymount stood confounded. What could the hussy mean? Was she going to pretend she was married to him?

Indignation and rage began to rise afresh. But if he gave way what might he not be guilty of a second time! A rush of shame choked the words that crowded to his lips. And with the self-restraint came wholesome doubt—was it possible he had married her?

Would it not be just worthy of him to have done so and never told one of his family! At least there need be nothing incredible in it! This girl—yes—plainly she had both cunning and fascination enough to make him not only run after her but marry her! How was he to know the truth of the thing? The coward would not have the courage to contradict her, but he would know if he were lying!

"Do—do you mean to tell me," he said, "that he has married you—without a word to his own father or mother?"

Then at last Cornelius spoke, rising on his elbow in the bed:

"Yes, father," he said with slow determination, "I have married her. It is all my fault, not a bit hers."

"Why did you not let us know then?" cried the father.

"Because I was a coward," answered Corney, speaking the truth with courage. "I knew you would not like it."

"Little *you* know of what I like or dislike!"

"You can soon prove him wrong, sir!" said Amy, looking up in his face through the growing light of the morning. "Forgive us, and take me too. I was so happy to think I was going to belong to you all! I would never have married him, if I had known—without your consent, I mean. It was very wrong of Corney, but I will try to make him sorry for it."

"You never will!" said Corney.

Now first the full horror of what he had done broke upon the mind of Mr. Raymount. He stood for a moment appalled.

"You will let me take him away then?" said Amy, thinking he hesitated to receive her.

Now whether it was from an impulse of honesty towards her, or of justification of himself, I cannot tell, but he instantly answered,

"Do you know that his money is stolen?"

"If he stole it," she replied, "he will never steal again."

"He will never get another chance. He cannot get a situation now."

"I will work for us both. He belongs to me as much as I do to him. If he had only kept nothing from me, nothing of this would have happened.—Do come, Corney, while I am able to walk, I feel as if I were going to die."

"And this is the woman I was such a savage to last night!" said Mr. Raymount to himself.

"Forgive me, Amy!" he cried, stretching out his arms to her. "I have behaved like a brute. To strike my son's wife! I deserve to be hanged for it. I shall never forgive myself. But you must forgive me, for God's sake!"

Even before he had finished, she was in his arms clinging to him.

The strong man was now the weaker. The father, not the daughter, wept. After a moment she drew back her head.

"Come, Corney," she said, "out of your bed and down on your knees to your own blessed father, and confess your sins to him. Tell him you're sorry for them, and you'll never do them again."

Corney obeyed. In some strange, lovely way she had got the mistressship of his conscience as well as his heart. He got out of bed at once, went straight down on his knees, and, though he did not speak, was presently weeping like a child. It was a strange group in the gray of the new morning—ah, indeed, a new morning for them!—the girl in the arms of the elderly man, and the youth kneeling at their feet, both men weeping and the girl radiant.

Gerald Raymount closed the door on his son and his son's wife and hastened to his own to tell her all.

Immediately when the emotional strain was off her, Amy fell into a severe and fevered illness, brought on by her exposure to the cold and rain and pain. She was brought almost to death's door. Corney in his turn became nurse, and improved not a little from his own anxiety, her sweetness, and the sympathy of every one, his father included.

But such was Amy's constitution that when she began to recover she recovered rapidly, and was soon ready for the share lovingly allotted her in the duties of the house.

—Forty-Seven—

The Message

But the precious little Mark did not get better, and it soon became very clear to the major that, although months might elapse before he left them, he must go before long. It was the only cloud that now hung over the family. But the parting drew upon them so softly, with so little increase of suffering, and with such a mild but genuine enjoyment of existence that only he was thoroughly aware that death was at the door. The rest said the summer would certainly restore him. But the major expected him to die with the first of the warm weather. The child himself believed he was going soon.

Most of his dreams, which now seemed to be coming with greater frequency, he told to the major.

One day he said, "I was trying to tell Saffy a dream I had while you were resting. And when I told her she said, 'But it's all nonsense, you know, Mark! It's only a dream!'—What do you think, majie?"

"Was it a dream, Mark?" asked the major.

"Yes, it was a dream, but do you think a dream is nothing at all? I think if it is a good dream, it must be God's. For you know every good thing is from God. He made the thing that dreams and the things that set it dreaming, so he must be the master of dreams—at least when he pleases. Do you know, majie, I used to think he came and talked to me in the window-seat when I was a child! What if he really did, and I should be going to be made sure that he did—up there, I mean, you know—I don't know where, but it's where Jesus went when he went back to his papa! Oh, how happy Jesus must have been when he got back to his papa!"

Here he began to cough and could talk no more for the present.

A great silent change had been passing in the major, for the child's and the soldier's souls had gotten nearer to each other than until that time any two other souls in the house had been able to. Mark was not only an altogether new influence on him, but he had helped to stir up and bring alive in him a thousand influences besides. Those were not merely of things hitherto dormant in him, but memories of unconscious memories—words of his mother, a certain Sunday evening with her, her last blessing on his careless head, the verse of a well-known hymn she repeated as she was dying, old scraps of things she had taught him. Dying little Mark gave life to these and many other things. The major had never properly been a child but now lived his childhood over again with Mark in a better fashion.

"I have had such a curious, such a beautiful dream, majie," he said, waking up in the middle of one night. The major was sitting up with him—he was never left alone now.

"What was it, Markie?" asked the major.

"I should like Corney to hear it," returned Mark.

"I will call him and you can tell us both together."

"Oh, I don't think we should wake Corney up. He would not like that! He must hear it sometime—but it must be at the right time, otherwise he would laugh at it and I could not bear that. You know Corney always laughs without thinking first whether the thing was made for laughing at."

By this time Corney had been to see Mark often. He always spoke kindly to him now, but always as a little goose. And Mark, the least assuming of mortals, always being in earnest, did not want his dream made light of. Hence he was not often ready to speak freely to Corney.

"But I'll tell you what, majie," he went on "—I'll tell *you* the dream, and then, if I should go away without having told him, you must tell it to Corney. He won't laugh then—at least I don't think he will. Do you promise to tell him, majie?"

"I will," answered the major, drawing himself up with a mental military salute, ready to obey to the letter whatever Mark would require of him.

Without another word the child began.

"I was somewhere," he said. "—I don't know where. Jesus was there too. 'Ah, little one,' he said when he saw me, 'I have been getting your eyes open as fast as I could all the time! We're in our father's house together now! But, Markie, where's your brother Corney?' And I answered and said, 'Jesus, I'm very sorry, but I don't know. I know very well that I'm my brother's keeper, but I can't tell where he is.' Then Jesus smiled again and said, 'Never mind, then. I didn't ask you because I didn't know myself. But we must have Corney here—only we can't get him until he sets himself to be good! You must tell Corney, only not just yet, that I want him. Tell him that he and I have got one father, and I couldn't bear to have him out in the cold, with all the horrid creatures that won't be good! Tell him I love him so that I will be very sharp with him if he doesn't hurry and come home. Our father is *so* good, and it is dreadful to me that Corney won't mind him! He is *so* patient with him, Markie!' 'I know that, Jesus,' I said. And I don't know what came next.—Now, what am I to do, majie? You see why I couldn't bear to have that dream laughed at. Yet I must tell it to Corney because there is a message in it for him!"

The major did not speak, but looked at the child with his soul in his eyes.

"I do not think," Mark went on, "that he wanted me to tell Corney the minute I woke. I think when the time comes he will let me know it is come. But if I found I was dying, you know, I would try and tell him, whether he laughed or not, rather than go without having done it. But if Corney knew I was going, I don't think he would laugh."

"I don't think he would," returned the major. "Corney is a better boy—a little—I do think, than he used to be."

A feeling had grown upon the household as if there was in the house a strange lovely spot in direct communication with heaven— the room where Mark lay shining in his bed, a Christ-child, if a child might bear the name. Whenever the door opened, loving eyes would seek first the spot where the sweet face, the treasure of the house, lay.

That same afternoon, as the major dozed in his chair, the boy suddenly called out in a clear voice,

"Oh, majie, there was one bit of my dream I did not tell you. I've just remembered it for the first time.—After what I told you, do you remember?"

"I do indeed."

"After that, Jesus looked at me for one minute—no, not a minute like on Mama's watch—but perhaps just a few seconds, and then said just one more thing, 'Our father, Markie!' and then I could not see him anymore. But it did not seem to matter the least tiny bit. There was a stone near me, and I sat down upon it, feeling as if I could sit there without moving forever, I was so happy. And it was because Jesus' father was touching me everywhere. My head felt as if he were counting the hairs of it. And he was not only close to me, but far and far and farther away, and all between. Everywhere was the father! I couldn't see or feel or hear him, yet I knew he was so near that I couldn't see or hear or feel him. I am talking nonsense, majie, but I can't do it better. It was God, God everywhere, and there was no nowhere anywhere. All was God, God, God. And I felt I could sit there forever, because I was right in the middle of God's heart. That was what made everything look so right that I was anxious about nothing and nobody."

Here he paused a little.

"And then after a while," the boy resumed, "I seemed to see a black speck somewhere. And I could not understand it. I did not like it, and it made me miserable. But, I said to myself, whatever the black speck may be, God will rub it white when he is ready! For you know, he couldn't go on forever with a black speck going about in his heart. And when I said this, all at once I knew the black speck was Corney, and I started to cry. But then the black speck began to grow dim, and it grew dimmer and dimmer till all at once I could see it no more. The same instant Corney stood beside me with a smile on his face, and the tears running down his cheeks. I stretched out my arms to him, and he caught me up in his, and then it was all right. And then I woke, majie."

The days went on. Every day Mark said, "Now, majie, I do think today I shall tell Corney my dream and the message I have for him." But each day passed and the dream was not told. The next and the next and the next passed and he seemed to the major not likely ever to have the strength to tell Corney. Still, even his mother, who was almost constantly in the room during the day, did not perceive that his time was drawing nigh. Hester also was much with him now, and sometimes his father, occasionally Corney and Mrs. Corney, as Mark called her with a merry look—very pale on his almost transparent face. But none of them seemed to think his end quite near. When several were in the room, he would lie looking from one to another like a miser contemplating his riches—and well he might! For such riches neither moth nor rust corrupt, and they are the treasures of heaven also. He took everything that came to him as in itself right. He seemed in his illness to love everybody more than even while he was well.

One evening most of the family were in the room. A vague sense had diffused itself that the end was not far off, and an unspoken instinct had gathered them.

A lamp was burning low, but the firelight was stronger.

Mark spoke. In a moment the major was bending over him.

"Majie," he whispered, "I want Corney. I want to tell him."

The major went to find the brother, and on his way met the father and told him that the end was near. With a sorely self-accusing heart, for the vision of the boy seated in the middle of the cold moor the day of their walk haunted him, he went quickly to the boy's room, the anteroom of heaven.

Mark kept looking for Corney's coming, his eyes turning every other moment to the door. When his father entered, he stretched out his arms to him. The strong man bent over him and could not repress a sob. The boy pushed him gently back far enough to see his face.

"Father," he said—he had never called him *father* before—"you must be glad, not sorry. I am going to your father and my father. He is waiting for me."

Then seeing Corney come in, he stretched his arms toward him past his father.

"Corney! Corney!" he cried, just as he used to call him when he was a mere child. Corney bent over him, but the outstretched arms did not close around him. They fell.

But he was not yet ascended. Feebly he signed to the major.

"Majie," he whispered, with a look and expression for which the major tried the rest of his life to find the meaning. "Majie! Corney! You tell!"

Then he went.

I think it was the grief at the grave of Lazarus that made our Lord weep, not his death. One with eyes opening into both worlds could hardly weep over any law of the Father of Lights! I think it was the impossibility of getting them comforted over this thing death, which looked to him so different from what they thought it, that made the fearless weep, and give them in Lazarus a foretaste of his own resurrection.

The major alone did not weep. He stood with his arms folded, like a sentry relieved and waiting the next order. Even Corney's eyes filled with tears and he murmured, "Poor Markie!" It should have been "Poor Corney!" He stooped and kissed the silent face, then drew back and gazed with the rest on the little pilgrim-cloak the small prophet had dropped as he rose to his immortality.

Saffy, who had been seated gazing into the fire, called out in a strange voice, "Markie, Markie!"

Hester turned to her at the cry and saw her apparently following something with her eyes along the wall from the bed to the window. At the curtained window she gazed for a moment, and then her eyes fell and she sat like one in a dream. A moment more and she sprang to her feet and ran to the bed, crying again, "Markie! Markie!" Hester lifted her and held her to kiss the sweet white face. It seemed to content her. She went back to her stool by the fire, and there sat staring at the curtained window with the look of one gazing into regions unknown.

That same night, before the solemn impression should pass, the major took Corney to his room and, recalling every individual expression he could of the little prophet-dreamer, carried out the commission entrusted him, not without the shedding of tears.

And Corney did not laugh. He listened with a grave, even sad face. When the major ceased, his eyes too were full of tears.

"I shall not forget Markie's dream," he said.

Thus came everything in to help the youth who had begun to mend his ways.

And shall we think the boy found God not equal to his dream of him? He made our dreaming. Shall it surpass in its making his mighty self? Shall man dream better than God? Shall God's love be inferior to man's imagination or his own?

—Forty-Eight —

A Family

When Mark's little cloak was put in the earth, for a while the house felt cold—as if the bit of Paradise had gone out of it. Mark's room was like a temple forsaken of its divinity. But it was not to be drifted up with the sand of forgetfulness! The major put in a petition that it might continue to be called Mark's, but should be considered the major's. He would like to put some of his things in it and occupy it when he came!

Every one was pleased with the idea. They no longer would feel so painfully that Mark was not there when his dear majie occupied the room!

To the major it was thenceforth chamber and chapel and monument. It should not be a tomb except as on the fourth day the sepulchre in the garden! He would fill it with live memories of the risen child! Very different was his purpose from that sickly haunting of the grave in which some loving hearts indulge! We are bound to be hopeful, nor wrong our great-hearted father.

Mark's books and pictures remained undisturbed. The major dusted them with his own hands. Every day he read in Mark's bible. He never took it away with him, but always when he returned in whatever part of the bible he might have read in the meantime, he resumed his reading where he had left off in it. The sword the boy used so to admire for its brightness he had placed it unsheathed on the wall. In Mark's bed the major slept, and to Mark's chamber he went always to shut the door. In solitude there he learned a thousand things his busy life had prepared him for learning.

The master had come to him in the child. In him was fulfilled a phase of the promise that whosoever receives a child in the name of

Jesus receives Jesus and his father. Through ministering to the child he had come to know the child's elder brother and master. It was the presence of the master in the child, that without his knowing it, opened his heart to him, and he had thus entertained more than an angel.

Time passed, and under the holy influences of duty and love and hope their hearts began to cover with flowers their furrows of grief. Hester's birthday was at hand. The major went to London to buy her a present, determined if he could to make the occasion a cheerful and memorable one.

He wrote to his cousin, Helen, asking if he might bring a friend with him. He did not think, he said, she or her husband knew him, but Hester did. He was a young doctor by the name of Christopher. He had met him among "Hester's friends" and was a great deal taken with him. He had been ailing for some time and had persuaded him to take a little relaxation. After Hester told them something of the man's history, saying that she had the highest esteem for him and the work he was doing among London's poor, Mr. and Mrs. Raymount expressed their delight in the major's proposal.

Corney gradually began to show a little practical interest in the place—first in the look of it, and then in its yield. Next he took to measuring the land and the major gave him no end of help. Having found a point of common interest, they began to be drawn a little together and to develop a mild liking for each other's company. By degrees, Corney saw that the major knew much more than he, and the major discovered that Corney had more brains than he had given him credit for.

Everything was now going on well at Yrndale—thanks to the stormy and sorrowful weather that had of late so troubled its spiritual atmosphere, and killed so many evil worms in its moral soil!

As soon as the distress caused by Corney's offences was soothed by reviving love for the youth and fresh hope in him, Hester informed her parents of the dissolution of her engagement to lord Gartley. Her mother was troubled, for the simple reason that she knew how the tongue of the world would wag against her daughter. But those who despise the ways of the world need not fret that low minds attribute to them the things of which low minds are capable. The world and its judgments will pass. The poisonous tongue will one day become pure, and make ample apology for its evil speaking. The tongue is a fire, but there is a stronger fire than the tongue.

Mr. Raymount and the major cared little for this aspect of the matter, for they felt that the public is only a sort of innocent, whose behaviour may be troublesome or pleasant, but whose opinion is worth considerably less than that of a wise hound. The world is a fine thing to save, but a wretch to worship. Neither did the father care much for lord Gartley, though he had liked him. The major, we know, both despised and detested him.

Hester herself was annoyed to find how soon the idea of his lordship came to be altogether a thing of her past. But she was able to look on the whole blunder with calmness, and a thankfulness that kept growing as the sting of her fault lost its burning, lenified in the humility it brought.

There was nothing left her now, she said to herself, but the best of all—a maiden life devoted to the work of her master. She was not willing any more to run the risk of loosing her power to help the Lord's creatures, down trodden of devils, well-to-do people, and their own miserable weaknesses and vices. Now she would hold herself free! What a blessed thing it was to be her own mistress and the slave of the Lord, externally free! To be the slave of a husband was the worst of all slavery except self-slavery!

Nor was there in her conclusion anything of disappointment or self-humiliation. St. Paul abstained from marriage that he might the better do the work given him by the Lord. For his perilous and laborious work it was better, he judged, that he should not be married. It was for the kingdom of heaven's sake.

Her spirits soon returned more buoyant than before. Her health was better. She found she had been suffering from an oppression she had refused to recognize—already in no small measure yoked, and right unequally. Only a few weeks passed, and, in the prime of health and that glorious thing feminine strength, she looked a yet grander woman than before. There was greater freedom in her carriage, and she seemed to have grown. The humility that comes with the discovery of error had made her yet more dignified. True dignity comes only of humility. Pride is the ruin of dignity, for it is a worshipping of self, and that involves a continuous sinking. Humility, the worship of the Ideal—that is, of the man Christ Jesus, is the only lifter-up of the head.

Everybody felt her more lovable than before. Her mother began to feel an enchantment of peace in her presence. Her father sought her company more than ever in his walks, and talked about his own wrong feelings toward Corney and how he had been punished for them by what they wrought in him. He had begun, he told her, to learn many things he had supposed he knew—he had only thought and written and talked about them before! Father and daughter were therefore much to each other now. Even Corney perceived a change in his sister. Scarcely a shadow of what he used to feel of "superiority" remained in her. She became more and more Amy's ideal of womanhood, and she showed her husband how few sisters would have tried to protect and deliver him as she had done, and would have so generously taken herself, a poor and uneducated girl, to a sister's heart. So, altogether, they were growing toward becoming a true family as God intended families to be.

Along with Mr. Christopher, Hester invited Miss Dasomma to come and spend a few days to help her celebrate her birthday.

—Forty-Nine—

A Birthday Gift

Hester's birthday was the sweetest of summer days, and Hester looked a perfect summer-born woman. After breakfast all except the mother went out for a walk. Hester was little inclined to talk, and the major was in a thoughtful, brooding mood. Miss Dasomma and Mr. Raymount alone conversed. Mr. Raymount had taken them to a certain spot for the sake of the view, but Hester had fallen a little behind, and Christopher went back to meet her.

"You are thinking of your brother," he said in a tone that made her feel grateful.

"Yes," she answered.

"I knew by your eyes," he returned. "Why don't you tell me something about him?"

As they walked and talked, he drew her from her sadness with gentle words about children and death, and the look and reality of things. And so they wandered about the moor for a little while before joining the others.

Mr. Raymount was much pleased with Christopher, and even Corney found himself drawn to his side, feeling, though he did not know it, a strength in him that offered protection.

The day went on in the simplest, pleasantest fashion. After lunch, Hester opened her piano, and asked Miss Dasomma to sit down and play. A rosy conscious silence pervaded the summer afternoon and the ancient drawing-room, in which the listeners were one here and one there—except Corney and "Mrs. Corney," as for love of Mark she liked to be called, on a sofa side by side, Saffy on the floor playing with a white kitten. Mr. Raymount sat in a great soft chair with a book in his hand, listening more than reading. His wife lay on a couch, and soon passed into dreams of pleasant sounds. The major stood erect by Miss Dasomma, a little behind her, with his arms folded across his chest, Hester sat on a stool beside her mother and held her sleeping hand, and Christopher sat on a low window-seat where the balmiest of perfumed airs freely entered. He could neither play nor sing—at least anything more than a common psalm-tune to lead the groans of his poor—and understood little of music. But there was in him a whole sea of musical delight.

Following an early dinner, the major stood, raised his glass, and proposed the health of his cousin Hester, and then made a little speech in her honour. But his praise did not make Hester feel awkward, for praise which is the odour of love is genuine and true and therefore does not sicken its hearers.

"And now, cousin Hester," concluded the major, "you know that I love you like a child of my own. But it is a good thing you are not, for if you were, then you would not be half so good or so beautiful or so wise or so accomplished as you are! Will you honour me by accepting this little gift, which I hope will serve to make this blessed day yet a trifle more pleasant to look back on when I am gone and when Mark has got his old majie back. I hope you will fill this gift with many good deeds of the sort which only you know how to perform."

With this enigmatic introduction, the major made Hester a low bow and handed her a small piece of white paper, twice folded, and tied with a bit of white ribbon. She took it with a sweetly radiant curiosity.

It was the title deed of the house in Addison Square. She gave a cry of joy, got up, threw her arms around majie's neck, and kissed him.

"Ah!" said the major, "if I was a young man now, I should not have had that! But I know what she means by it—the collective kiss of all the dirty men and women in her dear slums, glorified into that of an angel of God!"

Hester was not a young lady given to weeping, but she did here break down and cry. Her long-cherished dream had come true! She knew she had no money to go with the house, but that did not trouble her. There was always a way of doing when one was willing to begin small!

And this is, indeed, a divine law. There shall be no success to the man who is not willing to begin small. Small is strong, for it only can grow strong. Big at the outset is but bloated and weak. There are thousands willing to do great things for every one who is willing to do a small thing. But there never was any truly great thing that did not begin small.

In her delight, without unfolding it all the way, Hester handed the paper to Mr. Christopher. He took it and, with a questioning look, opened it farther.

The major had known for some time that Mr. Raymount wanted to sell the house, and believed from the way Hester spent her time in London that he could give her no greater joy than to purchase it for her.

"There is more here than you know," said Christopher, handing her back the paper. She opened it and saw several notes, amounting to something about a thousand pounds. But before the evening was over she learned that it was not a thousand pounds the dear major had given her, but the thousand a year he had offered her if she would give up lord Gartley. Thus a new paradise of God-labour opened on the horizon in the delighted eyes of Hester.

In the evening, when the sun was down, they went for another walk. I suspect the major, but am not sure:—anyhow, in the middle of a fir-wood Hester found herself alone with Christopher.

The wood rose towards the moor, growing thinner and thinner as it ascended. They were climbing westward full in face of the sunset, which was barred across the trees in gold, blue, rosy pink, and a lovely indescribable green, such as is not able to live except in the after sunset. The west lay like the beautiful dead not yet faded into the brown dark of mother-earth. The fir-trees and bars of sunset made a glorious gate before them.

"Oh, Hester!" said Christopher—he had been hearing her called *Hester* all day long, and it not only came of itself, but stayed unnoticed of either—"imagine if that were the gate of heaven, and we climbing to it now to go in and see all the dear people!"

"That would be joy!" responded Hester.

"There is no harm in dreaming."

"Sometimes when Mark would tell me one of his dreams, I could not help thinking," said Hester, "how much more of reality there was in it than in most so-called realities."

Then came a silence.

"Suppose," began Christopher again, "one claiming to be a prophet appeared, saying that in the life to come we were to go on living just such a life as here, with the one difference that we should be no longer deluded with the idea of something better, that all our energies would then be, and ought now to be spent in making the best of what we had—without any foolish indulgence in hope or aspiration."

They emerged from the wood, the bare moor spread on all sides before them, and lo, the sunset was countless miles away! Hills, fields, rivers, mountains, lay between! Christopher stopped, and turning, looked at Hester.

"Is this the reality?" he said. "We catch sight of the gate of heaven, and set out for it. It comes nearer and nearer. All at once a something they call a reality of life comes between, and the shining gate is millions of miles away!"

He was silent. They were on the top of the ridge. A little beyond stood the dusky group of their companions. And the world lay beneath them. At length they saw the major approaching them.

"Who would live in London who might live here?" he said.

"No one," answered Hester and Christopher together.

The major looked at them almost in alarm.

"But I *may not*," said Hester. "God chooses that I live in London."

"Christ would surely have liked better to go on living in his father's house," said Christopher, "than go where so many did not know either him or his father! But he could not go on enjoying his heaven while those many lived only a death in life. He must go and start them for home! Who in any measure seeing what Christ sees and feeling as Christ feels, would rest in the enjoyment of beauty while so many are unable to desire it? We are not real human beings until we are of the same mind with Christ. There are many who would save the interesting, but let the ugly and unlovely take care of themselves! Not so Christ, nor those who have learned of him!"

Christopher spoke in quiet contrast to the fervour of his words.

"I would take as many in with me," he said, turning to Hester, "as I might, should it be after a thousand years I went in at the gate of the sunset—the sunrise rather, of which the sunset is a leaf of the folding door! It would be sorrow to go in alone. My people, my own, my own humans, my men, my women, my little ones, must go in with me!"

And so the two did return from those peaceful valleys and hills to London, to the men and women and children who drew their hearts.

Hester laboured, and Christopher laboured. And if one was the heart and the other the head, the major was the right hand. But what they did and how they did it, would require a book, and no small one, to itself.

It is no matter that here I cannot tell their story. No man ever did the best work who copied another. Let every man work out the thing that is in him! Who, according to the means he has, great or small, does the work given him to do, stands by the side of the Saviour and is a fellow-worker with him. Be a brother after thy own fashion, only see it be a brother thou art.

The one who weighed, is found wanting the most, is the one whose tongue and whose life do not match, who says, "Lord! Lord!" and does not the thing the Lord says—the deacon who finds a good seat for the man in fine apparel and lets the poor widow stand in the aisle unheeded, the preacher who preaches on the love of God in the pulpit and looks for a rich wife in his flock, the missionary who would save the heathen but gives his own soul to greed, the woman who spends her strength for the poor and makes discord at home.

Books and series by and inspired by
GEORGE MACDONALD

This new series of MacDonald's stories culminates a forty-year attempt that began in the 1970s to acquaint new generations of readers with the works of the man C.S. Lewis called his spiritual "master." Throughout that time, it has been my prayerful life's work to make MacDonald's writings and ideas accessible and understandable to persons of all backgrounds with a complete range of literary interests. I have tried not only to expand availability of MacDonald's writings, I have attempted also to shed light on how those writings can most fruitfully be read, interpreted, and placed in the context of MacDonald's life. Listings of my own original writings, both fiction and non-fiction, are easily accessible from many sources in which, often indirectly, I try to point readers toward MacDonald. Most of the publications that bear specifically on MacDonald, as well as my new and edited editions of his books, are listed below.

M. P.

EDITIONS OF GEORGE MACDONALD'S BOOKS
Edited and published by Michael Phillips

The Bethany House Reprint Series
    (18 Edited novels)—1982-1990

The Sunrise Centenary Editions of the Works of George MacDonald
    (Original facsimile collector editions)—1988-1998

Edited compilations: *Discovering the Character of God, 1989*
         Knowing the Heart of God, 1990
         Wisdom to Live By, 1996

Young Reader Editions: *Alec Forbes and His Friend Annie, 1990*
         Wee Sir Gibbie of the Highlands, 1990
         At the Back of the North Wind, 1991
         The Boyhood of Ranald Bannerman, 1991

Edited and annotated sermons: *Your Life in Christ, 2005*
            The Truth in Jesus, 2006

The Cullen Collection of the Fiction of George MacDonald, 2018-19

By Michael Phillips

George MacDonald Scotland's Beloved Storyteller, 1987
Universal Reconciliation, 1998
The Garden at the Edge of Beyond, 1998
The Commands of Jesus, 2012
Hell and Beyond, 2013
Bold Thinking Christianity, 2014
Heaven and Beyond, 2015
The Commands of the Apostles, 2015
George MacDonald and the Late Great Hell Debate, 2014
George MacDonald and the Atonement, 2014
George MacDonald's Spiritual Vision: An Introductory Overview, 2016
George MacDonald's Transformational Theology of the Christian Faith, 2017
George MacDonald A Writer's Life, 2018
George MacDonald, Cullen, and Malcolm, 2019

Available titles may be purchased at TheCullenCollection.com, from WisePathBooks.com, from FatherOfTheInklings.com, or from Amazon